THE OUTCAST

Book One: The Empire's Corps
Book Two: No Worse Enemy
Book Three: When The Bough Breaks
Book Four: Semper Fi
Book Five: The Outcast
Book Six: To The Shores
Book Seven: Reality Check
Book Eight: Retreat Hell
Book Nine: The Thin Blue Line
Book Ten: Never Surrender
Book Eleven: First To Fight
Book Twelve: They Shall Not Pass
Book Thirteen: Culture Shock

THE OUTCAST

CHRISTOPHER G. NUTTALL

The characters and events portrayed in this book are fictitious. Any similarity to real persons, living or dead, is coincidental and not intended by the author.

Text copyright © 2017 Christopher G. Nuttall
All rights reserved.
No part of this book may be reproduced, or stored in a retrieval system, or transmitted in any form or by any means, electronic, mechanical, photocopying, recording, or otherwise, without express written permission of the publisher.

ISBN: 1542341043
ISBN 13: 9781542341042

http://www.chrishanger.net
http://chrishanger.wordpress.com/
http://www.facebook.com/ChristopherGNuttall

All Comments Welcome!

DEAR READERS

When I first started to outline the series that would become *The Empire's Corps*, I intended to alternate mainstream books – stories following the characters on Avalon – with stand-alone books set somewhere else within the collapsing Empire. *When The Bough Breaks* was set on Earth, but still followed the Terran Marines. *The Outcast* follows a character who is not a Marine and the Marines themselves are barely mentioned. However, she will be very important as the ruins of the Empire give way to successor states and interstellar war.

I hope this meets with your approval. Please feel free to post your opinions on my website discussion board or Facebook page (links above.) And if you liked the story, please don't hesitate to write a review.

Chronologically speaking, part one of *The Outcast* starts four years prior to *The Empire's Corps* and the epilogue takes place a few months after *Semper Fi*.

As always, if you spot any spelling errors and suchlike, drop me a line. I offer cameos!

Thank you for your attention.
Christopher G. Nuttall

DEDICATION

There are hundreds of thousands (perhaps many more) people trapped in bad situations, from a troubled marriage to a repressive state or religion that refuses to allow them their freedom. And yet sometimes the oppression can feel safer than trying to escape, without quite knowing what might be waiting for you…

This book is dedicated to those who have the courage to escape.

PROLOGUE

From: *The Rise of the Trader Queen.* Professor Leo Caesius, Avalon Publishing. 49PE (Post-Empire).

When did the Galactic Empire fall?

It seems an absurd question. A cursory glance at a history book will reveal the dates that Earth was destroyed, the Sirius Sector declared independence, the war between Hecate and Heartland began and a thousand other events that formed part of the final collapse of the Empire. But when did the Empire actually die? At what point did the fall become unavoidable?

I think it truly became unavoidable when the economy started to collapse.

The empire was held together by a combination of military force and economic ties. Together, they held thousands of worlds in a common union. But the former was wearing away and the latter was being destroyed by the Grand Senate. The economy was being strangled at precisely the moment it needed to breathe. In short, the Grand Senate was not only robbing Peter to pay Paul, it was also eating its own seed corn.

This was disastrous. As imperial taxes grew ever-higher, more and more freighters and interstellar shipping companies were forced out of business – or became smugglers. Entire planetary systems and even sectors started opting out of the Empire's economic network, forming their own units that existed in isolation. Indeed, as the big corporations started to lose their profits, they pulled out and abandoned hundreds of planets to their own devices.

Chaos spread across the Rim. Pirates went on the rampage, attacking trading starships and entire planets. HE3 supplies started to run out, forcing planets to revert to an earlier stage of technological development if they couldn't build their own cloudscoops. Isolated colonies fell completely off the trade routes, such as they were; entire planets died out because they could no longer maintain their life support systems…the end of history seemed at hand.

But this also offered opportunities for those who were prepared to think outside the stifling centralised control of the Empire.

One such person was Sameena Hussein.

Or, as she became known, the Trader Queen.

CHAPTER ONE

A very famous philosopher once referred to the study of economics as the 'Voodoo Sciences,' suggesting – in effect – that there was no true science behind economics. Human experience tends to agree. All attempts to devise a science for economics have failed.

- Professor Leo Caesius, *The Science That Isn't: Economics and the Decline and Fall of the Galactic Empire.*

"Good work, Sameena."

Sameena beamed with pride at her father's words. It was unusual for a girl to receive any formal education on Jannah, let alone be granted the chance to use it, but her father had recognised her talent from a very early age. The family business would be passed down to her brother Abdul – a girl running a business was unheard of – yet he'd already promised her that she could continue to work behind the scenes. Her brother had no talent for business and knew it.

"Thank you, father," she said, as she looked down at the figures. Honestly, they weren't very complicated at all. "I could do the next set right now."

Her father made a show of stroking his beard in contemplation, then shook his head. "Your mother will want help in the kitchen," he reminded her dryly. "Or we will have no food tonight."

Sameena rolled her eyes. "I burn water, father," she said, hoping that he would change his mind. "You should put Abdul in the kitchen."

Her father's eyes twinkled with amusement. The only male cooks on the planet were the ones who cooked in the mosques, feeding the men who travelled from town to town spreading the word of Islam. It was unlikely, to say the least, that Abdul would ever join them. He was simply too fond of games to take up a career in the mosque.

"Cheeky brat," he said. He reached out and patted her on the head. "Go help your mother while I check the figures. You can do more sums tonight."

Sameena stood up and bowed, then walked out of her father's study and down towards the kitchen, where the smell of cooked meat was already starting to waft through the house. Her mother was a wonderful cook, she knew, but Sameena herself had no talent for cooking. In her fanciful moments, she wondered if she had inherited the gene for trading from her father, rather than the gene for cooking she should have had. Most of her friends saw nothing wrong with spending most of their time in the kitchen.

She stopped in front of the kitchen door and hesitated, catching sight of her own reflection in the mirror her mother had hung on the door. A dark-skinned face looked back at her, surrounded by long dark hair that fell down over her shoulders. She looked almost mannish, her mother had said, apart from her hair. The doctor they'd taken her to had said that she was simply a late developer. Shaking her head, Sameena pulled her hair into a ponytail and pushed open the door to the kitchen. Her mother was standing in front of the stove, boiling a piece of beef in a large pan.

"There you are," her mother said, crossly. A strict traditionalist, her mother had little time for the work she did with her father. Only the tradition of female obedience had stopped her from making more of a fuss. "Go wash the pots and pans."

Sameena sighed. "Yes, mother," she said, as she walked over to the sink. As always, her mother seemed to have gone out of her way to use as many different pans and utensils as possible. "Why don't you get Abdul to do it?"

Her mother gave her a sharp look. "Because he is at study," she said, sharply. It was her latest scheme to make something of her son and she'd nagged her husband until he'd agreed to pay for it. "And because men don't work in the kitchen."

It hardly seemed fair to Sameena. She was better at maths than her brother, better at reading…why did she have to get married and spend her life in the kitchen? If her father had wanted to marry her off, he could have done so from the moment she'd become a woman. She'd been lucky. Some of her girlfriends had already been married, or had been practically chained to the kitchen inside their houses, permanently supervised by their mothers. But why was it that way?

She pushed the thought aside and started to work on the pots and pans. Her mother kept adding to the pile, or scooping up items she'd washed and using them again, forcing Sameena to wash them again and again. She just wanted to walk away, but there was no point in leaving. Her mother would be angry and her father would be disappointed in her. Where could she go if she left?

"Take this out to the dining room," her mother ordered. "And then come *straight* back."

Sameena took the dish of curry gratefully and carried it out of the kitchen, down towards the dining room. It was the largest room in the house; her father used it to entertain his business partners or the bureaucrats from Abdullah every few weeks. Sameena had been allowed to listen to some of the discussions – although she hadn't been allowed to speak – and she'd learned more about how the world worked than she'd learned from her mother, or the tutor her father had hired for her education. They hadn't bothered to conceal anything from her.

Her father was already sitting on the floor. "Put it down there," he ordered, tiredly. "And then you…"

There was a crash as someone opened the front door. Sameena looked up to see Abdul as he stepped into the room, grinning from ear to ear. Her brother was handsome, some of her girlfriends had said, but Sameena didn't see it herself. But then, he'd been two years old when she'd been born and they'd practically grown up together. She'd been very lucky in her brother as well.

"You're late," her father said, sternly.

"I had to talk to the teacher," Abdul said. He was still grinning. "Can you believe that he got something wrong?"

Their father stared at him. "…What?"

"The teacher, the one who came all the way from Abdullah," Abdul said. "He was basing his arguments on a discredited *hadith*, so I had to tell him…"

Sameena looked at her father and saw the blood draining from his face. "What did you tell him…?"

Abdul dropped into classical Arabic and started to explain. Sameena scowled at him – girls were not encouraged to learn classical Arabic and she could barely follow one word in ten – before looking at their father. He'd gone very pale.

"You utter *idiot*," he said, when Abdul had finished. "You…you've ruined us all!"

"But I was right," Abdul protested. "I…"

"Fool of a boy," their father thundered. "Do you really think that matters?"

He started to pace around the room. "He will have complained about you to the Guardians of Public Morality," he snapped. "You will come to their attention. And anyone who comes to their attention is lost forever."

Abruptly, he turned and headed towards the door. "Eat your dinner, then stay in your room," he ordered. "And *don't* talk about it with your mother."

His gaze moved to Sameena. "You too," he added. "Don't talk to your mother about *anything*."

Sameena watched him leave, unable to suppress the nervous feeling in her chest. She'd seen the Guardians of Public Morality – dark men in dark robes, carrying staffs – from a distance, but she'd never spoken to one. And yet she'd heard the rumours of what they did to people who stepped too far outside the lines drawn for Jannah's population. Those who came to their attention *always* regretted it.

She would have asked Abdul, but their mother bustled just after their father left and started putting the rice and bread down on the mat. Instead, she ate and worried.

Two days passed before her father returned to the house. He must have said something to her mother, Sameena had decided, if only because she didn't seem worried by his absence. But then, he'd often had to make business trips, either to Abdullah or to the spaceport out in the desert. Having to leave at short notice wasn't uncommon. Even so, she couldn't help worrying about what was going on. Abdul hadn't been very talkative and had spent most of his time in his room.

Sameena was sitting in her room, reading a book, when her father opened the door and came inside. As master of the house, he could go anywhere without bothering to ask permission, but he normally respected her private space and knocked before entering her room. It was so out of character for him to barge inside that she almost panicked. Just what was going on?

"I have arranged for you to marry," her father said, without preamble. The look in his eyes chilled her to the bone. "You will marry Judge Al-Haran and…"

Sameena gaped at him. "Father," she protested. "He's married! He has *two* wives!"

"You will be his third," her father said. He put a small purse of gold coins on her bedside table. "He has agreed to take you. It is a very great honour."

Sameena felt her world crashing down around her. She had known that she would be married, sooner or later; it was very rare for a woman to remain unmarried past her late teens. Even those whose morals had been called into question were married off; they just had to become second or third wives. But *she*…

Her father had promised her – *promised* her – that she wouldn't be married off unless she approved of the groom. And her brother, who would become her guardian if her father died before she married, had made her the same promise. She'd *trusted* them – and yet now they were selling her off to the highest bidder. How could she be a third wife? She'd heard the older women chatting, when they thought their children couldn't hear, and she knew what it would be like. The third wife was a slave, in all but name. She would be bullied by the senior wives as well as her husband.

And she'd met the Judge, once. He hadn't impressed her.

"Father," she said, gathering herself as best as she could, "I will not marry the Judge. He's fifty years old, and smelly, and…"

Her father slapped her.

Sameena fell backwards, more shocked than hurt. Her father *never* hit her. She'd been slapped by her mother more than once when she'd been disobedient, but her father never hit her – or Abdul. Her cheek hurt… she lifted a hand to it and touched her skin, feeling it throbbing in pain. She'd never been *scared* of her father before.

But when she met his eyes, she realised that he was scared too.

"Your idiot of a brother has made powerful enemies," her father said, very quietly. "I have it on good authority that the Guardians of Public Morality have already been alerted and that they're just waiting for permission to act. No matter what bribes I offer, I cannot save my son, or my wife, or myself. You know how many enemies merchants have on this world."

Sameena nodded. Merchants kept the world going, yet the local governments often disapproved of them. She'd done the sums and knew how much money her father had to pay out in taxes – or bribes – just to keep going. A charge of disbelief, of unorthodoxy, might be impossible to bury underneath a mass of bribes. Even their friends might back away if they realised that the fallout might land on them as well.

And all it took to unleash the Guardians of Public Morality was a brief dispute in a mosque between a young man and a teacher…

"But I can save you," her father insisted. "You'll go to the Judge, you will become his wife and they won't be able to touch you. We can go to his house and he can perform the ceremony…don't you understand? There is *nothing* he can do to you that is worse than what the Guardians of Public Morality will do, if they get their hands on you."

Sameena remembered the worst of the rumours and went cold. How could their lives have turned upside down so quickly? But there was no point in crying over spilt milk, as her mother had said more than once. If her father was right, she had no other choice. There was no one else who would give her the same protection as the Judge…

A thought struck her. "But father, given what Uncle Muhammad has been doing for the government…"

"They won't take that into account," her father assured her, grimly. "He isn't your *real* Uncle, after all. If we're lucky, he won't be involved at all."

He tapped the purse of gold. "You won't be able to take much with you," he added. "But take that – in a few years, maybe you'll be able to seek an alternate arrangement. Legally, he has to leave that with you…"

Sameena shook her head in absolute despair. Maybe, just maybe, the Judge would grant her a divorce once the whole affair had died down in a year or two. But if he refused, there was no way that she could find a legal separation. The law wouldn't be on her side, whatever he did to her. And he could take her gold and no one would be able to stop him.

She looked out of the open window towards the darkening sky and shuddered.

"I can't do anything else," her father said. "All I can do is make the best arrangements I can for you. And pray."

He gave her a hug, then stood up. "I'll come back in an hour to take you to the Judge's house," he told her. He sounded almost as through her were pleading. "Please don't do anything stupid."

Sameena felt hot tears prickling at her eyes as he closed the door, leaving her alone. Her thoughts danced in crazy circles through her head. How *could* he do that to her? But what choice did he have? Abdul had ruined the whole family and her only hope of escaping the coming dragnet was to surrender to a lecherous old man. No doubt the Judge had struck a hard bargain. Everyone thought that merchants were rich, even when they weren't.

She picked up the purse and counted the coins silently. Nearly five thousand sultans – and, buried at the bottom of the purse, an Imperial Credit Coin. There were only a handful on the entire planet; whatever Imperial Law happened to say, Jannah rarely used any currencies apart from its own sultans. She doubted that she could find someone who would accept the coin, at least outside the spaceport. Mere possession of the coin would raise suspicions of spiritual contamination by off-worlders.

There was no formal law against women possessing such sums of money, but it was almost unheard of. Her dowry would go to the Judge; if he knew that she had the rest of the money with her, he would be within his rights to take it for himself. All that was hers would become his. She would have to hide it, somehow. And then…

And then what? She asked herself. Her life was utterly ruined.

She heard a dull crash from downstairs. Worried, she stood up and opened the door very quietly. A harsh male voice echoed upstairs, demanding that everyone in the house present themselves for arrest and formal interrogation. Sameena felt her blood run cold as she realised that her father had been too late, after all. The Guardians of Morality had arrived to take them all into custody.

Her mother started to scream. There was the unmistakable sound of a scuffle and the screaming cut off, abruptly. They'd knocked her mother down, she guessed; how long would it be before they searched the house? She'd heard too many rumours to go gently into their custody, but there was no point in fighting. Even if she'd known how to fight, there were just too many of them.

She turned and scooped up the purse of coins and stuffed them into her pocket. At least she'd worn loose trousers rather than a dress; it would have been far harder to escape in one of her dresses, even if her mother *did* like seeing her in them. She picked up her headscarf a moment later – she normally didn't wear them in the house – and then slipped over to the window. Was that footsteps she could hear coming up the stairs? She couldn't tell, but there was no longer any time to hesitate.

It had been five *years* since she'd last scrambled out of her window and climbed down to the garden below, but her hands and feet still remembered where to go. She was heavier now, she realised, as one of the footholds almost broke under her weight and she slipped, thankfully only a few inches above the ground. As soon as she touched the ground, she turned and fled into the woods behind her house. There were no guards outside to catch her before she could escape.

She and her brother had used to play in the woods and she knew them like the back of her hand. If the Guardians of Public Morality came after her, they'd have problems…she hoped. They'd played hide-and-seek before, but never with adults…catching her breath, she looked back towards the house. No one seemed to be coming after her.

But they would, she knew. Everyone knew that the Guardians of Public Morality never gave up. Give them a day or two and everyone in the town would know that they wanted Sameena, dead or alive. No one would shelter her, not even the Judge. And going to him would mean swapping one kind of captivity and torture for another.

And yet...where could she go?

A thought occurred to her. It wasn't something that she would ever have considered before, but what did she have to lose? And besides, the Guardians of Public Morality would never expect it, not of a girl.

And if it worked, she would be *far* outside their reach.

CHAPTER TWO

Humans being what they are, considerable attention is focused on the handful of people who have successfully predicted the future of the stock markets. Those winners have made vast sums of money. It is generally ignored, however, that thousands of people have lost money by predicting the future… unsuccessfully. The separation between winners and losers is as much a matter of luck as judgement. They, of course, would not agree.

- Professor Leo Caesius, *The Science That Isn't: Economics and the Decline and Fall of the Galactic Empire.*

The call to prayer was echoing through the air when she reached the other side of the woods and paused, staring at the house ahead of her. It belonged to a very religious family, one that had two daughters who had been her friends before their parents had decided that a merchant's daughter was an unsuitable companion for their children. They were so religious, Sameena knew, that everyone in the house would make their way to the local mosque for prayers, even the women and servants. The house would be left empty.

She waited in the woods until she heard the prayers begin, then slipped into their garden and walked over to where the clothes were hanging from the washing line. The family had a younger son who was about Sameena's height; she took his shirt and tunic from the line, then found a turban that would cover her hair. Theft bothered her, but there was no choice, not with the Guardians after her. They could only kill her once.

Back in the woods, she pulled the shirt and tunic on, then wrapped up her hair inside the turban. Wearing clothes belonging to the other sex was asking for a whipping, but most people wouldn't look past the male clothes to see the girl underneath – or so she hoped. She bundled up her former clothes, glanced down at herself to ensure that she didn't look very feminine, then walked down to the road and headed eastwards, down into the town.

She felt terrifyingly exposed as she walked down the street, catching sight of a handful of Guardians on the other side of the road. If they caught her…women were not supposed to go anywhere, anywhere at all, without a male escort. Sweat was trickling down her back as she walked past the Guardians and headed towards the bus station in town. Getting caught meant that there would be nowhere left to run. But no one tried to stop her as she entered the bus station and climbed onto a bus. Four stops later, she was near the spaceport – and near Uncle Muhammad's house.

Uncle Muhammad wasn't really her uncle, at least not in any biological sense. He had been her father's partner, once upon a time, before they had separated their businesses and gone their own ways. Sameena's father had told her enough for her to realise that he could not be trusted, but there was no other choice. Besides, it was quite likely that the Guardians would pick him up as well, unless he had enough warning to round up some political support from his allies. She hesitated, looking at his huge house, then walked forward towards the main entrance. There was no point in backing out now.

She pushed the bell and waited. Moments later, Muhammad's son appeared and peered at her suspiciously. He'd been mentioned as a potential candidate for Sameena's hand, she knew; it was quite possible that he would recognise her, despite the flimsy disguise. But there was no point in concealing herself any longer. She pulled off the turban, allowing her hair to spill down over her shoulders, and smiled at him. He looked utterly flabbergasted.

"I need to speak to your father," she said, before he could say a word. "Now."

He *must* have been shocked, she reflected, as he led her into the house. Normally, a man would grow stubborn at the mere thought of taking orders from a woman. She smirked inwardly as they walked down luxurious corridors and past artwork that would probably give the Guardians heart attacks, including several that were rather indecent. Uncle Muhammad seemed to believe that one should flaunt the wealth one had, despite the Guardians. So far, his services to the government had been enough to keep him safe. Sameena hoped that was still true.

"I should fetch my mother," Muhammad's son said, as they reached his father's office. "I…"

"No need," Sameena said. Her reputation was hardly a concern any longer. Oddly, the thought made her feel freer than she'd felt ever since she'd realised the difference between male and female. "I just need to talk to him in private."

She ignored his doubting look and strode into the office, leaving him outside. Uncle Muhammad was a tall man, considerably overweight, with a neatly-trimmed beard that tried to give him an air of distinction. Sameena, who had been raised by a trader, knew better than to take him for granted. He would keep the letter of any agreement, but would have to be watched carefully to prevent him using any loopholes to his own advantage. No wonder her father had preferred to separate himself from his former friend.

"Sameena," Uncle Muhammad said, carefully. "Why are you here?"

Sameena couldn't blame him for being surprised – and alarmed. It was almost unheard of for girls to travel on their own, certainly outside the towns…indeed, it was quite rare for girls to travel at all, no matter what their husbands did. The Guardians believed that women should remain at home and enforced their beliefs on everyone they could reach. Her presence here, without her father or brother, spelt trouble.

"The Guardians came for my family," she said, and outlined what had happened. "I need your help."

Uncle Muhammad narrowed his eyes. "And if they're prepared to arrest the Judge," he said, "what makes you think that *I* can protect you?"

Sameena stared at him. "They arrested Judge Al-Haran?"

"He was taken away a couple of hours ago," Uncle Muhammad informed her. "Your father was evidently unaware of how many enemies he had. Quite a few of the Guardians thought that he was too merciful to captured criminals."

His eyes bored into hers. "And I ask again," he said. "What makes you think that I can protect you?"

He was talking to her, Sameena realised numbly, as if she were a man rather than a woman. It would have pleased her under other circumstances, but right now…she couldn't help wondering if the religious tutor who'd lectured on a woman's place in the world had had a point after all. She would have liked to put the whole matter aside…angrily, she shook her head. Denying reality wouldn't make it any less *real*. And she could only rely on herself.

"You have connections to off-worlders," she said, remembering the credit coin her father had given her. "I want you to get me off the planet."

Uncle Muhammad's eyes went very wide. "You want to go off-world?"

"Yes," Sameena said. "Where else can I go?"

He considered it for a long moment. Sameena knew what he was thinking. The Guardians would not stop hunting her – and she couldn't live on her own, not as a young woman. She could hide in Uncle Muhammad's house, but that couldn't last forever – and besides, she wasn't sure that she would *want* to stay even if she could. She certainly couldn't get married without announcing her identity to the clerics, who would alert the Guardians.

"The alternative would be to…ah, *marry* someone without registering it," Uncle Muhammad said, finally. "You would be safe and…"

Sameena felt her blood run cold. She'd heard about such marriages – and about how they lacked the handful of legal protections offered to registered marriages. It was effectively prostitution, something she wasn't supposed to know about. But her brother had always talked too loudly and Sameena had listened carefully. Knowledge was power.

"No," she said, flatly. "I am *not* a whore."

Uncle Muhammad flinched, as if she'd struck him. "Getting you into space would be risky…"

Sameena threw caution to the winds. "So will trying to sell me to a brothel," she said, sharply. "I will go to the Guardians and tell them everything, all the details of your trade with the off-worlders, if you refuse to help me now."

He clenched his fists. She realised, suddenly, just how easy it would be for him to crush her neck. They could bury her in the garden and make sure that no one would talk. Perhaps the Guardians would realise that there was a connection between Uncle Muhammad and Sameena's father in time, but it would be far too late to help her.

"I also know a few details of my father's business that you need to know," she added, lowering her voice. "They will be yours."

Uncle Muhammad muttered a word she didn't recognise, then glowered at her. "What do you want?"

Sameena fought to keep her face expressionless. "Get me onto a ship leaving the system, with something I can use to support myself," she said. She didn't want to admit to having the Credit Coin, not if it could be avoided. "And then I will be out of your hair for good."

"And you will tell me what I need to know," Uncle Muhammad said. He paused. "I should warn you that the Guardians patrol the spaceport quite heavily. You'll need to be smuggled onboard and that could be risky."

Sameena surprised herself by smiling. "I have made it here," she said. Few women on her homeworld could have done that, even if it was a bare fifty kilometres from her hometown to the spaceport. "I understand the risk."

"I will take you to the library," Uncle Muhammad said, standing up. "I'll give you pen and paper; you will write down everything you know that I might need to know. In the meantime, I will make the arrangements to get you onto a freighter. After that, you're on your own."

He could still betray her, Sameena knew, as he led her down the corridor and into the library. Or simply kill her outright. But there was no other choice. She had to trust that he would do as he had promised.

"Here," Uncle Muhammad said, shoving a piece of paper at her. "I'll be back as soon as possible."

Sameena watched him go, then looked around the library. It was crammed with books, ranging from the standard textbooks on Islamic thought to a number of volumes that would thoroughly displease the Guardians, if they found them. Several of them, she realised, were on off-world science and cultures, a number clearly imported rather than produced on her homeworld. But that wasn't surprising, she knew. Her father had told her, more than once, just how many restrictions there were on printing new books. It could be very hard to gain permission to publish a book.

She took the piece of paper and wracked her brains, writing down almost everything she could remember that she thought Uncle Muhammad would like. Her father would be angry, she knew, if he knew...but he would never be released. Nor would anyone else in her family...they'd want to make a horrible example of her brother, just to ensure that no one else dared to question the religious tutors. Sameena felt tears welling up in her eyes, now that she was somewhere relatively safe. She wanted to weep for her family.

Uncle Muhammad took almost an hour to return to the library. When he did, he was accompanied by his third wife, a thin-lipped woman who gave Sameena a stern look that would have promised trouble, if she'd just made a normal visit. Sameena ignored her and looked directly at Uncle Muhammad, no longer caring to remain demure and downcast. It wasn't as if she could get in more trouble.

"I have made some preparations," he said, shortly. "You will be transported into a cargo pod that will be shipped into orbit and loaded onto a freighter. After that, you will be on your own. I trust that you speak Imperial Standard?"

Sameena nodded, wordlessly. Her father had insisted that she learn along with her brother, although Imperial Standard wasn't something that women – or men, for that matter – were encouraged to learn. Talking to off-worlders risked contamination, the Guardians insisted – and besides, there were few opportunities to practice. But she knew how to speak to the off-worlders if necessary.

"Good," Uncle Muhammad said. He gave his wife a sharp look when she began to splutter in disbelief. "Now, you need to take a careful look at these."

He pulled a set of sealed plastic bags out of his pocket and dropped them on the table. "Most of our trade goods are impossible for me to obtain on such short notice," he said. "These, on the other hand, will be worth a considerable sum of money off-world. I suggest that you treat them with considerable care – and *don't* let anyone know what they are, at least until you're sure that you can trust them. I've attached a set of instructions for using the berries and producing more."

Sameena picked up one of the bags and frowned. Inside, there were a dozen berries and seeds, just waiting for soil and water. What *were* they?

"Sunflower Berries," Uncle Muhammad said, seeing her puzzlement. "They're almost worthless on this world, but off-worlders are very fond of them." He tapped the set of instructions. "I think you would be able to grow new ones, if you tried. Is gardening one of your skills?"

Sameena shook her head.

"Don't worry about it," Uncle Muhammad said. He nodded to his wife, who scowled at Sameena. "My wife has taken the liberty of preparing some additional clothes for you, as well as food and drink. However, I honestly don't know *what* will happen once you're in orbit. You may end up staying in the cargo pod for days before the ship reaches its destination."

He looked back at Sameena. "You *could* stay here," he added. "I would hide you."

Sameena saw the look on his wife's face and knew that wouldn't be safe. Uncle Muhammad wasn't her *real* uncle, after all; there would be no legal objections if he wanted to marry her, particularly if he didn't register the marriage. And she had no strong male protector to help her escape. The Guardians would probably thank her for betraying her new husband right before they killed her for daring to try to escape them.

But she knew next to nothing about life off-world. There were stories and rumours, but nothing concrete, nothing she could trust. She might starve to death in the cargo pod, or be caught and killed by the freighter crew, or…the only thing she could trust, really, was that there would be no Guardians. She would be well away from them.

"I'm going off-world," she said, firmly. She passed him the sheet of paper. "This is everything I can remember. I hope you can use it."

Uncle Muhammad nodded. "My wife will help you dress," he said, as he turned to walk out of the library. "And then we'll be on our way."

Away from her husband, Uncle Muhammad's wife seemed to warm up slightly as she helped Sameena to wash and then dress in a new set of male clothes. Sameena glanced at herself in the mirror, wondering if she shouldn't hack her hair off while she had the chance. Her hairless chin was far too revealing, but if someone pulled off her turban they'd see long hair and know that she was female. Then again, if someone came that close to her she was in deep trouble anyway.

"The cargo pods are unloaded outside the spaceport," Uncle Muhammad explained, as she joined him in the car. "One of them is being sealed in an hour or so; I want to get you inside before then, along with your supplies. After that, you're on your own."

He passed her a small vial. "This is a sleeping drug," he added. The car roared to life and bounced out of the driveway, heading towards the spaceport. "Once you're inside, I suggest you take it. You don't want to make any sound before you reach orbit, or they'll hand you over to the Guardians."

Sameena took the vial and studied it, thoughtfully. It was utterly unmarked. She scowled, realising that it could easily be poison; Uncle Muhammad was unlikely to forgive her for her blackmail threat, no matter her reasons for threatening him. Her dead body wouldn't be discovered until she was hundreds of light years from the Guardians or anyone else who might care to identify her. Maybe she shouldn't take it…

…But he was right. There was no choice.

She sat back and forced herself to relax as the car entered the loading compound and braked to a halt. Uncle Muhammad climbed out of the car and beckoned for her to follow him into the warehouse, where a large metal crate sat in the centre of the room. It was open…and completely empty. The men surrounding it were sealing it up, piece by piece."

"I'm going to call the men away," Uncle Muhammad said, very quietly. "When they go, you get inside and hide in the shadows. And good luck."

Sameena gave him a surprised look, then watched as he walked away to speak to his men. As soon as they followed him out of the warehouse, she ran forward and slipped into the cargo pod. Inside, it was as dark and silent as the grave. She held her breath, not daring to make a sound, as she heard the men returning and slamming the final seals closed. Darkness surrounded her like a living thing.

Bracing herself, she opened the vial through touch and swallowed its contents. It tasted foul.

Moments later, she fell asleep.

CHAPTER THREE

This should not be surprising. The number of variables involved in any sophisticated economy can be staggering to contemplate. Game theory admits of too many separate variables to allow accurate predictions – and, of course, each difference between theory and reality only serves to render theory even more useless. In order to explore economics, we must go back to the very start of human civilisation.
- Professor Leo Caesius, *The Science That Isn't: Economics and the Decline and Fall of the Galactic Empire.*

Awareness came back to her slowly, in fits and starts. She was lying on a hard metal surface, in absolute darkness. It was so cold that her clothes were completely inadequate. For a long chilling moment she thought that she had died and gone to Hell, before her memory returned and reminded her that she had stowed away in a cargo pod. Where was she now?

A dull *thrumming* noise seemed to be everywhere, pervading the cargo pod and echoing through her ears. It was growing louder, sending tiny vibrations echoing through the metal hull; she realised, dully, that the ship was actually accelerating. Or so she assumed. In truth, she knew almost nothing about starships. It wasn't a field of study that the Guardians encouraged. Jannah had no starships and liked it that way.

Should have brought a flashlight, she told herself, as she fumbled through the knapsack she'd been given by Uncle Muhammad. He'd packed a small supply of food for her; carefully, she pulled out a piece of bread and chewed on it, feeling her stomach threatening to rebel. There was something about being on the ship that was making her feel queasy, almost unwell. And then the vibration simply seemed to *stop*.

The next thing she heard was something scrabbling at the outside of the cargo pod. Sameena tensed, remembering the rats that had once found their way into her mother's stockpile of rice and flour, before realising that someone was trying to get into the pods. Were the pods opened in transit or...it struck her, suddenly, that they'd realised that she was there. A moment later, the pod cracked open and blinding light blazed inside. Sameena gasped in pain and covered her eyes, unable to resist as strong hands grabbed her shoulder and hauled her out of the pod.

"It's a girl," an accented voice said, in Imperial Standard. "What the *fuck*?"

Sameena blinked in surprise. How had they seen through her disguise so quickly? There was no time to think about it, though; her captor grabbed her arms, pulled them behind her back and wrapped sticky tape around her wrists. No matter how she struggled, she couldn't break free. She was trapped.

"Language," a second voice said, reprovingly. "And you ought to know that the female of the species can be more deadly than the male."

They were *both* male, Sameena realised, as her eyesight returned to normal. One of them was young, with a pale face and blonde hair, wearing a tight-fitting uniform that moulded itself to fit his body. The other was older, his face so badly scarred that she couldn't tell his age, wearing a pair of grubby overalls decorated with hundreds of patches. He should have scared Sameena, yet there was something about him that put her at ease. But he was still holding her down.

"A stowaway," the second man said. He looked down at Sameena, thoughtfully. "You'll have to face the Captain."

Sameena winced as he frisked her, removing everything from her pockets and piling them up beside her head. He didn't seem to understand what the berries were either, or why she didn't have a weapon. Eventually, he helped her to her feet and marched her through a metal door, his younger companion bringing up the rear.

She couldn't help looking around as they made their way through the giant ship. The walls – bulkheads, she reminded herself – were all metal, but decorated with children's drawings and a handful of certificates written in Imperial Standard. There was no time for a proper look as they kept pushing her onwards, towards what she assumed was the starship's bridge. They passed through a solid metal door and into a large compartment, crammed with consoles and computers. The sight was so alien to her experience that she felt her legs buckle. She would have collapsed if her captor hadn't been holding her upright.

"Captain," her captor said, addressing an older man who reminded Sameena of her father, "we found one incredibly stupid stowaway."

"Or ignorant," a woman said, as Sameena flushed. "Tom?"

The Captain leaned forward. "I am Captain Hamilton, majority shareholder and commander of the *Logan*," he said, briskly. He looked very much like an older version of the younger man who'd helped catch her. "What are you doing on my ship?"

Sameena hesitated, unsure of what to say.

"She is incredibly lucky, sir," her captor said. "She brought food, but no air or toilet supplies. If we hadn't detected the faint consumption of oxygen, she would have suffocated to death when we sealed the cargo holds and pumped out the air. And she had no weapon."

The woman stepped forward. "You need to tell us what happened," she said, seriously. "Or we will have no choice, but to turn about and return you to the planet."

"No," Sameena said, desperately. "I won't go back."

"I don't blame you," the Captain said, "but we really need to know what happened to you – and why."

Sameena nodded and started to recount the entire story, starting with her brother mouthing off to a religious tutor and ending with the drug she'd taken, once she was safely in the cargo pod. It was hard to read the Captain's reactions – he was as skilled at controlling himself as some of her father's more formidable friends - but the others seemed alternatively shocked or amused.

"Your uncle might have set you up to die in space," her captor said, when she had finished. "Or perhaps he was just too ignorant to realise that we would pump the air out of the cargo bay when we left orbit."

"That's not our concern," the Captain said, firmly. He looked down at Sameena. "Does your homeworld still want to arrest you?"

"Come on, Tom," the older woman interrupted. "You can't send her back to that…"

"Ethne," the Captain said, "you know what is at stake…"

"Bugger all," Ethne snapped. "You really *want* to go back? Because *I* don't."

"They might come after us, if they thought we were harbouring a fugitive," the younger one of her captors said. "We're not armed to stand off a warship."

The older captor snorted, rudely. "Come after us with what?"

Captain Hamilton looked over at him. "Paddy," he said, "what did she have on her?"

"An Imperial Credit Coin, which should suffice to pay her way, and some…berries," the older captor – Paddy – said. He looked towards Sameena. "Care to explain what *they* are?"

"Sunflower Berries," Sameena said, and explained. "I think they're very popular off-world."

The Captain scowled. "I cannot *imagine* why your uncle might have thought that," he said, when she had finished. "We'll have them analysed before we do anything with them."

Sameena watched as the crew continued to argue. Some of them seemed willing to take her with them, others wanted to turn around and dump her back on Jannah. It was difficult to follow their argument; every time she thought she knew who held what position, they seemed to change. The only person who remained quiet, merely listening to the discussion, was the Captain.

"I don't want to go home," she confessed, miserably. There was nothing left for her on Jannah, but death. Or a fate worse than death. "If…"

She swallowed and pushed onwards. "If you let me stay, I will marry your son."

"That settles it," Ethne snapped. "We are *not* returning her to her homeworld."

"And she won't have to marry me either," the younger one of her captors said. "I'm sure we can take her to Madagascar and drop her off there."

"Except she has little to attract people apart from her looks," the Captain mused, as if Sameena wasn't in the compartment. He picked up her Credit Coin and looked down at it, thoughtfully. "And even if we give her the lowest possible rate, she won't have enough to live on afterwards."

"Then she can stay onboard," Ethne said, firmly. "I've always wanted another daughter."

Captain Hamilton smiled and looked over at Sameena. "You are utterly unprepared for life outside a planetary gravity well," he said, simply. "And you are incredibly lucky that we noticed your presence before you died. How long were you intending to spend inside the cargo pod anyway? You would have been in there for a month before we unloaded the pod."

He scowled. "You would have starved if you had not suffocated," he added. "That gives us a problem."

"But one we can overcome," Ethne said. "She would hardly be the first groundhog to come into space with us."

The Captain nodded. "You have two choices," he said. "It will take us a month to reach Madagascar, our next port of call. In that time, you can study and learn enough to become part of the crew. We might as well start with basic safety precautions; space is a harsh environment and a single mistake can kill. Or we can put you in the stasis pod and offload you when we reach Madagascar. You'd be on your own from then onwards."

Sameena hesitated, cursing her own ignorance. It had honestly never occurred to her – and she had no way of knowing if it had occurred to Uncle Muhammad – that they might pump the atmosphere out of the cargo hold. How many other dangers were lurking for her, hiding in plain sight…and shielded by her own ignorance. Perhaps Madagascar would be better for her.

But I know nothing of the greater universe, she thought. All she really knew was composed of vague generalities that her father had told her, when she'd been younger. *I need to know more.*

"I'll stay with you," she said, making up her mind. They'd refused her suggestion that she should marry their son, thankfully. It spoke well of them. "And I will do my best to learn."

"See that you do," the Captain growled. "We do have the two kids onboard. They'll be happy to help you – or I'll know the reason why."

He nodded towards his wife. "If Jannah tries to hail us, ignore them," he ordered. "It isn't as if they can come after us anyway. If we weren't so desperate for credits, we would never have come here in the first place."

"Understood," Ethne said.

Sameena frowned as she tried to understand their relationship. On Jannah, no wife would argue with her husband in public. The man was the head of the family and arguing and pleading had to be done in private, if it was done at all. Sameena knew a few families where the wife had been beaten into mute compliance soon after marriage. But Ethne seemed more than willing to argue with her husband in front of the rest of the crew.

The Captain smiled at Sameena. "Welcome aboard," he said. "Can I have your name for the ship's log?"

"Sameena," Sameena said. "I think I want to discard my family name."

"Good idea," Ethne agreed, bluntly. She nodded towards her son. "Brad Hamilton; my oldest…"

"And best," Brad put in quickly.

"I did better the second and third time around," Ethne said. "Steve and James are busy working on the drive; you'll meet them later. Jayne should be in the medical compartment right now." She waved a hand at the scarred man. "Paddy, my son-in-law; Jayne's husband."

"And the kids are at their schooling," Paddy said.

Sameena found her voice. "You're all related?"

"Most of us are," the Captain confirmed. "The kids, on the other hand, are here to gain experience from someone who *isn't* related to them. When they grow up, they will probably marry into another ship's crew or try to buy their own ship."

"Don't worry about it," Ethne added. "You're part of the family now."

She looked over at Paddy. "Speaking of which," she added, "take her to see Jayne and tell my daughter that I want a full medical workup on Sameena before we start teaching her how to survive in space."

"And tell her to take a look at those berries," the Captain added. "I want to know what they are and if they are of any real value."

He held out his hand to Sameena, then scowled. "Cut her hands free," he ordered. "She needs to be welcomed into the family properly."

Sameena held herself very still as Paddy cut her bonds. Once her hands were free, she took the Captain's hand, even though she knew that it would have been considered indecent on Jannah. Shaking an unrelated man's hand, no matter how innocently, could call her chastity into question. But somehow it was no longer even remotely important.

"Welcome to the crew," the Captain said, shaking her hand firmly. "I hope that the Great Traders will smile on you."

Paddy offered his hand next, followed by Brad, who gave her a wink and a smile. Ethne gave her a hug, then gently pointed her towards the hatch. Paddy stepped past her and opened the hatch, then led her out of the bridge and down another metallic corridor. The gravity seemed to be fluctuating slightly – one moment, she felt heavier; the next, she felt lighter – making her feel dizzy as Paddy stopped in front of a hatch in the deck. He opened it up, revealing a ladder leading downwards into the bowels of the ship.

"There are three decks in all," Paddy explained, as he climbed down the ladder. "Our living quarters are on decks one and two, along with the exercise room, the school and a few other compartments. Deck three is almost entirely cargo space; both decks one and two have their own holds too. You'll get used to it. I suggest that you stay in your cabin unless you're escorted, at least until you know what you're doing. Space is a *very* unforgiving mistress."

Sameena said nothing as he stopped in front of a hatch and keyed a switch. There was a long pause, then he stepped forward and pushed against the metal, forcing it to open up. Inside, there was a small compartment, with a woman seated in front of a tiny desk. Jayne, Sameena assumed. The woman's eyes went wide when she saw Sameena.

"I thought Brad was pulling my leg," she said. She stared at Sameena as if she expected her to vanish the moment she looked away. "A real live stowaway!"

Sameena stared back. She had never seen such an immodest girl in her entire life. Jayne was tall and blonde, just like her older brother, but she wore a very tight uniform with a cut in it that exposed the top of her breasts. The suit followed the curves of her body, revealing almost everything she had. How could she show off so much in front of her family, let alone a complete stranger? Sameena had never been so immodest even when it had just been her mother in the room.

"A real live stowaway," Paddy confirmed, gruffly. "The XO wants you to perform a complete medical scan, then analyse these berries and see what they are."

He put the berries down on Jayne's tiny desk and stepped backwards. "I have to get back to duty," he admitted. "The XO should have designated a cabin for our guest after you've checked her out, so please take her there. And I'll see you tonight."

Jayne smiled at her husband. "I look forward to it," she said. "And thank you."

Sameena felt herself flushing as Paddy stepped out of the compartment and closed the hatch. Paddy had to be at least two decades older than Jayne, perhaps more. The Judge – whatever had happened to him – had been older than Paddy, but that had been different. Paddy and Jayne seemed to really love each other.

"I had to stay on the ship while the boys went down to the surface," Jayne said, tapping the bed. "I don't think I'd like your homeworld very much."

"No," Sameena agreed. The Guardians would have a collective heart attack if they saw Jayne wearing her outfit. If they could beat a woman for daring to show a single strand of hair – and her husband, if he didn't have any powerful connections – she hated to think what they would do to Jayne. "I didn't like it much either."

"Smart girl," Jayne said. "Undress and get onto the bed."

Sameena hesitated. "You're a *doctor*?"

"I have the qualifications to prove it," Jayne said, tartly. "Don't you have female doctors on your homeworld?"

"No," Sameena admitted, silently thanking God that she had never been ill. Male doctors were not allowed to touch female patients, merely ask them questions. And that was if they were lucky. If the husband was very traditionalist, the doctor would have to ask *him* questions instead. There was no such thing as a female doctor on Jannah, only midwives. "There are none on my homeworld."

"Barbarians," Jayne said, crossly. She tapped the bed meaningfully. "Come on and undress. I really don't have all day. And then we will find you something a little more appropriate to wear. If you want to be part of the crew, you have to look the part."

Sameena swallowed hard and started to undress. She had never been completely naked in front of anyone, except her mother – and that only when she'd been very young. Now, a complete stranger was going to be looking at her...she bit her lip as she lay down on the bed, hoping that it would be quick.

At least she isn't the Judge, she thought. *I won't ever have to marry him.*

CHAPTER FOUR

The basic law of economics is summed up in the interaction of supply and demand. If demand outstrips supply, prices will rise; if supply outstrips demand, prices will fall. This seems outrageously simple in theory, but in practice it can become alarmingly complex.

- Professor Leo Caesius, *The Science That Isn't: Economics and the Decline and Fall of the Galactic Empire.*

"Interesting," Jayne said, twenty minutes later. "Very interesting indeed."

Sameena gritted her teeth. Being naked made her feel vulnerable…and she wasn't entirely sure that she trusted Jayne enough to be vulnerable near her, even if she *was* female. The doctor had waved…*devices* over her body, taken a sample of her blood and poked and prodded at her orifices. Sameena was honestly uncertain just what, if anything, was going on, or what Jayne hoped to find out. It seemed rather more like pointless sadism to her.

"What," she demanded finally, "is so interesting?"

"Your homeworld was founded by a religious sect that banned genetic engineering," Jayne said. She saw Sameena's blank look and hastened to explain. "The science of modifying the human genome in hopes of improving it. Quite a few low-tech worlds have the same blanket ban in place, forbidding any form of human improvement. But there are definite traces of genetic engineering in your bloodstream."

Sameena frowned, not understanding. "What did they do?"

"I think they gave you – your ancestors, I should say – a basic upgrade package…probably around seven hundred years ago," Jayne said, after a long moment. "You have improved resistance to disease, you heal quicker than pureblood humans...there may be other modifications beyond my ability to detect. That isn't too uncommon, really. A low-tech world means low-tech medical science. Giving you some improvements might have been intended to prevent you from rediscovering medical science for yourself."

"I don't understand," Sameena confessed. "*How?*"

Jayne gave her a vaguely superior smile. "You do understand how humans produce more humans, don't you?"

Sameena nodded, sharply. Her mother had told her when she'd asked, then threatened the whipping of a lifetime if Sameena ever mentioned the fact she knew to *anyone*.

"The child combines...*aspects* from both mother and father," Jayne added. "In this case, the original colonists were *improved* and then the improvements were passed down through the generations until you were born."

"I see, I think," Sameena said. Had the Guardians known? Or the powerful people Uncle Muhammad had worked for? "What else did they do?"

"Your eyesight and hearing are both excellent," Jayne said. "That's probably intended to remove another incentive to rediscover science. I was worried that they might have done something to your brain, but it seems they weren't quite *that* foolish. A low-tech world might not have the ability to deal with the problems when they cropped up – and they would."

She glanced down at the terminal in her hand. "Virgin, of course," she added. "That's uncommon at your age."

Sameena blushed, furiously.

"Nothing seems to be wrong with your reproductive system," Jayne continued, smirking openly now. "I'll give you an implant for coping with your time of the month – there's no reason why you should have to put up with it on the ship, or anywhere else for that matter. The implant will also serve to prevent pregnancy, should you decide you wish to have sex with someone. You can get it removed just about anywhere..."

She chuckled as Sameena's blush grew worse. "Don't worry about it," she added. "If you're not interested, just say so."

Sameena sat upright and swung her legs over the bed, allowing them to dangle down towards the deck. "Are we finished yet?"

"Almost," Jayne said. She reached into a small cupboard and produced a white uniform, which she passed to Sameena. "This is a basic shipsuit, providing limited protection from the vacuum of space. If you hear the emergency alarm, pull the mask" – she demonstrated – "over your face, then head to the nearest emergency airlock or cache."

Sameena frowned. "What if there isn't one nearby?"

"Then you need to bend over and kiss your ass goodbye," Jayne explained, shaking her head. "Space can *kill*, easily. If you happen to be caught up in a disaster without emergency supplies, you're screwed."

"Oh," Sameena said.

She pulled the shipsuit over her head and frowned at the way it moulded itself to her body, outlining her breasts and hips for everyone to see. Jayne was far better developed, she knew, but Jayne was related to all of the adult males on the ship. *Everyone* could stare at Sameena…

"You can wear something else over the suit," Jayne said. She dug into another cupboard and produced a long white coat. "But not wearing the suit while you're outside a secure compartment will be severely punished. Wear it at all times until you know where you can safely remove it."

Sameena pulled the coat on, then watched as Jayne poked and prodded at the berries. "Not an Earth-origin fruit," Jayne observed, thoughtfully. "The…ah, *construction* is completely dissimilar to anything from Earth."

She looked up, suddenly. "What do they tell you about Earth on your homeworld?"

Sameena struggled to remember the lessons Abdul had recited to her, back when she'd been younger and the world had seemed to make a little more sense. The male children had been expected to learn by rote, without actually *thinking* about the material; female children had been lucky if they'd had any schooling at all, beyond limited religious education.

"Just that it turned into a nightmare and so the founders left to find a place where the religion could flourish," she recalled. "And that we were the last bastion of Islam."

Jayne snickered. "I can name a dozen planets where Islam is the dominant faith," she said, "and I'd be surprised if there weren't hundreds more. Your founders lied to you, girl."

Once, Sameena knew, the thought would have been inconceivable. But she'd already been questioning, even before Abdul had run into real trouble. She knew that she was smarter than her brother, certainly better suited to run the family business; why should the mere fact that she had been born female stand in her way? And yet, she knew that she wouldn't have been allowed to take control openly. The law would side with her brother.

"I know," she said, quietly. "I know."

There was a *ding* from the machine. "Let's see," Jayne said, peering down at the screen. A moment later, she began to laugh. "Oh, this is *hilarious*."

Sameena stared at her. "*What* is hilarious?"

"The berries," Jayne said. "We *know* what they are."

She straightened up. "I have to go speak to my father," she said. "Coming?"

Puzzled, Sameena allowed her to lead the way out of the medical compartment and through a series of corridors until they reached a single large room, dominated by a set of large computer-like machines. Two children – a boy and a girl – were sitting in front of the machines, supervised by Captain Hamilton, who was tapping away on a smaller terminal in his hands. The children turned to stare at Sameena as she entered the compartment, their eyes going wide. None of them had expected a stowaway from Jannah.

"These machines teach the children what they need to know," Jayne explained, briefly. "You can take the standard tests, then start developing your knowledge from there. We'll have to open you an account with the examiners on Madagascar, at least if you want the qualifications, but you can go quite some distance without them."

"As long as you're careful," Captain Hamilton said. He dismissed the kids, who took one final look at Sameena and then fled the compartment. "What did you find?"

Jayne started to titter. "The berries she brought with her," she said, indicating Sameena. "There's a direct match to Firewater Mead. I checked it twice, dad. Jannah is the source of Firewater Mead."

Captain Hamilton stared at Sameena. "Did you *know* about this?"

Sameena, puzzled, shook her head.

"They kept her completely ignorant, dad," Jayne said, flatly. "I would venture a guess that she knows absolutely nothing about Firewater Mead." She looked over at Sameena. "Do you?"

"No," Sameena admitted.

Captain Hamilton cleared his throat. "Firewater Mead is…one of the most expensive drinks in the Empire," he said. "It's sold by a cartel based in the Core Worlds, with absolutely staggering price tags. No one knows where it comes from; as far as anyone can tell, the cartel has an absolute monopoly."

"Allowing them to set prices as they see fit," Sameena said, just to prove that she wasn't a *complete* ignorant. Her father had ensured that she knew something about basic economics and she doubted that the laws would be any different in the Empire. "And this…*stuff* comes from my planet?"

"So it would seem," Jayne said. "Do you know *anything* about the berries?"

"They're called Sunflower Berries," Sameena recalled. "Other than that…nothing."

The Captain scowled. "That makes a certain kind of sense," he admitted. "Your homeworld's leadership would *not* want their little secret exposed; once the galaxy knew the source, there would be hundreds of starships heading to Jannah, intent on claiming control of the berries for themselves. Selling them to the cartel would allow them to keep the trade under control, while the cartel would have its own motives to keep its collective mouth shut."

He started to laugh. "Used properly," he said, "those berries you bought with you would be worth an absolute fortune."

"Uncle Muhammad knew," Sameena said. She hesitated as a thought struck her. "This…Firewater Mead, sir. Is it alcoholic?"

"I don't think so," Jayne said, before her father could answer. "It's derived from a plant that was probably native to Jannah, rather than a modified part of the standard terraforming package. But if we were to grow the berries ourselves…"

Pity, part of Sameena's mind thought. The tutors regularly castigated the outside universe for being sodden with alcohol. If she'd managed to convince the world that the Guardians were selling alcohol to the off-worlders…what would it do? It might give them some bad moments before they regained control.

"We'd have to be very careful," Captain Hamilton warned. "The cartel would not take it lightly if we were undermining its sales."

He looked over at Sameena. "It's lucky for you that I'm honest," he said. "As it is…you can start using the berries soon enough, but I *will* expect a cut of the profits."

Sameena nodded. "Yes, sir," she said.

"We cross the phase limit in five hours," the Captain added. "I think you'll want to be on the bridge for that, just as I was on my first voyage. Jayne can take you to your cabin and help you get settled in. We'll work out a duty and educational roster for you tomorrow."

"Put her on cooking duties," Jayne said. She pulled a face. "I love Paddy dearly, but when I think about his cooking…"

"People who live in glass starships shouldn't throw stones," her father said. "Your cooking is no better than his."

Sameena looked from one to the other in stark disbelief. *Paddy* – the scarred man who had caught her and dragged her up to the bridge – was the cook? And not Jayne or Ethne, the Captain's wife? *Men* didn't cook, not on Jannah. But she was starting to realise that the rules were different on the ship.

"I can try," she said, remembering all the recipes her mother had taught her. But they all depended on having the right ingredients and she had no idea if they were available in outer space. "I do know how to cook."

"But not on a starship," the Captain said. "Still, you can try."

He looked over at his daughter. "Take her to her cabin, then sit with her for a while," he ordered. "She will probably need company."

Jayne opened her mouth, as if she were going to object, then nodded brusquely and led Sameena out of the compartment and down towards a set of hatches in the bulkheads. Most of them had a name stencilled on them – one read PADDY + JAYNE – but a handful were blank. Jayne keyed a switch outside one of the blank ones and the hatch hissed open, slowly.

"There are too many parts of this ship that are wearing out," she said, by way of explanation. "The ship is really too big for the handful of crew we have, but dad won't hear of exchanging her for something smaller. Nor should he, really. I was *born* on this ship."

Sameena nodded. "How did you meet Paddy?"

"He signed on as a general crewman, with experience in engineering and helm control – and weapons," Jayne explained. "After a few weeks, he'd proved himself and I asked him to marry me."

She smiled at Sameena's disbelieving expression. "That's quite common among the clans," she added. "Marriage and blood ties bind us together, even when we fight – and that's quite common too. One day, Paddy will go to another ship and I will probably go with him."

Sameena shook her head as she followed Jayne into the tiny cabin. It sounded absurd, yet…her own homeworld had been a great deal worse. If she hadn't had such an understanding father, she might be married by now…having met her husband on their wedding day. The marriage would have been arranged by both sets of parents and the bride and groom wouldn't have had any say in the matter.

"Keep the hatch firmly closed at all times," Jayne explained. "This is one of the sealed compartments, where you can undress – although I do recommend that you keep the suit on when you don't specifically need to be without it. You'll notice the telltales at the corner of the airlock" – she pointed to a glowing green light – "that confirm that it is safe to leave the compartment. If they turn red, stay inside and use the terminal to alert the rest of the crew."

Sameena nodded. The compartment was tiny, barely large enough for one person…but it felt better than her bedroom on Jannah. She couldn't have said why.

"The toilet is in the tiny section at the end of the compartment," Jayne continued. "There's a shower at the end of the corridor; you're restricted to only one shower a day, unless you manage to convince someone to trade with you. Water is in short supply on the ship, so learn to be quick when you shower. Luckily, we have plenty of hot air to help dry you."

She smiled, then pushed on. "The terminal is connected to the ship's interior communications network and memory core," she said. "If you want to watch a movie, listen to music or read a textbook, you can access them through the terminal. There are no restrictions on what you can see, but…given where you're from, you might want to give the *Green-Skinned Alien Space Babes* series a miss. And anything else with such a rating."

"I see," Sameena said, although she didn't. Green-skinned alien space babes? "What should I be reading now?"

Jayne glanced at her chronometer. "Mum will probably want you to start early tomorrow," she said, "so I'd honestly advise getting some sleep. But as we're going to be crossing the Phase Limit and you won't want to miss it…"

She picked up the terminal and tapped on it, then passed the device to Sameena. "That's a tutoring program," she explained. "Basically, it teaches you how to use the interface to pull information and entertainment out of the system. But it won't take you long to pick it up."

She was right, Sameena decided, as she experimented with the terminal. It was quite user-friendly, even though she didn't have even the faintest idea of how the technology behind it worked. Once she mastered the basic system, she skimmed though a brief overview of the Empire's history, looking specifically for anything on Jannah. There was almost nothing, beyond a description of the government that was clearly outdated. And a link to a controversy over the removal of the Holy City of Mecca from Earth.

The article reminded her of something she'd been forgetting. "Which way do I pray?"

"I have no idea," Jayne said. She frowned. "Is it really that important to you?"

Sameena hesitated. She had been told that infidels – non-Muslims – were perplexed by even the simplest parts of Islam, or the strict requirements that Muslims were obliged to honour. But part of her wanted Jayne to understand, even though Sameena herself was wondering about the faith. How much of her previously-restricted life had been dictated by the Guardians, rather than Islam itself?

"I think so, yes," she admitted, finally. It was still important to her, after all. She didn't need the Guardians – or the Clerics – to be a good Muslim. "How did they do it in the past?"

"Get the terminal to tell you the direction of Earth, or New Mecca," Jayne said, after taking back the terminal and glancing at it. "There are programs that will keep track of it for you."

She pulled a smaller device off her belt and settled down to read. "Read as much as you like," she added. "You can't trust everything written down in the shared databases, but much of it has been verified by the clans. I guess that's what we get for allowing everyone to contribute. But it's better than the standard Imperial-issue databases. You might learn something useful reading these, while those are full of lies."

Her eyes narrowed. "Just like the ones on your homeworld," she concluded. "How many lies do you think you can uncover with a quick search? A hundred?"

Sameena shrugged. After everything she'd seen and done in the last twenty-four hours, she didn't doubt it for a second.

CHAPTER FIVE

> This is, to some extent, caused by the fact that value is relative. A desire shared by one person may not be shared by others. For example, bras are worn by almost every mature woman, while the number of men who will willingly wear a bra is vanishingly small. Men, simply put, place less value on bras than women. Women, likewise, will not place so much value on male-specific items.
>
> - Professor Leo Caesius, *The Science That Isn't: Economics and the Decline and Fall of the Galactic Empire.*

Despite herself, Sameena had to admit that crossing the Phase Limit and jumping into Phase Space was not particularly exciting. Her homeworld's star was little more than a dot of light, while Jannah itself had vanished somewhere in the darkness of space. On the other hand, the moment they went FTL she knew that she was completely safe. The Guardians could no longer even demand that she be returned to the planet.

"Brad, you have the bridge," Captain Hamilton said. The viewscreens all showed the same inky darkness, an unholy sight that sent a chill running down Sameena's spine. "The rest of us will go eat dinner."

"Bring me something nice," Brad said, quickly. "Or should I wait until the end of my shift?"

Captain Hamilton looked over at Sameena, ignoring his son. "How are you feeling?"

"Relieved," Sameena admitted, finally.

"No nausea?" Ethne asked. "Or even mild discomfort?"

Sameena shook her head. Jayne had warned her that some people felt uncomfortable when entering Phase Space, while a tiny minority of the human race took it so badly that they had to be sedated or placed in a stasis pod before they could leave their home system. But she'd felt almost nothing, apart from a faint quiver passing through her as the starship jumped into Phase Space. She hoped that was a good sign.

"A natural-born spacer," Paddy said, cheerfully. The older man gave Sameena a twisted smile. "Welcome to the clan, my dear."

"Food," Ethne said, firmly. "We can have a small party later."

She led the way down to a small kitchen on deck two. Sameena took one look and knew that she wouldn't be able to cook for her new family, at least until she worked out how to handle the cooking equipment. Almost nothing was recognisable, apart from the kitchen sink. Even when Paddy went to work, providing a running commentary as he produced food from a preservation locker and dumped it into a pan, it was hard to follow what he was doing.

"We took on a consignment of fresh food at Jannah," Paddy explained, as he cracked eggs and dropped their innards into a pan. "After we finish it, we're back on ration bars – hello, constipation and irritation. They used to feed us exclusively on ration bars while I was in the military, just to make sure that we were ready to take it out on anyone fool enough to challenge us."

"He's off telling war stories again," Jayne said, as she pulled the table down from the bulkhead. "I suggest you take everything he says with a grain of salt."

Sameena watched quietly as Paddy placed the pan on a metal surface and tapped a switch. The surface – the stove, she realised – started to glow red, cooking the eggs. She stepped forward, studying the stove carefully. It was hard to see how it worked; it certainly seemed more sophisticated than the gas-fired stove her mother had used.

"Fresh bread," Paddy said, as he started to ladle out the scrambled eggs. "And jam. And butter. And fruit."

Sameena took her plate and started to eat, watching with some amusement as Paddy doled out fruit and vegetables to the two kids. They seemed even more reluctant to eat their vegetables than Abdul had, back on Jannah. The thought caused her a pang of grief. Her brother might have been responsible for her family's arrest, but he'd been a good brother and she missed him. She knew that she would never see him again.

Paddy's cooking wasn't too bad, although the meal was unfamiliar. Sameena couldn't understand why Jayne had grumbled about her husband's cooking, particularly when she didn't have to cook herself. Or maybe it was just part of their odd relationship…if there was something she had learned from the terminal, it was that the outside universe had more complex relationships than anything that had existed on Jannah.

"Thank you," she said, remembering her manners. "Can I help with the washing up?"

Paddy gave her a blank look, then laughed, not unkindly. "No need," he said, as he took her plate and placed it in a drawer. "The automatic washer will take care of it."

Sameena stared as he tapped a button, then pulled the plate back out of the drawer. It was clean. Somehow, seeing the washer in action brought home to her just how much her homeworld had chosen to abandon when the founders had left Earth. Sameena had helped with the washing up almost as soon as she was old enough to walk. How much of her life, she asked herself, had been completely wasted? And how many other labour-saving devices had never been allowed on Jannah?

Jayne placed a hand on Sameena's shoulder and she jumped.

"You need to get some sleep," the doctor said, softly. "I'll lead you back to your cabin, then tuck you in."

"She can borrow Mr. Paws, if she likes," Regina said. The little girl smiled shyly at Sameena, then looked over at Jayne. "Maybe that would help her sleep."

Jayne laughed. "Would you like to borrow a stuffed animal?"

Sameena shook her head. "No, thank you," she said to Regina. "I should be able to sleep without him."

"I never slept without him for the first month on the ship," Regina said. "You can borrow him, if you would like."

"She said no thank you," Jayne said, firmly. She looked over at Sameena. "Coming?"

THE OUTCAST

Sameena nodded and followed her out of the hatch and down towards the cabins. "Mum will be waking you at 0900 tomorrow," Jayne said, once they were alone. "I suggest that you go straight to sleep. Mum will not be happy if you're too tired to wake up tomorrow."

The bunk was uncomfortable, Sameena discovered, but she was too tired to care. Instead, she closed her eyes and tried to sleep, struggling to ignore the omnipresent *thrumming* running through the entire ship. It was funny, she decided, as she rolled over and pressed her ear into the pillow, how she'd managed to ignore the sound when she was awake, but it had come back as soon as she was trying to sleep.

She must have fallen asleep, for the next thing she remembered was Ethne shaking her gently. For a long moment, she thought that everything from Abdul's stupidity to her escape had been a nightmare…and then reality came rushing back as she opened her eyes. The Captain's wife – and XO, according to Jayne – was standing right next to her bunk.

"Time to get up," Ethne said, sharply. "You need to eat something before you face the tutoring machines."

Sameena nodded, climbed out of the bunk and splashed water on her face, careful to allow the drops to fall back into the sink. Jayne hadn't said *much* about how the ship processed and reprocessed water, but some of the technical documents she'd read on the terminal had stated that the ship had no facilities for mining water from interstellar space. They had only a limited supply until they reached their next port of call.

Breakfast consisted of a pair of ration bars and a mug of coffee. The coffee tasted awful compared to the coffee she'd drunk on Jannah, something that puzzled her until Ethne pointed out that the freighter had to carry processed coffee and the planet's inhabitants could obtain fresh coffee. Sameena was still puzzling it over in her head when Ethne introduced her to her other sons, Steve and James. James was so like Jayne that it was easy to tell that they were twins.

"Welcome aboard," Steve said, shaking her hand. By now, it no longer felt strange to be shaking male hands. "I hope you become an engineer. There's no shortage of work for qualified engineers these days."

"Bit too late for her now," James said. "Engineers really start quite young."

"We'll see," Ethne said, crossly. She gave her sons a look that cowed them instantly. "I shall be expecting you to find something for her to do in the next few days."

Sameena was impressed. Boys on Jannah rarely listened to their mothers, certainly not once they were old enough to realise that women were second-class citizens. The clerics preached absolute obedience to fathers – and the clerics themselves, naturally – but they never spoke of obeying one's mother. Abdul had been a nightmare for Sameena's mother – and he'd been one of the better-behaved young men. Ethne, on the other hand, seemed quite capable of dominating her children.

"This way," Ethne said, breaking into Sameena's thoughts. "You can chat to the boys later."

Sameena felt herself flushing as they stepped down the corridor and into the schoolroom, or so she'd come to think of it. There was no sign of the kids, or anyone else. Ethne motioned for her to take a chair, then sat down on the opposite side of the table.

"Ignorance can kill," she said, simply. "But you already know that, don't you?"

"Yes," Sameena said. She'd made a vow to herself when she'd started studying the terminal and making a mental list of documents to read. "I will never be ignorant again."

Ethne's lips twitched. "A very good idea," she agreed, dryly. She cleared her throat, preparing to lecture. "The Empire firmly believes that everyone must attend a standardised educational program from four to twenty years old, complete with mandatory school attendance and constant testing. We disagree – and we take advantage of a loophole in the law to school our children while they are onboard ship. You fall into an odd category as none of the qualifications you have earned on your homeworld are valid outside your solar system."

"I earned none," Sameena admitted. "My father would never allow me to be tested."

"Education comes in three sections," Ethne continued. "First, the student spends an hour a day using one of the educational programs." She nodded towards the tutoring machines. "Second, the student completes assignments handed out by a tutor, which are then passed back to the tutor when the ship returns to port. Third, and perhaps most importantly, there are practical lessons supervised by a qualified starship officer.

"In order to start you on the first – and to prepare you for obtaining assignments from the tutor – we need to know where you are. What I've done is program the tutoring machine to give you an examination, starting from the first level and moving upwards to the highest levels. It will measure your basic skills, knowledge of the standard curriculum and a handful of other important points. Don't worry if you find that most of the questions are impossible for you to answer. There are questions in the machine that *I* would have trouble answering."

Sameena winced. It was hard to imagine *anything* that would defeat Ethne.

Ethne gave her a reassuring smile. "After that, we will run through basic starship safety," she added. "You really have to *understand* just how dangerous life in space can be."

She stood up and walked over to one of the tutoring machines. "Sit here," she said, pointing to a stool in front of the machine. The console came to life as Sameena sat down. "Would you rather read the questions off the screen or have them read out to you?"

"Read the questions," Sameena said, after a moment.

"Smart choice," Ethne said. She pointed to the image of a talking face. "If you need a question read out to you, push that button."

She tapped a switch and a question appeared on the screen. *What is the first letter in the Imperial Standard alphabet?*

"Tap the screen to select the answer you believe to be accurate," Ethne said. "It will automatically move on to the next one, without telling you if you were right or wrong. You'll get a full breakdown of your answers at the end of the session. *Don't* try to guess the answer, just skip the question."

She smiled at Sameena. "Ready?"

Sameena nodded, mutely.

"Go," Ethne ordered.

The questions, as Ethne had promised, started out easy and rapidly grew harder and harder, forcing her to skip past them. Basic maths was straightforward – her father had insisted that she studied maths with the same intensity as her brother and she *knew* that she was good at it – but questions on history, science and biology left her feeling slow and stupid. Jannah had taught her next to nothing about the Empire's history, save only that it was a wretched hive of scum and villainy that the founders had been glad to abandon. Even a couple of questions on comparative religion left her wondering how many other lies she'd believed...

Several other questions tested her problem-solving skills. Once she realised that the precise details were there to hide the nature of the problem, she found them easier to solve. Some of them were even practical applications of math skills she'd mastered as a child, then discarded as useless. But then, they *would* have been useless to a girl on Jannah. There was no way that she would be allowed to seek employment as an engineer.

"Good work," Ethne said, as the volley of questions finally came to an end. She'd been sitting at the table, reading from her terminal. "The machine will analyse your performance and then determine the best path of study for you."

Sameena slumped, feeling uncomfortably sweaty. Her head *hurt*; she'd wondered why Abdul had complained so much after examinations, but now she knew. Besides, she had a feeling that *his* examinations had been more focused on rote learning and recitation than actually forcing him to *think*. *Her* exam had been much tougher, even if she hadn't been threatened with a beating for mispronouncing a single word.

"Drink this," Ethne said, passing her a flask. The liquid inside tasted odd, but refreshing. "I remember my first exam *far* too well. Training can be very taxing."

She smiled, as if she had made a joke. Sameena didn't understand.

"My father was a trader," Sameena said, instead. "He tried to make sure that I learned..."

"He failed in his duty to you," Ethne said, shortly. "Imagine denying someone an education because of their *sex*!"

Sameena hesitated, unsure of what to say. On one hand, her father *had* seen to it that she had received some education, certainly far more than any of the other girls she knew. But on the other hand, he had never insisted that she take exams or tried to enter one of the few career paths open for women. She might have made a good *teacher*, if she'd been given a chance.

"I wouldn't have been able to do anything with it," she confessed. "Jannah has little place for educated women."

"You're not on Jannah now," Ethne reminded her. There was a bleep from the tutoring machine. "Let's have a look."

She skimmed through the details as they flowed over the screen. "Interesting…you rated high in problem solving and maths, poorly in most other fields. Basic comprehension is good; advanced comprehension is very limited, despite your age. There are concepts that you would never have been exposed to on your homeworld, I suspect. Picking them up is going to take time. Still, there's plenty we can work with. But you probably won't make an engineer."

Sameena blinked in surprise. "Why not?"

"It can take years of study to become fully qualified," Ethne explained. "Steve started when he was nine, practically apprenticing himself to my younger brother. By the time he was sixteen, he could dismantle a Phase Drive and put it back together…which, by the way, is *not* something we are supposed to do. You, on the other hand, are missing plenty of background knowledge that Steve picked up from birth."

She shrugged. "On the other hand, you would make an excellent trader," she added. "I think I'll treat you as my apprentice. That will give you some background you will desperately need. But you will still have to work all over the ship."

Sameena nodded. She had expected no less.

"I'm going to work my way through your results," Ethne said. "In the meantime, I want you to study basic safety precautions. Ignorance can kill."

"Ignorance can kill," Sameena repeated. She had a feeling that she was going to be sick of that phrase before too long. But she knew that Ethne was right. "Show me what to study."

Ethne grinned and tapped on the tutoring machine. "This is a very basic program," she admitted, as the screen changed. "And it can be very graphic. But it is still deeply important that you study it. After that…"

Her smile grew wider. "I want you to write a report," she added, "and list everything that could have gone wrong with your harebrained plan to escape your homeworld. The program will show you just about everything, but I want you to use your imagination too. Do you understand me?"

"Yes," Sameena said. She hesitated, then admitted something she'd realised while watching Jayne at work. "I don't know how to type."

"The machine has a basic tutoring program. You'll pick it up," Ethne assured her. "And once the report is done, we can go for lunch and then Paddy will teach you how to cook. Maybe you would be a better cook."

"His food wasn't *bad*," Sameena insisted. "I rather liked it."

Ethne grinned. "He is good with the simple recipes," she admitted. "It's when things get complicated that he tends to run into problems."

Chapter Six

> However, value also depends on time and place. If I may borrow a term from a good economics primer, the value of a bagful of gold is quite high in the world – but almost worse than useless on a desert island. Would you rather have a bag of potatoes or gold on a desert island? You could not eat the gold.
> - Professor Leo Caesius, *The Science That Isn't: Economics and the Decline and Fall of the Galactic Empire.*

Over the next two weeks, Sameena felt her life beginning to settle down into a routine that was both strange and comforting. Her mornings were spent in front of the tutoring machine, working her way through educational programs she knew to be designed for children much younger than her, while her afternoons were spent gaining practical experience around the freighter. Steve and James taught her a great deal about basic maintenance, while Brad taught her how to operate the helm console and Paddy taught her how to cook. Most of what her mother had taught her was still relevant, but the technology he used added its own wrinkles. The microwave alone would have revolutionised her life on Jannah if the technology had ever been imported.

"And to think that this technology actually predates space travel," Paddy informed her, when she broke down and cried in the kitchen – the galley, as he called it. "Your planet's founders were fools."

Once, she would have found such a statement insulting – if not outright blasphemous. But after a week of reading as much as she could, she had the feeling that he was right. Jannah's founders had wanted to preserve their own power base as much as they had wanted to preserve their religion and they'd done it by banning most technology from their world. If men and women had to work hard every day just to survive – and the schools taught rote learning rather than actual *thought* – there would be less opportunity for people to start to question the way things were. And, if people *did* question, there were always the Guardians, ready to step in and remove the questioner before it was too late.

The version of history she'd pulled out of the starship's database had been far more complex than anything she'd learned on Jannah. Jayne had been right; there were plenty of Islamic worlds in the galaxy, all claiming to be the sole possessor of the true faith. Some of them didn't seem to differ from Jannah much, if at all; others seemed to embrace high technology or political and social innovations that threatened to turn the world upside down. Who would ever have imagined a world that *wasn't* governed by clerics? Sameena hadn't…until she'd realised that clerical worlds were in the minority.

"That's what tends to happen," Paddy told her, when she outlined her thoughts. "The planet's founders try to get away from the" – he held up his hands in makeshift quotation marks – "evil demon called *technology*. And then their sons and daughters discover what their parents left behind and start demanding change – or simply emigrate in vast numbers, leaving the world behind to die on the vine. It's amazing how being forced to live rough convinces you that technology is actually a *good* thing."

He smirked at her expression. "You'd better get on with scrubbing the corridors," he added, not unkindly. "You're going to be learning how to use a weapon later and I don't want to have to wait for you because the XO insists that you do it again."

Sameena nodded and headed down towards the engineering compartment, where the vacuum mops and other cleaning supplies were stored. Everyone onboard took a turn scrubbing the corridors, she'd been told, along with cleaning out the pipes and several other duties that were thoroughly disgusting. Sameena didn't mind it as much as Steve and James, both of whom had complained about it endlessly when their mother handed out a list of chores, but then she'd spent plenty of time scrubbing floors on Jannah. The tools here made it much simpler to do the work.

She took a moment to check the berries as they floated within a nutrient solution. Once they had explained to him what the berries *were*, Steve had rigged up a hydroponics compartment using some of the emergency supplies Imperial Law insisted that all starships carry. Steve had explained that being able to force-grow algae for rations wasn't really a good idea at all – if they were stranded, they would probably grow old and die without hope of rescue – but the bureaucrats had insisted. Sameena had heard enough about *them* to realise that they were just as bad as the clerics back on Jannah, without the excuse of serving God.

The berries were growing at surprising speed, as the instructions from Uncle Muhammad had promised. Steve had suggested that they take the first harvest and use it to expand production, then start processing the berries into mead after they had enough to produce a few dozen bottles. Captain Hamilton was still thinking about the best way to sell them onwards, but it would be several weeks before they had to come to any final decision. Sameena took one last look, then hurried down to the supply cupboard. Ethne was a strict supervisor and she didn't want to let her down.

"You did well on your last set of tests," Ethne said, as soon as Sameena appeared. "How have you been getting along with everyone else?"

Sameena hesitated. She'd grown to like everyone on the ship, although there were times when she was reminded just how *different* they were from her. Paddy and Jayne seemed to have no shame; they kissed regularly in front of the entire crew. Steve, meanwhile, had stripped to his shorts while working on the drives, embarrassing Sameena when she'd walked into the compartment and seen his bare chest. And Brad seemed torn between being friendly and being unable to look at her without blushing.

"I'm learning how to get along," she said, finally. She hadn't dared ask anyone, but a quick review of the database had produced files on culture shock. It seemed to be a common problem in the Empire, particularly when dealing with isolated planets like Jannah. The trader clans didn't seem to have any problems with it. "But I have a long way to go."

"Everyone speaks well of you," Ethne said. "Steve was very pleased with how precise you were with the machine tools."

Sameena felt herself flushing. It was good to think that her mother's endless lessons in how to be a young lady had come in handy for *something*, even though her mother would have been horrified at where she was using them. Precision and dedication had been important to her, Sameena knew, and she'd used them in working with Steve's tools.

Ethne bounced other questions off her as she went to work, removing as much dust as she could from the deck. Basic maintenance, Steve had told her time and time again, was the key to keeping the independent freighter functioning. It was easier to prevent a problem from arising than deal with it once it was too late. There were times when Sameena felt that she'd personally replaced every component on the ship twice over, although she knew that was absurd. *Logan* was colossal. It was strange to realise that there were other starships in the galaxy that made the medium freighter look tiny.

"Your bargaining skills aren't too bad," Ethne said, afterwards. "All you really need is an appreciation for how much something ought to be worth."

Sameena nodded. Jannah had valued gold and silver…and both were almost absurdly cheap in the Empire. She'd puzzled over that until she'd realised that gold and silver – and other valuable metals – could be mined from asteroid belts. HE3, on the other hand, was important almost everywhere, as it powered everything from starships to planet-side fusion plants. It was tricky, sometimes, to figure out what was important – and would therefore bring a profit – and what was a waste of space. In the right place, even canisters of oxygen could be worth a fortune.

"I'll be taking you to Madagascar, once we get you an ID card," Ethne added. "You can see the bargaining process for yourself. The kids will complain, but…"

"You don't have to," Sameena objected. "They might deserve it more."

"It's your first chance to see somewhere away from your own planet," Ethne pointed out. "And besides, it isn't as if you have assignments to hand in…is it?"

Sameena nodded. Richard and Regina would be handing their assignments to the tutor at Madagascar when they finally arrived – and, if they did well, they would be allowed to visit the station rather than spending time rewriting their assignments. They'd pointed out that Sameena, who was actually *behind* them despite being older, should be subject to the same rules. Ethne hadn't bothered to say anything in response, apart from ordering the kids to carry on with their own assignments.

"Don't worry," Ethne added, dryly. "We'll get you some assignments while we're there."

She inspected Sameena's work, then nodded. "Very good," she said. "I believe that you have an appointment with Paddy?"

"Yes," Sameena said.

"Take weapons training seriously," Ethne warned. "Anyone who fucks around with a weapon is lucky to live long enough to regret it."

Sameena was still mulling over Ethne's words when she entered the empty cargo hold that Paddy was using for training. The kids grinned at her as they finished cleaning their weapons, then headed out of the hatch, chattering excitedly to each other. Sameena felt an odd rush of affection as she watched them go – she'd always liked kids – before Paddy coughed, drawing her attention back to him. He was holding a single metal box in his hands.

"It is possible to make a fantastically complex weapon," he said, as he pressed his thumb against the sensor on the box. "But we don't use them. Why?"

"Because the more complex a device is, the more likely that it will break down," Sameena said. Steve had told her pretty much the same thing when she'd been working on the ship's internal systems. Much of the technology actually predated spaceflight. "The more things that can go wrong, the more likely that something *will* go wrong."

"Steve *does* have such an elegant turn of phrase," Paddy said, dryly. He smiled, as if there was something he found funny. "But he's basically right."

He opened the box and passed it to her. It held a simple pistol, gleaming silver under the single light mounted overhead. Sameena hesitated, feeling an odd sense of trepidation, and then touched the weapon with her fingers. It felt reassuringly solid as she brushed her fingertips across the handle.

"There are several rules you need to bear in mind at all times when dealing with weapons," Paddy said. His eyes hardened suddenly. "If you break any of them, you will *not* enjoy the consequences. Do you understand me?"

Sameena nodded, wordlessly.

"Do *not* point your gun at anyone unless you mean to use it," Paddy said, his eyes never leaving her face. "Do *not* trust anyone to tell you anything about your gun. Do *not* carry your gun off the ship without checking the local laws first. And do *not* give it to anyone else, unless there is no other choice.

"The gun has no mind of its own," he added. "You, the bearer, are the one who will determine what it does, either deliberately or through fucking up. You are the one who will be held responsible for whatever it does. So be careful!"

He pulled the weapon out of the box and held it in front of Sameena's face. "This is the safety," he said. "When on, the gun will not fire. Make sure you keep the safety on unless you actually intend to use the gun. I've known people do themselves a serious injury through jamming the gun into the holster – or their pockets – without bothering to click the safety on first. Bear that in mind at all times.

"The gun needs to be taken apart, cleaned and then put back together regularly," he continued. "Make sure you do it every day; if the gun gets jammed up, it will be unable to fire. Or it might explode in your hand."

Paddy scowled. "The Army claims that this particular brand can take a great deal of mistreatment before it is rendered unserviceable. They're right, I suppose, but people who take care of their weapons can expect their weapons to take care of them."

Sameena sat down on the deck and carefully took the weapon apart, following his instructions. It was actually simple, compared to some of the components Steve had made her dismantle for practice; she oiled the interior and then put the gun back together again. Paddy passed her a clip of ammunition, then caught her hand before she could start loading it into the gun. Sameena winced in pain at his grip.

"You have the gun pointed at your leg," he said, releasing her. "Be *careful*."

She flushed, then loaded the gun. It felt deadlier, somehow, with ammunition loaded into the weapon. She touched the safety, smiling inwardly. The Guardians would be horrified if they saw a woman holding a gun. Women – and most men - were barred from all means of self-defence on Jannah.

"That's the target," Paddy said, pointing towards the silhouette at the far end of the compartment. "Take aim and shoot him."

Sameena lifted the gun, took aim and pulled the trigger. It clicked.

Paddy laughed at her embarrassment. "Take off the safety," he reminded her, dryly. "And then try to learn how to do it quickly."

This time, the weapon jerked in her hand and produced a deafening sound. She saw a spark where the bullet had struck the far bulkhead, missing the target by several metres. Paddy patiently corrected her and told her to fire again. This time, she hit the target in the arm.

"It takes time to master a handgun enough to shoot accurately," Paddy said, when she had run through the whole clip. "We shall be practicing every second day."

He took back the weapon, removed the empty clip and then passed it back to her to clean.

"The Empire has a blanket ban on civilians owning weapons in the Core Worlds," Paddy lectured, as Sameena took the weapon apart for the second time. "Outside the Core, the laws tend to differ depending on where you are. Keeping the weapon on the ship is almost always legal, but there are places where you cannot take it off the ship without special permits. If you are caught carrying a weapon there, they'll ship you off to a penal colony faster than you can blink."

He snorted. "Not that it really works," he added. "There are enough illegal weapons on Earth to keep a revolution going for years.

"You need to research the laws *thoroughly* if you intend to go planetside," he warned. "The first-stage colony worlds tend to permit hunting rifles and pistols, but frown on anything military-grade. There's a balance between making sure that the settlers can defend themselves from wild animals and not defend themselves from tax collectors."

He shook his head. "And there are corporate sponsored worlds where weapons are banned completely. They know that an armed population will rise up against them at once."

Sameena frowned. "My homeworld banned weapons too," she said.

"Probably afraid that someone would start shooting at your Guardians," Paddy said. He took back the weapon and examined it with a cynical eye, then nodded and put it back in the case. "They tend to disguise it behind concern for public safety, but that's the usual motive."

He snorted. "You *can* take the weapon with you when you go to Madagascar," he explained, "but you need to be careful. If you punch a hole through the walls, they'll put you through it before they seal it up. Or worse."

Sameena nodded. She'd looked up the Empire's laws – and then the simpler laws written for colonies that rarely saw an Imperial Navy starship. Most of them were brutally simple; a murderer was executed, a thief spent a lifetime on a penal world…or indentured servitude. It didn't seem a very pleasant life.

"I shall be expecting your shooting to match that of the kids in a month," he concluded. "Believe me, you *will* need to carry a weapon in some places."

"Thank you," Sameena said.

He passed her the case. "Keep it in your cabin, but remember what I said about responsibility," he said. "Clean it every day. And *don't* practice shooting without someone else to supervise – one of the adults. The XO came very close to strangling the kids after they started to practice on their own and then claimed that they were supervising each other."

"I won't do that," Sameena promised. "Besides, I don't have any ammunition."

Paddy's lips quirked into a smile. "You'd be surprised by how many recruits manage to miss *that*," he said. "All those idiotic war movies show the characters possessing unlimited ammunition so they can fire madly towards the enemy. It doesn't work like that in real life."

He passed her a pair of clips, then pushed her gently towards the hatch. "You'd better go catch some sleep," he ordered. "You'll be helping me cook tonight. Unless you want to do it yourself…?"

Sameena made a face. "I think you'd better be there to supervise," she said. There had been no way to know that putting metal in the microwave was asking for trouble…at least until Paddy had pointed it out, sarcastically. It had been sparking like mad when she'd pulled it out. "I am not quite ready for it yet."

Paddy snorted. "They'll love your cooking," he told her. "Besides, if they ever tasted military rations, they'd praise mine to the skies."

Chapter Seven

> This can be clearly seen with a cursory glance into the past. Salt, now so commonplace, was once used as a currency by the Roman Empire (and other states of that era.) Aluminium was once hideously expensive; now, it is almost worthless. The claim that the Prophet Muhammad was promised seventy-two raisins rather than virgins, which seems laughable on the surface, actually makes a great deal of sense. Raisins would have been immensely valuable to a merchant like Muhammad.
> - Professor Leo Caesius, *The Science That Isn't: Economics and the Decline and Fall of the Galactic Empire.*

The inky darkness of Phase Space suddenly flared with light, then dimmed down to show a starfield outside the starship's hull. Sameena caught her breath as she realised that she was seventeen light years from Jannah, far away enough that the light of the planet's star originated from a time before she had been born. It was a concept she would never have understood – or even realised existed – before stowing away on the freighter.

"Local space seems empty, Captain," Brad said. "Picking up beacons from Madagascar, dead ahead."

Captain Hamilton smiled. "Shoot them our beacon," he ordered. "And then take us in towards the station."

Sameena settled back into her chair and watched as Brad worked his console. Space travel seemed to be both very fast and very slow, even though she knew that they were moving fast enough to circle Jannah within seconds. It would still take the ship hours to travel deeper into the system and match orbits with Madagascar. She pulled up the system display on her terminal and studied it with interest. Madagascar was a far more *interesting* star system than Jannah.

There was no Earth-like world in the system, merely a Mars-like world where genetically-engineered lichen and other modified crops were slowly attempting to turn the barren world into a garden spot. The terraforming process, according to the files she'd read, had been underway for nearly two hundred years and would take at least another five hundred more, unless the Empire chose to make an additional investment in the system. Instead, it seemed that the settlers were content to wait. There was no shortage of Earth-like worlds in the sector that didn't need extensive terraforming before settlement.

Madagascar itself was a large moon orbiting a gas giant, which was surrounded by a handful of cloudscoops, industrial nodes and an Imperial Navy shipyard. Sameena found herself studying the cloudscoops with considerable interest as the freighter approached the moon; she knew, from her research, that the cloudscoops underpinned the interstellar economy. A dozen large ships she recognised as tankers were heading away from the gas giant as they approached, escorted by a handful of smaller ships. Pirates, according to Captain Hamilton, had been growing bolder in the last few years, pressing attacks against isolated colony worlds and starships travelling independently. A HE3 tanker would be a valuable prize.

"Steer us towards Orbit Three," Captain Hamilton ordered. "We'll have to see what sort of contract we can find here."

Sameena frowned, inwardly. *Logan* hadn't taken much from Jannah, apart from a handful of sealed crates that were intended to be passed on to a shipping agent unopened. She had a suspicion she knew what was in the crates, but Captain Hamilton had told her that they weren't allowed to open them or they might be sued. There would be a flat fee for delivery and little else. Perhaps they really needed to sell some of the mead. But producing it was going to be difficult.

Orbit Three came into view. Sameena stared, her brain unable to quite process what it was seeing. The orbital station was a massive rock, studded with domes and long struts that reached out towards incoming freighters. Hundreds of tiny lights bustled around the structure; it took her a moment to realise that they were shuttles, going to and from the moon below. Some of the struts were attached to freighters, she saw as they came closer; others were empty, just waiting for someone to arrive.

"We have permission to dock," Ethne said, softly. "Captain?"

"Take us in," her husband ordered. "Gently, if you please."

Sameena barely felt the faint quiver that ran through the ship as they docked with the station. There was a flicker of discomfort as the artificial gravity field adjusted itself to match the field inside the station, then nothing. The omnipresent *thrumming* echoing through the ship slowly faded away to nothingness. Oddly, its absence made her feel uncomfortable.

"Good work," Captain Hamilton said. "I shall see to the transhipment of our goods. Ethne, if you would care to take Sameena…"

"That isn't fair," Richard protested. Like Sameena, he and his sister had been invited to watch as the ship came into port. "She didn't complete her assignments."

Captain Hamilton gave him a stern look. "And yours, I trust, are perfect?"

Richard reddened, but said nothing.

"Besides, she has yet to start properly," Ethne added. She looked over at Sameena. "Keep the shipsuit on, but wear the clothes you brought from your homeworld over it. Luckily, no one here is likely to recognise your point of origin as long as you don't wear the scarf."

Sameena nodded, hiding her embarrassment. She knew that she was supposed to wear a headscarf when near an unrelated man – and there were six unrelated men on the freighter – but she'd given up after the second day. Now…the thought of not wearing it made her cringe, yet she didn't have a choice. She didn't want to be publically identified as a refugee from anywhere.

"And take your pistol," Paddy added. "Madagascar allows open carry, but be careful you don't shoot the wrong person."

"I won't," Sameena assured him.

She went back to her cabin, pulled the clothes she'd brought from Jannah out of her drawer and peered at them. Compared to what Jayne wore, they were almost ridiculously covering…but they still felt comfortable. She dressed quickly, then walked down to the airlock. Ethne was already standing there, holding a terminal in her hand.

"Don't say a word, unless you get asked a direct question," she warned, as she started to open the airlock. "Stick to the script, if you do get asked something – anything. Madagascar generally minds its own business, but sometimes there are changes."

She led the way through the airlock, down a long tube that seemed dangerously fragile, and through a second airlock. The smell struck Sameena as soon as the airlock hissed open, a strange mixture of unwashed humans, spices, alien cooking and plenty of other smells she couldn't quite identify. She remembered what she'd been told about everywhere smelling differently, particularly to newcomers, but it was still hard to take a deep breath. Inside, Ethne spoke briefly to a black-uniformed man and then walked past him. The man gave her a sidelong glance as she passed, but said nothing.

"Madagascar doesn't have much of a permanent population on the surface, despite the presence of the cloudscoops," Ethne explained, as they walked down a long corridor. "Most of the inhabitants prefer to live in orbit."

They reached the end of the corridor. Sameena stopped, dead. Ahead of them was a tangled mass of tiny stalls, shops built into the walls…and thousands of people, walking around in hundreds of different clothing styles. There were women who were completely topless, men wearing clothes so bright that it hurt her eyes to look at them…one man seemed to be dressed in living snakes and little else. One of the topless woman caught her eye and winked at her; Sameena flushed and shrank back behind Ethne. The sight was completely overwhelming.

A man and a woman walked past her, wearing drab clothes. There was something wrong with their faces, she realised, but she couldn't see what until the woman turned slightly, revealing that she had pointy ears. Sameena stared; she'd researched body-modification technology, back when she'd realised what it could do for her, but pointy ears seemed a little extreme.

"They're a…religious sect," Ethne explained, when Sameena asked. "Dedicated to the principles of pure logic and absolute emotional control. It's quite rare to see them this far from their homeworld."

Sameena found herself looking back at the pair. "And they do that to themselves deliberately?"

Ethne shrugged. "The changes to their ears – and a few others intended to make life on their homeworld more bearable – are actually quite minor," she said. "There are others who are far more extreme. I know a world that is inhabited by mermen and mermaids, humans with fishy tails and a thoroughly weird outlook on life."

"I don't believe it," Sameena said. "You're pulling my leg."

"Go look it up," Ethne said. She gave Sameena a thin-lipped smile. "I've always found it useful never to underestimate the limits of human stupidity."

She led Sameena forward into the mass of stalls. Sameena looked around, seeing men and women who were huge and others who were tiny; she would have thought they were children if they hadn't looked physically mature. Some had white, black, brown or yellow skins; others seemed to have gifted themselves with biologically impossible skin tones. One man, with bright blue skin, seemed to be arguing loudly with another man over the price of foodstuffs at his stall.

There seemed to be no rhyme or reason to the stalls, she realised as they moved deeper into the crush. Food stalls – her stomach rumbled as she smelled something hot and spicy – were right next to stalls that sold clothes or weapons. One large stall was crammed with weapons, ranging from pistols like the one Paddy had given her to massive weapons that were taller than Sameena herself. Behind the weapons, there were walking suits of armour, all pitted and scarred from years of active service. She felt herself flushing as she saw one suit of armour with very prominent breasts, suggesting that whoever had ordered it was larger than Jayne.

"In here," Ethne said, pulling her towards a wall. There was a door half-concealed behind a large clothing store. "You and Jayne can go clothes shopping later."

The racket behind them faded away as the door closed with a loud thud. Sameena frowned as she saw the darkened corridor, blocked by two of the oversized red-skinned men. They didn't seem to be carrying any weapons, but their clenched fists seemed larger than her head. She had a feeling that if she shot one of them he probably wouldn't notice.

"We're here to see Jack," Ethne said, briskly. If she was intimidated by the men, she didn't show it. "I think he knows who we are."

There was a long pause – long enough for Sameena to realise that the men were using some form of communication system to talk to their superiors – and then they stepped aside, motioning for Ethne and Sameena to walk past them. Ethne led Sameena down the corridor and through a door that opened as they approached. Inside, a man with a curiously immobile face sat at a desk facing them.

"Be seated," he said. His voice was flatter than the standard voice produced by the tutoring machine. "Madame Hamilton. What can I do for you?"

"We need a set of false ID papers," Ethne said. She motioned to Sameena. "Something that will suffice for the nonce."

Jack's gaze shifted to Sameena and she had to fight not to look away. His eyelids were completely missing, rendering his stare truly terrifying. She couldn't understand how he could sleep without being able to close his eyes.

"That should be doable, provided that she has no record," Jack said. He looked back at Ethne. "*Does* she have a record?"

"No," Ethne said, flatly. "There should be no record of her birth outside her homeworld."

"A black colony, then," Jack said. He picked up a terminal and peered down at it. "I'll give her residency papers from the Lumpur Cluster. They send hundreds of people to the Empire every year, so that won't raise any eyebrows. That can be leveraged into getting her an Empire-standard ID card. There's nothing particularly special about her genotype, is there?"

"Just a little hackwork," Ethne said. "Nothing specific to her homeworld."

"Good," Jack said. He gave Sameena a creepy smile, then passed her the terminal. "Press your fingertips against the indicated places."

Sameena obeyed, then passed the terminal back to him.

"Good," he said. There was a brief pause. "No trace of your fingerprints or DNA code in the Imperial Criminal Database." He looked over at Ethne. "Did you bring the other documents?"

Ethne produced a datachip from her pocket and dropped it on the table. "Medical profile, starship schedules, guardianship and sponsor records, a handful of educational certificates from a Class-A rated machine. We plan to get more of them this week."

"Educational certificates aren't *that* important," Jack said, dismissively. He looked back at Sameena. "Come back in two days to pick up your documents. Welcome to the Empire."

Ethne didn't say anything until they were back onboard the freighter. "Jack isn't exactly cheap, but he's the best in the business," she explained. "I think it would be better not to have to answer too many questions about where we actually picked you up. Given our flight path over the last two years, it would be difficult for someone to pick holes in your story. As long as you don't try to lie too blatantly, it should be safe enough."

She paused. "We listed ourselves as your guardians" – she looked apologetic as Sameena flinched at the word – "and sponsors. Try not to get in trouble, as we will be liable for everything you do. It's basically the same arrangement as we have with the kids, but you don't have anyone else to speak for you. So be *careful*."

"Thank you," Sameena said, giving Ethne a hug. "But…why did he think I was a criminal?"

"You're not the only person who might want a false ID," Ethne pointed out, rather dryly. "If you'd had a criminal record, Jack would have had to work harder to ensure that there was nothing to encourage a suspicious customs officer to carry out a more thorough check. As it is, you're clean, just unregistered. Which would have made life difficult for you if you wanted to find a job without registering."

Sameena frowned. She could, in theory, apply for asylum, but a careful review of the databases had exposed the problems with that approach. The Imperial Navy might view her as underage, and therefore not considered capable of making decisions for herself, or they might conclude that local law held priority and return her to Jannah. Even if they allowed her to stay on Madagascar or another colony, she had no qualifications they would recognise, ensuring that she would be doomed to eternal poverty. Or be forced to join a colony mission to a low-tech world.

"Thank you," she said, again. It was funny how quickly she'd lost her respect for the law…what little respect she'd had in the first place, she had to admit. If she'd respected her homeworld's law, she would never have striven to learn what her father had been trying to teach her. "But how do we know he won't betray us?"

"Too many people would want him dead if he spoke the name of even *one* of his clients," Ethne explained. "And he has an implant in his skull that will kill him if it thinks he's being interrogated. He's as trustworthy as a forger and hacker ever gets."

She sobered. "Which isn't very far, really."

Sameena shivered. "What do we do now?"

Ethne smiled, nastily. "You have a couple of days, which I would suggest you spend with the tutoring machine," she said. "The tutor on Madagascar will want to examine you personally once you have the papers, so you can prepare for your exams. Unless Steve wants you…he has some components he was talking about stripping out and replacing, assuming that we can find the money to pay for them. Costs of spare parts keep going upwards."

Sameena scowled. "Why?"

"There's a shortage, of course," Ethne said. She nodded as they reached Sameena's cabin. "Have a nap, then join us for dinner tonight. We'll be bringing food back from Madagascar rather than cooking for ourselves, which should be a relief."

"Anyone would think that you don't like my cooking," Sameena said, deadpan. Part of her felt a little insulted. Paddy had allowed her to take over the cooking full time one week away from Madagascar. "I do try to cook well."

"But there are limits to what you can do with the equipment on hand," Ethne said. "I used to cook myself. It's a very useful skill, but you don't get high-class meals in space unless you happen to travel on a luxury liner. And that costs more money than most people make in their entire lives."

Sameena nodded, then stepped into her cabin and picked up her terminal. This time, a new icon appeared on the screen when she clicked it on, inviting her to access the datanet binding Madagascar together. Carefully, she accessed the network and downloaded a list of prices from the seven main distribution companies in the system. Ethne had been right, she realised grimly. Prices *were* going up. She'd thought about using the money on her Credit Coin to fund the purchases, but it was clear that she simply didn't have enough. Not if she wanted to pay Jack too.

"That's interesting," she mused to herself, as she started asking questions. The basic laws of economics should be the same on Madagascar as they were on Jannah, even if the two worlds were completely dissimilar. "Now, where do the spare parts actually come *from*?"

Slowly, very slowly, the germ of an idea started to form in her mind.

CHAPTER
EIGHT

> The foundations of basic economies rested on the barter system, which might operate through a cobbler (shoe-maker) exchanging a pair of shoes with the blacksmith, in exchange for the blacksmith producing his tools. The blacksmith might also have an understanding with the local butcher, who would give the blacksmith some meat in exchange for the knives he used to cut up the animals. And so on.
>
> - Professor Leo Caesius, *The Science That Isn't: Economics and the Decline and Fall of the Galactic Empire.*

Two days later, she sat back from the terminal with a sigh of relief.

"Congratulations," Professor Sorrel said. He was an elderly man with an air of fussy precision that reminded Sameena of the clerics back on Jannah. "You have completed the placement exams. Welcome to the program."

He held out a hand. After a moment's hesitation, Sameena took it and they shook hands.

"I shall work out a lesson plan for you this afternoon and relay it to your ship," he continued. "You will be expected to turn in essays and reports upon your return to Madagascar or another associated port, which will be marked by myself or one of the other tutors. This chip" – he pulled a datachip out of his pocket and passed it to her – "contains specific information for your guardian and for any other tutors, should you be unable to return. I should warn you that accessing it yourself will be considered cheating."

"Thank you," Sameena said, sincerely. The Professor might have watched her like a hawk as she struggled to answer some of the more complex questions, but he also treated her as a genuine student, not a girl pretending to be a boy. Or one who was overstepping her place. "I won't look at it myself."

The Professor smiled, slightly. "Asking someone else to look at it and tell you the answers is also considered cheating," he said. "But your guardian has done a good job in the past."

Looking after Richard and Regina, Sameena guessed. But then, all of the Captain's children had been homeschooled, rather than exposed to the tender mercies of the Imperial Education Service. From what she'd heard, the IES was even less inclined to actually *teach* than the clerics on Jannah.

"I'll see you when you next return to Madagascar," the Professor concluded. "Send in the next person on your way out."

Sameena nodded and exited the examination room through an airlock that looked reassuringly solid. Orbit Three was honeycombed with airlocks and other emergency measures, ensuring that a disaster wouldn't kill everyone onboard. Steve had pointed out, rather darkly, that a single nuke could shatter the entire asteroid, then assigned her an essay on how Orbit One was poorly designed. It had taken her several hours to work out that the asteroid's life support systems were actually several separate systems jammed together.

Outside, there were a handful of other students – and Jayne. Sameena glanced at the students, feeling an odd sense of relief that some of them were older than her, then looked over at the ship's doctor. Jayne stood up, hooked her arm through Sameena's arm and then led her out of the compartment. It was quieter in this part of the asteroid, but Sameena could still hear the sound of people talking echoing through the corridors.

"Mum says that I am to take you clothes shopping," Jayne said, before Sameena could say a word. "And then take a look at whatever else you might want in the stalls."

Sameena hesitated. "I don't know how long my cash will last…"

Jayne snorted and passed her a Credit Coin. "You were paid standard wages for a very junior crewwoman," she said. "Didn't dad *tell* you?"

"No," Sameena said, looking down at the Credit Coin. It proclaimed her to have a balance of four thousand credits. "I didn't know…"

"He probably assumed that you knew," Jayne said, crossly. "There are centuries of tradition that state that a ship's commander is not allowed to advise his crew about how to spend or save their money. For example, you could take out insurance if you wanted – or save the money in the local bank, or spend it on just about anything. Teaching the kids is one thing, but pushing an adult…"

She shook her head. "I'll ask mum to go over that with you later," she added. She shot Sameena an inquisitive look. "I wonder how much else we take for granted that will be new and strange to you."

"This asteroid," Sameena said. There were times when she realised just how *alien* the whole environment was, at least to someone who had spent their whole lifetime on a planet's surface. "And much else, I'm sure."

"Don't be afraid to ask," Jayne said. "There's a healthy tradition of self-reliance too, but you don't have to be stupid about it."

Sameena mulled it over as she followed the doctor down the corridor and into one of the larger marketplaces. The noise grew louder the moment they stepped through the airlock; she looked towards the source and saw a handful of men playing instruments in one corner, producing a deafening racket. It sounded like one of the songs the kids listened to when they were off duty. Sameena had listened once and decided that she didn't like it.

"One of the touring bands," Jayne muttered, by way of explanation. "It's pretty hard for anyone to get famous away from their homeworld, unless they travel so often that they can outrun the bootleggers. Someone probably called in a favour and arranged for them to play for the Imperial Navy ships in the system."

She led Sameena away from the band and down towards a large stall, covered in fancy silk that provided some privacy. Inside, there seemed to be endless racks of clothes, ranging from basic tunics and dresses to underwear that made Sameena blush. An overweight woman, standing at the entrance, nodded to them both as they entered, then studied Sameena with frank interest.

"My sister needs a new outfit or two," Jayne said, shortly. "Some basic stuff for onboard wear, a couple of fancy dresses and suchlike. What do you have that might suit her?"

The woman smiled. "I'll have to measure her first," she said. "And then we can see what we have."

"Take a note of your measurements," Jayne ordered, as the woman started to measure Sameena's body. "We can save some time if we have to go elsewhere."

Sameena had never been very fond of clothes shopping, even though it had been one of the few legitimate excuses for young girls to be out of the house. She had known that no one was likely to see her in anything new, apart from her family – and her husband, when she was finally pushed into marriage. Now…part of her was intrigued by the possibility of new clothes. Others would be seeing her in them for the first time.

"You don't want anything too complex for onboard wear," Jayne said. She held up a loose tunic that could be worn over the shipsuit. "This wouldn't be too bad, as long as you wore a utility belt with it so you could carry your tools and terminal."

Sameena nodded, reluctantly. It would make a change from wearing the coat over the shipsuit, without showing off too much of her body. On the other hand, it didn't look very *new*.

"They never do," Jayne said. She grinned. "Everyone wears shabby clothes onboard ship, apart from dad. He thinks he has to look dignified."

"A regular delusion," the storekeeper said. "Get undressed and try the outfit on."

"No," Sameena said, quickly. "I can't…"

Jayne pulled the woman aside and whispered briefly in her ear. Sameena couldn't hear what she said to her, but the woman nodded, threw her a sympathetic look and then pulled the curtain over the entrance. No one could see inside without making it obvious.

"Better do it now," Jayne said. "You won't be able to come back if they don't fit."

Sameena hesitated, then undressed slowly. The woman's gaze was cold and clinical, but Sameena still felt uncomfortable as she pulled on the outfit. When she was dressed, she looked in the mirror. She had to admit that it was suitable for wearing on a daily basis.

"We'll take it," Jayne said, as Sameena undressed again. "And now for something fancier."

The woman held up a pair of shorts and a halter top, like the one Jayne wore. Sameena took one look and shook her head, firmly. Her breasts might not be anything like as big as Jayne's, but she would still be showing them off if she wore the top. And most of her legs…

"You do have nice legs," Jayne said, deadpan. "It would be a shame not to show them off."

Sameena felt her face redden. "I don't want to be so…immodest," she admitted, shaking her head. "I couldn't walk around like you."

Jayne snorted with honest amusement. "You're naked under the clothes," she pointed out, snidely.

Sameena rolled her eyes, recognising the terrible joke. "I couldn't be like that," she said. "I just…can't."

All of her life, she had been taught that a woman was meant to cover everything, but her face and hands in the presence of unrelated men. Some households on Jannah had even insisted that their womenfolk be covered completely, leaving them hidden behind layers of all-enveloping cloth. Now, having been exposed to a society that thought nothing of women – or men – walking around naked, she still couldn't do it for herself. It left her feeling far too vulnerable.

"Try this," the storekeeper suggested, holding up a long red dress. "I may have to take the hem in for you, but it should be *modest*."

Sameena pulled the dress over her head and then peered into the mirror. It was tighter than she wanted around her waist, but otherwise suitable. Her breasts were faintly outlined without being so clear that she might as well be naked. She brushed a hand through her hair and smiled at her reflection.

"Suits you," Jayne said, after a moment's contemplation. "I dare say that Brad will like it too."

The storekeeper smiled. "Is there a young man in your future? You'll need some proper underwear for *him*…"

Sameena cringed.

"Perhaps," Jayne said, quickly. "But we're not here for *special* underwear or anything else, apart from a couple of outfits."

"Shame," the storekeeper said. "I have a special offer on underwear that slowly becomes translucent as you become excited and…"

She pulled another dress off the rack and passed it to Sameena, who tried it on. It was green, but otherwise identical to the first dress. A third dress proved to be a little tighter than she would have preferred, yet when she looked in the mirror she was tempted to keep it. The fourth dress seemed to be almost transparent, revealing far too much...

"You need black underwear for *that* dress," Jayne said. "But it does make you look great."

Sameena shrugged as she pulled it off. "We'll take the others," she said, firmly. "But that one is too revealing."

Jayne nodded and picked up a selection of basic underwear. "Take this too," she said, seriously. "Even with the shipsuit, it can be good to have it too."

The storekeeper totted up the bill while Sameena pulled her original clothes back on. "Five hundred credits, the lot," the storekeeper said, finally. "Plus fifty credits for minor modifications."

Sameena scowled. That was a sizable percentage of her wages.

"Bargain," Jayne hissed.

"One hundred credits," Sameena said, wishing that she knew more about the specifics of clothing prices. Maybe they should have looked in the other stalls before buying. "And ten for modifications."

"The modifications are a flat rate," the storekeeper said. "But I can offer you *three* hundred credits for the clothes."

Sameena had watched her father bargaining with his customers. A sudden drop in price suggested that the cost had been inflated, she remembered. Two hundred credits was hardly a *small* amount. But had it reached the limits of what the storekeeper could reasonably give her or was she still trying to gouge out an additional profit?

"Two hundred credits for the clothes," she said, finally. She tried to read the storekeeper's face, but it seemed completely expressionless. "And you can have the fifty for the modifications."

"Done," the storekeeper said.

Sameena looked at Jayne, unable to escape the feeling that she was still paying more than she should, even after stripping out three hundred credits from the final bill. Jayne shrugged, then nodded. Sameena took out her new Credit Coin and gave it to the storekeeper, who pushed it against her own coin. There was a moment's pause and then she passed the conjoined coins back to Sameena.

"Push your finger against the reader," Jayne explained. "Then verify the amount and then let it scan your finger again."

There was a *bleep* as it processed the transaction. "I'll have the clothes ready for you to pick up this afternoon," the storekeeper said, as she passed Sameena a receipt. "If you need them repaired in future, I do a discount rate if you purchase something else from my stall."

"Thank you," Jayne said.

Sameena looked up at her as they walked away. "How did I do?"

"You didn't get bilked *too* badly," Jayne said, after a moment. "Two hundred and fifty credits gives her some profit, so she's happy, without overcharging you too badly."

"Thank you," Sameena said. She frowned, then asked the question that had been bothering her for some time. "Why does everyone assume that I am going to marry Brad?"

"You *did* offer to marry him," Jayne reminded her. "It *is* tradition for someone who wants to join the crew permanently to marry into it, if they don't already have blood ties. That's how Paddy joined us."

Sameena hesitated, unsure of what to say. Back home, she would have been pushed into marriage eventually…and she would have been lucky if she'd been allowed to meet the groom before their wedding day. But onboard ship…in truth, she liked Brad, but she didn't want to marry him. Or to commit herself to *anyone*.

Jayne seemed to sense her confusion. "Listen," she said, placing a hand on Sameena's shoulder, "you don't *have* to marry him – you can marry Steve instead."

It took Sameena a moment to realise that Jayne was teasing her. Steve *was* closer to her age than Brad, but he seemed to be wedded to his engines. Indeed, while she'd seen Brad staring at her when he thought she wasn't looking, Steve had shown little interest in her as a woman at all. Did he have someone on another ship, waiting for him?

"More seriously," Jayne continued, "if you don't want to marry or date *anyone*, you don't have to. If Brad ever works up the nerve to ask you out, just say no. Mum will *kill* him if he makes unwanted advances."

She hesitated. For a moment, she almost looked embarrassed. "You don't know anything about biology," she added. "I think you should look it up before doing anything with anyone."

Sameena felt herself flushing. One of the movie files she'd accessed on *Logan* had shown a man and a woman having sex. She'd stared in horror, then deactivated the terminal, despite the strange temptation to keep watching. Later, she'd worked out which entertainment files were pornography and gave them a wide berth.

They stopped in a small cafe to have lunch – as she'd been told, the food on the asteroid was considerably better than the food on the freighter – and then wandered through the marketplace, looking for anything interesting. Jayne seemed to take an unholy delight in pointing out anything that Sameena might find shocking, including a brothel and a stall that sold sex drugs and toys. Sameena hadn't wanted to know that drugs to improve male potency were cheap and easy to produce, or that she could buy a toy shaped like a penis and use it to give herself pleasure. Or, for that matter, that a simple implant could give her a jolt of pleasure every time she pushed a button.

"People can get addicted to that," Jayne said, darkly. "It doesn't do any physical harm, unlike some of the other drugs, but it creates a psychological dependency that can be completely destructive. I've known people to waste away, begging for enough money to buy themselves another boost."

Sameena frowned. "Why isn't it banned?"

"Most of the people out here on the Rim don't give two shits about what the Grand Senate thinks," Jayne admitted. "They don't know what it's like to be living out here. If someone wants to jolt themselves into a stupor…no one will care as long as no one else is hurt."

She shook her head. "But it is a waste of life," she added. "Once addicted, they are unable to break free without outside help."

They reached a stall heaving under the weight of hundreds of paperback books. Sameena found herself smiling as she picked up a book with a lurid cover, remembering the feel of the books in her father's study. The cover showed a man carrying a gun, with a naked woman clinging to his legs, while giant spacecraft flew overhead. Judging by the comment on the front cover, the publisher thought that it was great literature.

"Books are quite expensive out here," Jayne explained. "Normally, everyone reads from their terminals, rather than buying a book. Data files are cheap."

Sameena nodded, then looked for something she could stand to read.

She was still looking when Jayne's wristcom buzzed. "Jayne," Ethne said, "escort Sameena to the negotiation block. I have someone I want her to meet."

"Understood," Jayne said. She closed the channel and looked over at Sameena. "Don't get too excited, but it sounds as if my mother has found us work."

CHAPTER NINE

However, such a system is inherently limited. The cobbler might not be able to convince the butcher that the butcher needs a pair of shoes, ensuring that the cobbler cannot obtain any meat. With only one thing to trade, his ability to obtain products from others is limited. He might be able to convince the blacksmith to serve as a third party – shoes to the blacksmith, knives to the butcher, meat to the blacksmith and then to the cobbler – but the system would become very clunky. A new means of exchange is required.
- Professor Leo Caesius, *The Science That Isn't: Economics and the Decline and Fall of the Galactic Empire.*

The negotiation block proved to be a tiny handful of offices buried deep within the asteroid where – according to Jayne – freighter commanders and those who wanted to make use of their services could meet in conditions of strict neutrality. It was guarded by five oversized men – heavy-worlders, Jayne explained – who checked Sameena's ID before allowing her to enter. Jayne waved her goodbye, then headed back to the marketplace. She'd already promised to pick up Sameena's new clothes.

Inside, Ethne was standing next to a young man wearing the Imperial Navy's black uniform. He was a Lieutenant, Sameena realised – Paddy had made her memorise the different ways to tell a person's rank – but he seemed far too young, as if he were dressing up in his father's uniform. But the existence of rejuvenation treatments ensured that he might easily be twice Sameena's age and look younger. Indeed, apart from the blonde hair and pale skin, he reminded her of Abdul when he'd been fourteen years old.

"Sameena," Ethne said, beckoning her over. "This is Lieutenant James Cook…"

"Jamie, please," Cook said. His voice was softer than Sameena had expected, as if he were truly fourteen years old. He nodded to her instead of offering to shake hands. "It's a pleasure to meet someone new."

"Thank you," Sameena said. "It's a pleasure to meet you too."

Cook gave her a charming smile, then looked over at Ethne. "And Sameena is…?"

"My adopted daughter – at least for the moment – and apprentice," Ethne said. "I thought that she should sit in on the negotiations."

"I can't see any harm in it," Cook said. He led them over to a small table and motioned for them to sit down. "You drink tea?"

Ethne laughed. "It is socially *impossible* to not drink tea when dealing with the Imperial Navy," she said. "Of *course* I drink tea."

Sameena frowned, confused.

"There's a long-standing tradition that the Imperial Navy drinks tea, while the ground-pounders drink coffee," Cook explained, seeing her puzzlement. "It's complete nonsense, of course, but we just can't get away from it."

He picked up a tray containing a kettle, three mugs and a small jug of milk and put it down on the table. "There are traditions that tell us how to serve it," he added, "but I'm not going to bother. Besides, this place doesn't bother to buy *real* tea leaves to flavour its water."

Sameena looked over at Ethne. "Is there an opportunity there?"

"Maybe," Cook answered, before Ethne could say a word. "But I wouldn't expect too much outside the navy."

He poured three mugs of tea, then picked one up and passed it to Sameena. She took a sip and frowned. It tasted suspiciously like the powdered tea Paddy had made, the second night she'd spent on the freighter. The milk, on the other hand, seemed to add more flavour than the processed tea granules.

For a long moment, they sipped in silence – and then Cook leaned forward. "I understand that you are currently looking for a charter," he said. "We need a small consignment of supplies shipped from Madagascar to Sungai Buloh. Your freighter would be ideal for our purposes."

Ethne frowned. "I thought Sungai Buloh was a war zone," she said. "Or have the insurgents been suppressed?"

"You wouldn't be required to land, or do more than dock at the orbital station," Cook assured her. It wasn't quite an answer. "Once there, you would unload your cargo and then depart – if you couldn't find a charter there. We would be happy to alter the fees to ensure that you were not out of pocket."

Sameena considered it as she sipped her tea. *Logan* was permanently on a shoestring, needing to find a new charter in every port – or the ship's debts would eventually catch up with her crew. If they went to Sungai Buloh and couldn't find a charter there, they might be in real trouble. The offer to increase the fees accordingly was incredibly tempting. But didn't that make it too good to be true?

Ethne seemed to be having similar thoughts. "What sort of cargo will we be carrying?"

"Various supplies that have been urgently requisitioned by the garrison commander," Cook said, reluctantly. "Nothing dangerous…"

He pulled a datachip out of his uniform pocket and passed it to Ethne. "That's our proposed contract, our offer of fees and other such details," he added, as she slotted it into her datapad. "I think you will find it more than generous."

Ethne looked up. "Why can't you use one of your own freighters?"

Cook hesitated, just like Abdul had when he'd been on the verge of telling a lie, then made a visible decision to be honest. "Most of our transports have been pulled out of the sector," he said, reluctantly. "We are forced to improvise."

Sameena took the datapad when Ethne passed it to her and skimmed through the contract as quickly as she could. It looked very like the others she'd seen during Ethne's tutoring sessions, apart from the offer to provide an escort ship if one was available. The total fee was eight hundred thousand credits, half paid in advance. It was not a small sum.

"It looks good," Ethne said, taking the datapad back. "Will you be providing additional crew?"

"We are stretched too thin to detach anyone for your ship," Cook admitted. "However, you could take on temps from this station."

"We could," Ethne said. She looked down at the datapad for a long moment, rereading the contract thoughtfully. "When do you wish us to depart?"

"If you can be ready to leave in a day, a destroyer will escort you," Cook said. "After that...you'll have to leave alone, within the week."

"Understood," Ethne said. She pressed her thumb against the datapad. "We accept your contract."

Sameena fought to keep her surprise off her face. Ethne had just *agreed*, without consulting her husband...she'd known that Ethne enjoyed more independence than any woman on Jannah, but Sameena had never really comprehended just how independent Ethne was until seeing her make a unilateral decision for the entire ship's crew. Even her father would have exploded with rage if her mother had made such an agreement.

But the contract wouldn't be legal on Jannah either, she thought, sourly. *Her husband or father would have to undersign it.*

"There is a second matter," Cook said, once he'd countersigned the contract and uploaded a copy to the asteroid's datanet. "We need you to transport a message from us to an officer on the picket there, *without* using the standard datanet. If you will carry it for us, there will be an additional ten thousand credits for you two – personally."

Sameena frowned, then realised that he was suggesting that they didn't have to share the money with anyone else on *Logan*, including the Captain. Was that even legal?

"We'd be delighted," Ethne said, without looking at Sameena. "I assume that the message is encoded?"

Cook produced a small box from his uniform and passed it over to her. "The box is sealed, with the chip inside further encrypted," he said. "I shouldn't have to warn you that trying to decrypt the message will destroy the chip and we *will* notice."

He smiled, rather dryly. "There may be a reply," he added. "If so, there will be an additional payment upon delivery – one large enough to cover all of your costs."

"Thank you," Ethne said, pocketing the chip. "I look forward to doing more business with you in the future."

"I shall hope so," Cook said. He gave Sameena another charming smile, then passed her a small card. "Perhaps you would join me for a drink when you return?"

Sameena hesitated, looking down at the card. It showed Cook's name, his ship and a string of numbers and letters she vaguely recognised as a personal communications code. If a message was uploaded into the Imperial Navy datanet in any system, she had been told, it would eventually make its way to wherever Cook was stationed.

"She has a lot of work to do," Ethne said, softly. "I don't think she could make any promises."

"The lot of juniors everywhere," Cook agreed. He stood up and bowed to them both. "It was a pleasure doing business with you."

Sameena looked up long enough to watch him go, then looked over at Ethne. "What does he want?"

"A date, a drink...perhaps more, if you wanted to go further," Ethne said. She shrugged, then smiled. "You seem to have made a new friend."

"And you took his datachip," Sameena said. "Shouldn't you mention it to your husband?"

"I'll give you half the fee for keeping quiet," Ethne said. She laughed at Sameena's shock. "Don't worry, I *will* tell Tom about the chip. Tradition says we get to keep ninety percent of the fee, however."

She stood up and led the way back to the docks, bouncing questions off Sameena as they walked. "How did your exams go?"

"My brain was hurting afterwards," Sameena admitted, still a little bothered by how easily Ethne had decided to take the chip. "Is that a good sign?"

"Pain builds character, my father always said," Ethne said. "But once you start regular schooling, you should be able to build up some genuine qualifications. You're going to need them, unless you want to remain a lowly deckhand for the rest of your days."

She paused outside one of the shops. "I think you'll want to see this," she said, as she pushed a glass door open. "Look for something familiar. But keep your mouth shut."

Sameena frowned as she followed Ethne inside. The shop was larger than she had realised, but almost empty, save for a single table. But the walls were lined with shelves, each one holding a single glass bottle filled with coloured liquid. Short notes beside them indicated point of origin, alcoholic strength and a handful of other details that made no sense to her. There was nothing to indicate price…she couldn't help feeling that she was sinning just by stepping into the shop. Almost everything seemed to be thoroughly alcoholic.

"Whiskey from Nova Scotia," Ethne said, pointing to one of the bottles. Her finger moved from bottle to bottle. "Asteroid Ale from Ceres. Vodka from Stalin Prime. Fruit Punch from Tropicana. And Firewater Mead."

She smiled as Sameena stepped closer. "If you have to ask the price," she whispered, "you can't afford it."

The bottle of Firewater Mead seemed to be glowing, slightly…or was that just Sameena's imagination? It was small; she estimated that it held barely a pint of liquid…and it wasn't even the smallest bottle in the shop. The brief note beside the bottle didn't say anything about its point of origin, merely a note that it was not alcoholic and was rated safe for human consumption.

"One of the most popular drinks in the system," a voice said, from behind them. Sameena spun around to see a thin, elf-like man standing there, rubbing inhumanly long fingers together. His face looked equally inhuman. "That bottle is worth one hundred thousand credits."

Sameena blinked in surprise. Captain Hamilton had told her that the mead was expensive, but she hadn't quite believed him. But one hundred thousand credits…her wages for a month on *Logan* were barely four thousand credits. How could *anyone* afford to buy Firewater Mead?

The very rich buy it as a status symbol, she told herself. *That's what makes it so expensive.*

"We'll have to look elsewhere," Ethne said, leading Sameena out of the shop. "The Captain will need a cheaper gift."

She laughed as soon as the door was firmly shut. "Did you notice what he *didn't* do?"

Sameena nodded. "He didn't try to bargain," she said.

"Indeed not," Ethne agreed. "He knows that there is enough of a market for his products that he doesn't have to bargain. That should be useful, later."

They met Jayne outside the airlock, who passed Sameena a small plastic bag of clothing. "There were a couple of offers to do locum work on the station," she said, as Ethne opened the airlock. "How long are we staying here?"

"Ideally, we want to leave tomorrow," Ethne said. "But I'll explain it all once your father calls a crew meeting."

Stepping back onboard *Logan* felt almost like coming home, Sameena was surprised to discover. She started to head down towards her cabin, only to be stopped by Ethne who reminded her that there was going to be a crew meeting. The last one had left her feeling oddly out of place, but now she was being paid…it felt as if she should attend.

"Put on your new clothes first," Jayne suggested. "See if you can give Brad a heart attack."

Ethne glared at her daughter. "You're not so old I can't beat you," she said, crossly. "Or sentence you to clean the waste disposal pipes on your own."

The galley was barely large enough to hold the entire crew, even though the kids were off visiting friends on the asteroid rather than joining the meeting. Ethne waited until Paddy had passed out the drinks, then nodded to her husband who called the meeting to order.

"We have a contract," she announced, and outlined the terms of the agreement. "We're going to be hauling freight for the Imperial Navy. If we manage to get everything loaded up by tomorrow, we will be escorted as we leave the system."

"That's good," Hamilton said, once she had finished. "An escort would deter pirates from attacking us, if they found out what we were carrying."

Sameena studied him with some interest. If he was irked that his wife had committed him to taking the contract without consulting him, he didn't show it. Perhaps he was planning to yell at her in the privacy of their cabin, but it seemed unlikely. She was starting to realise that their relationship was built on love, trust and mutual respect, not subordination and submission. Ethne didn't *have* to take her husband's opinion as the last word in anything.

Jayne looked down at the contract, then over at her mother. "We do have to take on some more supplies from Madagascar," she said. "This contract stipulates that we have to pick up their cargo from the naval base. It will be tricky to do both in time, unless you want to pay premium rates."

"I'll see if I can call in some favours," Hamilton said. "Steve? How's the drive?"

"I switched out the vital components over the last two days," Steve said, "and laid in some more supplies. We do need to refuel, but that won't take too long. If worst comes to worst, we can do it at the naval base while loading the supplies and pay their rates. God knows they should help us if they're *that* desperate to get supplies to their destination."

Brad smiled. "There might be a permanent contract in it for us," he said. "A good report from the Imperial Navy would go a long way."

"But we don't want permanent contracts," Hamilton reminded his son. He looked around the compartment. "We'll undock tonight and move over to the naval base. Can we have our supplies by then?"

"Probably," Jayne said. "But we will have to pay."

Hamilton nodded. "See to it," he said. He raised his voice. "Is there any other business?"

"There was a second contract," Ethne said, and explained briefly about the message. "I don't know what it means."

"Odd," Hamilton mused. "If they're sending a destroyer to escort us, why couldn't someone on the destroyer hand-carry the message?"

He shook his head. "But it doesn't matter," he added, "as long as we get paid."

Sameena made a mental note to research the Imperial Navy more thoroughly. Jannah didn't really have an army, beyond the Guardians. There was certainly nothing resembling the Empire's colossal military machine, either on the ground or in space. But if the Imperial Navy was hiring civilian transports to move their supplies…what did it mean? Where were *their* transports?

She thought briefly about the small pile of notes she was collecting on her terminal, looking up details on spare parts for starships. Could the

Imperial Navy be having its own supply problems? Cook had given her his contact code; she could ask him…but she was sure that he wouldn't answer, not directly.

Hamilton snorted, drawing her attention back to him. "Anything else?"

"It's Regina's birthday in a week," Jayne said. "She'll be ten years old."

"Get a few party supplies from Madagascar," Ethne ordered. She looked over at Sameena. "When's your birthday?"

Sameena hesitated.

"It would have to be calculated," Paddy said, before she could hazard an answer. "Jannah's dating system is not based on the Imperial standard."

"Do it," Hamilton ordered. He gave Sameena a smile. "Now you're part of the crew, you deserve to have your own birthday celebrated."

"Thank you," Sameena whispered. Abdul's birthdays had been celebrated, but hers had been largely ignored, save by her mother and father. "I don't deserve you."

"Nonsense," Ethne said. "You're one of us now."

Sameena was still smiling hours later.

CHAPTER TEN

> This, in short, provides the impetus for the development of money. Money provides a common object of value that can be exchanged between people who would otherwise have nothing they could share. The butcher might not need new shoes, but money would allow him to buy knives instead. As long as people are willing and able to recognise the value of money, trade can take place.
>
> - Professor Leo Caesius, *The Science That Isn't: Economics and the Decline and Fall of the Galactic Empire.*

"I used to think about joining the navy," Brad said, as the Imperial Navy base came into view. It was an impressive network of tubes and spheres, with a dozen starships in close attendance. "But I never did."

Sameena didn't take her eyes off the viewscreen. "Why didn't you join?"

"Never had the patience for spit-and-polish," Brad admitted. "Besides, there's a lot of discrimination against independent traders and RockRats in the Imperial Navy. I would have been lucky to become a mustang; there was certainly no chance that I would be allowed to go straight into the Naval Academy. I get a better life out here."

He looked over at her. "Where do you want to be in ten years?"

Sameena smiled. "My own ship," she said. She did have other ideas, but she didn't want to discuss them too openly. "And go trading across the stars."

Brad grinned. "Me too," he admitted. "But I would have thought that you would have wanted to go home and exact a little revenge."

The thought had crossed Sameena's mind after she'd realised just what an advantage it would be to have a single armed starship in orbit around a defenceless world. She could drop rocks on the Guardians from orbit and batter the entire planet into submission, then punish the clerics for what they had done to her family. But there would be no shortage of problems in governing the world afterwards. Perhaps she would just offer free tickets off-world for everyone, male or female, who wanted to leave. The ones who remained behind would at least have had a choice.

"Maybe later," she said, reluctantly.

A dull thump ran through the ship as they docked with the naval base. "Rough arrival," Brad commented, ruefully. "Dad's going to yell at me later."

Sameena shrugged. No one had let her steer the ship outside simulations, not after she'd crashed it into the orbital station twice. Ethne had been *very* sarcastic afterwards, listing all the mistakes she'd made and loudly praising God that it had all been simulated. If it had taken place in reality, she'd concluded, over a thousand people would have died in a heartbeat, including the entire crew. Sameena had honestly thought that Ethne was going to hit her. Instead, she'd had to go through it again and again until she knew what she'd done wrong.

"Don't worry about it," Brad added. "You should have seen *my* mistakes when I was an apprentice. My uncle used to threaten to throw me out of the airlock every second day."

Sameena gave him a surprised look. Abdul would *never* have been so sensitive to her feelings, let alone tried to cheer her up.

Brad stood up as Ethne came through the hatch. "They're starting to load up the pallets now," she said. "Steve and James will handle it, while your father talks to the destroyer skipper."

"Seems a bit odd," Brad commented. "Why would they detail a destroyer to escort little old us?"

Sameena considered it. The destroyer was the workhorse of the Imperial Navy – few pirates, according to the files, would willingly take on a warship – but it had very limited cargo space. Much of its hull was composed of drives, weapons and control systems, with the crew squeezed into the remaining space. The images she'd seen on the datanet had suggested that three or four crewmen were crammed into cabins no bigger than her own. She could never have endured such an existence.

"They're short on transports," she muttered. "And they must *need* their supplies."

"Indeed," Ethne agreed. "Sameena, stay here until the loading is completed. Once we separate from the station you can go back to your cabin. For the moment, I suggest you review the files from your tutor. You have a lot of work ahead of you."

Sameena watched her go, puzzled.

"There's a bunch of horny crewmen on the ship right now," Brad said, once the hatch was closed. "She doesn't want you seen."

He smiled at Sameena's expression, then passed her a terminal. "There's never anything to do while docked," he added. "You may as well review the files."

Sameena frowned, remembering everything she'd been told about off-worlders on Jannah. "If they saw me…would anything happen?"

"I doubt it," Brad admitted. "They'll be working hard and there will be officers supervising…but it's best not to take chances. Some of the crewmen here have been on duty for years."

"Oh," Sameena said. She clicked on the terminal, accessed the file and read the first page. It was a blunt assessment of her first set of exams, concluding with a note that while she showed intelligence and promise, she was critically short of background knowledge that would be required for further qualifications. "This isn't good."

Brad took the terminal and read it, quickly. "It doesn't say you're stupid," he pointed out, bluntly. "Background knowledge merely requires research and some careful thought. I think you're better off than some others."

He smiled as he passed the terminal back to her. "I can help with some research," he said, "but mum would go ballistic if she caught me giving you more than basic help. Sorry."

Sameena smiled and read through the next set of pages. They outlined a study schedule, followed by a series of assignments that she would be expected to have completed by the time she returned to Madagascar. Two of them she thought she could answer immediately, but the remainder – fifteen in all – were completely beyond her. She felt her heart start to sink as she realised she would have to spend months studying, just to pass the exams.

"And you will have plenty more work to do on the ship," Brad pointed out, dryly. "You might find it more useful than exams and studies."

Sameena rolled her eyes. Steve had said the same, but he'd also admitted that exams could make it easier to get onboard a new ship. Shaking her head, she started working her way through the first study plan, reading the background notes the tutor had provided for her. Some of the titbits on history were actually quite interesting…

"That's often more important than you might expect," Brad said. "Worlds that joined the Empire willingly are often more likely to follow Imperial Law than those that were annexed by force. Quite a few worlds are fanatical loyalists because the Empire saved them from certain disaster. If the Imperial Navy asked them a favour, you can bet your…ah, rear that they would comply."

"I see," Sameena said.

"And then there's places like Han, where understanding history will tell you that it's a very good idea to stay away," Brad added. "Dad always downloads history modules when we move to a new sector, just so he can research our destinations. He'll be ready to bore us to death about Sungai Buloh tonight."

He shrugged. "Fortunately, you will have plenty of time to prepare for the practical exams," he warned. "Crashing a starship *then* will certainly get you booted out of the examination chamber."

It was nearly four hours before the hatches were closed and Captain Hamilton came back onto the bridge. "They're clearing us for immediate departure," he said. "The *Pinafore* will be escorting us to our destination."

Sameena smiled as Brad powered up the engines, ran through a brief checklist – he'd told her that the Imperial Navy were sticklers for following procedure, even though half of the steps could be omitted without risking anything – and then disengaged from the station. She glanced down at the near-space display as the freighter wallowed free and frowned, her eyes narrowing as she studied the display. Four of the starships near the station were radiating nothing, but their IFF beacons. They weren't powered up at all.

"Interesting," Brad said, as he took them past the weapons platform marking the outskirts of space claimed by the Imperial Navy. "The only time they're supposed to be powered down completely is when they're in a shipyard, being repaired. *Anything* could happen here and it would take hours to power up the ships to respond."

"If they *can* be powered up," Hamilton said, softly. "If…"

He cleared his throat. "It will take us three hours to reach the Phase Limit," he added. "Perhaps, Sameena, you would care to work on your berries? Richard and Regina will assist you."

Sameena nodded and slipped through the hatch, walking down to what she was starting to think of as her hydroponics lab. It had been expanded since they'd purchased more supplies from Madagascar, allowing Steve to set up a dozen additional vats. The berries were growing faster than she'd expected. Some of the second batch were already ripe for harvesting.

"They taste good," Regina called, as she entered. "We had one each."

"Oh," Sameena said. They'd bought a press, bottles and a handful of other supplies at Madagascar, as well as some instructions on how to turn the liquid into mead. "I wouldn't eat any more or some people will be very annoyed."

"We know that," Richard said. It was strange to realise that he was a mere eleven months older than his sister. But then, both of them acted older than they really were. "We're not stupid, you know."

"I know," Sameena said, remembering what she'd said to Brad. "You're not even remotely stupid."

She felt a flash of envy. The kids had grown up in an incredibly dangerous environment. They'd learned to wear shipsuits and check air pressure before they'd been able to walk. In some ways, they were far more mature than kids born on Jannah – and far more used to thinking for themselves. There were times when they made her feel slow and stupid beside them, even though she was five years older than Richard.

"Pluck off the ripe berries, then press half of them into liquid," Regina recited. She started to work, her brother right beside her. "The other half are to be put in the stasis pod until we can rig up a new set of vats."

Sameena watched as the small pile of berries grew larger, then started to work on the press. Steve had made her practice with the device before she actually tried to use it properly; it was harder than it seemed to crush the berries so that they released their juices. A sweet smell arose in the compartment as the liquid pooled under the press, then drained into the container.

"Smells nice," Regina commented. "How much do you think this is worth?"

"Lots," Sameena said, shortly. "We'll have to wait and see."

She'd done a little research into Firewater Mead when she had been on Madagascar, but there hadn't been much information on the datanet. Distribution was handled by a cartel – which she had already known – and they were incredibly close-mouthed about where the mead actually came from, originally. If Sameena hadn't already known about Jannah, she would have suspected that the mead came from the other side of the Empire. Someone had worked hard to obscure the source.

Odd, she thought, as she looked over at the bubbling vats. *Why didn't the cartel try growing the berries for themselves?*

It puzzled her. *They* had certainly had no trouble in growing the berries, let alone producing the mead. An interstellar cartel with more money in its pocket change account than the entire planet of Jannah possessed should have had no trouble doing the same. Could it be that the government on Jannah actually *ran* the cartel? It was bizarre, but she had to admit that it was possible. She couldn't think of any other explanation.

She added the handful of other ingredients, as dictated by Uncle Muhammad, and then stored the liquid in the refrigerator. It should be ready to drink in a month, according to the information she'd been given. And then they would have to find a way to distribute it.

"That won't be a problem," Ethne had assured her, when she'd asked. "You'd be astonished how many items can be found on Madagascar with the serial numbers filed off. The buyer might want to run a check first – people have been conned with bottles of coloured water before – but after that…hell, we could just copy the bottles the cartel makes and let them assume that we bought it in another sector."

"I think that's it for the day," she said, finally. The remainder of the berries would be placed in the vats, once they were cleaned and replenished, where they could start producing the next generation of fruit. "Thank you for your help."

"Oh, it was no trouble," Richard said, in an oddly formal tone. "The alternative was sweeping the corridors again."

Sameena started to laugh as the kids headed out of the compartment, back towards their cabin. It still felt strange to see boys doing anything useful, let alone domestic…but it also felt right. She took one last look at the vats, then frowned again. They'd managed to produce nearly a hundred pints in a month. Surely the cartel could have produced more.

But it would be spread out over the entire Empire, she thought, slowly. *Even if they produced a million pints, there would only be a small amount for each inhabited world.*

The thought nagged at her mind as she closed the compartment – like every other hatch, there was no actual *lock* to keep people out – and started to make her way back to the bridge. As far as she could tell, producing vast amounts of mead shouldn't be a problem. There were just too many things that didn't make sense.

Or maybe they're just keeping supplies deliberately low, she thought, remembering her discovery of just how useless gold sultans were in the Empire. Enough money to buy a small house on Jannah wouldn't have bought her more than a few meals on Madagascar. *That would allow them to keep the prices high.*

"Welcome back," Hamilton said, when she stepped onto the bridge. "As you can see, we have a friend."

He waved at the main display, which showed a single green icon effortlessly keeping pace with the wallowing freighter. Sameena wondered, briefly, what the destroyer's crew thought about having to tie their speed to a much slower ship, before deciding that it hardly mattered. An escort was about the only way to guarantee that the supplies would reach Sungai Buloh, rather than being captured and resold by pirates.

"And we're about to cross the Phase Limit," Brad said, from his console. "The coordinates are already set for the jump."

Sameena nodded, feeling a familiar throbbing at her temple as she remembered what she'd been told about Phase Space. One set of articles had called it an alternate dimension, where the laws of physics were different and starships could travel faster than light; another set had claimed that the starship actually *created* its own alternate dimension, once it was safely away from the massive gravity well created by a star. She honestly couldn't understand why the drive was used without being understood, but she had to admit that she used plenty of devices without knowing how they worked.

Besides, the fact it *worked* was all that mattered.

"Good," Hamilton said. "Confirm with our escort and then take us into Phase Space as soon as possible."

"Understood," Brad said. There was a long pause as he worked his console. "Crossing the border.... now. I'd prefer to wait longer before we jumped."

"Then do so," Hamilton said.

Sameena frowned, puzzled.

"The gravity well isn't a perfect sphere," Hamilton explained, noticing her expression. "A military ship can normally compensate for any last-minute flickers, but we can't. So we wait until we are well clear before we jump."

"They'll complain, of course," Ethne added. "But if they are *really* desperate for the supplies..."

"They won't dare complain too loudly," Sameena finished. A cursory look at the Imperial Navy's fleet list had convinced her that this contract would just be the first of many. If the navy *needed* civilian craft, they wouldn't be able to push too hard. "Or would they try to rewrite the contracts?"

"There is always some leeway built into contracts," Ethne observed. "You should know that by now."

She smiled, rather dryly. "Unavoidable delays happen – and no one wants to chance losing their ship over them," she added. "Suffice it to say that we would have to be over a week late before they could start using the penalty clauses."

"But once they start using them, we're in deep doo-doo," Brad offered. He looked down at his display, then up at his father. "I think we can jump from here, dad."

"Then tell them that we're going," Hamilton ordered. "And then jump us out."

Brad keyed a set of switches. This time, Sameena felt a faint sense that something wasn't entirely right blowing through her for a long second, before the universe snapped back to normal. There was nothing but inky darkness on the displays.

"Phase Space," Brad said. He smiled over at Sameena. "Next stop; Sungai Buloh. Estimated Time of Arrival: seven days, nine hours."

"Splendid," Ethne said. "And now you have nothing else to do, you can help Paddy and James with the corridors. The decks are a right mess."

Brad groaned theatrically, but obeyed.

"And Sameena, you have schooling to attend to," Ethne added. "You really don't want to waste those lessons."

Sameena nodded in agreement, then left the bridge.

CHAPTER
ELEVEN

> It is not easy, of course, to put a value to different items. The blacksmith may feel that the butcher's products are worth less than either his or the cobbler's. However, over time, the free (i.e. uncontrolled) market tends to find a definite value for specific items , if only through suggesting the prices that people are willing to pay. Something priced too high or too low would eventually price itself out of the market.
>
> - Professor Leo Caesius, *The Science That Isn't: Economics and the Decline and Fall of the Galactic Empire.*

"Happy birthday to you, happy birthday to you, happy birthday dear Regina, happy birthday to you."

Sameena found herself giggling as the song came to an end. It was so different from anything that she had experienced on Jannah that she couldn't help feeling happy…and a sense that she finally belonged somewhere at long last. Regina looked happy too, even as the older spacers thumped her back or rear ten times each, one whack for each of her years. She would never have to doubt her place among them.

"Congratulations," she said. "I hope you'll have many more birthdays to come."

Regina grinned as she sat down at the table and started to open her presents, all wrapped in duct tape and plastic containers that had once held food supplies. One of the containers, when opened, revealed another container; Steve giggled mercilessly as Regina worked her way through five successive containers before finally finding the multitool he'd purchased on Madagascar. Regina threw herself into his arms and gave him a tight hug.

"Just be careful what you unscrew," Ethne warned, sternly. "I had to speak quite sternly to your brother after he dismantled a terminal and then couldn't put it back together again."

Sameena felt her smile growing wider as Regina opened the next present and discovered a paperback book. Brad must have purchased it on Madagascar too, she realised, although she hadn't seen him on the rock. Regina looked at the front cover, then gave Brad a hug too. It was an omnibus edition of a famous novel series that refused to die, even if it was massively outdated by now.

Captain Hamilton and Ethne had given Regina her own ship's log, with a droll note advising her to write something in it each day. Sameena had never kept a diary – she had known that her mother would read it, if she found the book – but she had to admit that she understood the attraction. Regina opened it to the first page, carefully wrote her name and communications code on the crisp paper, and then placed it on the table. She stood upright and gave Captain Hamilton a salute, before collapsing into giggles and hugging his wife. The Captain returned her salute gravely.

"Welcome to being ten years old," Richard said, once Regina had opened his present. "I'll be ahead of you again in five months."

"Richard," Ethne said, although there was no real irritation in her tone. "It just means that you will grow old first."

"Hah," Regina said, and stuck her tongue out at her brother. She picked up the final package before Richard could retaliate, then looked up at Sameena. "From you?"

Sameena nodded, feeling a hint of nervousness. Present-giving wasn't a strong tradition on Jannah, where it was customary to give children – particularly boys – religious texts for their birthdays and then quiz them mercilessly about them for months afterwards. She'd thought long and hard over what to buy for the girl she had come to think of as her younger sister, but she honestly wasn't sure about her choice. In the end, she'd purchased a dress from Madagascar with a little help from Jayne.

"It's lovely," Regina said, when she unfurled the dress. It was sky-blue, matching her eyes and setting off her blonde hair nicely. "Thank you!"

Sameena watched as Regina pulled the dress over her shipsuit and spun around, showing off the skirt. It was considerably more modest than anything Jayne had suggested; Sameena had balked at the thought of giving a ten-year-old girl anything revealing, no matter what culture she had come from. But it also looked nice. The storekeeper had included, at Sameena's request, some material and tools to extend the dress if necessary. At least she knew how to sew. Neither Ethne nor Jayne possessed that particular skill.

She grunted as Regina gave her a tight hug. The girl was stronger than she looked – the result of genetic engineering, Jayne had told her – and seemed to be unaware of it, although she did spend most of her time wrestling with her brother or Jayne. The doctor had promised Sameena her own classes on self-defence, something that had definitely *not* been a possibility on Jannah. No doubt they hadn't wanted women – or men – defending themselves.

"You're welcome," she murmured, as the girl let go of her. "And I hope you have many more birthdays to come."

Paddy tapped the table, summoning Regina, Richard and Jayne to sit down, while everyone else gathered behind them. Once they were seated, he started to hand out small cakes in plastic containers, one of which bore Sameena's name. There was a small amount of alcohol in some of the cakes, Sameena had been told, but he'd picked one for her that didn't include alcohol or anything else forbidden in the recipe. Paddy, it seemed, was nicer than he wanted to let on.

"Eat up," Paddy urged. He grinned, as if he was enjoying a private joke. "And don't forget to do your teeth afterwards."

Sameena realised what he meant the moment she bit into the cake. It was astonishingly sweet, tasting sweeter than the sugar drops she'd eaten as a child. The icing – bright green – seemed to be nothing, but sugar. Thankfully, the cake itself was rather bland. She ended up leaving half of the icing behind. Richard promptly asked her if he could have it.

"Now that we have had our celebration," Captain Hamilton said, "it's time to get back to work. We arrive in two hours, remember?"

"I'll clean up here," Paddy said, scooping up the discarded containers. He looked over at Sameena. "You should be on the bridge for when we arrive."

"Good idea," Brad agreed. He gave Sameena a sidelong glance. "Did you ever work out when it was *your* birthday?"

"Four months, more or less," Sameena said. "I think, at least."

She had needed the computer to help calculate her age, if only because Jannah's years were longer than the Imperial Standard Year used by the Empire. It struck her as odd to realise that she was effectively an adult by the Empire's standards, although being an adult woman on Jannah wasn't *that* different from being a child.

"It's always tricky to be sure," Brad said. He shrugged as he led the way out of the galley and up towards the bridge. "Most spacers just go by the Imperial Standard Year, but it does cause problems. People have been arrested because someone failed to take different years into account."

Sameena nodded. She'd run across case studies while doing her reading for interstellar law, some complex and some so absurd she was at a loss to understand how they could ever have happened. A child could be considered sixteen years old on one planet and thirteen the next; one planet's legal age of consent was five, which had shocked her until she realised that five years on that planet were effectively comparable to nineteen standard years. Such problems cropped up regularly and, as Ethne had noted sardonically, made a lot of money for lawyers.

The bridge was deserted when they arrived, the automated systems monitoring their passage through Phase Space. Captain Hamilton had impressed upon Sameena – and the rest of his crew – that the bridge was never to be left unattended while they were in normal space, but nothing could threaten them in FTL. In fact, it was hellishly difficult to *track* a ship through Phase Space, let alone attack it. Brad sat down in front of the helm and checked it, briefly, before looking up at her. His face was faintly red.

"You look very good in that dress," he stammered. "It suits you."

"Thank you," Sameena said, flushing. She'd worn the green dress, which set her skin and hair off nicely. It felt odd to wear the shipsuit underneath, as if it was a piece of oversized underwear, but there was no choice. "I'm glad you like it."

Brad seemed tongue-tied afterwards, so much so that it was a relief when Captain Hamilton and Ethne came onto the bridge as the timer ticked down towards zero. A faint shudder ran through *Logan* as she returned to normal space, the stars flickering back into existence on the viewscreens. Sameena wondered, absently, how many of the stories of ships trapped forever in Phase Space were actually true. Ethne had pointed out that a trapped ship would never be able to get home to report, but the stories were still creepy. Richard seemed to enjoy hearing them from Paddy before he went to bed.

"Welcome to Sungai Buloh," Captain Hamilton said. "Brad; check with our escort, then take us into the inner system."

Sameena picked up the terminal and started to read through the files on Sungai Buloh, as Brad had suggested. The planetary system should have been well-placed for an economic boom – there was a large asteroid field and a pair of gas giants for fuel – yet the settlers had fallen into a prolonged civil war a bare two hundred years after settlement. It was difficult to reconcile the disparate versions of history stored in the database, but it seemed that the founding corporation had provoked an uprising, which had become civil war after the corporation cut its losses and retreated. Just to make matters more complicated, it seemed, there were a number of semi-legal settlements throughout the system. The Empire had landed a garrison in the hopes of dampening down the violence and preventing the system being used by pirates, smugglers and insurgents, but the reports suggested that they weren't having much success.

She frowned as the freighter and her escort made their way further into the system, studying the displays. There was a surprising amount of traffic moving through the system despite the civil war – or perhaps because of it. Technically, the entire star system belonged to the planet's government, but as the planet's government couldn't enforce its authority anyone could move in and start settling or mining for themselves. It was going to be a nightmare when the civil war finally burned itself out and the government started trying to assert itself outside the gravity well.

Good thing Jannah's founders picked such a worthless system, she thought, ruefully. *What would have happened to us if they had landed on prime real estate?*

"They want us to dock at Orbit One," Brad said, shortly. "Apparently, the Imperial Navy just took the whole place over, once they arrived in the system."

"Probably for the best," Captain Hamilton said. "Steer us towards the station."

"Maybe," Ethne said, doubtfully. "They may also wish to search the ship."

Sameena had never seen a life-bearing world from orbit before, not even Jannah. Sungai Buloh was a green and blue orb, hanging against the darkness of space, seemingly completely untouched by humanity. God had worked wonders in creating the universe, she realised, and yet few people on Jannah would ever see the results of His handiwork. Nothing human, not even the terraformed worlds like Mars, could match up to a natural planet.

Orbit One seemed cruder than Madagascar, she decided, as Brad slowly brought them into dock. It was a blocky structure, studded with sensor blisters, docking ports and open-space warehouses. A dozen heavy-lift shuttles were making their way to and from the planet below, transporting goods from orbit to the surface. Three Imperial Navy starships orbited near the station, watchfully. One of them was dropping projectiles on the planet below.

"KEWs – Kinetic Energy Weapons," Brad commented. "There's never any shortage of rocks in an inhabited star system."

There was a dull thud as the ship docked with the station. "We have arrived," Brad said. He looked down at his console. "The Imperial Navy is sending crewmen to help off-load the supplies. Apparently, we're welcome on Orbit One, but they advise us not to try going down to the planet."

"Quite right of them," Ethne agreed. She looked over at her husband. "Sameena and I will go onto the station and look for our contact. Can you see to the unloading?"

Captain Hamilton nodded. "Just remember to share the proceeds," he said. He shared a long smile with his wife. "And see if you can pick up on any other contracts here."

"Doubt it," Ethne said. "This place has little to offer the universe."

Orbit One's designers and operators seemed to agree, Sameena decided, as they stepped through the airlock and into the giant structure. Madagascar was a whole settlement in its own right; Orbit One seemed nothing more than a giant orbiting warehouse, with a handful of shops and other facilities tacked on as an afterthought. Apart from the Imperial Navy personnel, there was hardly anyone on the station. The single store for spacers contained nothing, but overpriced junk.

"That isn't too surprising," Ethne said, when Sameena pointed it out. "This system doesn't go out of its way to attract visitors."

"You'd think they could offer fresh food," Sameena objected. "Even if they don't offer anything else…"

"They do," Ethne said, darkly. She nodded towards a hatch that was decorated with an image of a naked woman. "They offer sex."

Sameena stared at her. "Why…?"

"War causes refugees to flee their homes," Ethne said. "Many of them have nowhere else to go, so they become prostitutes. The ones here are actually lucky, in many ways; they may be working as sex slaves, but they're not actually in danger of sudden death."

Sameena shuddered, but said nothing.

Ethne found a data terminal and typed in a name, hunting for their contact. "Got him," she said, after a moment. "He's currently stationed on one of the gunboats."

"One of the ships," Sameena said. "How are we going to get to him?"

"We message him and ask for a meeting," Ethne said, dryly. She typed in the message and then scowled. "No integrated system here. We'll have to wait for a reply."

It was twenty minutes before a reply arrived, requesting a meeting in two hours. Sameena wanted to go back to the ship, but Ethne insisted on taking a look around the station so she could memorise the layout. Orbit One was a standard design for a newly-settled colony world, she explained, and knowing one would give her a working knowledge of the others. If Sungai Buloh had developed normally, she added, the station would probably have been replaced by now.

Sameena had to admit that it *was* a fascinating tour, particularly when Ethne talked the crew into allowing them to see the command centre, which was a fancy name for a compartment only twice the size of *Logan's* bridge. Sungai Buloh just didn't have enough interstellar traffic to rate a larger station. Even so, it was a relief when they finally returned to the meeting place. Some of the looks the crewmen had been shooting at her suggested that they'd been mentally undressing her.

Their contact proved to be a middle-aged man wearing a white duty uniform, with gold stripes that proclaimed him to be a Commander. He looked almost fatherly; Sameena couldn't help wondering if he was deliberately trying to be a father to his men. But then, Imperial Navy crewmen would be even more isolated from their families than trader crews.

"Thank you for coming," he said. His voice was so calm that it was hard to imagine anything flustering him. "Do you have the datachip?"

Ethne smiled. "Do *you* have some ID?"

The Commander reached into his pocket and produced a wallet, then held up an Imperial Navy ID card. Ethne took it, pressed it against the reader in her datapad, then nodded grudgingly and handed it back to him.

"Commander Sebastian Viol," she said. She produced the box and passed it to him. "And we need the other half of the fee."

"One moment," the Commander said. He opened the box with his thumbprint, then checked the datachip in his reader. A line of text scrolled up in front of his eyes. "It seems to have been left untouched."

"We live to serve," Ethne said, tartly.

"We cannot be too careful," Viol admitted. He produced a credit coin and passed it over to Ethne, who took it and checked the amount. "When will you be leaving the system?"

"Four days, unless we find another contract," Ethne said. "Do you know of any possibilities?"

"I will have to send a reply back," Viol said. "There are, I believe, several groups that wish to leave the planet permanently. They will be offering cash to any freighter willing to take them out of the system."

Ethne lifted an eyebrow. "And where do they want to go afterwards?"

"I don't think they care about that," Viol admitted. He smiled, rather humourlessly. "I shall meet with you again in two days, same time and place. I'll give you the reply then."

"And the advance on the fee," Ethne added. "If we don't find a contract here, we're going directly back to Madagascar."

"I'll see what I can forward in your direction," Viol promised. He stood up. "Thank you for your time."

Sameena watched him go, then looked over at Ethne.

"That man is deeply worried about something," Ethne said, softly. "And they're paying far too much for courier duty."

She stood up and led the way back to the ship. Sameena followed her, mulling it over in her mind. What did it all mean?

CHAPTER TWELVE

However, the money itself rested upon items of almost universal value. Salt, as noted above, was immensely valuable in some primitive societies. It could serve as a symbol of wealth, although as people did tend to find uses for salt, it was hardly a stable material. Later, precious metals became the first coins of the region. Gold, for example, was almost worthless as anything but money.

- Professor Leo Caesius, *The Science That Isn't: Economics and the Decline and Fall of the Galactic Empire.*

"I found us a potential contract," Ethne said, two days later. "It may not be quite what we want, however."

"Beggars can't be choosers," Paddy pointed out. "Where do they want us to go? Han?"

Sameena looked around the galley, trying to judge their reactions. Captain Hamilton looked impassive; Steve and James seemed completely disinterested. Brad and Jayne, on the other hand, seemed rather more interested than Sameena would have expected. But then, Brad *was* planning to obtain a freighter for himself once he built up the funds for the first investment.

"Anywhere," Ethne said, softly. "There are five families who want to escape their homeworld. I told them that we would be going to Madagascar and they jumped at the chance."

"Sounds odd," Brad commented. "Where are they going to go *after* Madagascar?"

"They have money to book transport onwards, it seems," Ethne said. "All they really want to do is get to a system with regular interstellar travel. Madagascar would fit the bill nicely, with the added benefit of being where *we* want to go, so we can collect more money from the Imperial Navy."

Steve scowled. "Five families," he repeated. "How many people are included?"

"Twenty-seven, fifteen of whom are young children," Ethne explained. "They have basic medical certificates from their homeworld, nothing from the Empire. There's no reason why they would be denied entry to Madagascar."

"Not if they have money," Paddy growled. "Do they *really* have enough credits to survive?"

"They've been trading with off-world traders," Ethne said. "From what their representative said, their lives have been threatened and they just want to take their kids and run. Quite understandable, if you ask me."

Sameena nodded in agreement. She could understand people wanting to leave their homeworld, even if it *was* where they had grown up. Besides, nothing she'd read about the world below had suggested that it might be a decent place to live. The civil war had been going on for far too long, despite the best efforts of the peacekeepers.

Steve scowled. "We will need to redline the life support systems," he warned. "Assuming that we bed them down in the hold, we're still going to have problems. I assume we can't take the kids first and everyone else afterwards?"

Ethne gave her son a dark look. "You would assume responsibility for their safety on Madagascar?"

"Dumbass," Paddy agreed. He looked over at Captain Hamilton. "Permission to punch him, sir?"

"If we are to take *all* of them, we will need to install additional life support systems," Steve said, sharply. "The cold equations do not bend. As you should damn well know, *jarhead*."

Sameena shivered. Steve had ordered her to read the short story – apparently, it dated all the way back to the pre-space era – and explained afterwards that the universe didn't change its laws for anything, not even sentimentality. He'd *then* pointed out, once again, just how lucky Sameena had been to survive her first trip into space…and how the next mistake could easily kill her.

Captain Hamilton tapped the bulkhead, loudly enough to silence both of them. "Do we have an expenses account as part of the contract?"

"Not a big one," Ethne said. "But we can always resell life support technology on Madagascar, if we manage to obtain Imperial Navy-grade equipment."

"See what you can find," Captain Hamilton ordered. "Steve, you work out what we would need and then give me the list. Unless there are any serious objections, I intend to take the contract."

"We might want to add in a liability clause," Steve warned. "What happens if one of those idiots accidentally opens an airlock?"

"I'll see to it," Captain Hamilton said. "Anything else?"

No one said anything. Sameena wondered, absently, why *this* contract was up for debate while Ethne had signed the previous contract without consulting with anyone else, even her husband. But then, a live cargo was always a difficult problem. *Logan* simply didn't have enough stasis pods to transport all five families to Madagascar.

"Sameena, go with Steve to work out the requirements for life support," Captain Hamilton ordered. "Ethne and I will draw up the contract for their approval."

Sameena normally liked working with Steve, but he seemed to be in a dark mood as they went down to the engineering compartment to work through their sums. She knew how the life support systems worked, at least in theory; adding twenty-seven newcomers to the crew risked overloading it. They would need to produce more oxygen…

"Count them all as adults," Steve ordered, when she asked how old the children were. "You don't want to cut corners with the life support."

Sameena nodded, wincing inwardly at his tone. The life support requirements for children were considerably smaller than adults, but it was difficult to be sure precisely how much each child required. Adults, on the other hand, were fairly constant. He was right, she knew; counting them all as adults would be safer than trying to work out precisely how much they needed.

"Show me your results," he growled, once he'd worked it out himself. "And you check mine."

They had the same answer, Sameena noted with some relief. A mistake with the life support could be absolutely disastrous. All of her exercises over the last month had been torn apart and the mistakes highlighted, just to make sure that she knew exactly what she was doing.

"Excellent," Steve said. He sounded as though he was annoyed that they hadn't been able to prove that they couldn't take the families onboard. "And here is what we will need to provide for them."

The next four hours passed quickly, once they purchased the additional life support gear from Orbit One. Steve, Paddy, James and Brad did most of the installing, but they took time to explain to Sameena and the kids just what they were doing – and why. Next time, Steve promised, she could actually do a section herself, although he would be checking her work afterwards. Sameena felt vaguely insulted until she realised that everyone's work was being checked.

She caught a nap in her cabin, then awoke in time to assist Brad in preparing the hold for their guests. There *was* enough space for twenty-seven passengers, she realised, but it was going to be cramped – and there would be absolutely no privacy. The sole remaining cabin had been designated the toilet, with the kids charged with showing the newcomers how to use it. Sameena was just grateful that she hadn't been given *that* job.

"We're taking on additional rations too," Brad told her, once they had finished laying out the bedding. "It was rather worrying how quickly the Imperial Navy signed a case of standard ration bars over to us."

Sameena made a face. Paddy had told her that standard ration bars were nutritious, with everything a growing spacer needed, but they were *disgusting*. She had wondered why the producers didn't try to improve the flavour; Paddy had pointed out that they didn't want to *encourage* people to eat the bars and nothing else. It didn't make sense to her.

"We can probably hang a curtain to separate the sexes if they wish it," she said. She had no idea of the sexual mores on the planet below. "Or should we do that anyway?"

"See what they have to say," Brad said. "It would probably be better to let them choose."

Their wristcoms buzzed. "Come to the airlock," Ethne ordered. "They're ready to come onboard."

Sameena hadn't been sure what she'd been expecting to see. The children looked terrible, as if they'd spent their lives permanently on the run. Their eyes were haunted, their faces were pale and their clothes were tattered, despite the vast sum of money their parents had handed over to Ethne for transport out of the system. The adults looked more confident, particularly the younger men, but there was a wariness about them that bothered Sameena. How much of their confidence was an act?

"They got shipsuits on the station, thankfully," Brad muttered to her, as they escorted the refugees into the hold. "But we will still have to tell them about safety."

Sameena nodded, remembering the days when she hadn't been allowed to leave her cabin without an escort. There were just too many ways one of the children could get themselves killed, entirely by accident. Ethne stepped forward as soon as the last refugee was in the hold and started to warn them of the dangers. None of them showed much reaction.

"It's a seven-day trip to Madagascar," Ethne concluded. "It would be nice if you could stay in the hold until we reach our destination. Do *not* go beyond the airlock at the head of the corridor without an escort."

Brad pulled at Sameena's arm, leading her out of the hold. "Pity they can't be permanently sedated," he muttered. "You know the vast colonist-carriers? They're nothing, but thousands of stasis pods for the colonists. They don't experience *any* time passing until they reach their new homeworld. So much better than just waiting in the hold, staring at the bulkheads."

Sameena said nothing as they walked back up to the bridge. Steve was already there, monitoring the life support equipment. He didn't look happy; he was checking and rechecking the readings, as if he expected the system to break down at any moment. There were horror stories, Sameena had read, where starship crews had had to shoot their passengers into space, just to survive long enough for help to arrive. They never ended well.

"There's hardly any System Command here," Brad muttered, as he took his seat. "We could just leave orbit without waiting to ask for permission."

"You'd better ask for permission to undock first," Captain Hamilton said, dryly. "Or they will make a *terrible* fuss."

Sameena smiled as Steve chuckled, finally turning away from the monitoring systems. *Logan* couldn't hope to outrun one of the gunboats in the system, even if she were given an hour's lead. If the Imperial Navy chose to come after them, escape would be impossible.

"They've cleared us to depart," Brad said, after a moment. "And they're wishing our passengers a happy voyage."

"Not a chance," Steve said. "They'll be thoroughly sick of each other by the time we reach Madagascar."

Logan quivered to life as she undocked from Orbit One and then headed out towards the Phase Limit. Sameena studied the displays long enough to confirm her first impression of the system, then picked up her terminal and went back to work. There were five more assignments to complete before she returned to Madagascar or…she didn't know what the consequences would be, but it would probably delay her progress. Besides, Ethne hadn't been joking when she said that the kids weren't allowed to explore unless they had completed all of their assignments. Sameena would probably face the same restriction.

The hatch opened, revealing Paddy. "Jayne's just finished inspecting some of the kids," he said, as he sat down at one of the consoles. There was a hint of cold anger in his voice. "Someone slapped them around, quite a bit. That refugee camp was a very nasty place and the Imperials did bugger all to make it better. I'm surprised they kept their cash. It should have been stolen or used for bribes by now."

Sameena gritted her teeth. She'd done some research during a break and discovered that interstellar refugees rarely fared well. If they were lucky, they were shipped to a planet that allowed them to integrate into its population; if they were unlucky, they remained in refugee camps or were simply dumped on colonies like Madagascar, where they were ruthlessly exploited by the locals. How many of the women in brothels, she thought grimly, had been refugees? The Empire could be a very unfriendly place.

And how would Jannah react, she asked herself, *if a few thousand refugees from a different culture were dumped on us?*

Her research suggested that the answer to that was *poorly*. Some worlds were quite welcoming, or simply in desperate need of new colonists, but others resented unwelcome immigrants, particularly the ones who refused to assimilate into the local culture. Jannah, she was sure, would be *very* unwelcoming. And she had a feeling that few outsiders, even the ones from Islamic worlds, would be willing to assimilate completely.

Ethne and Jayne would refuse to wear the veil, but there's just two of them, she thought, bitterly. *How would a few thousand outsiders react to Jannah?*

"Poor bastards," Brad said. "But they're safe now."

"Once they get to Madagascar they'll be safe," Steve said. He didn't sound as though he believed himself. "Right now, I think we should keep a very close eye on the life support."

Sameena nodded and returned her gaze to her terminal. The assignment was driving her insane, but she didn't want to ask for help. Starship navigation was something she would definitely have to master if she wanted to pass the exams, let alone command her own ship. And navigating through Phase Space was incredibly tricky…every one of her first set of calculations had gone wrong because she hadn't been able to account for all of the gravity wells that warped and twisted Phase Space. Or made it harder for the drive to work properly.

There's a gravity well there, she thought to herself, rubbing her temple. *If we go too close, we'll wind up three light years from our intended destination. But if we give it a wide berth, we'll add several more days to our transit time.*

And to think the assignment wanted the *quickest* route between two points, with as few stopping places as possible…

She put it aside, deciding that she might be forced to ask Brad or Ethne for help. Brad might give her the answer; Ethne would show her how to avoid making the same mistake time and time again. Silently promising that she would ask them tomorrow, she searched through the other files on the database and brought up a textbook on interstellar biological quarantine procedures. She'd been warned that she would be expected to have a passing understanding of what could and could not be shipped in merchant hulls.

The hatch opened again. Sameena looked up, expecting to see Ethne or Jayne…and gasped as one of the refugees stepped onto the bridge. The young man didn't look *beaten* anymore; he looked…*dangerous*. And he was carrying a small pistol in his hand.

"I'd ask you all to remain still," he said, as the other young men filed onto the bridge. He spoke Imperial Standard with an oddly lisping accent. "If you do as we say, none of you will be harmed."

Captain Hamilton stared at him, his face twitching with rage. "What is this?"

"Your ship is under our control," the hijacker said. "Please, put your hands in the air."

Sameena hesitated, cursing her oversight. If she'd carried her pistol…but she'd known that she couldn't take it onboard Orbit One and so she'd left it in her cabin. It might as well be a thousand light years away for all the good it would do her.

And they have the drop on us anyway, she thought, remembering a couple of movies she'd watched with the kids. There was no way she could have drawn her pistol without being shot. If she'd had it, they would have taken it. *What could we do?*

"Do as he says," Captain Hamilton ordered. His voice was very controlled, but she was sure that he was furious. He was the master of his ship and his command was being violated. "Now."

Sameena lifted her hands. Brad and Steve did the same, their faces flushed with angry humiliation. Paddy complied a moment later, his face tight and expressionless.

"My wife," the Captain said, suddenly. Sameena heard the alarm in his voice and winced, inwardly. What had happened to Ethne? And Jayne? And the kids? "What have you done with her?"

"She's safe, just a little tied up," the hijacker said. He gave Hamilton a savage smile. "Now, I'd like the command codes to your ship. Now."

"The Imperial Navy already knows that you're here," Hamilton said, calmly. "You cannot hope to get across the Phase Limit in time to escape."

"You're lying," the hijacker said, simply.

Sameena suspected that he was right. They hadn't known that the refugees had bad intentions until they'd come crashing onto the bridge. There had been no time to contact the Imperial Navy and scream for help. If the hijackers kept their nerve, they could just keep going to the Phase Limit and vanish the moment they crossed it. There would be no help from outside.

The hijacker didn't even sound angry. "And you don't seem to be taking us seriously. How…*terrible*."

He reached forward and caught Sameena's arm, pulling her out of her seat and thrusting her towards two of his men. She winced, expecting to be molested or raped in front of her adopted family, but instead they pushed her towards the airlock. The hatch was open and she was inside before she quite realised what was going on. And then the hatch closed. Absolute silence descended as she beat her hands against the inner hatch…

…And then she heard air starting to hiss out of the compartment as the outer hatch began to open, revealing the inky darkness of space.

Chapter Thirteen

> Critics claimed that gold (and thus money) was the root of all evil. Ironically, there was a certain amount of truth to this, at least where the local economy was concerned. A sudden influx of gold and silver – the discovery of a new mine, for example – could badly undermine the economy by causing a shift in the balance between supply and demand. If the level of gold rose, prices would rise along with it. The Spanish Empire's access to the vast levels of gold and silver from the New World proved as much curse as blessing.
> - Professor Leo Caesius, *The Science That Isn't: Economics and the Decline and Fall of the Galactic Empire.*

Sameena felt one long moment of absolute panic as she felt the outrush of air pulling her out of the ship, then she forced the panic aside, remembering what she'd been taught from the very first day she set foot on *Logan*. She used one hand to grab hold of the handle, holding herself in the ship, while she used the other to pull her facemask over her face. There was only a limited supply of oxygen in the shipsuit – it was meant to keep the wearer alive long enough to find a proper spacesuit – but it would have to suffice.

The last traces of the atmosphere rushed out of the airlock, then the pull simply faded away to nothingness. Sameena pulled herself forward, feeling cold seeping through the shipsuit, and out onto the freighter's hull. Thankfully, she was still inside the ship's drive field; there was no danger of being left behind unless she threw herself away from the hull. She reached for the first handhold and made her way down towards the lower airlock. The cold seemed to be growing stronger, wearing away at her; it was awfully tempting to just let go and drift away into nothingness. But somehow she kept going until she reached the airlock and touched the emergency lever.

Galactic Law insisted that all airlocks had to remain unlocked, allowing someone on the outside to get into the ship quickly if there was an emergency. Steve had commented that the law had been written by engineers rather than bureaucrats, crediting the engineers with saving countless lives since most equipment had been standardised. Normally, the airlocks were also designed to trap any unwanted intruders – just in case someone attempted to board the ship and take control – but Sameena had a set of access codes for *Logan*. She plunged into the airlock and sighed in relief as she heard fresh air being pumped into the compartment.

She opened the second hatch and looked around, listening for any signs of trouble. There had been twenty-seven refugees, but half of them had been kids. Assuming all of the adults were hijackers, there were thirteen hijackers on the ship. Gritting her teeth – her skin felt odd, despite the protection provided by the shipsuit – she hurried down towards the cabins. She needed to arm herself before she did anything else.

Paddy probably has a stockpile of weapons elsewhere, she thought, as she opened the hatch that led into the cabins. *But I don't know where.*

Her cabin was, as always, unlocked. She slipped inside, noted to her relief that no one had attempted to search her possessions, then found the pistol where she'd buried it under her underwear. Once she slipped a clip into the weapon, she felt much better, even though she was vastly outnumbered. Keeping that thought in mind, she pocketed the remaining clips and slipped down to the cabin Richard and Regina shared. Bracing herself, she peeked inside. The kids were lying on their bunks, their hands and feet taped together. And they'd been gagged, just to keep them quiet.

No guard, she thought, relieved. *They must not have considered them worth the effort.*

Sameena tapped her lips, then found Regina's multitool and used it to cut their bonds. "I was thrown off the bridge," she muttered, as soon as they were free. "Do you have weapons?"

"No ammo," Regina said. "Uncle Paddy said he'd tan our hides if we touched the ammunition without permission."

She looked up at Sameena. "What happened to your face?"

Sameena touched her cheek...and felt a chilling numbness that spoke of the icy cold of space. It had left its mark on her, she realised. Part of her mind insisted that she would never be truly warm again, while the remainder dismissed that as a silly thought.

"Take these," she said, hoping that her ammunition was compatible with whatever weapons Paddy had given the kids. "He'll understand, I think."

Richard gave her a weak smile. "We'll blame you if he doesn't," he said. His face darkened. "What do we do now?"

"Follow me down to the hold," Sameena said. If they could find and free Ethne, she'd know what to do. "And if you see any of the bastards, shoot them."

She felt a twinge of guilt for giving the kids such orders, but there was no choice. Besides, the hijackers had thrown her into interplanetary space, fully expecting her to die in the cold vacuum. A few more minutes, she suspected, and they would have gotten their wish. She scowled as she felt the ship's drives suddenly growing stronger, as if the hijackers were trying to squeeze more speed out of the ancient systems.

Steve must be panicking, she thought, grimly. She knew just how much work he'd put into the drives over the years, replacing as much as he could just to keep them running for a few more months. But there was nothing he could do to save the ship he loved.

"Hold here," she ordered, and peeked down towards the hold. There was an unpleasant smell in the air, but no sign of anyone with a gun. Carefully, she slipped further down and peered into the hold itself, sucking in a breath when she saw the scene in front of her. The remaining refugees – and Ethne and Jayne – were lying on the deck, their hands tied behind their backs. Again, there was no sign of any of the hijackers.

She removed the strip of tape over Ethne's mouth, then released her hands. "I've got the kids," she muttered, "but everyone else is on the bridge, apart from James."

"He was meant to be in engineering," Jayne said, once she pulled the gag away. "What happened on the bridge?"

Sameena explained – and then had to endure the doctor examining her face and hands. "You may need some surgery later," Jayne said, finally. "Vacuum damage isn't hard to repair, but if you leave it too long it can leave scars."

"Leave that for the moment," Ethne said. "Why are they powering up the drive?"

She started to walk out of the hold. Jayne caught her. "What about them?" She asked, nodding to the remaining refugees. "They're clearly not on the wrong side."

"We can't trust them," Ethne said, flatly. "Leave them here until we regain control of our ship."

Outside, Ethne found some additional weapons and ammunition, then used her terminal to access the datanet. "We're heading back towards the planet," she said, in surprise. "And picking up speed. That's worrying."

Jayne nodded. "I thought they wanted to *leave* the planet," she said. "Or..."

"They're taking us right back to Orbit One," Ethne said. "I think they plan to ram the station."

Sameena frowned. She might not have known anything about orbital trajectories before she'd joined the crew, but she'd learned a great deal since then. "There are three starships in the system," she pointed out. "Surely one of them will intercept us before we hit the station."

"Almost certainly," Ethne said. "But there are children on this ship. They may hesitate – or they may simply blow us away. Either way, we die."

She looked over at Jayne. "I want you and the kids to go to engineering," she ordered. "If James is there, get him free and then shut down the drives. Don't worry about anything else, just stop us from heading towards the station. Sameena and I will go get them out of the bridge."

Jayne nodded. "Understood," she said. She looked over at Sameena. "You watch yourself, all right? And don't let my husband get himself killed. He's through with heroics."

Sameena nodded, although she didn't understand quite what Jayne meant. Ethne passed her a pair of spare clips of ammunition, then led the way towards the ladder leading up to deck one. If the terrorists suspected anything, Sameena realised, they'd have someone posted on the ladder, watching for trouble.

"It's possible," Ethne agreed, when Sameena said that out loud. "If this was a bigger ship, we could go through the tubes and surprise them, but there isn't any other choice."

"We could go through the airlock again," Sameena said. "Or…"

Ethne shook her head. "Far too easy to get trapped in the airlock," she reminded her. "That would be a good way to turn ourselves back into prisoners."

She scowled as they reached the ladder. "Once we get out of this, I'm going to insist that we strip-search everyone who comes onboard," she added. "We should have searched the bastards for weapons, but we just took it for granted that they wouldn't have been allowed to keep them in the camps. Someone must have taken a fairly hefty bribe."

Sameena looked over at her. "Who *are* they?"

"The Imperial Navy is backing one faction on the planet's surface," Ethne said, as she inspected her terminal. "Logically, one or more of the other factions would want to destroy Orbit One and make it harder for the Navy to operate here. Even if they failed, the new security precautions would be so irksome that fewer merchant ships would wish to visit."

She grinned, suddenly. "There's no one up there."

Sameena blinked in surprise. "How can you tell?"

Ethne showed her the terminal, which was linked to the life support monitors. "If someone was up there, there would be a higher concentration of carbon dioxide in the corridor," she said, shortly. She scrambled up the ladder and pushed open the hatch. "But you still need to be quiet."

Sameena nodded as she joined Ethne. *Logan* no longer felt entirely friendly, as if the ship had been violated by the enemy. Cold rage burned in her, fuelling her determination to help liberate her new family and destroy the hijackers before they could turn her new home into a weapon. She was *not* going to let them get away with this.

The ship trembled, then the sound of the drives faded away. "She must have succeeded," Ethne muttered. "If they'd burned out the drives, we would probably have lost gravity as well."

Ahead of them, the hatch to the bridge opened, revealing two of the hijackers. They stared at Sameena as if they'd seen a ghost, giving Ethne a chance to get the drop on them. She levelled her weapon at the pair, daring them to move. There was a long pause, then the hijackers started to stumble backwards. Ethne barked at them to stay where they were and keep their hands where she could see them. Instead, the leader peeked out of the hatch and stared at them. He had never expected to see Sameena again.

"We still have your friends hostage," he said, his voice inhumanly calm. "And we have control of your ship."

"No, you don't," Ethne said. "We have control of the drives now and the Imperial Navy is on their way. Tell me – what were you *thinking*? They would have blown this ship into little pieces of debris before they let it get within ramming distance of the station."

The hijacker glared at her. "So we wait and blow the ship when the Marines arrive," he said. "It's still a win."

"No, because the ship won't explode on your command," Ethne said. She snorted, rudely. "This isn't a warship with a self-destruct system, you know. You couldn't even convince the drives to explode if you worked on them for hours – and you knew precisely what you were doing, which you don't. You really need to surrender now."

"So you take us out of the system instead," the hijacker said. His voice was starting to crack, as if he'd realised that he might well be able to die for nothing. "Get us somewhere else, like you agreed…"

"I think our contract is moot now," Ethne said, dryly. "Besides, do you know that we cannot *hope* to outrun the Imperial Navy? They could give us a few hours to run and then still chase us down before we cross the Phase Limit. If you surrender, you might…"

The hijacker pulled a knife out of his sleeve and threw it at her. Sameena reacted on instinct, shoving Ethne to one side and then shooting the hijacker through the head. She saw, through a cold haze that had descended over her mind, him crumpling to the deck, like a puppet whose strings had been cut. The first two hijackers lunged at her; she shot them both, then staggered backwards as one crashed into her. She hit the deck and winced as her head smacked against the cold metal.

"Good work," she heard Ethne say, through a haze of pain. The weight on her body – the hijacker, she realised – was dragged away. "Very good work."

Sameena sat upright, feeling the world spinning around her. She'd killed. The mere thought of killing someone had bothered her after Paddy had started giving her shooting lessons, but when the time had come she'd just…acted. And she hadn't panicked when they'd tried to shoot her into interplanetary space without a spacesuit either. She'd remained calm and done what needed to be done.

There was a nasty red stain on her shipsuit, she saw. Blood; the hijacker's blood. Only one of the hijackers had survived, although she knew that the rest of the refugees had concealed them. Had they been forced into it or had they been willing collaborators? There was no way to tell.

"Call Jayne," Ethne was saying. Her voice seemed very distant. The deck seemed to be buckling under her weight, as if the internal compensators had started to fail. But that was impossible, wasn't it? They'd all be dead if the compensators failed. "Sameena needs help…"

The next thing she knew was that she was in the sickbay. Jayne was bending over her, examining Sameena's forehead. Her head was pounding unpleasantly – for a terrible moment, she was sure that she was about to throw up – and her body felt numb all over.

"Lie still," Jayne ordered. There was a flat tone in her voice that brooked no argument. "I've done basic repair work, but it will take some time for your body to settle down."

Sameena tried to nod, but even *that* motion made her head feel worse. Instead, she just lay still, fighting the urge to whimper. Tiny sparkles of pain were starting to break through the numbness, tearing away at her mind. Part of her just wanted to surrender to the darkness and go back to sleep forever.

"Diving into space like that," Jayne said. She shook her head in disbelief. "If you'd done that deliberately, sweetheart, there wouldn't be a single ship that would take you on as a crewwoman. As it is, we'll have to make sure that the story is told and retold before someone starts their own version. The clans chatter a lot, you know."

I didn't mean to, Sameena wanted to say, but her mouth refused to work.

"Your face, thankfully, didn't require more than basic repair work," Jayne added. "Some frostbite to your hands and feet, which is more serious, but I've injected you with quick-heal, seeing that the Imperial Navy is picking up the bill. They're quite embarrassed over what happened to us – and almost happened to the station."

Sameena tried to look a question at her. "It seems that they also want to offer a large cash reward," Jayne added, after a moment. "Those refugees" – she made the word a curse – "included one of the deadliest killers on the wrong side – the one the Imperial Navy isn't backing. Turns out that someone in the Navy took a huge bribe to look the other way when he and his team forced their way into the refugee camp and rounded up some women and children to go with them, pretending to be their families. They were told that if they didn't cooperate, the remainder of their families would be killed."

She smiled. "Mum was talking about taking them with us when we leave, but I don't know what will happen to them. They don't really have much to offer, apart from their bodies – and they've already been badly abused. Maybe we can find something else for them."

Set up some schooling, Sameena thought. It would tie in with the plan she was slowly putting together, piece by piece, in her mind. *Maybe see if we can turn the kids into proper engineers.*

Jayne shrugged, unaware of Sameena's thoughts. "Brad will be pleased," she said. "A large cash reward split between the crew will help him accomplish his dream much sooner. The rest of us will no doubt find uses for the cash, in time."

Good for him, Sameena thought. She already knew how she was going to spend hers. *Good for all of us.*

"I'm going to sedate you again now," Jayne added. "You're going to be in my sickbay for a few more days, unless the Imperial Navy can offer better facilities. When you wake up, you should be much better. And thank you. You saved us all."

She leaned over, kissed Sameena lightly on the forehead and placed something against the side of her head. Sameena felt a faint spark…and then she plunged down into darkness.

CHAPTER FOURTEEN

> This may seem contradictory. However, the true foundations of wealth lay in production, rather than stockpiles of money. Gold actually lost value while it rested in a bank vault; it was only when it was turned into produce that it gained value. A sudden influx of gold caused the overall value of gold to decline. In effect, the supply had suddenly outstripped demand. The Spanish failed to use the windfall to build up their position before the economy adjusted for its arrival.
>
> - Professor Leo Caesius, *The Science That Isn't: Economics and the Decline and Fall of the Galactic Empire.*

"They stiffed us," Brad said, four days later. "A lousy *ten thousand* credits each?"

"And a promise of supplies from Madagascar Base, *and* first dibs on any future contracts," Ethne said. "I don't think we did too badly."

"But they also want us to keep it quiet," Brad growled. "Other crews might make the same mistake."

Sameena tuned out the argument. She couldn't blame Brad for being annoyed; if *Logan* had been destroyed, they would have been unable to obtain a new starship with the compensation they'd been given. But it wasn't as if they'd had much choice. The only alternative had been to bail out and hope that the navy could rescue them. It hadn't even crossed their minds as they sought to recover their bridge.

She looked down at her hands, shivering. Jayne had repaired all of the physical damage – no one could tell that she'd ever been injured – but the whole affair had left scars on her soul. She'd *killed*…and she felt nothing, apart from mild regret. It bothered her that she felt so little. And that she'd done so well, even though she had been raised to avoid fighting at all costs. It wasn't considered a feminine occupation on Jannah.

Paddy snorted, loudly enough to catch her attention. "The Navy can't give us a few million credits each," he said, crossly. "Just be glad they're not trying to bill us for the rescue."

He stalked off the bridge, heading down towards the galley. After a moment, Sameena followed him. They would need to prepare water and ration bars for the remainder of the refugees, who had elected to go to Madagascar anyway. There was nothing left for them on their homeworld.

"I need to ask you something," she said, once they were alone. "You used to be in the military, right?"

Paddy studied her for a long moment, his gaze reminding her that – by the strict social mores of her homeworld – she shouldn't be alone with him, even if Jayne *had* been her biological sister. But she felt no particular guilt or shame any longer.

"I am a retired Marine," Paddy said, finally. "Why do you ask?"

Sameena hesitated. "I killed them," she said. She'd killed three of the hijackers personally; the remaining two had been handed over to the Imperial Navy, who would interrogate and then execute them. "And yet I feel…almost nothing."

"You handled yourself well in a crisis," Paddy said. "I've known more experienced officers and crewmen who would have panicked when they were thrust into space."

"All of your emergency drills helped," Sameena admitted. She'd hated being woken in the middle of the night and told that there was an emergency, but it seemed to have prepared her for a *real* disaster. "But why don't I feel anything now?"

"They would have rammed Orbit One and destroyed the station, along with us," Paddy said. "If a large chunk of the station had made it through the atmosphere and hit the surface, it would have devastated parts of the planet too. Thousands of lives were at risk. And they weren't going to surrender. I think you know that they *had* to die."

"I don't think I thought it through that comprehensively," Sameena said. "I just…I just don't know how to feel."

She looked up at him. "How did you cope with it?"

Paddy considered. "You want a honest answer? Most of the people I killed while I was in the Corps were trying to kill me at the time, or they were tormenting others, or they were not honourable opponents…they were people I wasn't going to waste time feeling sorry for. The real problem was remembering that just because some people come from a bad society isn't a good reason to hate the *entire* population."

Sameena frowned. "The *entire* population?"

"I was stationed on Moonstone," Paddy said. "The entire planet was run by…well, call them religious fanatics. By the time we landed, they'd sunk their propaganda bullshit into every man, woman and child on the planet. They would happily launch suicide attacks, use themselves as human shields, keep their mouths closed when we asked questions and turn on us at the drop of a hat. We could never trust anyone completely. After a while…"

He shook his head. "After a while, we just started to *hate* the entire population," he added, softly. "Our discipline began to break down. We shot people for looking at us funny, ignored problems that we could have fixed…thankfully, they pulled us out before we could go completely bad. The Imperial Army had it much worse. Some of their units had been stationed there for years and were little more than just another gang."

Sameena thought she understood. "Why did you leave?"

"The Marines?" Paddy asked. "Do you want a honest answer to that too?"

He smiled at her expression. "I joined because I was told that it was a brotherhood – and I *needed* some brotherhood in my life. And it *was* a brotherhood; by the time we fought our way through the Slaughterhouse, there wasn't one of us who wouldn't lay down his life for the others. I was proud to serve until I realised an ugly truth.

"We were the Grand Senate's enforcers," he explained. "When a planet defaulted on its taxes, we were sent in to bust heads; when a planet rebelled, it was our task to restore order; when a black colony was exposed, we were the ones who invaded and brought them into the Empire. I was a terrible coward. It took me *months* to decide not to re-up when I completed my first decade of service.

"The Grand Senate claims that the Empire is as strong as ever. I doubt it very much."

Sameena nodded. That fitted with her own observations.

"I miss the brotherhood," Paddy admitted. "I like Brad and Steve and James, but they haven't been where I've been. The Captain…had a different kind of experience. But I don't miss cracking skulls for the glory of the Grand Senate. I suppose I could join a mercenary band, but I'd just end up fighting for the highest bidder."

He gave her a long considering look. "Have you been having nightmares?"

"Some," Sameena said. They'd changed after the hijacking. One recurring nightmare had had her drifting out into space instead of making it to the second airlock. "But Jayne said that they might have been caused by the drugs."

"They might," Paddy agreed. "But then again they might be caused by your inner conflict. I sometimes have nightmares too."

"There isn't a Marine alive who would place any faith in the headshrinkers," he added, "but if killing them is really bothering you I'd suggest talking to Doctor Maritz on Madagascar. She does have her head screwed on properly, unlike most civilian doctors. And she won't bombard you with psychobabble."

"Thank you," Sameena said. She'd never heard Paddy talk about his past before, not even when he'd been helping her with her studies. "If you hadn't taught me how to shoot…"

"We're going to start self-defence too," Paddy said. "Jayne or Ethne would probably be better at teaching you – you need to fight like a bitch, not a girl."

"I don't understand," Sameena admitted.

"You're slight," Paddy said. He pulled back his sleeve to reveal a muscular arm. "If you tried to fight me directly, I'd beat you easily. You need to learn how to fight dirty. Carry a knife and a few other concealed weapons at all times and suchlike. It's a dirty little secret that, on average, a man can always beat a woman if she fights *fair*."

"That isn't fair," Sameena observed.

"Quite," Paddy agreed. "But a knee in the groin will give the average man something else to think about other than trying to get his grubby little paws on you."

He turned back to the cupboard and started to pull out ration bars. "For the refugees," he said, changing the subject. "You can take them in; I'll wait outside, stunner in hand."

Sameena nodded. After the attempted hijacking, the remaining refugees had been locked in the hold. It wouldn't be very comfortable, but the alternative was returning them to the planet, where they would probably be killed or sold into slavery. She picked up the tray of ration bars – at least the Captain had allowed them to have a water processor in the hold – and carried it down towards the hatch. Paddy picked up his stunner and followed her.

The hatch hissed open. Sameena winced as the smell struck her – Steve had rigged up a makeshift toilet, but the refugees were all unwashed and would remain so until they reached Madagascar – yet somehow managed to step inside. The refugee women looked almost listless; their children didn't seem much better. After everything they'd been through, Sameena couldn't blame them for breaking down.

She looked for Lamina – their spokeswoman – and nodded to her. Lamina wasn't more than a couple of years older than Sameena herself, but she looked almost thirty. Her whole bearing spoke of a woman who had been beaten down by life. She reminded Sameena of some of the older women she had known on Jannah, women who had been forced into unwelcome marriages. None of the others were much better.

"We need to talk," she said, quietly.

Jayne had carried out a full medical examination of the refugees – with Paddy and James standing guard – and what she'd found had shocked everyone. The children had been quite badly abused, but their mothers had been beaten and raped by the hijackers, just to make sure that they were too terrified to betray the hijackers to the Imperial Navy. Their husbands had vanished somewhere in the chaos sweeping over the planet. That, Ethne had said, was reason enough to ship them to Madagascar. At least they'd have a chance to build a new life there.

"You're going to be dropped off at Madagascar," she continued. "What are you going to do with yourselves there?"

Lamina looked blank. She'd been too badly beaten and abused to harbour the notion that there might be a future for her and her children. Sameena suspected she knew what would happen when they arrived on the asteroid. They'd be swept up into prostitution before they could find their footing. The kids might join them in the brothels before too long; the oldest girls were already pushing thirteen. It was a sickening thought.

"Your children need education," Sameena said. It was their only hope for a better life. "I would be willing to fund their scholarships, in exchange for a decade of service after they become qualified engineers."

She'd consulted with Steve and Ethne before making the offer. They'd checked her calculations and agreed that she had enough money to start the kids down the path towards becoming engineers, assuming that they had the aptitude. Once they started selling Firewater Mead, it shouldn't be too difficult to *keep* them in training…Steve had pointed out, rather dryly, that a half-trained engineer should still be able to find work. He'd even expressed interest in helping to fund the scheme.

"I don't want a ship of my own," he'd explained, when she asked. "But do you think that there would ever be a payoff?"

"You have to spend money in order to make money," Sameena had countered, quoting one of her father's favourite sayings. Apparently, the saying predated the Empire. "And some payoffs don't come in credits."

She watched Lamina carefully as she explained what she had in mind. If Lamina agreed, the other women would certainly do as she said…but just how far gone *was* she? Even Jannah, for all of its belief that women were incapable of handling their own affairs, wouldn't have tolerated such abuse. Or would it? What woman in her right mind would go to the Guardians with a complaint against her husband? How could she even leave the house without a male escort?

"It sounds very tempting," Lamina said, finally. "And what of *us*?"

The women, Sameena thought. What *could* they do, besides prostitution? She was damned if she was going to force *anyone* into a brothel. From what she'd heard Steve and James say, when they'd thought she couldn't hear them, they would be awful places for a woman. The women had no qualifications the Empire might recognise…

A thought struck her and she smiled. "Can you *cook*?"

"Of course," Lamina said. She sounded almost offended. "I wouldn't have trusted my husband to boil water."

"I can probably give you a loan to open an eatery on Madagascar," Sameena said, slowly. It wasn't something she had planned to do, but it might come in handy later. Besides, from what she'd seen, the inhabitants of Madagascar would be happy to try a new kind of food. "The four of you could make it work."

Lamina eyed her, suspiciously. "And you will claim the profits?"

"You can pay me back slowly," Sameena said. "I haven't worked out the details yet, but you would be able to keep most of the profits for yourself and provide a place for your kids to live."

She smiled at the thought. The kids would probably end up working in the kitchens or serving tables, just as similar kids had done on Jannah. It would help to cut costs…later, when they were qualified engineers, their mothers would be able to hire additional help. Assuming the eatery was a success, of course. She'd have to look into renting space on the rock. It should be reasonably cheap, thankfully.

The women held a brief, whispered consultation in their own language. Sameena looked over at the kids, wondering how many of them spoke Imperial Standard; they'd have to learn before they tried to join one of the educational programs. The Empire insisted that the entire population should be able to speak Imperial Standard, but there were plenty of worlds that only paid lip service to the concept. It was funny she'd never realised how that crippled opportunities off-world before.

But I never even imagined leaving Jannah until I had to run, she thought. *How many of these women expected to leave their homeworld too?*

Lamina looked over at her. "We accept your offer," she said. "Do you have a contract for us to sign?"

Sameena blinked in surprise. "I will have to write one out for the eatery," she said. "It might be better to do that on Madagascar, so we know the prices."

"Thank you," Lamina said. She hesitated. "Is there any way the kids could get some exercise?"

"I'll discuss it with the Captain," Sameena promised. He would be reluctant after the attempted hijacking, she knew. But maybe the kids could use the exercise machines under strict supervision. "We'll get you to Madagascar as quickly as we can."

She left the hold and nodded to Paddy. "That took longer than I had expected," she admitted. "I'm sorry for making you wait."

"It could be worse," Paddy said, dryly. He checked that the hatch was locked, then led the way back up to the bridge. "Captain wants to leave the system as quickly as possible."

"I don't blame him," Sameena said. After the hijacking, she was mildly surprised that they'd stayed in the system long enough to collect their reward from the Imperial Navy. There was nothing holding them from leaving. "I want to leave too."

Paddy snorted. "A very good idea," he said. "If we're lucky, we won't ever have to come back here."

He snorted again, then smiled. "And you're going to go back to your studies," he added. "Hijacking or not, you don't want to fail your assessments or people will point and laugh at you."

Sameena scowled. After the excitement of the hijacking, it would be hard to go back to her education…but there was no choice. She would have to arrange something for the refugee children as well, something that would help them prepare for their own studies. Perhaps she could convince Ethne to let her bring a few of the older children to the schoolroom. It was a shame they didn't have a real teacher…

Or maybe not, she thought, remembering some of the horror stories she'd heard. The Empire's educational system seemed designed to turn out drones, rather than people who could actually *think*. Ethne had told her that she would rather spend hours slaving over an assignment from Professor Sorrel than spend a day in a standard classroom. Discipline was non-existent, the curriculum was designed more for political correctness than actual learning and the kids were exposed to drugs, electronic stimulation and other addictions that tore them away from their studies. And teachers often poked their noses into their children's personal lives – or those of their parents. No *wonder* the trader clans preferred to have as little to do with the formal educational system as possible.

"I'll get back to work," she promised. Besides, the assignments *were* fascinating. It was certainly better than endless religious studies, where she'd learned to recite by rote, without any real comprehension. "And we also have to prepare more mead."

"Make sure you do," Paddy said. "But be careful. The cartel isn't the only organisation that might take an interest in someone else distributing Firewater Mead."

CHAPTER FIFTEEN

> As society became more developed – a result of the creation of national monetary standards, however imprecise – the economy developed alongside it. Workers would work for others and be paid wages, which in turn they would use to buy products…allowing the sellers of those products to keep the money moving themselves. This led to a steady rise in the economy; the more people who were employed, the more people who could be employed, as the first group would help fund the second group. And the money kept going round and round.
>
> - Professor Leo Caesius, *The Science That Isn't: Economics and the Decline and Fall of the Galactic Empire.*

The flight back to Madagascar was uneventful, much to the entire crew's relief. Sameena spent most of her time working on her studies, completing all but one of the assignments before *Logan* dropped back into normal space and headed in towards the asteroid. The remainder was spent with the refugee children, who proved eager to learn, and keeping up with her duties on the freighter. *They* never seemed to come to an end.

"You know," Ethne said, after they docked, "I should ban you from going to Madagascar."

Sameena winced. She hadn't completed her final assignment. This time, she had been looking forward to visiting the asteroid, even if it was still a discomforting environment. She had to organise care and feeding – and schooling – for the refugees, start selling Firewater Mead and then start her long-term plan. But Ethne wasn't likely to bend the rules for her again, not when the kids would complain about the unfairness of it all. They'd completed all of *their* assignments.

"I know," she admitted, finally.

"But you do have to visit Professor Sorrel," Ethne added. "You can do that, then attend your dinner date and…"

Sameena blinked. "Dinner date?"

Ethne smirked at her. "Lieutenant Cook didn't give you his card because he thought you might like it," she pointed out. "Besides, you have to hand over the datachip we were asked to take back for him. Drop him a message; ask if he wants to meet up with you this evening. And go somewhere nice."

"Oh," Sameena said.

The thought was terrifying. It had been hard enough to convince herself that the crew were her adopted family. Going to meet a complete stranger for dinner…it wasn't something she'd ever considered doing on Jannah. And she'd skimmed a couple of romance movies from the ship's database, all of which seemed to end up with the happy couple in bed together. What if Lieutenant Cook wanted to do *that*?

"I think you will discover that most of those movies are exaggerated," Ethne said dryly, when Sameena confessed her fears. "I'm sure he's interested in you, but he probably won't push if you want to take things slowly. There's no obligation to go any further than you want to with him."

She scowled. "Do you need the talk about the birds and the bees?"

Sameena flushed. She'd known almost nothing about sex while she'd been on Jannah, apart from a blanket statement that having it before marriage – or outside marriage – was bad and would certainly lead to eternal hellfire. Or at least punishment from the Guardians. It had puzzled her at the time because she'd wondered how she was supposed to avoid it without knowing what it actually *was*, but the one time she'd asked her mother had resulted in a slap and left her with the definite impression that there were some questions better left unasked.

"I watched some of the movies," she admitted, finally. She did have a rough idea of the mechanics now, although some of the women had sounded as though they were in pain rather than enjoying themselves. "Are they...real?"

"I shall have to have words with the boys," Ethne muttered, darkly. "And we'll talk about it later. For now, just don't do anything beyond kissing – if he wants to kiss you. We can ask Paddy and Jayne to go to the same place if you want someone friendly nearby."

She headed off, leaving Sameena to access the datanet and send a brief message to Lieutenant Cook. It was nearly an hour before a reply came back, inviting her to join him for dinner at an expensive restaurant on Madagascar that evening. Sameena checked its site on the datanet, winced inwardly at how many dishes it served that included pork, then decided that she could eat the fish if nothing else. She had never even *seen* pork until she'd visited Madagascar for the first time, but that hadn't stopped the Guardians claiming that off-worlders ate pork all the time.

I suppose a stopped clock is right twice a day, she thought, as she picked up a datachip containing her assignments and walked down to the schoolroom, where Steve was preparing to take the kids onto the asteroid. Ethne snapped at them the moment they started to complain that Sameena was joining them, pointing out that she was just going to visit her tutor and then going back to the ship. The kids still looked irked, but cheered up when Steve pointed out that Sameena wouldn't be doing any shopping. *That* was a fixed reward for completing one's assignments.

"You can finish it this evening," Richard said. His tone was so pompous that Sameena had to bite her tongue to keep from laughing. "And then you can spend the rest of the week on the asteroid."

"She'll be working tomorrow," Ethne said, crossly. "Steve, make sure they have a good time, but get them back to the ship before 2000. They have an early bedtime."

She looked over at Sameena. "Come with me," she said. "Professor Sorrel is waiting for you."

Sameena hid her amusement as she followed Ethne through the airlock and up towards Professor Sorrel's office. Madagascar was as alien – as discomforting – as ever, leaving her wondering how the refugees would fit in. She didn't *like* shopping, even with Jayne; forbidding her from going into the asteroid on her own wasn't much of a punishment. But then, a few more weeks cooped up inside the freighter and she might have a different attitude.

"I spoke to a friend in the maintenance crew," Ethne said. "The refugees will be given basic quarters and food until they find their feet."

"Thank you," Sameena said. One of the advantages of an asteroid settlement was that no one ever starved to death, even if they *did* become heartily sick of algae-based food. She'd checked and discovered that it was made to taste awful deliberately in the hopes of convincing the eaters to eat something – anything – else. "And their scholarships?"

Ethne smiled. "I really should charge you a consultancy fee," she said, dryly. "A consultant is working on drawing up contracts now. They'll have their eatery and the kids will have their shot at gaining a proper education. And *you* will have some very loyal allies."

She gave Sameena a long look. "What do you have in mind?"

"It depends on how much money we draw in from the Firewater Mead sales," Sameena admitted. "Can I tell you when we find out?"

"We get ten percent of the total sum," Ethne said. "So yes – you can tell us once you know."

Sameena smiled. Ethne had taught her a great deal about contracts, including safety clauses intended to prevent one party from charging right through a loophole and violating the intent – if not the written letter – of the contract. One loophole she'd pointed out would have allowed Ethne to sell the bottles of mead to *herself* at a very low rate, then sell them onwards as she saw fit. As she'd said, once Sameena had finished spluttering with indignation, poorly-drafted contracts made a lot of money for lawyers.

Professor Sorrel looked pleased to see her when she entered his office. "You didn't do badly," he said, once he'd inspected her first set of assignments. "There are a couple of minor problems with your assignment on interstellar law – generally, Imperial Law holds sway when there are parties from two or more star systems, unless all involved parties have agreed to operate under a separate set of laws. You also made a blunder with planetary law."

He passed her the datapad. "If local law states that something is a crime – and Imperial Law disagrees – the worst the locals can do to any

THE OUTCAST

tourist committing such a crime is expel them from the planet," he added. "Locals, on the other hand, can be held to account by local law."

Sameena scowled. It had been an understandable mistake, but an embarrassing one.

"I'll have these properly marked for you by the end of the week," Professor Sorrel added. "You'll also have the next set of assignments. Let me know if you want anything more specific."

"I will," Sameena promised.

"And she'll have the uncompleted assignment done in a couple of days," Ethne said, firmly. "Or I *will* know the reason why."

Sameena winced, but said nothing until they were out of the professor's office and heading back to the ship. "I'm sorry," she admitted. "It just got away from me…"

"You weren't expected to have to tend to the refugees," Ethne agreed. "But time management is important."

She smiled. "You'd better ask Jayne to help you get ready for your date," she added. "She'd be delighted to help."

Jayne was, Sameena discovered. It took nearly an hour to get her absolutely ready, trying on all of her dresses to see which one made her look her best. The white dress looked good, Jayne insisted, but Sameena refused to wear it. It just made her look far too much like a bride. In the end, she settled for the green dress and bound her hair into a long ponytail, silently thanking God that she hadn't followed Ethne's advice to cut it short.

"Just remember what I was saying," Jayne said, once she had finished admiring her handiwork. "We won't be too far away if you need help."

Sameena nodded, feeling her legs quivering. It felt strange not to be wearing a shipsuit, even if they *were* docked with the asteroid. Her nerves kept threatening to overcome her. She'd asked Jayne if she had anything to help with that, but Jayne had flatly refused. Even mild sedatives could have unpredictable or unfortunate effects.

"I think you'll be alright once you get there," Jayne assured her. "And good luck."

Lieutenant Cook was definitely impressed. Sameena saw his eyes go wide when he saw her, even though she was extremely modest and covered up compared to some of the other girls in the restaurant. It gave her an odd thrill as he took her hand and led her towards one of the smaller tables. Was this something she would ever have experienced if she'd stayed home?

"I've been told that the steak is very nice," he said. "They're all imported from the Lone Star Republic."

Sameena nodded in understanding. Madagascar didn't produce any food, but algae. There weren't even any hydroponic farms anywhere in the system. The steaks would have to be imported, along with almost everything else. It was something else she would have to look into once she built up her funds.

"I'll stick with the fish," she said. "And yourself, Lieutenant?"

"The steak," Cook said. "And please call me Jamie. I'm off duty."

Sameena listened as he gave their orders to the waiter, trying hard to hide her amusement when he ordered two glasses of Firewater Mead. He shrugged at her expression and confessed that he had almost nothing to spend his paycheck on, not while he was stationed at the naval base. The Imperial Navy, he admitted, picked up the tab for food, drink and recreational activities.

"Tell me about yourself," she said. Jayne had told her that men liked to brag about their accomplishments, given half a chance. "How did you end up here?"

"I was born on Terra Nova," Cook – Jamie – said. "My family has always been in the Navy, so it wasn't hard to choose my career. I graduated from the Academy as a Lieutenant and was sent out here. I think I must have annoyed the wrong person."

Sameena wasn't so sure. Paddy, once he'd unbent a little, had told her quite a bit about junior officers who had no real experience – and were utterly unaware of what they lacked. Jamie might have been sent to Madagascar in the hopes of picking up the experience without placing the station or a starship in serious danger. Besides, Madagascar was a good place to make contacts among the merchant traders.

"Tell me about yourself," Jamie said, when he'd finished. "How did *you* end up here?"

"I ran away from home," Sameena said, which was technically true. "Ended up on a freighter ship and went on from there."

"Good choice," Jamie said. "Business may be picking up over the next few years."

The waiter returned with their food before Sameena could ask him what he meant. Her fish was cooked in cream, garlic and a herb she couldn't quite identify, although it was vaguely familiar. Her mother's cooking had been better, but *that* wasn't a surprise. There were times when she dreamed of being home, tasting the curry her mother had taught her how to make. But her mother might well be dead by now.

Jamie reached over and touched her hand. "Are you all right?"

"I just…I just remembered home," Sameena said. She pushed the sudden sense of loss aside, firmly. "I'm sorry."

She took a sip of her mead and smiled as the taste exploded on her tongue. It was easy to see why the cartel had managed to keep the price so high; it tasted absolutely fantastic, without any sense of guilt that came from drinking alcohol. She had to force herself to put the glass back down and finish her dinner. Uncle Muhammad had been right. The berries *were* worth a fortune to the off-worlders.

Jamie was easy to talk to, she discovered. He chatted happily about moving between his ship and the station, then about plans for hiring more freighters to service the Imperial Navy. She wasn't sure how to probe for details, but it seemed that the Imperial Navy was having supply problems too. In fact, the price of spare parts seemed to have jumped upwards again since her last visit to Madagascar. It crossed her mind that her plan might have formed too late, but she pushed that thought aside too. She had to *try*.

"There haven't been enough replacement crews too," Jamie continued. "We should have had several thousand new officers and crewmen heading out here. Instead, we get nothing, which forces us to keep the old ones in place. It isn't doing morale any good at all."

He scowled. "Chances are that we will have to abandon Sungai Buloh and a handful of other worlds," he added. "Even with freighters helping, we're stretched too thin. They're already warning us that we might have to give up our Marines. And *that* will force us to arm crewmen and use them for boarding parties."

Sameena listened, realising – to her surprise – that Jamie *wanted* to talk, yet there was almost no one he could approach. His superiors wouldn't listen and he wasn't allowed to talk about his frustrations with his subordinates. There were times, she suspected, when he was crossing the limits of what he *should* be talking about, but he hadn't told her anything she couldn't have figured out for herself.

It boded ill for the Empire, she thought, numbly. If the Imperial Navy could no longer meet its obligations, what would happen to the isolated star systems along the Rim?

"I'm sorry for boring you," Jamie said, finally. "I just…"

"Don't worry," Sameena said. "I do understand."

The waiter came back, took their plates and offered the dessert menu. Sameena considered it briefly, then shook her head. Jamie smiled and nodded in agreement, then passed the waiter his credit coin. He didn't seem inclined to let Sameena help pay for the meal.

"I pay for the next one," Sameena said, firmly.

Jamie smiled. "I'll walk you back to your ship," he said. He hesitated, then took the plunge. "Do you want to see me again?"

"Yes," Sameena said. She'd enjoyed herself more than she'd expected. "And besides…"

She passed him the datachip, which he pocketed without comment.

"I'll have to send the money to your account later," he said. "You don't want to be accepting money here."

"Understood," Sameena said, feeling her face heating up. "And thank you."

"Thank *you*," Jamie said, as he offered her his hand. "You may have done us a very important service."

It was almost unknown for a woman and a man to walk hand-in-hand on Jannah – normally, the woman would walk two or three steps behind the man – but Sameena discovered that she liked it. She was almost disappointed when they finally reached the airlock and he let go of her, then leaned forward and kissed her cheek. Part of her wanted to run; the rest of her wanted to kiss him back. She couldn't quite decide what to do.

"I'll see you again," he promised. "Soon."

Sameena stepped through the airlock and stopped, trying to reconcile her conflicting impulses. It was almost a relief when the airlock hissed open again and Paddy and Jayne entered, both wearing surprisingly decent clothes. But then, they *had* been keeping an eye on her.

"That seemed to go well," Jayne said, as Paddy nodded to her and headed off towards the bridge. "How are you feeling?"

"Strange," Sameena admitted. She absently touched her cheek, where his lips had touched her. "Is that normal?"

"Yep," Jayne said. She gave Sameena a brilliant smile. "Get some sleep. Mum will be forced to resort to extreme measures if you don't get your assignment completed before we find a new contract."

Sameena nodded. "I will," she promised. "And thank you for being there."

CHAPTER SIXTEEN

> But this booming cycle was matched by a busting cycle that deflated the economy whenever it moved too far beyond what it could reasonably support. These events wreaked economic havoc because unhealthy businesses often took down healthy businesses with them. An otherwise healthy business, for example, might be crippled by an association with a failed business.
>
> - Professor Leo Caesius, *The Science That Isn't: Economics and the Decline and Fall of the Galactic Empire.*

"Not too bad a set of sales, I suppose," Ethne said, three days later. "You're a rich young woman."

Sameena studied the credit coin, feeling a sense of genuine accomplishment. Her father must have felt the same, she knew, when he'd made his first sale. *This* was something he'd loved – and she loved too, now that she knew what it was like. If only she'd been able to do it for him, while he'd been alive. But that had never been a real possibility. She would have had to ensure that Abdul received all the credit.

The Firewater Mead, sold over two days, had brought in a staggering amount of cash. It would be sold onwards by other freighters, probably passing through several sets of hands before it was drunk. No one had asked questions when offered such a valuable cargo. In the end, Sameena had been almost disappointed.

"The children will have their education," Ethne said. "And the women can open their eatery. And you still have a *lot* of money."

Sameena hesitated. Money was important, her father had taught her, but it also needed to be invested. The Prophet, canny merchant that he had been, would have understood that long before he'd first encountered an angel. It dismayed her to realise just how few Islamic colony worlds embraced *that* particular aspect of the Prophet's life. But then, trading brought in ideas from all over the universe, ideas that would upset the *status quo*.

"I have plans," she said. "I think we should discuss them with your husband."

Talking to Captain Hamilton wasn't easy. Respect for the elderly – male and female – had been hammered into her on Jannah; it was difficult not to think of the Captain as yet another elder. If she hadn't known how often her elders could be wrong, she would have felt compelled to obey him in everything. *That* was something that she'd never dared admit to anyone else.

But there was no alternative. She needed his help.

The Captain smiled at her as he joined them in the schoolroom. "You brought us luck," he said, cheerfully. "Ten percent of the profits will keep the old girl ticking a while longer."

"Sameena wishes to talk about her plans," Ethne explained. "You might want to listen to her."

Sameena nodded, carefully formulating her thoughts. "The price of spare parts is going up," she said. "And they've been going up slowly, but steadily for years. Even the Imperial Navy is having problems keeping their ships in working order. Half of the ships at the naval base have been cannibalised to keep the rest going."

"That's a known problem," the Captain said, after a long moment. "Prices are going up everywhere."

"But this is going to cause major problems, if it hasn't already," Sameena said. "As shipping prices rise, demand falls because people cannot meet the prices. But if shipping prices *don't* rise, freighter crews will be unable to pay their debts and they'll lose their freighters. Either way, shipping in this sector becomes sharply reduced."

The Captain shared a long glance with his wife. "Go on," he said, shortly.

"But shipping isn't the only problem," Sameena continued. "We need a steady supply of spare parts to keep the cloudscoops functioning and shipping to move the HE3 from its source to destination. If both of them happen to be sharply reduced, the supply of HE3 will be reduced too – either because they can't *get* it to where it's needed or because the cloudscoops are breaking down. The price of HE3 will go upwards sharply. And that will be devastating."

"Almost everything is powered by HE3," Ethne said, quietly. "It's why hardly anyone fired on the cloudscoops during the wars."

"True enough," Captain Hamilton said. There was a hint of challenge in his tone. "And what will happen then?"

"The lights will go out," Sameena said. It had taken her several days to work out the whole scenario and she wasn't sure of the precise details, but she was sure she had the general idea right. "The only worlds that will be marginally untouched will be the ones that don't depend on HE3 – or have the facilities to build and maintain new cloudscoops. For everyone else, interstellar trade will just wither away and much of the Empire will fall back to barbarism."

"It will be worse than that," Ethne predicted. "There will be civil war. Officers who feel slighted by the Grand Senate will see its grip weakening and make a grab for power. Worlds that were brought into the Empire by force will see their chance to try to regain their independence. Loyalists will see their support bases crumbling around them – God alone knows what will happen on Earth when the food shipments stop coming in from the Core Worlds."

"There are eighty *billion* people on Earth," Captain Hamilton said. "Eighty *billion*."

Sameena couldn't even *begin* to comprehend such a number. Jannah's population was just under a billion people, assuming that the census was accurate. The thought of so many people crammed onto a single world was terrifying. How could they possibly be fed and watered? They'd be eating each other within the week.

"It will be the end," Ethne said, simply.

The Captain cleared his throat. "I think that many of us know that you're right," he said. "What do you propose to do about it?"

Sameena lifted the datapad she'd used to make her calculations. "There are quite a few pieces of industrial machinery dumped in the system," she said. "All outdated, by the Empire's standards, but still usable with a little work. I could start buying it, along with a really old colonist-carrier that was placed into mothballs hundreds of years ago. Then we'd have a mobile factory that could produce spare parts."

"Given time, you could create a much larger industrial base," Captain Hamilton mused. "But it would be vulnerable…"

"Not if it was mounted on a starship," Sameena insisted. "The carrier remains in Phase Space, or outside the Phase Limit; smaller ships bring raw materials and HE3 to the mobile yard. I was thinking that we could start supplying spare parts to the freighters and cloudscoops, keeping the prices low. Apart from a handful of weapons systems, nothing we *need* has been patented."

"There *will* be complaints," Ethne observed. "Most spare parts are produced by corporations in the Core Worlds. Planets that try to set up their own space-capable industries either have to sign agreements or get stomped on, hard. It's not *technically* illegal, but…"

"Jamie hinted that the Imperial Navy might have to withdraw from Sungai Buloh," Sameena said. "How long are they going to stay in the rest of the sector?"

"It's *Jamie* now, is it?" Ethne asked. She grinned as Sameena flushed. "Glad to know that you had a good time."

Her husband smiled. "A contact with the Imperial Navy might help you," he said, seriously. "But you're right. They may well withdraw…in which case there would be no one to do the corporation's dirty work."

Ethne and her husband shared another long look. It struck Sameena, not for the first time, that they not only loved each other, but they *understood* each other. They had an easy companionship that Sameena's parents had never shared, even after twenty years of marriage.

"You have a source of income," Ethne said, finally. "You could probably build it up into a small industrial base."

"Steve might be willing to help you," Captain Hamilton added. "He'd be fascinated by the challenge. Brad, on the other hand, wants his own ship. What do *you* want?"

"To find other opportunities to make money," Sameena said, firmly. Spare parts would just be the start. There were plenty of other pieces of abandoned equipment out there – and, once the children were trained up, a cadre of engineers to help restore them. Who knew what *else* she could find and put to use? "It won't do any good just sitting on my credit coin."

"And it will lose its value quickly," Captain Hamilton added. "We've been looking at ways to spend half of our percentage quickly."

"You'd be welcome to invest," Sameena said, giving him a cheeky grin. "I owe you everything."

"What do *you* want to do?" Ethne asked. "I mean with yourself, personally. Do you want to stay onboard?"

"Yes," Sameena said, quickly. She'd grown to love the crew. They were her family now. "If you'll have me, I'd like to stay."

"You're our lucky charm," Captain Hamilton teased.

"Besides, you have an education to finish," Ethne added, firmly. "We can't get rid of you yet."

Sameena spent the next two days outlining her plans to Steve, then working with him to sort out the practicalities. The colonist-carrier would require some minor refitting, but it was apparently intact, just waiting for a buyer. Steve professed himself unsurprised that it hadn't been sold, even for spare parts. It was simply too outdated even by the standards of the Empire, where technology seemed to have frozen for hundreds of years.

"They did take the stasis pods," he commented, after receiving an updated statement from the merchant who owned the junkyard. "Without them, the ship seems valueless."

"Because it can't carry colonists?" Sameena asked. "Or because no one thought of turning it into a mobile factory?"

"There was an emergency program, hundreds of years ago, to use such ships to evacuate small colonies, if there was a need," Steve explained. "A star flared once, catching the new colonists by surprise and destroying much of their equipment. Most of them died before the Imperial Navy could ship in emergency supplies. If it had been an older colony the death toll would have been in the millions."

He scowled. "If every starship in the empire was sent to Earth, it would still take years to evacuate the entire planet," he added. "And, as time wore on, precautions like having a ship on permanent standby were allowed to fade away."

Sameena frowned. "Could someone deliberately cause a supernova?"

"Not as far as I know," Steve admitted. "But it isn't as if there aren't thousands of other ways to wipe out vast populations with the touch of a button."

He finished skimming through the document, then looked up at her. "It shouldn't be too hard to refit it," he said. "You'll have to hit the engineering crew with some pretty tough secrecy contracts, I'm afraid. Someone talking out of turn would be…inconvenient."

Sameena looked at him. "Would you be interested in the job?"

"Brad wants a ship, not me," Steve said. He looked back down at the datapad. "But you will need someone like me to handle the refitting. And not everyone will take you seriously."

Sameena nodded. On Jannah, being a woman automatically made her opinions irrelevant; on Madagascar, her limited experience counted against her. But she could *gain* experience…irritatingly, providing a new source of Firewater Mead would have made her a hero, if she hadn't known that advertising her success would also attract trouble. Steve, on the other hand, was a qualified engineer and Captain Hamilton's biological son. People would *listen* to him.

"I don't know who else to ask," she admitted. "Are you interested?"

"You might have to marry another engineer," Steve teased. "I've repaid Dad's investment in me, but he might be mad if I leave without much warning."

Sameena swallowed, hard.

"Don't worry about it," Steve advised. "There should be one or two qualified engineers on the asteroid. James was dating one a while back…maybe he'd be interested."

"*He*?" Sameena repeated. "A *man*?"

"James likes men," Steve said. "I used to twit him that meant more women for me."

Sameena shook her head. Homosexuality was rare on Jannah, probably because the Guardians killed men who showed interest in other men. She had no idea what, if anything, they did to lesbians, but she doubted that it would be anything pleasant. The whole idea would have shocked her, months ago. Now...she found it hard to really care.

"I'll take on the job," Steve said. "Of course, we *will* have to discuss salary..."

Steve drove a hard bargain, Sameena decided, thirty minutes later. He would have a share of the profits as well as limited discretion in picking the refit crew and crewmen for the modified colonist-carrier. He'd also get to look for other pieces of industrial equipment that might come in useful, including a set of mining equipment for obtaining HE3 from moons and even asteroids. It would be inefficient compared to using a cloudscoop – or even a skimmer – but it would allow them to set up operations in an otherwise worthless star system.

"You could go back to your homeworld," he suggested, mischievously. "There aren't any starships there to prevent you from mining their moon and building factories."

Sameena considered it for a long moment, then dismissed the thought. Jannah might not have any starships, but the cartel presumably sent ships to and from the system regularly, where they might be able to do something about illegal installations. If nothing else, they wouldn't want potential spies in the system. Besides, tempting as it was to return and rub her success in her homeworld's collective nose, she didn't want to do it until she was far wealthier. And wealth equalled power.

"Maybe somewhere more isolated," she said, finally. "I'll leave that in your capable hands."

"I'd better go tell dad," Steve said, once they'd written out the contract. "And if he gets mad, just hide behind me."

Sameena gulped.

There *was* a shouting match going on when they returned to the schoolroom, Sameena was alarmed to discover. Ethne was giving Richard a loud lecture on something, while Regina was watching with a sly half-smile on her face. Steve strode in, caught Regina's arm and pulled her out. Ethne glanced sharply at her son, then nodded. Steve shut the hatch firmly, muffling her voice.

"That sounded bad," Steve said. "What happened?"

"Richard ran into Osco," Regina said. "They started exchanging insults, then they graduated to throwing punches. And then Auntie Ethne and Uncle Hobe separated them by force."

"Brilliant," Steve said, sarcastically. "And you weren't involved?"

"I was just watching," Regina said. "I..."

"Go back to your cabin and stay there," Steve ordered. He smacked Regina's rear when she hesitated, jerking her into motion. "Now."

He looked over at Sameena, apologetically. "Herding the clans is like herding cats," he admitted, as they resumed their path towards the bridge. "Fights and feuds can get in the way of serious business."

Sameena nodded. "What happened between Richard and Osco?"

"Their families are rivals," Steve explained. "No doubt the moment they saw each other they just started throwing insults and punches. It never fails. Mum is going to be *really* annoyed with them."

He shrugged. "Don't worry about it," he added. "Luckily, they didn't pull this shit during a Meet. Mum would have murdered the pair of them if they'd embarrassed us in front of the rest of the clan."

Sameena nodded as she followed him onto the bridge. Captain Hamilton was sitting at one of the consoles, working his way through several contracts offered by the Imperial Navy. Two of them promised a low, but steady income; the other three were apparently one-offs.

"Dad," Steve said. He gave his father his best grin. "I've been offered a job."

"I thought you might have been," the Captain said. He gave Sameena an unreadable expression, then looked back at his son. "I think you'd better go over the ship and equipment in cynical detail before you purchase it."

"I will," Steve promised. "But it *has* been verified."

The Captain snorted. "Have you forgotten what happened the last time you didn't verify something for yourself?"

Steve turned red. "Yes, sir," he said. "But I'm still trying."

"We have been offered several different contracts," Captain Hamilton said. "This one calls for us to depart within nine days. If you want to take up this new job" – he threw Sameena another unreadable glance – "you have until then to help me find a replacement. I would prefer not to leave without a qualified engineer."

"Understood, dad," Steve said.

"And get your mother to start setting up a limited corporation for you," the Captain added. "You might as well shield yourself as much as possible. It can handle the educational programs for the refugee kids too."

"Mum is currently raging," Steve admitted. He didn't sound pleased about having to explain. "Richard ran into some trouble on the asteroid."

"I see," his father said, once he'd finished explaining. "Talk to her later, once she's calmed down. And tell Richard that I will want a few words with him before he goes back onto the asteroid. It will not be a pleasant discussion."

He dismissed Steve, then looked over at Sameena. "You've done well," he admitted, "very well. I'm pleased I made the decision to let you stay on my ship."

"Thank you," Sameena said. She would have loved to hear those words from her own father, but that was impossible. "I…"

"You're going to have to work harder over the next few months," Captain Hamilton warned her. "We can't have a corporation controlled by someone without qualifications."

He grinned, then sobered. "And I am proud of you," he added. "But you have a long way to go. You have to master quite a few skills if you want to take control of your destiny."

"Yes," Sameena said. "I know."

INTERLUDE ONE

When he was a child, growing up in the corporate hell of Asteroid ETU828348 – the corporation had never bothered to give it a name – Marcus Vespasian had sworn a simple oath to himself. He would never be poor or hungry again – or another corporate slave. The alternative was an endless life of drudgework, drunkenness and an early death, just like his father and grandfather. By the time he was sixteen, he had taken control of the asteroid's flourishing criminal underground and used it to escape the corporation once and for all.

Legality meant nothing to him. His parents and grandparents had been nothing more than legal slaves, their servitude enforced by contracts signed by their ancestors when they'd believed the corporate lies and moved to the asteroid. If the Grand Senate couldn't be bothered enforcing laws that banned indentured slavery – indeed, if they profited from it – he refused to take any account of their other laws. At thirty, he ruled a criminal empire that stretched across thirty star systems, with a finger in just about every pie. He would ship anything anywhere, as long as there was money in it.

And some clients were prepared to pay so much that he actually met them in person.

"This is quite an interesting request," he said, as he studied the datapad. The client had agreed to meet him in a legitimate business Marcus controlled, walking into the building as if he hadn't a care in the world. "You want as many military or combat-capable starships as possible, right?"

"Correct," the client said. He'd given his name as Mr. Black, but Marcus would have bet most of his fortune that was a false name. It was easy to pick up a fake identity in the Lumpur Cluster. "I was informed that you buy and sell starships for those who wish them."

"It's a buyer's market," Marcus agreed. The Imperial Navy was going through yet another round of cost-cutting, decommissioning hundreds of starships and sending them to the breakers. It was quite simple to redirect a few of them to less than savoury interests. "But this really is quite a large request."

He studied Mr. Black, but came up with nothing. The man was… bland, his features no doubt sculptured by someone with a dab hand at cosmetic surgery. An hour on the table and Mr. Black would be completely unrecognisable. There was nothing to say who he was, or who he represented, merely an expense account – Marcus had checked – that a Grand Senator's son would envy. Buying an entire fleet would be…possible.

But who was he working for?

Marcus shrugged, dismissing the thought. It wasn't his concern. The Imperial Navy might make a fuss about pirates, but the *real* pirates were on Earth, draining the life out of the Empire. Besides, Mr. Black was probably working for a planetary defence force rather than pirates, or he wouldn't have wanted so many large ships. Having a contact with such a government might come in handy when the Empire finally collapsed. Marcus had seen enough to be sure that the crash would come within his lifetime.

He felt no regrets. What had the Empire ever done to earn his loyalty?

"I can start shipping you the ships within the month," he said. "It's a pleasure doing business with you."

CHAPTER SEVENTEEN

>Alternatively, as the economy constricted, workers would be laid off by their employers. As they were no longer earning money, they could not afford to buy products…which had a negative impact on the companies producing those products. They, in turn, were forced to lay off their own workers, prolonging the economic depression.
>
>- Professor Leo Caesius, *The Science That Isn't: Economics and the Decline and Fall of the Galactic Empire.*

"It's beautiful," Sameena breathed.

Brad patted her shoulder, never taking his eyes off the viewport. The shuttle was hanging in space, watching from thousands of kilometres away as two blue worlds converged on each other. Their combined gravity created, for a brief few hours, a funnel of water that stretched between them. It was the most remarkable sight Sameena had ever seen.

"Forward's Dream," Brad said, softly. "One of the nine hundred wonders of the universe."

Sameena smiled. The two moons had developed an extraordinary ecosystem of their own, one that might produce intelligent life in a few million years. Or it would have, if humanity had not foreclosed the possibility by settling on both water worlds. Even so, she'd been told that the two worlds were biological treasure troves, worthy homes for the genetically-engineered humans who lived there. But the Empire's research station had been abandoned years ago.

"You should show this to everyone," she said. "If the groundhogs saw it..."

"They wouldn't understand," Brad told her. "How could they?"

He was right, Sameena suspected. Groundhogs had no real comprehension of the size and wonder of the universe. Even a single star system was unimaginably vast by their standards, their worlds little more than grains of sand on an infinite beach. The freedom to travel enjoyed by the vast majority of the Empire's citizens was hardly ever exercised – and when it was, they mostly travelled in stasis pods, where the trip seemed to take almost no time. They never saw the wonders of the universe.

"You deserve to see it," Brad said. "After how hard you worked..."

Sameena gave him a sidelong look. The exams she'd taken for Professor Sorrel had been hard, but the ones she'd taken for the clan over the last two weeks had been much harder, even if they had been largely practical. It wasn't *easy* to earn papers from the trader clans that certified that one could work in space, certainly not if one wanted to work up to starship command. There were times when buying a starship outright had seemed the better option.

She looked down at the display. There were nearly a hundred starships orbiting the gas giant, each one a trader starship belonging to the clans. Meets – where the vast extended network of families actually met in person – were rare. Even though she'd been a trader for two years - and Captain Hamilton's adopted daughter - Sameena had never been to a Meet before. There simply hadn't been one taking place that she could attend.

It had been a fascinating experience, even though it had also been a rigorous one as the certified examiners tested her thoroughly. She'd met countless people who were related to her adopted family – and others who seemed to be feuding with them, although feuds weren't allowed at the Meet. And it had confirmed for her that she belonged in space. The trader clans had welcomed her without hesitation. No family on Jannah would be so welcoming.

"Thank you," she said, finally.

She hadn't been quite sure what to make of it when Brad had invited her to join him on the shuttle, after she'd finished the final set of exams. Part of her knew that he was attracted to her – and therefore being alone with him might not be a good idea – but the rest of her knew and trusted him as a brother. He and Abdul, she suspected, would have gotten along, if they'd ever met. They were really quite similar in many ways.

But Brad has little to rebel against, she thought. *Abdul had far too much.*

It was an odd thought, one that bothered her even though she no longer had nightmares about her homeworld. By Jannah's standards, Captain Hamilton and Ethne were ridiculously permissive parents – but what rules they did have were taken seriously by the kids. Brad was too sensible to rebel against rules that were intended to protect him and the rest of his siblings, if only because he understood the reasoning behind them. Abdul had never truly comprehended the reasoning behind Jannah's endless series of laws.

"You passed your first set of exams," Brad said. "And I know that you will pass the rest of them, once they finish marking you."

Sameena blinked in surprise. "How do you know?"

Brad grinned. "If they'd failed you, everyone would know by now," he said. "They'd want to make sure that no one tried to hire you until you had actually *completed* the exams."

He sobered. "Have you given any thought to your own future?"

"Some," Sameena admitted.

She'd earned millions of credits from the sale of Firewater Mead, all of which she'd plunged into her own personal project. Building up a stockpile of old or decommissioned industrial equipment hadn't been difficult; refitting it so it could actually be used was *much* harder. There were reasons, it seemed, why no one else had invested in mobile factories…but she knew that there was no choice. Having a fixed industrial base was just asking for someone to come along and take it from her. Much as she liked Jamie Cook, she had no doubt that the Imperial Navy would seize her ships when the supplies ran out for good.

Brad hesitated, then plunged ahead. "I finally signed the contract for a freighter of my own," he said. "The *Lead Pipe* is a smaller ship than *Logan*, but much faster. And it doesn't need so many crew. Would you be interested in shipping with me?"

Sameena hesitated. "Why me?"

"Keeping it in the family," Brad said. "Besides, you need to broaden your experience for the day you come out into the open."

He had a point, Sameena knew. She might own seventy percent of Khadijah Incorporated – the limited corporation she'd set up to handle her affairs – but she had never revealed her involvement to anyone outside the family. Spacers looked to experience rather than money or family contacts and they simply wouldn't take her seriously, not until she had far more experience. A few months or years as Brad's XO would definitely bolster her credentials.

"True," she agreed.

"And mom and dad aren't going to move on," Brad added. "If you happen to be ambitious…"

Sameena nodded. Captain Hamilton and Ethne owned majority interests in *Logan*, ensuring that they could never be displaced – and, unlike the military or the big corporate shipping lines, they would never be promoted upwards to clear the decks for younger officers. If she wanted experience as an XO – or a Captain – she would have to go elsewhere.

"*Lead Pipe*," she mused. "How many crew do you need?"

"She's a *Poseidon*-class fast freighter," Brad said. "Heavily automated. I'd only need one other crewman, apart from myself."

Sameena mentally ran through what she knew about the class. The ships were small, barely forty metres long, with very limited carrying space. But they made up for that by their speed; they were in considerable demand to serve as courier vessels or simply to transport goods from one star system to another at breakneck speed. They'd originally been a military design, she recalled. The civilians had found another use for them.

Experience told her that maintenance was going to be a problem. Even a relatively small starship would need plenty of maintenance – and two people would be pushed to the limits as they struggled to handle it all. But if the ship was newer…perhaps they could work out a schedule that would work. On the other hand, it would be tricky…perhaps they'd be safer taking on a couple of other crew.

"I'd prefer to avoid it," Brad admitted. "The funds are running *very* low."

Sameena nodded in understanding. The down payment on a freighter could be staggeringly high, particularly if the freighter was relatively new. Brad would need years to pay off his debt to the banks and assume full ownership of his new vessel. Limiting the number of crew would help save money…assuming, of course, that he didn't run into problems that only a larger crew could handle.

I could pay for it, she thought. But she knew that Brad's pride would never allow him to accept money from her. Captain Hamilton and Ethne had had qualms about collecting their share of the Firewater Mead money and Sameena would never have disputed that they'd earned it. If they hadn't taken her onboard, she would be dead – or worse – by now.

And then she realised that she'd made her decision.

"I think it would be a good idea," she said. She'd *wanted* a new challenge. "What sort of contract should we sign?"

Brad flushed. "I…would you be interested in a marriage contract?"

Sameena couldn't keep her surprise off her face. A marriage contract…she should have seen it coming, but she hadn't. Jannah cast a long shadow over her; the thought of a man asking her to marry him – and that was what Brad was doing, to all intents and purposes – still seemed alien. But it wasn't as if his family could approach *her* family.

She hesitated, thinking as fast as she could. Brad *was* a nice guy, but she didn't love him…and she'd grown to value the freedom of living in space too much to simply give it up. And yet…the traders respected marriage contracts far more than anything else. Refusing one would definitely raise eyebrows.

"I don't know," she admitted, miserably. She knew that there were hundreds of traders who would jump at the chance. But a combination of old and new cultural mores told against it. "I do like you…"

"But you don't love me," Brad said. "I do understand the need for a trial period…"

Sameena fought down the urge to laugh. There was no such thing as a trial marriage on Jannah. The wife went to her husband's house – normally, her husband's family house – and was effectively trapped there from that moment on. She would be the lowest person on the family tree, treated as a servant by her mother-in-law and her new sisters…it would be hard, almost impossible, for her to leave the house. And there were whispered stories of worse horrors awaiting disobedient wives.

She reached out and clutched Brad's hand. "I can't marry you," she said. Would she *consider* it? The hell of it was that she didn't *know*. Thanks to Jayne and modern medical science, it would be years before she had to have children. In fact, she could keep that option open until she died of old age. "It's too soon."

Brad tilted his head. "Are you still seeing that Lieutenant?"

"Just for dinner, every once in a while," Sameena admitted. "But I don't know how I feel about him either."

He surprised her by laughing. "You've been seeing him on and off for two years," he said, dryly. "Do you know how far the relationship might have gone by now?"

Sameena flushed. Jayne had told her in far too much detail for her peace of mind. Outside a marriage contract, traders and other spacefarers enjoyed a sexual freedom utterly unknown on Jannah. Even *inside* a marriage contract, there were clauses that would allow for affairs and periods of separation…there seemed to be nothing sacred, as long as the contract allowed for it. But she still felt reluctant to take part.

"If he finds someone else," she said, "I will be happy for him."

But she wouldn't be, she knew. Part of her *did* find him attractive, did enjoy the kisses he gave her…and would hate it if someone else married him.

"I think you protest too much," Brad said, reading her face. "But there are other contracts we could use."

"Let me buy my way onto the ship," Sameena said, quietly. "I don't want to be just a hired hand."

"You'd never be just a hired *anything*," Brad said. He sounded reluctant, even though it would help solve some of his money problems. "Forty percent?"

Sameena pretended to consider it. Forty percent would give her a share of the profits – assuming that there *were* profits – but it wouldn't give her any actual authority. But then, it was well understood that a starship could only have one commander. Brad would be the final authority in any case. And offering her so much was a gesture of complete faith and trust. If she left the crew, she could cripple him merely by demanding repayment.

No wonder they prefer to keep these matters in the family, she thought. *One person leaving at the wrong time could cost them the ship.*

"Forty percent," she agreed, finally. "And what other terms should we have?"

She'd learned more than she wanted to learn about writing contracts over the last two years, thanks to Ethne. Starship commanders couldn't afford loopholes when they lived far too close to the margins. Brad haggled for a few minutes, but it was clear that he wasn't really interested in negotiations. That, Sameena had to admit, was a very good sign.

"Leave room for a marriage contract," he insisted, when they'd finished haggling. "You might change your mind."

Sameena looked back out of the viewport. The two worlds were slowly disengaging, the stream of water that linked them together breaking up and falling back into the gravity wells. It would be ten years before their orbits pulled them back together, she knew…and one day they would probably come too close and collide. What would happen when two large bodies crashed together?

"There are people," Brad said quietly, "who believe that this entire system is artificial."

Sameena sucked in her breath. Humanity, in the thousands of years it had explored space, had never encountered another alien race. Hell, relatively few worlds had even had the same biological complexity of Earth. Normally, when a terraforming package was dropped on a newly-discovered world, the newcomers rapidly overwhelmed and replaced the local flora and fauna. There weren't *many* non-Earth animals on the same level as dogs or cats, let alone humans.

But there were always rumours, whispered tales of strange encounters out along the Rim…

"God created everything," Sameena said. She gave him a smile. "Or wasn't that what you meant?"

"No," Brad said, dryly. "That *wasn't* what I meant."

Sameena shrugged. She hadn't had the time to engage in a full study of religion in the Empire, but she *had* learned that there were no shortage of religions claiming to know the One True Way to God. Islam had thousands of different sects that Jannah had never acknowledged; it still stunned her when she thought about just how much had been cut out of the history books. Ali had been listed as one of the Rightly Guided Caliphs, the successors of the Prophet, but she'd never even *heard* of the Shia until she'd left her homeworld. History had been rewritten to suit the Guardians.

And Islam was just one of thousands of religions.

"Tell me," Brad said, quietly. "Are you refusing my offer because of religion?"

"No," she said, firmly. It was true enough. "I just don't want to be tied down, not…not like I would have been back home."

Brad squeezed her shoulder. "This is your home now," he said. "Why don't you take us back to the ship?"

Sameena smiled as she took control of the shuttle. Learning to fly had been fun, if hair-raising; Paddy had later confessed that he'd borrowed the training program from the Imperial Navy. *Their* pilots were expected to fly through the atmosphere at breakneck pace, avoid defensive fire and drop down to the ground before they could be shot down. It wasn't something the average trader had to do, which was a relief. Sameena knew that the two cargo shuttles on *Logan* would have been easily blasted out of the sky by any halfway competent defence force.

She took one last look at the water worlds, then steered the shuttle back towards *Logan*. Several other ships were clustered nearby, linked together by tubes that allowed their crews to move freely without spacesuits or shuttles. Sameena hadn't been too sure about allowing outsiders such unrestricted access to the ship, but Captain Hamilton had insisted that it was perfectly normal. The Sunflower Berries had been carefully hidden away before they reached the system.

"Take us in to dock," Brad ordered. "And then we will have to have a long talk with mum and dad."

Sameena nodded. "When are we going to say goodbye?"

"There's always a few dozen crewmen wanting berths at the Meet," Brad said. "They won't have any difficulty finding replacements for us."

The airlock clanged as they docked with the freighter, then hissed as it opened. "Welcome back," James called. He was working on an opened hatch, just down the corridor. "Did you have a good time?"

"We did," Brad said. "Where are mom and dad?"

"Dad's just talking to Captain Vinson," James said. "Mom should be on the bridge."

"Come on," Brad said. "Let's go give her the good news."

Sameena had half-expected Ethne to raise objections to her leaving the crew. The guardianship they'd assumed over her *did* give them certain rights, even if they hadn't used them to control her in the past. But instead Ethne's only comment was that they would be better off with a marriage contract. Sameena kept her thoughts to herself.

"Just make sure you take care of each other," Ethne cautioned. "After that, everything will take care of itself."

She hesitated. "And we'll take care of the Mead production," she added. "You won't have to worry about that."

Sameena, who was more worried about accidently flooding the market, nodded.

CHAPTER EIGHTEEN

Matters were made worse by the damage this could cause to the law. In order for the economy to grow, or at least remain stable, the law had to be impartial, without taking sides in economic disputes. However, the rapidly-changing economy often raced ahead of the law's ability to keep up, while those on top attempted to use their vast political power (through cash) to subvert the law and use it against their rivals. This allowed them to warp the free market to their advantage, at least in the short term. In the long term, their houses of cards always came crashing down. The results were not pleasant.
- Professor Leo Caesius, *The Science That Isn't: Economics and the Decline and Fall of the Galactic Empire.*

No one knew, at least as far as Sameena had been able to discover, just who had founded Tabasco Asteroid. It was a simple rock, one hundred kilometres across, drifting in orbit around an otherwise planet-less star. The Imperial Navy and Department of Colonisation had taken one look and dismissed the system as worthless. In their wake, smugglers and black colonists had turned the asteroid into a semi-legal trading port. It was nowhere near as civilised as Madagascar.

She sat at a table in the cantina, keeping her expression firmly under control. The large compartment was heaving with humans, many looking far more disreputable than anyone she'd seen on Madagascar. On a stage, several naked or near-naked girls were dancing to a tune so loud that it was a wonder that anyone could hear anything; the stench of desperation and hopelessness was strong in the air. Sameena mentally checked and rechecked the location of her concealed weapons. She'd never felt so threatened since the day the Guardians had invaded her father's house.

Brad's insistence on visiting Tabasco had puzzled her, even though he'd explained that it was a good place to make contacts that might help him to find work. *Lead Pipe* required a steady inflow of money and he refused to allow her to offer him funds from selling Firewater Mead, even though she could have paid off the entire debt. Instead, the money had been reinvested and they were looking for more contracts. The only upside of the whole episode, Sameena had decided, was that it allowed her to gather more data for her theory. It was no longer possible to deny that the Empire was in serious trouble.

She looked up, one hand reaching for her weapon…and then smiled as Brad sat down on the other side of the table. A topless waitress appeared out of nowhere, took his order and then retreated. Sameena couldn't help noticing that the cantina's denizens seemed to take an unholy delight in groping her as she passed…and that she did nothing to stop them. Like so many others, she had no choice but to sell herself. It was all she had left.

"I found us a contract," Brad said, cheerfully. He put a privacy generator on the table and clicked it on, wrapping them in an invisible sphere that should prevent anyone on the outside from overhearing them. It wouldn't draw comment. Almost everyone used such devices when they could get away with it, even though they were technically illegal. "And it's a good one."

Sameena nodded. The very first contract they'd been offered when they'd reached the asteroid had been to ship children from one star system to another. It had seemed odd to her…and Brad, despite his money worries, had flatly refused to take it. He'd explained, afterwards, that the children would be sold into slavery. The thought of children being used as slaves was disgusting. They would be lucky, Brad had said, if all that happened was that they were farmed out to new colonists and treated as spare labour.

"Go on," she said. "Where are we going?"

"Rosa," Brad said. He made a face. "They want us to transport weapons to the planet."

Sameena frowned. It sounded much better than shipping children into slavery, but it raised its own problems. Transporting weapons was technically illegal without permits and the Imperial Navy would take a dim view of it, if they happened to be caught. The last thing she wanted was to wind up on a penal world, staring up at the stars and knowing that she would never be able to fly amongst them again.

"Weapons," she repeated. "And do they have the proper permits?"

Brad shrugged. "They have permission from the government to import weapons," he said. "I checked the papers very carefully."

He shook his head. "We're quite short, Sameena," he admitted. "We're going to *need* a contract soon."

Sameena gritted her teeth, cursing male pride under her breath. Tabasco had almost no laws at all, but the ones they *did* have all revolved around paying debts. A person could rape or murder with impunity, yet those crimes were regarded as harmless pranks when compared to failing to pay what one owed. There would be no extension or mercy if they failed to meet their payments.

And we might have to do something dreadful just to survive, she thought. *Weapons would be preferable.*

"Very well," she said, tiredly. Their first two contracts had been simple, if boring. This promised to be far too exciting. "Let me see the contract."

Brad passed her his datapad, allowing her to skim through the document. It was relatively simple; they would be paid half of the money upfront, while the remainder would be paid by the shipping agent on the planet's surface. The attached certificates stated that the shipping agent was an authorised weapons dealer, representing the interests of the planet's government. But that didn't explain why they needed to send to *Tabasco* for weapons.

"I think they don't think that the Empire will help out," Brad said, when she asked. "They might well be right."

Sameena nodded, sourly. Two months after they'd escaped Sungai Buloh, the Imperial Navy – as Jamie had predicted – had pulled out of the system, abandoning it completely. Sameena had never been back, but from what she'd heard at the Meet the entire system had fallen into chaos, with dozens of factions fighting it out for supremacy. And it hadn't been the only system to be abandoned. Rumour had it that a third of the

Imperial Navy in the sector had been pulled back to the Core Worlds, leaving the rest of the sector fleet to pick up the slack as best as they could.

"It seems legit," she said, finally. It was clear that Brad had already made up his mind. "And when are we taking the weapons?"

"This afternoon," Brad said. "We'll leave early tomorrow morning."

"Before the prices go up again," Sameena said. Tabasco charged an immensely high price for HE3 and just about everything else, taking advantage of its odd position in the gray area between legal and illegal. Quite a few black colonies used the asteroid as a source of supplies. "I don't want to come back here."

Brad nodded in agreement.

They walked back to the ship in silence. Once they were onboard, Brad headed to the small bridge while Sameena went to her cabin to look up Rosa in the database. The official download from the Imperial Library stated that it was a fairly new colony world, settled late because of problems deploying the terraforming package. Apparently, the founding corporation had appointed a governor, shipped in several hundred thousand colonists…and then nothing. Doing the maths, Sameena realised that it had been settled for just over seventy years. Surely there should have been something else in the database.

The trader database wasn't much more informative. Rosa had four gas giants and an asteroid belt, which would allow it to develop a spacefaring economy in a few hundred years, but for the moment there wasn't much to attract independent traders. The founding corporation was known for its aggressive pursuit of unwanted settlers in their star systems, so there were no known black or gray colonies there. There wasn't anything at all on the planet's political situation.

She was still mulling it over when the weapons arrived, an hour later. Brad supervised the loaders as they moved the crates into the hold, then checked them off against the list he'd been supplied by the agent. It was rare to have sealed crates – the Imperial Navy always assumed that the Captain knew what he was carrying – and checking the list ensured that they couldn't be blamed for anything missing. By the time they were finished and the hold was sealed, both of them were tired and ready to sleep.

"Make sure the hatch is sealed," Brad reminded her. It was an irritating habit he'd picked up from his parents, but it was also a very useful one. "Do you want to play chess?"

Sameena smiled, despite her exhaustion. Chess wasn't regarded as a feminine pastime on Jannah, which hadn't stopped her father from teaching her how to play. The rules seemed to have remained largely unchanged over thousands of years, much to her relief. There were variants on Chess that made the game almost unrecognisable. And Brad didn't make a terrible fuss when she won. It probably helped that he beat her at most of the other games onboard ship.

"One game," she said, firmly. "And then we need to get some sleep."

Sharing a ship with Brad was…different. *Logan* had had several crew she could talk to; *Lead Pipe* had precisely one other crewman. If they argued, there was no one to get in the way and tell them that they were being silly. But she also had a larger cabin – although the hatches were unlocked, they had a mutual agreement to stay out of each other's personal space – and plenty of time to get on with her studies. It almost made up for her awareness that if they ran into trouble, it would be extremely difficult to deal with it.

Brad was a fairly good player on the chessboard, although he did have his odd little quirks that puzzled her. Chess was one of the strings binding the trader clans together, with players exchanging moves over the course of several months whenever their ships passed one another in the endless darkness of space. Brad seemed to take a long time to decide on each move, as if he thought he had weeks to make up his mind. Sameena had sometimes considered insisting that they played with a timer.

"Good game," she said, finally. Her victory had been hard won. "I'm going to get some sleep."

"We undock tomorrow at 0900," Brad agreed. "Don't be late."

Sameena snorted as she made her way back to her cabin. She had never been allowed to stay in bed past the crack of dawn; once morning prayers had been completed, there was an endless series of house chores to be done. It hadn't been any better on *Logan* either; she'd been given a schedule and expected to live up to it. Ethne would have given her a sharp lecture if she'd dared to be late for one of her duty shifts.

She couldn't help feeling relieved as they undocked from Tabasco the following morning and slipped across the Phase Limit. The asteroid seemed to confirm everything the Guardians had said about the universe outside Jannah's atmosphere, a place of horrors and depravities fit to turn a person's stomach. If Madagascar had been like that…she thought, grimly, of the refugees she'd provided for. What would have happened to them if she hadn't been there?

"Jumping…now," Brad said. *Lead Pipe* quivered as she jumped into Phase Space. "I feel cleaner already."

"Me too," Sameena agreed. She glanced down at the course calculations. It would be twelve days before they reached Rosa. "Why do people *tolerate* places like Tabasco?"

Brad frowned, considering. "People do what they have to do to survive," he said, finally. "And there are always other people willing to take advantage of their desperation. The children…the children might *not* have been meant for sex slavery. They might have been intended to go to a black colony that discovered, too late, that their population was too small for long-term survival."

Sameena frowned, horrified. "But where did they get the children?"

"Too many possibilities," Brad admitted. "Earth expels everyone who commits a crime, unless they can bribe their way out of the holding cells. Children aren't spared because of their youth. The indents tend to get shipped out to colony worlds and told to work off their debt to society. Most of them die off because they don't have survival skills that they can use on an undeveloped world."

"Why?" Sameena asked, remembering Paddy's survival training. "Don't they *care*?"

"There are eighty *billion* people on Earth," Brad pointed out. "Even with algae-based foodstuffs, feeding that many people is extremely difficult. The government thinks that expelling criminals will take some of the pressure off, while founding corporations encourage it because it gives them a source of cheap labour to help develop new worlds. And as for the people themselves…it doesn't matter. There are plenty more where they come from.

"And then there's the worlds that actually *buy* women and children," he added. "Do you think *Jannah* did that?"

Sameena looked down at the viewscreen. It seemed unlikely, but she'd already learned just how easily the Guardians could rewrite history. If they'd taken in children too young to have proper memories, how would anyone know? And even if they *did* recall…the Guardians had ways to deal with disruptive people.

"I hope not," she said, finally. "It *stinks*."

"It's the Empire," Brad said, reluctantly. "People do whatever they have to do to survive."

Sameena left him on the bridge and walked back to her cabin, where she accessed the trader database. It was dependent on updates being provided by the traders themselves – if there was an editor, he or she didn't seem to do much – but she'd discovered that it was more honest than any of the downloads from the Imperial Library. She worked her way through some of the files and realised that Brad was largely correct. Earth seemed bent on expelling as many people as possible. So did some of the older Core Worlds.

She had never worked on a life support system larger than a medium freighter, but the basic principles should be the same. Eighty *billion* people crammed together on a planet that was effectively one giant city. They'd be eating themselves to survive. The Imperial Library stated that everyone on Earth had enough to eat; the trader database suggested that large parts of the planet were effectively poisoned no-go areas. She knew which one she believed.

The indentured colonist program, according to the trader database, was exactly as Brad had described it. It was nothing more than a way to get cheap labour into the hands of corporations and newly-settled colony worlds, with no concern about their future. The whole scheme was appalling to her; the indentured colonists *might* end up in a good position…or they might end up as slaves or prostitutes – or rebels. In the long term, they might blur into the rest of the colony's population…or they might form a permanent underclass.

Something will have to be done, she thought, grimly. But what? The refugee children were doing well on their studies – Professor Sorrel forwarded her copies of their examination results – and they might make good engineers, but she couldn't offer a scholarship to everyone. Maybe later, when she had more resources under her control…she pushed the thought aside and closed down the datapad. She really needed to get her daily exercise before she started to gain weight.

"We should have put in a bathtub," she said, when she stepped into the exercise compartment and saw Brad already there. It no longer bothered her to see him wearing nothing more than a pair of shorts, although she averted her eyes politely every time. "You're far too sweaty."

"The water recycler isn't *that* good," Brad pointed out. "Besides, we don't have the water to waste. God knows if we will be able to get more at Rosa."

Sameena nodded as she took the machine next to him. It reminded her of a bicycle on Jannah, although naturally *she* had never been allowed to ride one. She started to ride, feeling her legs pumping as she pushed them through the motions. Paddy had insisted that she – and everyone else – do at least an hour of exercise every day. It was strange to look at her arms and realise that she was stronger than she'd ever been on Jannah. But she would never be as strong as the retired Marine.

"Put on some music," Brad suggested. "Or even a movie."

"Please," Sameena said. She'd discovered that she rather enjoyed Brad's collection of older movies, although he'd admitted that many of them were utterly unrealistic and played for comic relief. "Something *funny*."

"*Stellar Star* would be funny," Brad commented, as he climbed off his machine. "But you don't like it."

Sameena rolled her eyes. *Stellar Star: Queen of Space* had been scripted and produced by a whole team of groundhogs. If there was a single fact right in the entire series, it had been inserted by accident. And Stellar Star's uniform popped open at the slightest provocation, revealing a chest that was far too large to be natural. The only reason anyone living in space watched it, as far as she could tell, was to gawk at the lead actress and her harem of subordinate girls, who pretended to be a starship crew. God knew that there was little else to sell the show.

"Put it on if you want," she said. "Or something older."

She smiled at Brad. It was a strange relationship – being friends, almost family, with a boy – and yet she liked it. It was where she belonged.

"Thank you," Brad said. "We can watch something else afterwards."

CHAPTER NINETEEN

> The stereotype of evil money-grabbing corporations and greedy robber baron bankers comes from such events, it should be noted. Leaders of those corporations would often turn their attention to manipulating and swindling the law – and exploiting their workers – rather than attempting to help grow their productive base. Their short-term interest often caused long-term havoc, all the more so as CEOs grew distanced from the inner workings of their businesses.
>
> - Professor Leo Caesius, *The Science That Isn't: Economics and the Decline and Fall of the Galactic Empire.*

"It's very quiet," Sameena commented, as Rosa came into view. "Very, *very* quiet."

"That isn't uncommon for a first-stage colony world," Brad explained. "They haven't even bothered to install an orbital station yet, just plunked everything down through the atmosphere and onto the planet's surface. The corporation must be running short of funds."

Sameena nodded. She'd researched how colony worlds were founded over the last few days and the basic pattern was almost always the same. Farmers would be landed first, to start taming the land and preparing food supplies, then the rest of the population would slowly filter down and start turning the world into a human colony. Over the years, an industrial base would be built up to allow the colonists to produce most of what they needed on the surface, although their industry was always limited.

It hadn't taken long to confirm that the founding corporation wanted to keep the settlers dependent on them for outside tech.

There was almost no development at all outside the planet's atmosphere, save for a handful of orbiting satellites. They hadn't even *started* work on a cloudscoop. But then, the planet – according to the standard development pattern – wouldn't actually need a cloudscoop for at least another fifty to one hundred years. They could import their fuel from a nearby star system until then.

And what will happen, she asked herself silently, *when the transports stop coming?*

If there was one thing she had to admit was a workable idea for developing first-stage colonies, it was the dependence on animal labour and the determination to ensure that a planet could feed itself as quickly as possible. Rosa might well be able to continue to survive even without off-planet trade, but it would be years before it could reach back out into space…if it didn't collapse back into barbarism. It had happened before, according to the files, and it would happen again.

"They don't even have a system control," Brad said, ruefully. He worked his console for a long thoughtful moment, "Or a basic datanet. All we can do is ping them and see who responds."

It was nearly forty minutes before the response arrived, directing them to land their shuttle at a small landing strip some distance from the sole city. Grosvenor looked, from orbit, like a mass of converted shipping containers surrounding a handful of prefabricated structures that had probably been part of the original colony supplies. No matter how they looked, they couldn't even *find* a proper spaceport.

"Odd," Brad commented. "A spaceport and an orbital station are *always* part of the package for a new colony world."

Sameena frowned, noticing something else that didn't quite make sense. Rosa had been settled for seventy years, so they should have managed to replace the original buildings by now. There was no shortage of wood or stone to convert into houses, given proper equipment. And that too should have been included in the first drop.

"Maybe we shouldn't land," she said. "We could take the weapons…"

"We wouldn't get the other half of our fee," Brad said. "And we'd have to explain the weapons to the Imperial Navy. And we'd probably get sued. And we'd…"

"I know," Sameena said. She shook her head, chewing on a long strand of hair. "I just don't like it."

She looked over at him. "I could take the shuttle alone," she added. "You could stay here."

"We're both going to be needed on the surface," Brad said, shaking his head. "The ship will just have to be left on automatic until we return."

Sameena nodded and headed down to where the shuttle was docked to the hull. It had taken several days to move the cargo pallets into the shuttle, but there had been no choice. Without an orbital station, they couldn't simply pass it over and allow the station's crew to take it to the ground. They'd have to ship it down themselves. By her count, it would take at least two round trips before they could deliver all the weapons.

"Ready," she said into her wristcom, once she had checked the pallets one final time. "How about yourself?"

"I just loaded some emergency programs into the computer," Brad said. "No one will be able to board and take control without our permission."

He came through the airlock and joined her in the cockpit. "There's no ground control here," he added. "Do you want to fly the shuttle yourself?"

Sameena nodded, firmly. "Yes," she said, as she ran through the pre-flight checklist. "How often do we get a chance to land on a planet's surface?"

She smiled as she disengaged the shuttle and tapped on the thrusters, slowly moving away from *Lead Pipe*. Rosa was a colossal green and blue sphere against the viewport as she turned the shuttle and then headed right towards it. It grew larger and larger until her perspective seemed to flip, shifting it from a sphere to a living world. The shuttle rocked slightly as it entered the atmosphere, but she ignored it. She *loved* to fly.

"Remember we're heavily loaded," Brad warned, as they dropped through the atmosphere and headed towards the landing strip. Oddly for a newly-settled world, the main settlement was in the middle of a continent, rather than on the coastline. "She may handle a little roughly as we get lower."

"I can cope with it," Sameena assured him. The shuttle vibrated again as she dumped speed, taking the craft on a wide berth around the settlement. Flying directly over a large settlement was forbidden. "Can you find the beacon?"

"Pulsing away," Brad said, nodding to the main display. "They're waiting for us."

The landing strip didn't *look* very suitable, even to Sameena's inexperienced eye. It was nothing more than a large concrete field, with a pair of hangers at one end and a single large helicopter at the other. She slowed the shuttle to a hover, then lowered the craft down towards the ground. It rocked – hard – as it touched down.

"There's always a problem when you touch down," Brad commented. "The simulations never quite manage to duplicate it."

Sameena nodded, feeling the subtle difference in gravity as the shuttle's onboard field faded away. Rosa was slightly smaller than Earth, according to the files, and Earth had provided the standard for gravity throughout the Empire. She would be able to jump higher on the planet than she could onboard ship.

Pity it won't give us superpowers, she thought, remembering some of the older movies they'd watched together. One of them had implied that travellers from space would develop strange abilities under an alien sun. *You need to be a heavy-world native for the super-strength.*

Brad unstrapped himself and headed down to the hatch. "I think I see our welcoming committee," he said. "You coming?"

Sameena nodded and followed him through the airlock, taking her first breath of the planet's atmosphere. It smelt…*sweet*, as if there was a life about it that was simply lacking onboard ship. She felt an odd pang of homesickness as she stepped onto the concrete ground, catching sight of a handful of butterflies buzzing through the air. Perhaps, if she'd had a better life on Jannah, she would never have wanted to leave.

"I don't understand how they can live on Earth," she muttered to Brad. "Wouldn't they prefer to live here?"

"The average citizen on Earth sits in his poky little government-provided flat, eating his government-provided ration bars, watching government-provided entertainments and fucking his no doubt government-provided wife," Brad muttered back. "They are kept deliberately ignorant, fed propaganda instead of being taught how to think...do you think that they would *welcome* the chance to leave? Those that do leave willingly are the rarity."

He smiled at her expression. "Paddy was quite detailed when I asked him about it," he admitted. "Earth is not a nice place to live."

Sameena looked up as she saw their welcoming committee. Two men, both with sun-tanned faces and grim suspicious expressions. One of them held out a datapad, the other merely watched as Brad read the datapad and then checked it against his own.

"Half of the weapons are in the shuttle," he said. "The other half will have to be brought down from orbit."

"Understood," the man said. His accent was so thick that Sameena could barely understand him. "We can start unloading…"

There was a loud whistle from the other side of the field. A small army of men had appeared and started running towards them. Sameena glanced around, one hand reaching for her pistol, and saw other groups coming in from every direction. They were surrounded! Their greeter drew a pistol and started firing towards the men; Sameena grunted in pain as Brad tackled her, knocking her to the ground and lying on top of her body. It took her a moment to realise that he was trying to shield her as the newcomers started returning fire. Seconds later, a body crumpled to the ground. The newcomers had shot their greeter dead.

Brad swore as someone hauled him off Sameena and slammed him down to the concrete. She had a moment to see his attacker yanking his hands behind his back and slipping on the cuffs, then her own hands were wrenched out from under her and cuffed too. A man rolled her over and searched her roughly, removing everything from her pistol to the wristcom that linked back to the ship, then sat on her as his comrades pulled Brad to his feet and dragged him off towards one of the hangers. Sameena tried to struggle, but resistance was futile. She could barely move at all.

She twisted her head and stared at the two bodies. Something had gone very badly wrong, she knew now, but she didn't know why. If she'd listened to her instincts…she gritted her teeth, fighting to breathe. Her captor leered down at her, then stood up as a small vehicle drove across the landing strip and stopped beside them. Sameena had only a moment to feel relieved before they shackled her ankles and forced her into the vehicle. It was a mobile prison cell.

"Sit down and wait," her captor ordered. "You are under arrest."

He slammed the metal door shut before Sameena could say a word. Instead, she looked around, wincing at the pain in her wrists. The cuffs were far too tight. She concentrated, remembering what Paddy had taught her, and forced herself to consider her predicament as best as she could. The vehicle was nothing but bare metal walls. Even if she had free use of her hands and feet, she doubted that she would be able to get out. And she was completely cut off from the ship – and Brad.

The vehicle roared into life, lurching forward towards an unknown destination. Sameena sat down hastily, then closed her eyes and tried to think. They were trapped, under arrest…and that meant…what? Could it be that they'd been caught up in a civil war? But the government had ordered the weapons, hadn't it? She had the nasty feeling that they'd been conned.

It was nearly forty minutes before the vehicle finally lurched to a halt. Sameena felt nothing, but relief; the ride had made her want to throw up. Jayne could probably have explained why she had a bad reaction to the vehicle when she'd never had a problem with spacecraft…Sameena considered the problem briefly, then pushed it aside. There were more important matters to worry about. Where was Brad, for a start, and what was going to happen to them?

The door was yanked open, revealing the interior of a garage. A pair of uniformed men pulled her out of the vehicle and half-carried her down the corridor, rather than letting her walk for herself. Sameena forced herself to show no reaction, even when one of them allowed his hand to reach down to her breast and squeeze. He seemed disappointed by the lack of any response and stopped prodding her. There was no time to feel any relief before she was thrust into a small room and pulled to a halt in front of a table.

"That will be all," a woman's voice said. She stepped out of a door set into a wall, unmistakable authority in her tone. "Let's have a look at what we have here."

Sameena shuddered inwardly when she saw the woman, instinctively knowing that she would have been better off with the men. The woman was short, mildly overweight and had an expression that suggested that Sameena was even less than an insect in her eyes. She reminded Sameena of one of her mother's friends, a woman who had had two daughters who had always looked fearful when they thought no one was looking. And her children had always had nasty bruises on their faces.

The woman studied her back, her piggish eyes showing a hint of glee at having someone so completely in her power. Sameena had known that there were men who stared at her – and she was never comfortable with it – but this was different. She had the feeling that the woman wouldn't need much of an excuse before she began to hurt someone.

"I am Colonel Desiree," the woman said. Her Imperial Standard was better than the guard's. "Let's see now."

She made a show of consulting the sheets of paper on her desk. "You were caught smuggling arms to the surface to arm the rebels. You were in cahoots with the treacherous Osaka. You landed on our planet without permission. Tell me – do you think that anyone in the Empire will care what happens to you?"

Sameena gritted her teeth, but said nothing. Osaka had been the name on the permits to import weapons; assuming the woman was telling the truth, he'd been a rebel ally until he'd been caught. And that meant… what? She knew almost nothing of what was really going on.

"They won't," Desiree said, answering her own question. "No one will ask *any* questions about you, ever. Your only hope is to cooperate with us."

She nodded to the guards, who stepped up behind Sameena and removed the shackles, followed by the cuffs. There were ugly red marks on her skin, she discovered, as she rubbed at them frantically. Desiree watched, making no effort to hide her amusement. Sameena felt sick, but forced it down. She couldn't afford to make a mistake.

THE OUTCAST

Desiree smiled. "Take off your shirt," she ordered. "Now."

Sameena looked back at the guards. They were leering, anticipating the show. She turned back to Desiree, but saw no mercy in her eyes, merely a cruel sadistic amusement that chilled Sameena to the bone. Power had turned her into a monster.

And she was already trying to manipulate her captive, Sameena realised. Pushing her into an involuntary striptease would make her more cooperative in future. And it would serve to underline just how vulnerable she was…Paddy's Marine textbooks had gone into considerable detail on how someone could be broken down and rebuilt.

"No," she said, firmly.

Desiree quirked an eyebrow. "No?"

She nodded to the guards. Sameena had no time to react before one of them grabbed her and started to tear off her clothes. The shirt tore instantly, but the shipsuit was much tougher, giving her an opportunity to kick the guard in the shins. He yelped, shoved her to the floor and used a knife to cut the shipsuit away from her skin. She braced herself as his hands gripped her buttocks, but then he hauled her back to her feet. The remains of her clothing fell away, leaving her completely naked.

"They all *think* that they can resist," Desiree said. "But no one ever fails to give me what I want."

Sameena did her best to block out the next ten minutes as hands prodded her body, exploring every last inch of her skin. Anywhere she might have hidden something was examined, while Desiree watched, her face twisted into a smile. Eventually, she was cuffed again and made to stand upright in front of the sadistic woman. If she had come straight to Rosa from Jannah, part of her realised numbly, the experience would have broken her. As it was…

"You will have some time to contemplate what you will say to me next," Desiree informed her. She looked over at the guards. "Take her away."

They obeyed, shoving Sameena down a long corridor that opened into a room filled with cages. Several of them were inhabited by prisoners, all female. Sameena shuddered at the stench as the guards opened one of the cages, then pushed her inside and used another pair of cuffs to lock her to the bars. Finally, they released her hands and stepped backwards, slamming the door shut. She was trapped.

"Wait," she said. The guards paused and looked at her, expectantly. "Where's my...my friend?"

"Somewhere," one of the guards said. "I suggest that you start thinking about how to satisfy the Colonel. She's really quite demanding when she wants something."

She could hear them sniggering as they walked away, leaving the prisoners alone.

For a long moment, Sameena felt absolutely helpless. She was naked, unarmed, cuffed...there seemed to be no way out. But she knew never to give up. There would be an opportunity, Paddy had insisted when he'd discussed disaster scenarios with her, and when it came she would have to take it. But would it ever come?

And what were they doing to Brad?

"Hey," a female voice said. "What are *you* doing here?"

"I just landed," Sameena said. She looked over at the woman in the next cage. "What are you doing here?"

"Long story," the woman said.

Slowly, she started to talk.

CHAPTER TWENTY

> This in turn fuelled a demand for worker power, a demand that would eventually lead to both the trade union movement and communism. The former was often quite reasonable when the management could crush any individual worker effortlessly; collective bargaining was often the only weapon they could use against their employers.
>
> - Professor Leo Caesius, *The Science That Isn't: Economics and the Decline and Fall of the Galactic Empire.*

"My name is Ginny," the woman said. "My father wanted to leave Earth. He'd kept trying for promotion and he never got it. Eventually, he booked all of us on a transport and signed up with the RDC – the Rosa Development Corporation. I was four years old at the time."

Sameena listened, studying the woman. She was badly bruised, the marks clearly visible even in the dimly-lit room. The damage would leave her permanently scarred without proper medical treatment, although Sameena suspected that hardly anyone left the jail once they arrived. Desiree and her guards didn't seem too worried about future complaints from their former prisoners.

"It was difficult at first," Ginny continued. "My older brothers and sisters bitched like mad beasts over losing all the benefits of Earth. Father insisted that we get a homestead and learn how to farm. We were lucky enough to apprentice with a decent farmer and his wife, so we had good tutors. Didn't quite manage to make ends meet for five years, but eventually...I learned to love the farm. I don't think my siblings always felt the same way."

"I know the feeling," Sameena said, remembering how her adopted brothers had different aspirations. Even if the horror stories about Earth were exaggerated, she wouldn't have wanted to leave outer space – and its technology – and live on Jannah. "What happened?"

"The development corporation simply abandoned us," Ginny said. "One day, the starships simply stopped coming. There were no new colonists, no new supplies...and the governor went mad. All of a sudden, he turned into a dictator and started imposing his own rule on us. Some of us tried to fight..."

She tapped one of the scars on her body. "I was one of them," she admitted. "We attacked a supply convoy...I think it was a few weeks ago. They caught me and dragged me here. I haven't seen the outside world since."

Sameena shuddered. It would be easy for someone to make a bid for supreme power if a stage-one colony world had been cut off from the Empire. *She* wouldn't have considered it worth trying, but the governor clearly disagreed. And such a regime would attract sadists and psychopaths as shit attracted flies. She wanted to talk about their contract, about what had happened when they arrived, yet she knew that might be far too revealing. Who knew who might be listening to them?

Someone had ordered weapons from off-world. The rebels, according to Desiree...but the governor had clearly managed to detect the shuttle and send troops to intercept Sameena and Brad before the weapons were unloaded. They hadn't even known to try to conceal their landing, even though it would have been easy. Rosa didn't have a dedicated monitoring service for tracking starships and shuttles entering the system.

But if we'd known that we had to make a covert landing, I wouldn't have agreed to take the contract, she thought, cursing her own mistake – and Brad's desperation to pay off his debts. *I should have hired him myself and to hell with his pride.*

"Tell me about the governor," she said, instead. Knowledge was power, after all. "What sort of government does he run?"

The average stage-one colony had very little government, she knew; the corporation might hold all the power, but it had problems running every aspect of the population's lives. Mostly, the government would only step in if there was a serious problem…such as bandits or raiders in the hinterlands. Rosa's governor, freed from all constraints, had armed indents and turned them into a personal guard. He'd then established control over the city and created the basics of a police state.

"We can't get him out of the city, but he hasn't been able to break us," Ginny said, with a hint of pride. "But he might have won by now."

Sameena said nothing. She *did* have evidence that the fight was far from over, but she didn't want to say that out loud either. But the governor might be able to use either her or Brad to get up to *Lead Pipe* and then… the freighter wasn't armed, yet it wouldn't be hard to find small rocks and drop them on selected targets. Or he could simply use the craft to bring in mercenaries from off-world. There was no shortage of people who would fight to uphold his government if the price was right.

She shuddered. Brad was devoted to his ship – he seemed to have fallen in love with *Lead Pipe* the moment he set eyes on her – but the governor's thugs could simply threaten Sameena's life to make him comply. Or they could torture him until he broke…she considered, briefly, if she could convince them to take her back to the ship. There were computer overrides she could use that would render it useless, if she couldn't take back command. But it would be far too risky.

Only one of us should have gone down, Sameena thought, grimly. In hindsight, the mistake was glaringly obvious. But Brad had been desperate and the papers had seemed legit – hell, they *were* legit. *If one of us had remained on the ship, that person could have threatened the planet or simply left to get reinforcements from the clans. Or even summoned the Imperial Navy.*

But no one cared enough to intervene, she knew. Planets were being abandoned all over, even the worlds that had once showed promise for future development. Even Jamie, if asked, might shrug and leave Rosa to collapse into chaos.

She looked over at Ginny. "Tell me about yourself," she said, seriously. "What was life here like, before the governor went mad."

Ginny gave her an odd little smile. "Tell me about *yourself*," she said. "Where do you come from?"

Sameena hesitated. "The traders," she said, finally. "And I never meant to end up here."

They were still deep in conversation when the guards returned, swaggering down between the cages and leering at the prisoners. Sameena watched them coming, fighting to keep her thoughts and emotions under control. Surrendering to fear would cripple her, according to Paddy, making it impossible for her to fight back. There would be an opportunity, she told herself. She just had to be ready for it when it came.

"Good luck," Ginny muttered, very quietly.

"Silence, bitch," one of the guards barked. Clearly, Ginny hadn't been quiet enough. "And you, outsider. Give me your hands."

Sameena scowled as they cuffed her, shackled her legs and then pulled her out of the cage. She had to admire the cruel ingenuity of whoever had devised the shackles, part of her mind noted; it was impossible to walk at anything more than a shuffle, at least not without falling over. If she tried to run, she would trip over herself. There was no way she could escape as long as she was wearing them.

The guards inspected her briefly – as if she could have somehow hidden a weapon on her person in the cell – and then marched her down the corridor, slapping at her buttocks when she failed to move fast enough to suit them. It was yet another tactic to break her, she knew, yet knowing what it was didn't stop it working. She gritted her teeth, promising herself that the guards would suffer later. The part of her mind that always remained cool and collected refused to simply give up.

They entered an office and pushed her into a corner, then left her standing there to wait. It was an uncomfortable position – and another intimidation tactic - but Sameena did her best to relax and listen to the sounds behind her. The guards seemed to have found seats and had sat down, waiting themselves. She forced herself to ignore the fact that they were staring at her naked body. Giving them the satisfaction of knowing that it bothered her would be a mistake.

"Good," a female voice said. Desiree. "Take her to the van and transport her to the palace."

Sameena had no time to think about what it might mean before the guards caught her arms and dragged her from the room. They seemed almost fearful themselves now, as if they believed that they would face punishment...but for what? Judging by Ginny's condition, prisoner abuse was common on Rosa – and the guards hadn't *acted* like their superiors would punish them if they abused, raped or murdered any of the prisoners. In fact, some of the prisoners hadn't moved at all while she'd been in the cell. Were they even alive?

The van was another mobile prison cell, identical to the first one. Sameena was pushed into the back, then the doors were slammed shut and locked. The engine roared to life a moment later. They were definitely in a hurry to go somewhere...

Brad must not be talking, she thought, with a sudden flicker of pride and affection. She'd known that he was stubborn – stubborn enough to want to make his own way, even though it would have been simple to use the proceeds from Firewater Mead to fund a ship – and he wouldn't want to talk.

The thought made her shiver. If they couldn't make Brad talk through torture, they might hurt her in front of his eyes to make him talk. Brad might be stubborn enough to keep his mouth shut, even when he was being beaten half to death, but would he remain silent when they were hurting *her*? His feelings for her might compel him to do whatever they wanted.

She breathed in the stink of burning hydrocarbons as the vehicle lurched into motion, heading out of the prison. Burning gas was an inefficient source of power compared to fusion power, but without a source of HE3 Rosa probably didn't have any alternative. They wouldn't be the first world to fall back on older technology when the supplies of HE3 came to an end and they definitely wouldn't be the last. The thought made her scowl as she remembered her own predictions. Low-tech worlds like Jannah might be the only ones to survive the fall of the Empire unscathed.

The sound of the engines was growing louder, despite her best efforts to ignore it. It was more penetrative than the ever-present sound of starship drives, louder and nastier...she tried to clear her mind, only to discover that her head was starting to throb uncomfortably. The physical aches and pains the guards had inflicted on her were growing worse. And God alone knew what was going to happen next.

Something struck the vehicle, hard. Sameena had barely a second to react before it toppled over, sending her falling downwards against the wall. She gasped in pain as her shoulder struck the metal, cursing the handcuffs and the guards out loud. A moment later, the doors were wrenched open and two masked men looked in at her, then caught her arms and dragged her outside.

"She's shackled," one of them said.

"Carry her," the other snapped. "Hurry!"

Sameena grunted in pain as one of the men – rebels – she guessed – threw her over his shoulder, then started to run. She caught glimpses of their surroundings; a handful of buildings, several dead bodies…all wearing the same uniforms as the guards who had held her prisoner. Her head started to spin as they thrust her into a car, then started the engine and drove off. She must have blacked out, because the next thing she remembered was lying on a bed. Someone had removed her cuffs and started to tend her wounds.

"Hi," a female voice said. "How are you feeling?"

Sameena looked over to see a young girl, barely entering her teens, looking back at her with wide anxious eyes. "Sore," she admitted, reluctantly. "Where am I?"

"Somewhere safe," the girl said. She reminded Sameena of herself, when she'd been younger, although the girl had short blonde hair rather than long black locks. There was something waiflike in her wide blue eyes. Her skin was very pale. "I…I have some medical training. Can you tell me where you hurt?"

"My head, my shoulder, my…" Sameena broke off and looked over at the girl. "Who are you?"

"Barbara," the girl said, shortly. "I can give you something for the pain, but we don't have a proper hospital."

"I heal quickly," Sameena said. It still amused and annoyed her in equal measure that Jannah's founders had used genetic engineering to shape the population – after having condemned genetic engineering as a tool of Satan – but it did have its advantages. "Don't worry about it."

Barbara passed her a mug of water. Sameena sat upright and sipped it, glancing around the room. If it was intended as a hospital, she decided, it wasn't a very good one. The floor was clean, but there was almost no equipment apart from a table of very basic medical tools and supplies. Jayne would have been horrified at the thought of trying to perform surgery without proper equipment.

The throbbing in her head slowly faded away as she drank the water, allowing her a chance to think. Barbara watched her, showing no trace of fear, which either made her naive or confident that Sameena wouldn't harm her. Or, perhaps, because she knew that they were being watched. It seemed odd to leave a young girl alone with a potentially dangerous prisoner.

She looked the girl in the eye. "What sort of medical training do you have?"

"My father was a doctor," Barbara admitted, squirming under Sameena's gaze. "I grew up watching him work. He even let me help."

Sameena had to smile. The Empire insisted on doctors undergoing a rigorous training and assessment process before they practiced – Jayne had said a lot of sarcastic things about doctors on Earth – but the colony worlds didn't have that luxury. If Barbara had been willing to learn, her father would probably have been delighted to teach her – and then to allow her to practice medicine.

"He was taken away a year ago," Barbara said, when Sameena asked. "I haven't seen him since then."

Dead, Sameena thought, grimly. Or worse. A trained doctor might be forced to work for the governor, rather than simply being killed outright. But then, the governor hadn't managed to round up his daughter…she shook her head. She was speculating without anything like enough data.

Barbara gave her a long look. "I have orders to call the leader when you recovered enough to speak with him," she said. "But would you like some clothes first?"

"Yes, please," Sameena said. She wasn't sure if she could pass for a planetary native, but she would feel much better if she was wearing *something*. "Anything."

Barbara passed her a dressing gown, which she donned rapidly. "I'll find you something else to wear," Barbara added. "I don't have anything that will fit you, but if you don't mind wearing male clothing…"

Sameena surprised herself by laughing. "I have worn it in the past," she said, remembering how she'd escaped Jannah. "Male clothing will be fine."

Barbara nodded and stepped out of the door, leaving Sameena alone in the room. She looked around, but didn't touch anything, convinced that she was still under observation. Instead, she waited to see what would happen next. It was nearly ten minutes, she thought, before the door opened again, revealing a grim-faced man. He strode into the room in a manner that reminded her of Paddy, followed by Barbara.

"We tried to meet you when you landed," he said. His Imperial Standard was almost completely unaccented. "But you were captured too quickly for us to respond."

Sameena nodded, but said nothing.

"The codewords are Firefox, Brainy and Horses," the man continued. "Did *all* of the supplies fall into the governor's hands?"

"No," Sameena said, remembering the authorisation codes on the manifest. "But they also captured the shuttle and my communicator. And they have my…friend prisoner."

"So they might be able to take your ship," the man said. "Or at least put the weapons into service themselves."

Sameena gave him a long look. Barbara was eying the man with an expression of almost worshipful admiration, which – to his credit – he seemed to be ignoring. It spoke well of him, she decided; her instincts were telling her that he wasn't one of the governor's allies, or even a dangerously unstable rebel. Perhaps they could work together…

Besides, there isn't much choice, she told herself. *Without help, I can't get back to orbit.*

"It's possible," she admitted, reluctantly. An idea crossed her mind and she smiled. "What sort of forces do you have on the ground?"

"Hundreds of farmers, mainly armed with small weapons," the man said. "The governor has conscripted indents, all of whom have been terrorising the planet. So far, the war has stalemated. I was hoping that weapons from off-world would tip the balance in our favour."

Sameena nodded. "We need to try to recover the shuttle," she said. "Or perhaps find another shuttle. A way of getting back into orbit."

"That will not be easy," the man admitted. "*Your* shuttle is still on the landing field, but it is under heavy guard. The other shuttles are hundreds of years old. Would you be able to fly them?"

"Probably," Sameena said. The Imperial Navy had standardised everything centuries ago. Each shuttle might have different flight characteristics, but the basic control system would be unchanged. "I've had an idea."

CHAPTER TWENTY-ONE

> Perhaps one might have more sympathy for them if one realised that unemployment often led to total disaster. Social security networks were often more limited in practice than anyone not dependent on them realised. The idea that someone should 'do what they enjoyed' was simply impractical. People needed money to live.
> - Professor Leo Caesius, *The Science That Isn't: Economics and the Decline and Fall of the Galactic Empire.*

Sameena couldn't help feeling uneasy as night fell over Rosa. She'd been born on a planet and she'd visited several others – nightfall was hardly a new experience – but there was something about the darkness that bothered her. Or perhaps it was the grim awareness that she was about to gamble, risking her life in a desperate attempt to save Brad and return to their trading life.

"Only seven guards," Fox muttered. The rebel leader had finally told her his name – or, at least, the one he was currently using. From what he'd said, Sameena was sure that he was ex-military, rather than just another farmer. "And the shuttle is just inside the hanger."

Sameena nodded. Rosa had ignored so many regulations when it came to founding colonies that she wouldn't have been surprised to discover that they'd ignored the regulation that demanded that all colonies keep a handful of shuttles on the surface, ready to jump to orbit at a moment's notice. As it was, Rosa had five shuttles on the ground, if only to help unload the corporation's interstellar freighters when they came calling.

They hadn't been used, according to Fox, for at least three years. Sameena could only hope that they were still in working order.

They're built to be durable, she reminded herself, as the butterflies in her stomach had babies and multiplied. *It should still be flyable, unless someone drained the power cells.*

Fox motioned for her to stay where she was – well out of danger – and crawled forward with the rest of his best strike team. The rebels didn't seem very professional, at least to Sameena's untrained eye, but they'd clearly learnt the basics of stealth and concealment. If they hadn't, they would have been wiped out by now.

But the war has effectively stalemated, Sameena thought, grimly. *The governor can't wipe out the rebels and the rebels can't get at him. Not until now.*

She waited, hoping against hope that she wouldn't hear the sound of shooting. Moments passed, each one seemingly a year in itself, before someone crawled back up to her and poked her in the side. Sameena almost yelped before she caught herself, then saw one of the rebels – a grim-faced woman - nodding towards the landing strip. The coast had been cleared. She nodded back to the woman and then walked towards the strip. A handful of bodies, their throats cut, lay on the ground in front of the hanger.

"Not a single word of warning," Fox muttered. He sounded disgusted. "And to think that this bunch were among the most *professional* in the governor's service."

Sameena realised what he meant as she stepped into the hanger. Barbara and some of the other rebels had told her of the horrors inflicted on the planet's population, particularly after the governor had started using indents as a personal police force. Looting, rape and murder had become common. But this group of guards hadn't been abusing anyone, or drinking themselves into a stupor, or anything other than doing their job. Perhaps, in another life, they might have served well.

She pushed the thought aside as she clambered into the shuttle and touched the console, bringing it to life. The shuttle ran a self-check, then reported that everything seemed to be in working order apart from a minor problem with the rear hatch. Flying to orbit would be impossible,

Sameena concluded, grimly. Luckily, she hadn't counted on being able to get back to the ship.

Fox stuck his head through the hatch. "Well?"

"The shuttle is functional, but can't get into orbit," Sameena said, keying in the next sequence of commands. The shuttle's systems flash-woke, readying themselves for action. It would take a few years off the estimated lifespan of some of the more delicate components, but it hardly mattered. They couldn't afford a long drawn-out process for bringing the shuttle to life. "But we should be able to get to Grosvenor."

"Good," Fox said. "I don't suppose you can just crash it into the palace?"

Sameena shook her head. God alone knew where Brad was – and besides, the shuttle's autopilot was one of a notoriously unreliable design. It might simply refuse to fly a suicide course, or it might accidentally crash into the wrong building. Brad had taught her that trusting an autopilot was asking for trouble. The slightest programming glitch could lead to a dreadful accident.

"No," she said. "Load up."

She finished powering up the shuttle, then waited as the rebels climbed into the shuttle and took their places. Ideally, they would have used one of the assault boats or Marine Raptors Paddy had talked about, but they had neither. Instead, Sameena knew, they were going to push the advantage of surprise as far as it would go. She closed the hatch, then took control of the shuttle and moved it forward, out of the hanger. Outside, the stars seemed so close that she could almost reach out and touch them.

"Here we go," Fox said. "Take us up."

The shuttle lurched alarmingly as it stumbled into the air, but Sameena kept control and guided it rapidly towards the city. Grosvenor was a tiny handful of lights against the darkness, the governor's palace and a handful of other buildings brightly illuminated to demonstrate his power. Sameena remembered just how dark Jannah had been between sunset and sunrise and shivered, inwardly, as she directed the shuttle towards the palace. There was no way that any of the defenders would fail to hear them coming. They were committed now.

"Five seconds," she snapped, as the shuttle came to a hover and then dropped out of the sky, the antigravity units barely cancelling out the worst of the impact. It was a far rougher landing than her first landing on Rosa – or anywhere, for that matter. She hadn't performed so badly outside her first simulations. "Go!"

"Go," Fox bellowed. The rebels seemed a little shaky – few of them had ever flown before – but they scrambled out through the hatch and opened fire on the defenders. "Move, you bastards!"

He looked over at Sameena. "And you'd better get out of the firing line," he added. "We may need you again."

Sameena picked up the rifle they'd given her and shook her head. "I'm coming," she said, firmly. "Brad's in there, somewhere."

The governor's madness, she decided as she followed Fox out towards the building, was quite definitely proven when he called his home a palace. It was nothing more than a giant prefabricated building, clearly designed to serve as a temporary base of operations for the planetary government. She was mildly surprised that he hadn't started building a newer and greater palace to *really* put his stamp on the planet, before deciding that he probably intended to do it after he'd defeated the rebels.

Fox led her up towards the first entrance, where the guards had already been cut down, allowing the rebels to storm the building. No mercy was being shown, she realised, although she found it hard to be sympathetic. Desiree and the others like her had taken advantage of their position to abuse innocent civilians and travellers who had landed on their world. If even a quarter of the stories she'd been told were true, they all deserved to die a hundred times over. Fox fired on a pair of guards who were trying to flee, then kept moving through the metal corridors. The sound of fighting was deafeningly loud.

Paddy had talked about combat awareness, about knowing what was going on despite the chaos. Sameena discovered that she didn't have the mindset to make it work. It all blurred together into a series of impressions in her mind; the defenders, trying to fight or run; the attackers, pressing their advantage as best as they could; the slaves, caught in the middle and mown down by both sides…she felt thoroughly sick as the fighting finally started to die away, leaving behind nothing, but silence.

"Space combat is far cleaner than fighting on the ground," Paddy had said. He'd been trying to comfort her after a training session that had left her feeling as if she would never learn how to defend herself properly. "It's easy to ignore the fact that an icon on the display is actually a starship full of living people – easier, too, to get used to the stresses of combat."

Looking at the desolation, Sameena suspected that he was right.

The governor just didn't *look* very impressive when they dragged him out of his basement lair. He was a short man, with dark hair, wild staring eyes and an emaciated body that reminded Sameena of the drug addicts on Madagascar. His ravings made no sense to her; he seemed convinced that he was the absolute ruler of all he surveyed, even as Fox and his men took aim at his head. Moments later, he lay dead on the ground.

A crazy man, she thought, *who took advantage of the chaos to establish himself as a ruler.*

She couldn't help thinking of it as a harbinger of things to come. The governor had had one planet, a stage-one colony world. What if he'd had a far more populated world and a handful of starships? He might have been able to start his own interstellar empire when the Imperial Navy pulled out of the sector altogether – or worse. Maybe he'd even make a bid for the throne on Earth. It would be insane on the face of it, but who knew what might be possible when the Empire fell?

"Tell his men that if they stop fighting, they can live," Fox ordered. He looked over at Sameena. "We're heading to the main prison. Do you want to come with us?"

Sameena nodded, wordlessly.

The streets of Grosvenor seemed almost deserted as the rebels took control. Most of the population had learned hard lessons about not showing anything other than submission to the governor and his thugs. Sameena had been told that hundreds of urban dwellers had fled into the countryside before the governor had ordered them to build a wall around the city, trapping the remainder of the population inside. She couldn't help spotting a handful of dead bodies on the ground as they drove up to the prison. It seemed almost deserted.

"They've fled," one of their escorts commented.

"Be careful," Fox ordered, as they slipped through the open doors. "It might be a trap."

It was worse than the prison they'd held her in, Sameena realised, as the rebels shone lights into the darkness. The male prisoners were crammed together in cells that were barely large enough to allow them some freedom of movement, all naked. And the stench was unbelievable. Sameena forced herself to breathe through her mouth – behind her, she heard some of the rebels retching – as she searched for Brad. But there was no sign of him.

"In here," one of the rebels called. "Hurry!"

The room was an interrogation chamber. Brad lay on the table, his arms and legs strapped down…and his body badly mutilated. Sameena let out a cry of horror as she saw the blood dripping down, then the twists in his arms that suggested broken bones…she was too late.

"Get a doctor," she screamed. The rudimentary first aid she'd learned, at Jayne's insistence, was nowhere near enough to save his life. Panic – not for herself, but for him – bubbled into her mind. "Hurry!"

"Not a chance," Brad wheezed. "Kept telling them that they were shitheads or worse. Wanted them to keep looking at me."

Sameena stared at him, then understood. Brad had wanted them to focus on him, rather than her. He hadn't known that she'd been liberated by the rebels; he'd encouraged them to torture him, rather than her. Sameena felt tears prickling at the corner of her eyes as she realised just how much Brad cared for her.

"My fault," Brad said, weakly. His hand twitched, struggling against the restraints – and the damage inflicted by the interrogators. "Should have listened to you. Never should have come here. But needed the money. I'm sorry."

"They didn't harm me," Sameena lied. She would give him that consolation, if nothing else. "And I got you free."

She looked back towards the door and raised her voice. "Where's the doctor?"

"Know too much," Brad said. "Internal bleeding and worse. I won't survive the day."

"I'll find a stasis pod," Sameena promised, urgently. "I'll get you back to Jayne. *She* can put you back together and…"

"No stasis pods on this planet," Brad said. He giggled, suddenly, as blood trickled out of his mouth. "Primitive shithole, isn't it? And I brought you here."

"I could have said no," Sameena insisted. "I didn't…"

There had been options, she realised. She could have used another shell corporation to hire Brad and his ship, leaving him unaware that she was secretly funding him. Given enough care, he might never find out. But she'd thought that she should let him have his pride…in a way, she was just as guilty. She could have made sure of his survival.

But he would never have forgiven me if he'd known, she thought. *And his pride would not have survived. Men*!

Brad's arm twitched again. "Tell mum and dad…sperm samples stored at the Meeting Place," he said. "Maybe find a host mother, if they want my line to go on. And tell them I'm sorry. And tell them that it wasn't your fault."

His eyes suddenly sharpened. "There's a marriage contract in my cabin, in the safe," he added, weakly. He coughed as he spoke. "Sign it. I signed it already. Be my wife. The ship will be yours. No one will argue."

"I can't," Sameena said. Tears were trickling down her cheeks. "It wouldn't be *right*."

"Mum and dad knew that I was planning to work on you," Brad said. "Mum will understand…"

"She won't want to see me again," Sameena said. "I might as well have killed you."

They'd say that she'd killed Brad for his ship. Even if Captain Hamilton and Ethne knew better, there would be plenty of others who would level the charge at her. Rumours and innuendo flashed through the trader community like wildfire, often bearing absolutely no resemblance to reality. There would be hundreds of spacers who would believe that she'd deliberately led him into a trap.

Jannah had stories of wives who murdered their husbands when they finally snapped. They were branded as monsters in religious education, women who had not lived up to the ideal – never mind the fact, Sameena had realised at a very early age, that their husbands hadn't lived up to the ideal either. The traders had stories of marriage contracts gone wrong, of gold diggers who had married into a clan and then ripped it apart from the inside…they'd say that Sameena was just another one of them.

"Tell them to give you truth drugs," Brad said. For a moment, he showed a hint of his old personality. "Do I have to think of *everything* here?"

Sameena couldn't help giggling, despite the tears. "I'm sorry," she said. "I…"

Brad coughed. More blood spilled from his mouth. "Have my child," he suggested. "And please…sign the contract. It will save you problems later on."

He choked suddenly. His eyes closed. Sameena stepped forward, but it was far too late. As she watched, the life went out of him. She found herself praying softly, realising just how much she was going to miss him. Maybe she *would* have his child, even though giving birth to a child out of wedlock was one of the greatest shames a woman could suffer on Jannah.

The door opened, revealing Barbara. "I'm sorry," she said, tearfully. "I came as quickly as I could."

Sameena looked at the child, then started to cry. Barbara reached out for her and enfolded her in a tight hug, providing what consolation she could. Part of Sameena wanted to lash out at her for not coming faster, but cold logic told her that Barbara could have done nothing to save her adopted brother. Like so many others, she was untrained…and she didn't have the equipment she would have needed to save Brad's life. Even a stasis pod would have given him a chance of survival.

"I can give you something to help you sleep," Barbara offered. "Because you need to sleep and…"

"Just find me somewhere to pray," Sameena said. "And then somewhere to sleep."

She was barely aware of Barbara talking to one of the rebel leaders, then of being helped to a small room inside the governor's palace. It was odd how her faith had actually grown stronger in space, when she'd seen some of the wonders God had created with her own eyes, even if it had also changed. The Guardians would say that Brad was doomed, merely for being an infidel. Sameena could no longer believe that to be true. Brad had been kinder and more honourable than any Guardian, or anyone else she'd met on Jannah. She refused to believe that he might go straight to hell.

The bed was hard and lumpy. She lay down on it and closed her eyes, realising just how little time had passed since they'd landed on Rosa. Had it really been under a day? It felt like much longer…and Brad was gone. She'd been talking and laughing with him yesterday…

That night, the nightmares started again.

Chapter Twenty-Two

> However, this could also do considerable damage to the economy. The idea that the government could redistribute the wealth was tempting, particularly to those who had none – or had no experience of actually working with money. However, attempting to do so caused other problems. Sharing out the wealth often meant that the money needed to rejuvenate the economy wasn't there, while putting power in the hands of those who claimed to represent the workers only meant trading one set of masters for another - as it did, when the communist governments took power.
>
> - Professor Leo Caesius, *The Science That Isn't: Economics and the Decline and Fall of the Galactic Empire.*

"I'm sorry for your loss," Osaka said.

Sameena scowled at him. Osaka's involvement with the rebellion had been discovered several months after he'd dispatched agents to obtain weapons from Tabasco or another grey colony, but apart from some minor torture he'd barely been touched by his captors. He should have died, part of her thought, and Brad should have lived. If he'd told them what they were getting into, they would never have travelled to Rosa.

"Me too," she said, finally. "I trust that the remaining weapons are acceptable?"

Fox – he swore blind that Fox was his real name – nodded. "I distributed them to the farmers and others, just to help hunt down the remainder of the indents," he said. "And the payment – was that acceptable?"

Sameena nodded, feeling numb. Imperial Credits were almost completely worthless on Rosa; she'd been paid enough to allow her to buy out the remainder of Brad's debts, but it wouldn't be enough to bring him back. His body had already been shipped up to orbit and placed in the stasis pod. All she could do was consider having his child…she hadn't even been able to sign the contract yet, even though she knew she should.

"Thank you," she said, finally. "What are you going to do now?"

"Try to rebuild," Fox said. "The prisoners can be put to work as slave labour, rebuilding the damage they caused during the war. Maybe we can survive even without the corporation's support – they just abandoned us, so our debts to them are null and void."

"They might feel differently," Sameena pointed out, waspishly. Ethne had taught her that in legal disputes, might tended to make right. One of the reasons the Empire was in so much trouble was because the bigger corporations encouraged the Grand Senate to pass laws in their favour, squashing their smaller competitors like ants. "And you're not in a good position."

Fox lifted an eyebrow. "How so?"

"You don't have the base to maintain a technological civilisation," Sameena said. "It would take you years to build up again, particularly after the tech you do have starts to fail. And it will, once you run short of HE3."

"We're already short," Osaka admitted, after a brief glance at Fox. "I don't know how long we can afford to keep the fusion reactor going."

"Not that we need it, outside the city," Fox said. He looked back at Sameena. "What do you have in mind?"

Sameena blinked in surprise.

Fox laughed. "I was a Civil Guardsman," he admitted. "I know when someone is trying to lead up to making a bargain. Cut to the chase, Captain. What do you have in mind?"

Captain? She *was* a Captain now, Sameena knew. As Brad's XO, she would have automatically succeeded him in any case, at least until the ship returned to port and the bankers started trying to claim it. But then, it hardly mattered. She had a sudden mental image of barking orders at herself, saluting herself and obeying herself and fought down a giggle. Brad would have understood.

"I've been looking at ways to set up other production plants," she said, slowly. She didn't want to tell them everything, but they had to understand that she was serious. "Plants that could produce spare parts for technology, which would eventually lead into producing new machines and then development; schools that would teach children how to become doctors or engineers or mechanics or whatever else we actually need…eventually, set up newer cloudscoops and shipyards to keep the sector going. I'd like to set one of them up here."

She smiled at their expression. There were limits to just how much Steve and his gang of engineers could do with the mobile factory, even if they were starting to produce a steady stream of spare parts. Building one in a populated star system would allow her to give the system a push in the right direction…and make it harder for anyone hostile to do anything about it. The RDC had effectively conceded Rosa's independence when it had abandoned the planet.

They might not see it that way, as she had warned them. But she had a feeling that it would be a long time before the RDC returned to the sector. By then, who knew what might have changed.

"I see," Fox said, finally. "And you think that we'd want this?"

Sameena looked at him, evenly. "Do you want to watch the remnants of your technology fade away and die?"

"Point," Osaka agreed. "However, we are not in a good place to offer investment, merely…people. And you may discover that you are producing more spare parts than we can reasonably absorb."

"There are plenty of other worlds and inhabited asteroids that need them," Sameena pointed out. "And you can offer food – Madagascar, for example, has to import almost everything it needs to survive. And you could even offer a home to refugees."

"I suppose that would be true," Osaka said. "It would need to be discussed by the new government, once it is established. However, I believe that there would be no real objections. You are, after all, quite a hero."

Sameena felt a pang of guilt. Brad had died when he should have lived. What did heroism matter compared to losing him?

"Thank you," she said, softly. "I'll have some of the equipment shipped in within the next two months."

Once, she would have been pleased at how the plan was coming together. Steve and she had collected an astonishing amount of old equipment – mostly outdated, but still functional. Some of it could be moved to Rosa…perhaps the RockRats could be convinced to help out by establishing an asteroid settlement in the system. They'd expressed some interest in her program, although – as always – they kept their own counsel about the future of the Empire. But then, their relationship with the Empire had always been fraught.

And she had some of the older children – adults now – who had come to Madagascar as refugees. Professor Sorrel and his assistants had done an excellent job. The children might still be inexperienced, but they were trained and ready to start work on the production plants – and to help train others. Given enough time, Rosa might even be able to produce a dedicated workforce.

"Start small," Steve had advised. "Work on basic spare parts, then simple machines – and then work your way up to starships and shipyards."

She should have been pleased. But all she could feel was the aching sense of loss.

"We look forward to it," Fox said. "And thank you."

He hesitated. "I believe that Barbara wants to speak with you, as do others," he added. "Can you make time for them before you depart?"

"I suppose," Sameena said, reluctantly. She didn't really want to talk to anyone. "Where is she now?"

Barbara's father had been lucky, she discovered as she stepped inside the makeshift hospital; he'd been enslaved rather than simply shot out of hand. A trained doctor was simply too valuable to waste, Sameena knew, and the governor evidently agreed. Barbara waved to her, beckoning her over to a tall man who looked like an older version of herself. Sameena found herself liking him on sight.

"Good afternoon, Captain," he said. "I am Doctor Hamblin."

"Pleased to meet you," Sameena said, After so long, shaking hands was no longer a problem for her. "I believe you wanted to speak with me?"

"I did," Hamblin said. He led the way into a private office – Barbara following them – and closed the door firmly. "I am very sorry for your loss. I had a look at him before he was placed in the stasis pod and I do not believe that he could have been saved with the equipment on this planet. They really were desperate to get him to talk."

"I know," Sameena said, sharply. She didn't wanted to be reminded – yet again – of her own failure. "What do you want from me?"

The Doctor gave her a long considering look, as if he was having second thoughts. But about what?

"Barbara needs medical training," he said, finally. "I would like you to transport her to Madagascar, where she can take up her studies."

Sameena hesitated. She'd expanded the scholarship program twice since she'd started it; there was no reason why Barbara should be denied one, if she was prepared to agree to the conditions. More doctors would be very helpful. On the other hand, she was young and would need supervision. But Lamina was proving to be an excellent supervisor.

She looked down at Barbara, who was looking up at her pleadingly. "I may not be very good company over the next two weeks," she warned. "And it will be just you and me on the ship."

"I will be fine," Barbara said. "And I can help…"

Sameena's first inclination was to snort…and then she caught herself, remembering the day she'd faced Captain Hamilton and pleaded to be allowed to stay. *She'd* had no formal training on shipboard life and he'd still given her a chance to prove herself. How could she do any less, particularly when the young girl wouldn't be staying on the ship permanently?

"I suppose you can," she said. "Do you want a scholarship?"

"I'm a qualified first-rank graduate of Hestia," Doctor Hamblin said. "That gives one of my children the right to study there, free of charge. I can pass that right on in exchange for Barbara's studies."

"Or she could have a scholarship," Sameena suggested. She could see why Hamblin wouldn't want his daughter to go to Hestia. It was right on the other side of Earth, nearly nine months away from Rosa. "There are always options that wouldn't force you to trade in your reward…"

"Maybe," the Doctor said.

Sameena looked back at Barbara. "Listen carefully," she said, and outlined the basic safety rules of living on a starship. She hadn't really known how seriously to take them when she'd stowed away, not until Ethne and Steve had gone through everything that could have gone wrong with her escape plan in considerable detail. "If you have problems coping with the rules, I suggest that you stay here."

Barbara looked nervous, but nodded firmly.

"And you won't be able to see your father again for months, if not years," Sameena added, grimly. "You may not even be able to send messages."

"I understand," Barbara said.

Sameena smiled, inwardly. *She* would have given up half her fortune to have her parents back, even though she knew that her mother would have been horrified at everything she'd done since travelling into outer space. Barbara had just recovered her father and yet she wanted to part from him again, immediately. Maybe she just wanted to be away from her homeworld for a while, where she'd been forced to grow up too quickly and play at being an adult. It was understandable, she supposed.

And Doctor Hamblin wasn't going to stand in her way.

"Very well," Sameena said, finally. She held up her hand before either of them could say a word. "I'll draw up the travelling and guardianship papers" – she scowled inwardly as she realised that meant that she would have to delay her departure – "and then you can both sign them. You might also want to review the legal issues surrounding such papers."

She looked at Barbara, wondering at the girl's enthusiasm. "You'll effectively be my daughter, at least until you graduate," she warned. "And there will be another guardian while you're on Madagascar. You'll have two people bossing you around."

Barbara giggled. "I get that a lot from father," she said. "And Fox, even though I was the doctor."

Sameena laughed. "You'll need to behave yourself anyway," she said. "And I *won't* be very good company on the trip."

Leaving them to make their goodbyes, she left the hospital and started to walk towards the landing strip nearest the ramshackle city. The shuttle was waiting there, ever since she had brought the remainder of the weapons down to the surface. She couldn't help thinking that Rosa was going to have problems even though the governor was now dead, but at least it would have a chance to bloom without him. Her production plants might help.

But the settlers didn't want to turn their backs on the universe, she thought, sourly. *Not like Jannah's founders, who wanted to pretend that the universe didn't exist.*

"Hey," a voice called. "Wait up!"

Sameena spun around, one hand reaching for her pistol…and stopped when she saw Ginny limping towards her. The former captive still looked bruised and beaten, although Sameena suspected that her life was no longer in real danger. Half of her face seemed to be frozen; the remainder seemed to be curved up in a twisted smile.

"I wanted to thank you," Ginny said, as she staggered to a halt. "You saved us all."

"You're welcome," Sameena said. She found it hard to even *look* at her. Under the dim lighting of the prison cell, she hadn't realised just how badly Ginny had been hurt. "Do you want to go into space too?"

Ginny gave her an odd look. "No, why?"

Sameena shook her head. "Never mind," she said. "Did you find your family?"

"Two of my brothers are dead," Ginny admitted. "The others were all up in the hills, fighting. It may be a long time before we get back to farming."

She shook her head. "I would have died too, without you," she added. "Do you know that some of my wounds were infected? I might have died within the week."

Sameena wasn't surprised. The prison had been extremely unsanitary. Islam prized hygiene – Steve and Jayne had explained why, when Sameena had first started to work on the waste disposal tubes – but Desiree hadn't cared about what happened to the prisoners under her care. It was sobering to reflect that she'd actually gotten off very lightly, compared to some of the other prisoners. The handful of reports she'd heard had been shocking. Male and female prisoners had been abused, raped and murdered, without restraint.

"The governor must have gone mad," she said, softly. How many more people in positions of power would go mad when they realised that the Empire was no longer there to enforce its laws? "I am glad you survived."

"Me too," Ginny said. "They caught up with the Colonel, you know. Silly bitch tried to plead instead of running. Her former prisoners tore her apart,"

Sameena shuddered. The capital city had been wracked by revenge killings, despite the best that Fox's men could do. One by one, those who had served the governor had been killed, thrown into a penal camp…or forced to flee into the countryside. The mob hadn't calmed down for three days, during which time hundreds of people had died. Some of them had simply been the victim of personal vendettas and hadn't had anything to do with the governor.

"Good," she said, finally.

She watched Ginny limping off, then turned and walked towards the landing strip, shaking her head sadly. The space-born seemed to know the limits from birth, growing up as they did in an immensely dangerous environment, while the groundhogs seemed quite willing to run riot whenever they were even slightly displeased. Jannah was no different, she knew; if the Guardians branded someone a disbeliever – or worse – the howling mobs would form and the victim would die. Law and order died when the mobs ruled the streets. Anyone even the slightest bit unpopular might become a target.

Inside the shuttle, she downloaded a copy of the standard contract from the starship and then altered it slightly to suit Barbara's particular circumstances. Technically, the girl was too young to take on an apprenticeship, but her father's high rank would ensure that would be overlooked. It was odd to realise that a graduate from Hestia would be working on a stage-one colony world, rather than Earth, yet Sameena found it hard to blame him. She couldn't see any way in which the crash of Earth could be averted. Anything the Grand Senate might try would only trigger the crash earlier.

She finished writing out the contract, copied it to her datapad and stood up to go find a printer. There was no real datanet on Rosa, not even a basic emergency system. It was strange – very few worlds lacked an emergency datanet, even if it was forbidden to the average citizen – but yet another sign of decay. She'd have to give them both a printed copy to make it legal. Once, the whole concept of printing a document would have awed her. Now, it just seemed far too primitive for words.

Laughing at herself, she left the shuttle and headed back towards the Imperial Library, where she should be able to get the contract printed out. If nothing else, taking Barbara onboard would save her from brooding – and she knew that she would have brooded all the way to Madagascar, if she'd been completely alone. Brad might be dead, but she would still feel his presence looking over her shoulder. And she knew that she would have to tell his parents.

She wasn't looking forward to that at all.

CHAPTER
TWENTY-THREE

> Even when the government was not communist (or fascist) the results of interference in the marketplace could be dire. The influx of money from the government (which came from taxpayers, which further damaged the economy) often warped the marketplace. For example, an unprofitable product could be continued because it was being funded by outside sources, rather than its own profits (or lack thereof).
>
> - Professor Leo Caesius, *The Science That Isn't: Economics and the Decline and Fall of the Galactic Empire.*

The marriage contract was simple, yet elegant.

She took it out of Brad's safe once *Lead Pipe* was in phase space and read it carefully, unable to avoid wondering just when Brad had drawn it up. It granted both parties certain rights over the other, acknowledged any children as their mutual heirs and even provided a framework for separation, should the marriage not work out. The only thing missing was any provision for extramarital lovers, which made her smile sadly. Brad had been more of a romantic than anyone had guessed.

Brad's signature at the bottom, accompanied by his thumbprint and a drop of blood, mocked her. He'd intended to court her – and he'd had faith that he would succeed. Or, perhaps, he'd set the whole thing up in the belief that she would need it after his death. He was smart enough, unlike some men, to anticipate the possibility. She felt another pang of grief and rage as she read the contract one final time, trying to decide what to do. It felt like a crude parody of a marriage.

She'd always had mixed feelings about the whole concept. Marriage on Jannah was for life – at least for the woman. It was a rare court that would grant a woman separation from her husband, let alone custody of her children. And marriages were almost always arranged by the parents, with neither party having much say in the affair. For every marriage that worked out – and her parents had come to love one another – there were several that were permanent battlegrounds, or so cold it was a wonder they didn't freeze. She'd known that she didn't want such a marriage, but she'd also known that she might not have a choice. One day, her father would have had to marry her off.

Marriage in the Empire was different. There was no taboo on pre-marital sex or on divorcé, ensuring that marriages were rarely permanent. It seemed to cheapen the concept if a couple could marry on Monday, fall out on Wednesday and separate on Friday. And the traders used marriage as a way of binding people together, at least as long as they shipped together. She had been unable to avoid wondering if Paddy and Jayne would one day separate without recriminations. It was a question that she had never dared ask.

And then…she looked down at the contract, feeling bitterness seeping through her soul. All it would take was a signature, a thumbprint and a drop of blood…and she would be Brad's wife, a woman married to a dead man. There would be trouble, she knew; the banks would know that she'd married him to ensure that she inherited the ship. And she wasn't even sure that she *wanted* the ship. *Lead Pipe* belonged to both of them. Now that Brad was gone, part of her wanted to find a new freighter. She could…

…But that would have felt like a betrayal.

My father would complain, she thought, as she signed her name to the contract. *He would certainly protest the marriage.*

She couldn't help smiling at the thought, although she knew that none of the traders would understand. On Jannah, a woman's protector – her father, her brother or her husband – would be required to countersign any contract she entered into, particularly marriage. Sameena could not have married *anyone* without her father's consent. But as a trader, she had freedom the moment she came of age. She could legally marry anyone she wanted.

The contract seemed to glow faintly as she pricked her finger and added a drop of blood to the paper, then placed it back in the safe. She had to be imagining it, she told herself as she stood up and looked around the cabin. Brad's clothes, his tiny collection of books and dozens of datachips lay everywhere, as if he'd just nipped out to go to the bridge and would return at any moment. Sameena sat down on his bunk and put her head in her hands, feeling an aching sense of loss that threatened to overcome her. She would have given up her entire fortune to see him again.

"I'm sorry," she whispered, quietly. "I'm so sorry."

There was a photo album on his table, she saw. She picked it up and flicked through it, realising that Brad had collected and printed out photos of himself as a growing man. Brad as a child, with a pair of babies that had to be James and Jayne; Brad wearing his first set of overalls over his shipsuit; Brad and his family in front of a shuttle, waiting to go up to orbit; Brad with a set of men and women she didn't recognise; Brad wearing a full-sized shipsuit; Brad and Sameena, standing together when they'd transferred to their new ship…when had *that* been taken?

She put the album down and forced herself to stand up and leave the cabin. It was her duty, as the starship's commander, to go through it, box up his possessions and store them until they could be passed on to his heirs. But she couldn't bear it, not now. It was something that would have to wait until they got to Madagascar. Once she stepped through the hatch, she closed and locked it behind her.

Barbara looked up at her in surprise as she entered the schoolroom. "Are you all right?"

Sameena scowled at the child. She really was astonishingly perceptive. "No," she said, sourly. "I'm not alright."

Brad hadn't been able to afford a full-sized tutoring machine for his ship, but thankfully she had progressed beyond having to need one. She picked up her datapad and tried to concentrate on Professor Sorrel's latest assignment, but her thoughts refused to focus on the aspects of Imperial Law as they related to interstellar trade. Instead, they kept coming back to Brad. He'd died…and part of her insisted that she could have saved him, if she'd done more. And yet, once they'd landed on Rosa, it had been out of her hands.

Barbara leaned forward and touched her arm. "Do you want to talk about it?"

Sameena almost slapped her as a hot flash of anger boiled through her mind. She didn't want to *talk* about it, she wanted to curl up and surrender to grief. And yet the part of her that was always cold refused to allow her to give up. Maybe talking about it would make it easier to handle…

"No," she said, firmly. "Why don't you tell me what happened on Rosa instead?"

Days passed as they travelled towards Madagascar. Much to her surprise, Sameena discovered that bringing Barbara along had been the right decision, even though the child was terrifyingly inquisitive. Talking to her, answering her questions – even if she refused to talk about Brad – prevented her from just slipping into her shell and giving up. Barbara kept her from being alone with her thoughts. And then there was the endless series of maintenance tasks that had to be carried out. Being busy helped push the pain aside.

"That's Madagascar," she said, two weeks after they left Rosa. The asteroid came into view slowly, hanging against the gas giant. It was almost as spectacular as she remembered from her first visit. "Welcome to a strange new world."

Barbara stared at the viewscreens, while Sameena tapped a switch and sent a pair of messages into the asteroid's datanet. One was to Professor Sorrel, asking him to start arranging Barbara's apprenticeship; the other was to Captain Hamilton. She wasn't going to send the news over the datanet when she could take it to him in person. And she would have to visit the banks, report *Lead Pipe's* change in ownership and pay the next instalment on Brad's debts. They'd be less likely to make a fuss, she figured, if they were still getting paid

"You need to remain onboard," she said, as they docked. Professor Sorrel had yet to reply to her, but Ethne had sent a message inviting her to visit *Logan*. "Do *not* try to leave the ship."

Barbara looked mutinous. Whatever she had thought the trip would be like, being trapped on the ship for two weeks had given the child a bad case of cabin fever. Sameena, who hadn't really felt it herself, found it hard to comprehend, but then she had led a very restricted life before fleeing her homeworld. Barbara had been used to the wide open skies.

"I won't," she promised, finally. "But please hurry."

Sameena felt nervous as she made her way through the spaceport to where *Logan* was docked. The last she'd heard from Ethne had been that *Logan* had accepted a series of semi-permanent contracts from the Imperial Navy, hauling supplies across the sector. It gave them steady work, even though she suspected that Captain Hamilton would be growing bored by now. The man had a wanderlust that drove him to visit new worlds and meet strange new people.

Stepping back onto the freighter felt like coming home. Ethne met her at the airlock, her face grim. She had to have guessed, Sameena realised; Brad would have visited his parents, if he'd still been alive. It was easy to believe that Ethne would hate her for Brad's death, or that she would be angry about the marriage contract. She'd brought good luck and bad to *Logan's* crew in equal measure.

Captain Hamilton was sitting in the galley, waiting for them. He looked older, somehow, despite the genetic engineering that gave him a distinguished image. Sameena swallowed hard, part of her tempted to turn and run. How could she face the man she had come to think of as a second father and tell him that his son was dead? But there was no way to escape the task. It was her duty.

"Brad…Brad is gone," she said, trying to get it out before she choked up completely. "They killed him."

Ethne caught her as her legs buckled. "Tell me what happened," she ordered, as she pulled out a stool for Sameena. "*How* did he die?"

Sameena found herself telling Brad's mother everything, starting with the contract to ship weapons to Rosa – Captain Hamilton sighed at that point – and ending with Brad's death in front of her. She half-expected them to hit her, or to throw her out of the airlock; it was odd to see them both sitting there, listening calmly. But death was an ever-present risk on a starship.

"He really did want to pay off his debts alone," Captain Hamilton said, finally. There was a note of grief in his voice that stunned her. "I was just the same. Poor brave foolish child."

"And his tormentors?" Jayne's voice demanded. "What happened to them?"

Sameena jumped. She hadn't even heard Jayne come into the compartment. "Dead," she said, turning her head to see Paddy and James standing behind Jayne. There was no sign of James's lover. "They killed them all."

"Good," Jayne said, darkly. Her husband took her arm and squeezed it. "And are *you* all right?"

"…No," Sameena admitted, miserably. "It was all my fault."

Captain Hamilton shook his head. "Brad knew the risks, but he was determined to make his own way," he said, softly. "It was not your fault. And at least you avenged his death."

And won us a new trading partner, Sameena thought. Somehow, the urge to keep building her little empire no longer seemed so strong.

She hesitated, then told them about the marriage contract. Jayne swore at her, Paddy seemed shocked…and Ethne nodded, thoughtfully.

"Good thinking on his part," she said. "I knew that he liked you enough to keep asking you to marry him – and it will help you immensely…"

Jayne caught at Sameena's shoulder, almost pulling her off the stool. "And did you fuck my brother's dead body?" Tears were streaming down her face. She'd loved Brad, far more deeply than Sameena had ever loved Abdul. "You had to wait until he was dead, didn't you?"

"*Jayne*," Ethne snapped.

"He *liked* you," Jayne snapped, ignoring her mother. "He could have had his pick of girls at the Meet – God knows that there was no shortage of girls who wanted to marry him – but he stayed with you, because he *liked* you. And he got killed because of you!"

Sameena felt bitter tears streaming down her face. Jayne was right, she knew; Brad *had* liked her and given up his chance of finding another wife to be with her. God knew that a starship captain would have had no difficulty in finding a wife, not during a Meet. But he'd stayed with her instead.

"That will do," Captain Hamilton said. His voice was quiet, but there was enough authority in his tone to penetrate Jayne's grief. "Brad's death was not Sameena's fault."

"But it feels that way," Sameena confessed. "I…"

"It will *always* feel that way," Paddy said, softly. "People will die near you; some under your command, some merely close to you. And you will always feel that you were to blame. It never gets any easier for decent souls."

Jayne glared at her husband. "More Marine claptrap?"

"Common sense," Paddy said. He gently pulled his wife towards the hatch. "We'll find a place to talk about this properly."

Sameena watched them go, wondering if she'd just broken their marriage. Jayne had been angry, lashing out in all directions…but would Paddy understand that? In her experience, men were rarely good at comprehending female emotions. Or vice versa, for that matter. But Paddy was a good man and old enough to be mature. Surely they wouldn't separate because of one row.

"There will have to be a funeral," Ethne said. "Brad wanted to be buried in space. And then I…"

"It wasn't your fault," Captain Hamilton said. "Don't ever forget that."

"I won't," Sameena said. But she knew that it was almost a lie. Part of her would always consider herself responsible for Brad's death. "I…I *liked* him too."

Ethne looked up at her. "Are you going to carry his child?"

Sameena hesitated. She'd done some research during the long flight from Rosa to Madagascar, reading up on legal precedents. There *were* injuries that could sterilise a spacer, despite the best medical technology in the Empire. All of the traders stored sperm and eggs at several different locations, ensuring that they could still have children. Jayne had even insisted that *Sameena* store a dozen of her eggs in a stasis tube, just to be safe. There would be no legal objection to her using her husband's sperm to get pregnant, even if he was dead.

And she didn't even have to *carry* the child. A child could be brought to term in an artificial womb, where it would receive all the care it needed – without inconveniencing the mother. It was yet another reason to curse Jannah's founders. When she thought about how much time a woman had to spend carrying a child, making it harder for her to do anything else…it galled her. One day, she promised herself, she was going to return to Jannah and force it wide open.

"I think so," she said. She felt an obligation to keep something of Brad alive, even if the whole concept still struck her as slightly perverse. But then, it wasn't as if they'd married after she'd become pregnant – or something else that would have marked them out as sinners on Jannah. "Should I?"

"You're his wife," Ethne said. "But I'd advise you to go talk to the banks first. They may have something to say about the whole affair."

Sameena frowned. "Why would they?"

"The price of starships has been going upwards over the last six months," Captain Hamilton said, gruffly. "So has the price of spare parts and almost everything else. There are strange rumours from the Core Worlds, hints of civil war…and Han seems to be on the verge of flaring up again. The banks may wish to take possession of *Lead Pipe* and sell her for a higher price."

"They will certainly call the marriage contract into question," Ethne added. "You need to be prepared for that. Get a lawyer who *isn't* related to you on standby, just in case."

Sameena nodded. "Thank you," she said. "And I'm sorry."

Ethne looked up, her eyes glistening with tears. "I have always thought of you as another daughter," she said. "And I think that Brad would come back to haunt us if we didn't acknowledge the contract."

Returning to *Lead Pipe*, Sameena found a message from Professor Sorrel inviting Barbara to apprentice with a trained and experienced doctor on Madagascar, if she passed her exams. The child seemed fascinated by her first glimpse of the asteroid, even though the exam was punishingly difficult and Sameena practically had to carry her back to the ship when it was completed. Professor Sorrel, thankfully, didn't seem to think that there would be any problems with the apprenticeship.

"She's bright and has some experience," he said. "She will need formal training, but her tutor can handle that. You'll have to arrange accommodations and suchlike for her before leaving her on the asteroid."

Sameena nodded. She'd already asked Lamina to find Barbara a room on the asteroid. She wouldn't be quite part of the refugee family, but they would take care of her. At least that would be one problem out of her hair.

The bank sued her two days later.

CHAPTER TWENTY-FOUR

And yet when the outside funds were withdrawn, the company simply crashed, unable to support its own weight. The results were often worse than if the government had stepped aside.
- Professor Leo Caesius, *The Science That Isn't: Economics and the Decline and Fall of the Galactic Empire.*

"It's a legal issue," Salazar Hernandez said.

Sameena scowled. Hernandez was a good lawyer – Ethne had recommended him, back when she'd founded her corporation – but he reminded her of too many of the clerics back on Jannah for her to relax in his presence. He was handsome, in a bland sort of way, old enough to look mature and responsible at all times. And he smiled too much.

"Your husband took out a quite considerable loan to pay for his ship," he explained. He seemed to feel the urge to explain everything, as if he was being paid by the word. "If your marriage is genuine, his shares in the ship would go directly to you; if your marriage was annulled, the shares would revert to the bank. They would effectively have a controlling interest in the ship."

His smile thinned down. "Normally, I would not expect them to raise any objection," he added. "You would have inherited his debt too and thus the bankers would still be paid. Now, however, they might make more if they resold the ship, hence their attempt to claim it back. No long-term thinking any longer, I fear."

Sameena couldn't disagree. The bankers seemed to be aware that the Empire was slowly drawing back from the sector, leaving them high and dry; they wouldn't be able to claim back their money once the Empire was gone. Making a quick profit, even at the expense of considerable goodwill, might be all they had left.

"Right," she said. "How exactly do they intend to challenge me?"

"By claiming that the marriage contract is invalid," Hernandez said, simply. "Given that you signed it after his death, they could make a case that the whole situation was invalid. He could no longer marry you. Alternatively, they could claim that you're lying about him insisting that you marry him – or that you even forged his signature on the marriage contract. I'm afraid that his death and the lack of consummation means that the marriage could be called into question."

"And if the marriage is annulled, the bank gets the ship," Sameena said. *She* would still have her shares, but not enough to prevent the bank selling the ship onwards. "How do we oppose them?"

"You'd have to ensure that there was no doubt over what actually happened," Hernandez admitted. "At worst, you would have to testify while under the influence of truth drugs."

Sameena scowled. She didn't mind testifying about Brad's death, but there were quite a few other details she didn't want to talk about, certainly not in public.

"The banks might also push for a flat ruling that the marriage is invalid," Hernandez added. "You need to be prepared for that too."

The case was heard two days later by Commodore Pollock, an elderly Imperial Navy officer who had been sent to Madagascar – according to Jamie – to keep him from doing any harm elsewhere. He looked as old and doddering as some of the men in the mosque, Sameena decided, but his eyes were bright and intelligent. She rose to her feet along with everyone else in the makeshift courtroom as he entered, glancing over at the bank's lawyers. They looked terribly shifty to her eyes.

"Please be seated," Commodore Pollock drawled. His voice sounded as ancient as he looked. "Lieutenant Singh?"

A dark-skinned woman wearing a white Imperial Navy dress uniform stood up. "The question before us concerns the validity of the marriage contracted between Brad Hamilton and Sameena Hussein," she said. "This court must decide if the contract should be upheld or annulled."

"Thank you," the Commodore said, as the Lieutenant sat down. He looked over at the bank's lawyers. "State your case."

The lead lawyer stood up. "Marriage is more than just a bond between two or more people who wish to live together," he said. "In our society, it serves to create relationships that handle family matters such as children, finances, inheritances and so much else. As such, it requires a complex series of contracts to hold it together. All parties involved must understand and agree to the terms of the marriage."

And pay you a great deal while you're at it, Sameena thought, cynically. Brad's contract had been relatively simple, others had been downright torturous to read. One of them had even attempted to dictate how many times the couple had sex each week. She could easily see why lawyers encouraged such detailed contracts, but it was harder to understand why everyone else put up with it.

"It is an aspect of such contracts that the people involved must be capable of understanding what they're doing," the lawyer continued. "A contract where one of the signers could prove that he or she was under the influence of drugs or conditioning would be rendered invalid. In this case, the male party to the marriage was quite definitely dead when the female party signed the contract. A dead man cannot enter into a marriage contract."

There were some titters from the spectators bench. Sameena felt the back of her neck heat, but somehow managed to refrain from turning to glare at them. Captain Hamilton had come to show his support, dragging his family with him, yet they weren't the only spectators. The others had come for the show.

"Tell that to my mother-in-law," someone muttered, loudly enough to be heard.

"Quiet," the Commodore snapped.

The lawyer continued without missing a beat. "Had *Miss* Hussein signed the contract without being aware of Captain Hamilton's death, it would be one thing," he said. "However, she signed in the full knowledge that he was dead – and that she would inherit the ship if she was taken to be his wife, rather than surrendering it to the bank. But she could not enter into a contract with a dead man."

He sat down, ignoring the muttered comments from the spectators.

The Commodore nodded to Hernandez. "Your response?"

Hernandez stood up. "My learned colleague is quite right; a dead man cannot enter into a marriage contract," he said. "However, the contract was signed by Captain Hamilton prior to his death – when he was alive, should there be any doubt about that." There were more snickers from the spectators. "He also verbally instructed my client to sign the contract before actually dying.

"Furthermore, my client does not deny that she has also assumed the responsibility for paying off the debts incurred by her husband. Had they been married for a year prior to his death, there would have been no doubt over the issue. She would have inherited the debts along with the ship. This has been proven in so many cases that I hardly feel the urge to point to specific incidents. In this case, the bank's seeming fear that they will not be paid is groundless."

Sameena kept her face under tight control. Hernandez had just exposed the bank's attempt at bullying her to the crowd, threatening its reputation. It wouldn't seem like calling in a debt any longer, if indeed it ever had. But the bank had a great deal of influence. It could still go either way.

"We acknowledge that your client has assumed the responsibility for paying off the debt," the lawyer said. "However, we do not consider the marriage as valid. Even though he did sign the contract before he died, she *didn't*. Would the contract still be binding if it was signed after his death?"

"That would appear to be the legal question facing us," Hernandez said. "However, in the case of *Putney V. Rushford*, it was clearly stated that a verbal agreement constituted a binding contract."

"Which leads to a simple question," the bank's lawyer said. He looked over at the Commodore. "I request permission to use truth drugs to determine if such a contract can be said to exist."

There was a long pause. "Understandable," the Commodore said, finally. "Have you submitted a list of questions to the defence team?"

"I have," the bank's lawyer confirmed. "And they have raised no objections."

Sameena couldn't help feeling nervous as the Imperial Navy's doctor approached her, carrying a small case in one hand. She'd been carefully briefed on the whole procedure by Hernandez; the doctor would ask the questions, sticking to the script that both lawyers had agreed. There would be no other questions without the Commodore's prior approval, which would mean delaying the trial. But she still feared that she could accidentally blurt out something she didn't want them to know.

"I need a blood sample," the woman said. She pushed a device against Sameena's wrist and held it there for a few seconds, then studied the results. "I confirm that there are no hints of anti-interrogation drugs in her bloodstream."

She gave Sameena a reassuring smile, then pressed an injector against her arm. Sameena felt a faint prick, then nothing. For a long moment, she was convinced that the drug was completely worthless…and then she started to feel almost dislocated from the universe around her, almost as if she was swimming underwater. When the questions started, she found herself answering without quite being aware of what she was saying.

It felt like hours before she felt herself falling back into her own body. "You did well," the doctor said. "Do you require a recess to compose yourself?"

Sameena shook her head.

"Very well," the Commodore said. "We shall continue."

"A case could be made that there was no true contract," the bank's lawyer insisted. "She did not *tell* him that she would marry him. Indeed, she hesitated for a long time after his death before signing the contract."

Sameena winced. A case could be made that she had acted very badly indeed, she knew, whatever Brad had said to her. But then, the bank couldn't come right out and accuse her of all sorts of crimes without admitting their true interest in the affair.

"But he practically begged her to sign," Hernandez countered. "They both knew that he wasn't going to live much longer."

The Commodore cleared his throat. "This case requires some careful thought," he said. "I suggest that all parties take a break. Rooms have been prepared."

"This way," Hernandez muttered, as the spectators stood up and headed out of the courtroom. He led her into a side room that, in theory, was sealed. "Do you want to review your performance under the drug?"

Sameena shook her head. Her head felt…funny, as if she was still partly under the influence. She wanted to go back to the ship to sleep it off, but she knew that wasn't going to happen. If the bank won the case, the ship would be sealed and she wouldn't be able to retrieve anything without their permission. And she would certainly face *some* charges for effectively forging a marriage contract. If she'd known how much trouble Brad's dying wishes were going to cause…

I would probably have carried out the first one anyway, she told herself.

Hernandez glanced down at his datapad. "The bank's lawyers are already having words with Admiral Villeneuve," he said. "They probably want him to put pressure on the Commodore to see things their way."

Sameena gritted her teeth. Was her life always to be dominated by older men making deals behind the scenes?

"Right," she said. Cold determination flowed through her. "And can we get him to see things *our* way?"

"Officially, I could not condone bribery," Hernandez said. "Unofficially, it would have to be something fairly substantial. The Admiral has quite a few family connections with the Grand Senate."

Very substantial, Sameena thought. The Grand Senators were wealthy enough to buy entire sectors out of pocket change. Sameena's little empire would vanish without trace in the vast interstellar corporations they'd built up to support their position. But she did have something the Admiral might want…

"Call him," she ordered. "Tell him that I want to talk."

She recalled what Jamie had told her about his nominal superior officer and smiled inwardly as he was shown into her room. He spent most of his time in the pleasure dens, leaving the station's management in the hands of his XO…and he was deeply corrupt. Quite a few consignments of spare parts had gone missing while he'd been in charge. Nothing had been proven, of course. It would be a brave investigator who brought a complaint against a Grand Senator's relative, no matter how distant.

Admiral Villeneuve certainly *looked* corrupt, she decided. He was fat, wearing a perfectly-tailored uniform that couldn't quite hide the bulge and eyed her as if she was something on the table waiting to be devoured. Given a chance, she realised, he would be quite as unpleasant as Colonel Desiree. The rumours she'd heard about some of the more…extreme pleasure dens had chilled her to the bone.

"Miss Hussein," he said, with a half bow. "I must say that the case against you looks quite bad."

He was *definitely* angling for a bribe, Sameena decided, as Hernandez left them alone. "I told the truth," she said. "Your own doctor confirmed that."

"So she did," Admiral Villeneuve said. He gave her a lopsided smirk. "What can I do for you – and what can you do for me?"

Sameena winced, fighting down the urge to giggle. He wasn't even trying to hide what he was doing. It galled her to offer bribes, even though they had been a fact of life on Jannah and still were on Tabasco. But she couldn't think of an alternative.

"I can offer you a consignment of Firewater Mead," she said, calmly. "Fifty bottles, to be precise."

His eyes went very wide. "*Fifty* bottles?"

"I have been stockpiling them for a rainy day," Sameena said. Fifty bottles concentrated in one place wasn't entirely unbelievable. He'd know that *something* was fishy if she told him that she had over five hundred bottles stockpiled. "Would you be interested?"

"I can ensure that no charges are pressed against you," the Admiral offered. "The bank would get the ship, but you would be a free woman."

Sameena shook her head, unable to believe the man's gall. He was trying to take *both* sets of bribes by satisfying both the bank and herself.

"Fifty bottles would also be enough to get me out of trouble," she pointed out. "You get the bottles in exchange for my marriage being confirmed and the bank told to go" – she stopped herself from using a very unladylike word just in time – "pound sand."

"They will still get the money your husband owed them," Admiral Villeneuve pointed out, snidely. He reached across and patted her knee. "I can't cancel that so easily."

"I never refused to pay," Sameena said. She kept her voice calm, despite his unwelcome touch. Was he hinting that he wanted more than just money – or mead? "All you have to do is ensure that my marriage is declared legal."

She watched the thoughts passing over the Admiral's chubby face. The bank had probably offered him money, but money was growing increasingly worthless. Fifty bottles of Firewater Mead, on the other hand, would go a very long way. And if they'd offered to cancel his debts instead…well, he could sell a few bottles and pay them back.

"I shall see to it," he said. His eyes narrowed until they almost vanished in folds of flesh. "But I should warn you that cheating me will prove to be very bad for your health."

Sameena said nothing as he left.

Hernandez entered a moment later. "What did you offer him?"

"Something *substantial*," Sameena admitted. It was quite possible that she'd overpaid the Admiral – and the worst of it was that she didn't even know if he would *stay* bought. "But you don't need to know the details."

"I suppose not," the lawyer said. "But ignorance isn't always a defence."

Ten minutes later, they were called back into the courtroom, where the Commodore briefly stated that he had consulted the precedents and decided that the marriage contract was borderline legal. Sameena would still be liable for Brad's debts, on his original schedule, but she would get to keep the ship. The entire courtroom erupted in cheers once he had finished speaking, leaving the bank's lawyer looking furious. Bankers were always necessary, but universally despised.

"They may try to move up the payment schedule," Hernandez warned. He sounded mildly amused at the prospect. "If they are pissed at you, and they will be, they might just push it forward. There's normally a clause or two in the original contract that would give them a facade of legality. The court decision could go either way."

Sameena shrugged. Between the money from Rosa and her earnings elsewhere she had more than enough to pay back the entire debt. Perhaps she would do it now, just to rub their noses in their defeat. They wouldn't be able to claim any further interest once the debt was paid. But Brad was dead. Nothing she could do would ever bring him back.

"I'll deal with it if it happens," she said.

Captain Hamilton made his way over to stand beside her. "You did well," he said. "But I'd suggest getting some sleep now. Come back to *Logan* and sleep."

Sameena nodded. Barbara was sleeping in her own room now, right next to the other refugees. *Lead Pipe* was empty...she'd have to see about getting more crew before she left the asteroid. She couldn't continue to handle the ship on her own. But taking someone else on would seem almost like betraying Brad.

"I'm coming," she said. There was so much she wanted to say, but she couldn't find the words. "Thank you."

CHAPTER TWENTY-FIVE

> More commonly, governments looked upon successful businesses as sources of revenue. A business could be taxed heavily to support government spending. However, these taxes could often prove another burden on the businesses, forcing them to either work hard to avoid the taxes by corrupting the law or collapse when they were unable to make their payments.
> - Professor Leo Caesius, *The Science That Isn't: Economics and the Decline and Fall of the Galactic Empire.*

"We are those who are truly free," Captain Hamilton said.

Sameena floated in space, wearing a spacesuit, and listened, feeling tears forming in her eyes. Hundreds of traders – and even some Imperial Navy officers and crew – had joined them for the ceremony. It was strange, very different from anything she'd seen on Jannah…and yet it was somehow fitting. They were sending a child of the universe back home.

"We live among the stars," Brad's father continued. "We are untouched by gravity or the oppression of planetary societies. We are born with a wanderlust that drives us onwards, beyond the furthest star. We move freely, making our living as we see fit, bowing to none. And when we die, we go back to the stars so that we may add all that we are to the light that pushes back the darkness. We are those who are truly free.

"My son was born heir to a civilisation that predates the Empire and will still be here when the Empire is gone. He grew up among the stars, moving from system to system and learning his trade. It was his dream to command his own ship, a dream he came to realise before his untimely death. In the end, we will remember him well."

There was a tiny flare as Brad's coffin began to drift towards the local star. It would be years, Sameena knew, before it was vaporised, returning Brad to the universe that had given him birth. The whole ceremony both puzzled and touched her. There was no mention of God or of an afterlife. But she found it hard to believe that God would think ill of the ceremony.

Her suit came to life, pushing her back towards Madagascar. The others joined her, swooping through the airlocks and into a place where they could remove the bulky suits and head into the meeting room. They wore nothing, but demure black shipsuits. Even Jayne was wearing something modest for a change. But she'd taken her brother's death hard.

There were a handful of tables inside, crammed with food and drink, and a band playing in the corner. Dancing in low gravity was an art form, Sameena had discovered; Brad had tried to teach her once, although she hadn't enjoyed it much. Now, she found herself wondering if she should dance in his name. He would probably have laughed at her if he'd still been alive.

She wanted to run as hundreds of people came up to her and offered their sympathies. Most of them assumed, she had discovered, that Brad and she had been lovers prior to his death, an assumption she had been unable to deny. They found his death and her struggle to have her marriage confirmed dreadfully romantic. She couldn't help feeling an urge to strangle them if they kept babbling at her. How *could* they treat it as a nice little story?

"Brad always hated these things," Steve said. He caught her arm and pulled her into a corner, then brought out a privacy field generator. "He would have wanted to leave immediately."

Sameena scowled. Space was an unforgiving environment; Brad had lost family to the cold darkness of space long before he'd met her. The spacers seemed to…accept death; they might work hard to extract all of the possible lessons they could from the incident, but they didn't deny its existence. Jannah, on the other hand, had simply been fatalistic. If deaths happened, they were the will of God.

"I want to leave," she admitted. A handful of people had even asked her if she meant to marry Steve, just to keep in the family. She'd had to hold herself back from slamming her fist into their noses. "But your parents wouldn't understand."

Steve nodded. "I thought you would like to know that we sent the first shipment of equipment to Rosa yesterday," he said. "Along with someone to draft out an ironclad contract, although it may be harder to enforce it. Give our factories the status of embassies, give them a share of the profits in exchange for complete freedom…and rights to mine the gas giant."

"Good," Sameena said. It was a relief to concentrate on something else for a change. "And the first shipments of spare parts?"

"They're being sold now," Steve said. "I think we might have started to uphold the economy ourselves, now."

"I know," Sameena said. Shipments of spare parts – and just about everything else – had been falling sharply over the last few months. The decline was becoming far too noticeable. "Can we meet demand?"

"Maybe," Steve said. "The problem is establishing enough factories. Mobile ships are useful, but we really needed fixed bases and we might as well paint targets on their hulls."

Sameena nodded. A factory on Rosa might be independent, technically speaking, but the Imperial Navy could still take it by force if they came knocking. Mobile factories didn't have that problem, but required very large hulls. Outside of colonist-carriers and military battleships, there weren't many ships large enough to carry an entire factory.

"We could set one up in interstellar space," she said, thoughtfully. "They'd never be able to find it unless they got very lucky."

"But they'd still have to bring in supplies and suchlike," Steve said. "The more people involved, the greater the chance of a disastrous leak."

"I think we'd better proceed anyway," Sameena said, remembering the simulations she'd worked out. It wouldn't be long until the cloudscoops started to fail, along with the atmospheric domes on a dozen uninhabitable planets. How many worlds had been founded on the comforting assumption that there would always be a supply of spare parts? "Time isn't on our side."

Steve nodded. "I've hired a number of additional freighters and their crews," he said. "We can start hauling stuff into interstellar space. And we have people on the lookout for more useful technology."

"And see what bargains we can make with other newly-independent worlds," Sameena added. "They'll all need a source of technology from off-world."

"I'll see to it," Steve promised. He looked over her shoulder. "I think Jayne wants a word with you."

Sameena turned to see Jayne standing there, with Paddy beside her. "Thanks," she said. She honestly wasn't sure if she wanted to talk to Jayne or not. "Let me know how you get on."

She stepped out of the privacy field and nodded to Jayne. "Thank you for your assistance," she said, quietly.

Jayne scowled. "Brad would have been amused, I think," she said. "You were too scared to go into his cabin."

Paddy elbowed her. "The Reading of the Will is about to be carried out," he said. "You're on the list of people who are supposed to be there."

Sameena winced, but followed them through the crowd and into a private room. Apart from the whole family, there were all four of the refugee women and a handful of people she didn't know. One of them introduced himself as the clan's representative, the others chose to remain anonymous. Once the hatch was shut, the representative checked names against a datapad and then flicked a switch. A holographic image of Brad appeared in front of them.

"My name is Brad Hamilton, son of Thomas and Ethne Hamilton," Brad's voice said. "This is my seventh last will and testament, superseding all previous last wills and testaments. I have been poked, prodded and certified to be of sound body and mind. There might have been some doubt about the last one."

Sameena felt a stab of guilt as she listened to the recording. "There are four separate tracks on this will," Brad continued. "The right one, according to the lawyer, will activate upon certain conditions being met. I trust that whoever is in charge of the circus will be able to handle it?"

His image smirked. "Well? Get on with it!"

The representative snorted, pushing a button to pause the playback. "I have selected the correct track," he said. "You will have a moment to register your objections once he has finished his introduction."

"Blimey, that took forever," Brad's image said. "I thought people would be dying to see my will – oops, sorry, bad joke."

Sameena fought down a giggle. Even in death, Brad was trying to cheer her up.

"More seriously," Brad continued, "this track is to be activated if I have married Sameena and my immediate family are still largely alive, but I have no children of my body. Well, technically *Sameena's* body…anyway, you get the general idea.. If those conditions have not been met, sack the guy in charge and then get a new one to supervise the rest of the recording."

There was a long pause. "Good," Brad said, finally. "Now, I'm dead – I trust that you have at least dealt with the body before looking at the will. Let's see now…Sameena, I loved you and wanted to marry you. I even drew up a contract, which you must have seen if you're looking at this recording. I hope we had a long time together before my death, but if not…don't go wasting your life after my death. Find someone reasonably decent and marry him."

He leaned forward, as if he were whispering a secret. "I should warn you that Steve has a dreadful habit of eating beans late at night," he added. "Don't let him court you."

"Hey," Steve protested.

"In any case," Brad's image continued, "I'm leaving you all of my personal possessions, apart from anything specifically mentioned in this will, and my shares in the ship. And good luck with your other plans.

"To my mother and father, I leave my shares in *Logan*, to be split equally between them," he said. "If they wish to pass them onwards, they may do so.

"To my brothers Steve and James, I leave my collection of books. If they can't come up with a fair division, Sameena can split them both into piles and Steve can pick one at random.

"To my sister Jayne, and her husband Paddy, I leave half of my bank account with instructions to start popping out kids. Jayne, Steve can't marry his engines and James isn't going to be producing kids, so it's up to you. And name one of them after me. Paddy, you've been a good friend and loyal shipmate ever since I met you; raise a glass in my honour, all right?"

There was a pause. Ethne and Jayne were both crying, their husbands doing their best to comfort them. Sameena felt cold ice wrapped round her heart, realising just how far Brad had dared to dream. And in the end, their marriage had been little more than a legal fiction to satisfy a court.

Maybe she should just have given up the ship and purchased a new one herself.

"I got to like Lamina and her friends and the kids have been growing up well," Brad said. "Accordingly, I leave them the remainder of my bank account, with orders that it be used to ensure that the kids have the best possible start in life. I hope they manage to find work well away from their godforsaken homeworld. With their training, they should never have to go back."

Sameena heard the women crying behind her, but ignored them.

"Well, I can't say much else," Brad concluded. "Just this…I loved my life. I wouldn't change it for anything. Goodbye."

His image vanished.

"That was the last will and testament of Brad Hamilton," the representative said. "I am obliged to warn you that he added the standard clauses forbidding any challenge to the will by any of the named beneficiaries or anyone acting on their behalf. Brad's estate…was not large enough to render such challenges fruitful. Should you wish to decline your bequests, please inform me by the end of the week. I'll distribute the bequests on Monday."

"Stay here," Paddy ordered, as everyone else started to file out of the room. "We need to talk to you."

Jayne waited until the door was closed, then looked back at Sameena. "Have you hired a new crew?"

Sameena shook her head. She'd never had to interview prospective crewmembers before and she'd been planning to ask Captain Hamilton's advice. Brad and she had been alone; as far as she knew, Brad had never even *considered* asking anyone else to join the crew. Between the court case and arranging Barbara's education, there hadn't even been time to advertise for newcomers.

"I…*we*…would like to sign up," Jayne said. She glanced over at Paddy, who nodded. "I'd like to be somewhere else for a while."

"Oh," Sameena said, surprised. She hadn't expected either of them to ever leave *Logan*. "I thought…"

"We can show you our resumes, if you like," Paddy said. He gave her a grin. "I am a qualified technician as well as a Marine. Jayne has a degree in navigation. You might find us useful."

"It looks that way," Sameena said. She hesitated. "I don't know where we will be going, though."

The thought made her scowl. She wanted to go see the mobile factory and inspect it for herself, but after that…part of her wanted to find a contract and go visit a whole new world. Who knew *what* opportunities there might be to expand her holdings…?

"That doesn't matter," Paddy assured her. "Just let us know before you take us into a war zone."

"I didn't know about the war zone on Rosa until it was far too late," Sameena confessed. In hindsight, there *had* been signs; they just hadn't noticed them. "But this time, there will always be someone left on the ship."

"Get some weapons too," Paddy added. "You can't really turn a freighter, even a fast light freighter, into a warship, but you can certainly deter pirates."

Sameena hesitated. Part of her knew that they would be a constant nagging reminder of Brad, but she also knew that she would welcome their company. "What about your current contracts?"

"I can buy them both out," Paddy said. "Once Captain Hamilton finds a new doctor and gofer, we can leave with a clear conscience."

"Then welcome aboard," Sameena said.

Jayne shook her hand firmly. "Are you going to have Brad's child?"

"I don't know," Sameena admitted. Somehow, hearing his last will had left her feeling unsure of herself. Would it be *right* to bring such a child into the world, knowing that she couldn't look after him or her properly? How had Captain Hamilton coped with his four children, to say nothing of Richard and Regina? "I just don't know."

"Be sure of your choice," Jayne said. "But you are building up a small trading empire. You're going to need a heir, sooner or later."

"I know," Sameena said.

Her father would have liked the thought, she suspected. He'd built a much smaller trading empire on Jannah; his daughter was building one out among the stars. And one day she would go home and see what had become of her family. It was a quiet resolution, one she'd kept to herself, but she intended to keep it.

She walked out into the main room, stared at the people drinking, dancing and singing as part of the wake, then turned and walked back towards her ship. Brad would have appreciated so many people coming, she suspected, but it wasn't her style at all. Instead, she found herself walking past the airlock and out to one of the observation blisters. It was facing away from the gas giant and its moons, allowing her to see the cold stars. Brad had been born amongst them, his father had said. And he'd died on one of the planet's the spacefarers had hated.

"I'm sorry," she whispered, quietly. It was tempting to believe that Brad had become part of the stars he so loved. "I'm so sorry."

"He was a decent person," Jamie's voice said. Sameena looked around to see him standing in the hatch, wearing dark mourning clothes. Somehow, she'd missed him at the wake. "He deserved much better."

"Yes, he did," she said, shortly. Seeing Jamie gave her another pang of guilt. Brad had loved her and she'd never seen it, not really. Her own feelings were still a conflicting mess. "I will miss him."

Jamie smiled. "Rumour has it that you bribed the Admiral," he said. "No one is quite sure what to make of it."

"Me neither," Sameena admitted. "Why are you here?"

"I've been offered a promotion if I stay in place," Jamie admitted. "A jump forward to Commander – up two full grades. Apparently, two of my superiors have decided that they want to go right back to Earth and there won't be any replacements."

Sameena felt a flicker of sympathy. The promotion did seem like a poisoned chalice, under the circumstances. "What about the Admiral?"

"He's gone back to the pleasure dens," Jamie said. "But his XO is on the list of people to be relocated back to Earth, soon. I don't know what's going to happen then."

Sameena looked back out at the stars. It wouldn't be long before the Imperial Navy supply lines collapsed. At that point…she would start offering them her supplies and then…who knew *what* could happen then?

But as she looked at the stars, they seemed to grow fainter…

It was an optical illusion, she knew. And yet it still sent a shiver down her spine.

INTERLUDE TWO

They were not very promising candidates, Commodore Steven Philly told himself, but beggars couldn't be choosers, certainly not beggars who happened to be under sentence of death if the Imperial Navy ever caught them. There had been a slight accident when he and the unit training funds had taken the wrong direction, leaving behind enough evidence to frame a young officer for theft and murder. He still didn't know how they'd worked out that he'd survived, but he dared not go back to the Core Worlds. There weren't many positions for former training officers along the Rim. Beggars definitely couldn't be choosers.

He eyed the line of prospective naval crewmen doubtfully. They were *shockingly* ignorant, even by the lax standards of entry-level Imperial Navy crewmen, but they had a sense of entitlement that rivalled the scions of the Grand Senate. Many of them were happy to dress up in fancy uniforms and prance around as if they were trying to impress the girls – a moot point as there were no girls on the base – yet most of them weren't even *trying* to pick up the basics. And they were intending to be officers!

God knew the Imperial Navy had been working hard to compensate for a lack of basic education for years, but this was absurd. Half of them couldn't even read or speak Imperial Standard, even though just about everyone in space spoke it as their second tongue. And it was hard to motivate them to do any real *work*. The concept of serving before leading was utterly foreign to them. Even switching out one solid-state component and replacing it with another was nearly impossible.

And they didn't take him seriously, even when one of their officers was supervising training sessions. They didn't listen, they looked down on him…and they chose to disregard everything he taught them at the worst possible time. By now, even Prince Roland himself would have been kicked out of the Imperial Navy Academy if he'd pulled half of the shit they'd pulled. Didn't they even have the sense to stop and listen to the NCOs?

It was God's own miracle, he decided, that the tiny flotilla of destroyers hadn't destroyed itself long ago. Ramming an asteroid or another starship accidentally was almost impossible, but the crews had very nearly managed to do just that. And then there were the problems with the life support units…if he'd been allowed a completely free hand, he would have hired mercenaries or starship crews to handle the ships, or at least perform basic maintenance. As it was, he wouldn't have cared to take the flotilla up against a single Imperial Navy destroyer, even at five-to-one odds. The crews were just pathetic. And they didn't even *know* it.

But he was being paid a hefty paycheck to get them ready for action.

Damn it, he thought, bitterly.

He should never have taken the job, he knew, but he hadn't been offered much of a choice. The promise of vast payment, a new identity and other perks – and the unspoken threat of handing him over to the Imperial Navy – had convinced him. And he'd needed the cash desperately. It had stopped him asking questions; indeed, no questions had been one of the terms of his contract. He didn't even know where the crewmen came from. Or why they were so…unconcerned when one of the little idiots did something stupid like accidentally walking out the airlock. Or why they held their enemies, whoever they were, in absolute contempt.

But in the end, he hoped he would never have to join them in battle.

He didn't know if they frightened the enemy, but he knew they frightened him.

CHAPTER
TWENTY-SIX

Government added yet another issue to supremely-complex economies. In order to avoid civil unrest, governments were forced to spend money on 'bread and circuses' – social security networks, in modern terms – to provide a safety net for their population. However, these safety nets became more and more expensive, forcing the governments to spend more…and thus collect more from sources of revenue.

- Professor Leo Caesius, *The Science That Isn't: Economics and the Decline and Fall of the Galactic Empire.*

Director Quemoy didn't look happy – but then, he had good reason to be very unhappy indeed.

"This contract is quite harsh, Captain," he said, as he signed it. "But we seem to have no choice."

Sameena nodded. Marigold's Folly orbited alarmingly close to its parent star, a tidal-locked burned ember of a world that would have been completely useless, save for the rare raw materials that could be found under its blackened surface. Over the years since the mining station had been established, it had grown into a small community, largely buried beneath the surface. But, without constant supplies from the outside universe, it was simply unsustainable. The corporation that ran the station had largely abandoned it, leaving the miners and their families to die. It had been sheer luck that she'd realised what was happening in time to intervene.

The contract was simple enough. Marigold's Folly would supply her growing industrial base with raw materials, mined from the surface of the planet. In exchange, her freighters would ship in food, spare parts and anything else the locals might need. She also intended to run internships through Marigold's Folly, although *that* might be a long time in coming. Most of the miners knew almost nothing about how their technology worked, despite its simplicity.

"No, you don't," she said, softly. The founding corporation had deliberately crippled the planet's development. They hadn't even included an algae farm. If interstellar trade broke down completely, the miners would have starved to death. "But I have no intention of treating you any worse than the corporation."

She smiled inwardly. Marigold's Folly was the ninth world to sign up to her growing trade empire, an empire that largely existed outside the Empire's awareness. With the big corporations pulling out, something had to take their place if *anything* was to survive. Given time, Sameena calculated, she would be ready to keep at least one sector going. And, once she was established, she could keep expanding into the ruins of the Empire.

The Empire had relied on physical force – directly or indirectly – to keep planets in line, even though it was pushing the Empire towards collapse. Sameena had a different idea. The colony worlds could have full control over their internal affairs, but *she* would control interstellar shipping and production. It would give her a formidable position without needing to resort to force. Or so she hoped.

"That's good," the Director said. "And thank you."

Sameena felt a twinge of guilt. Her walk through the domes on the dark side of the world had convinced her that the mining station was breaking down. The miners were nervous; their food stocks had been rationed for months, while there had been no visitors from outside the solar system. Sameena couldn't blame them – or their wives and children – for panicking, not really. Their world's life support system was on the verge of breaking down.

The Director wasn't a bad man, according to her contacts. He hadn't *asked* to serve as the final director of the mining station, abandoned – like the rest of the crew – by the corporation he had served. But he had to know that law and order were on the verge of breaking down, threatening to rip the station apart. A single riot might kill them all.

"You're welcome," she said, standing up. "I'll have the food supplies transported to the surface at once."

She'd never quite lost the thrill that came from seeing strange new worlds, even though what little she could see of Marigold's Folly looked identical to Madagascar and a thousand other asteroids. Corridors hewed through rock, massive chambers that had become everything from bedrooms to dining halls, all illuminated by flickering lights that seemed permanently on the verge of burning out. Their supplies of HE3 were running low too, she knew. If they ran out completely, the power would die and they would suffocate in the darkness. The corporation hadn't even bothered to introduce the oxygen-producing grass that carpeted the floors of most asteroids or settlements on airless worlds.

The Empire hadn't *quite* regarded Marigold's Folly as a penal world, but it *had* seen it as a dumping ground. Reading between the lines, Sameena had concluded that many of the women sent to the outpost had been refugees or convicts, purchased by the corporation and treated as slaves. Some of them had married miners and had relatively good lives, others had been forced into brothels where they serviced the unmarried miners. The Empire simply didn't care.

"There's little else for them to spend their money on," the Director said, when she asked. "Miners spend two weeks down in the darkness or in exploration vehicles, probing for new seams of ore. And then they come back and blow their cash on alcohol, women and song."

Sameena scowled. The miners had been trapped on Marigold's Folly even before the corporation had abandoned them. Their contracts ensured that, no matter how much money they made, they could never really hope to pay off their debts and leave the planet. The whole system was thoroughly rigged, she'd discovered. On the surface, the miners were paid well…but they were charged for each and every little thing. They had no hope of escape, so they wasted their savings. What else did they have to do with their lives?

She caught sight of a handful of children and shuddered. There were no tutoring machines on Marigold's Folly and certainly no teachers. Kids learned what they could from entertainment programs, all the while growing up into replacement miners who didn't even know what they were missing. The corporation, she realised grimly, must have seen it as a chance to make their workforce self-sustaining. But most of the kids had no hope of becoming more than grunt workers, if that.

I could do something about that, she told herself. *And about the women.*

They reached the shuttlebay without incident, despite a handful of angry stares that were directed at them from the off-duty miners. Sameena shook hands with the Director, pretended to ignore the wistful look he cast at the shuttle and stepped inside, breathing a sigh of relief as she tasted the shuttle's air. It was dry, but sweet compared to the colony's atmosphere. The growing stench outside suggested that the atmospheric scrubbers were beginning to break down.

She sat down in front of the console, catching sight of her reflection. Brad's death had left scars on her soul, scars that she could see on her face. Even two years after his death, she still missed him – and blamed herself. It would have been so easy to slip him a contract without him ever realising just who he was working for.

"He signed the agreement," she said, keying a switch on the console. "You can tell Ivan to send down the first shuttle now."

"Understood," Paddy said. "Are you coming back up now?"

"In a few minutes," Sameena said. She wanted to relax before heading back up to orbit and supervising the unloading. She'd brought two medium freighters, crammed with food, from Rosa. Between them, there would be enough supplies to keep Marigold's Folly alive for another few months. "Have you heard from the survey team?"

"The raw materials seem to be of good quality," Paddy said. "Steve will be pleased."

Sameena smiled and shut down the connection. Mining in a gravity world was inherently inefficient, but the reward was worth the extra expense. Or so the founding corporation had judged. She allowed herself a long moment to relax and focus her mind, calculating and recalculating their course back to Madagascar. Steve was meant to be meeting her at the hidden industrial plant.

The shuttle shook, violently. Sameena sat upright, one hand going automatically to the pistol at her belt before remembering that she'd left it in the locker. Marigold's Folly didn't allow weapons on the surface. She stood up and glanced out of the viewport, cursing out loud when she saw the miners gathered around her shuttle. They were pushing at the hull, shaking it. What the hell were they doing?

She saw their desperate faces and knew the answer. They wanted to leave the planet, sensing – perhaps – that they had been abandoned. Sameena hesitated, unsure of what to do. Bare hands couldn't break the shuttle's hull, even if it wasn't starship hullmetal, but miners tended to have mining tools. A simple debonder would be enough to break through the hatch and allow entry. And it would render the shuttle unserviceable. She wanted to take off, yet the hatch overhead was still sealed. Opening it would kill the miners outside as the atmosphere raced out of the shuttlebay.

There was no sign of the Director – or the handful of security men he had to maintain order. She wasn't surprised. They weren't armed with anything more dangerous than stunners – the corporation had been nervous of people letting guns off inside the mining colony – and they would be heavily outnumbered. He had to know that letting Sameena be lynched would destroy the agreement he'd signed to supply his people, but he had few options. And he was probably dithering in his office.

Should have bought that suit of armour Paddy kept recommending, she thought, as she keyed the console. *Bare hands couldn't break that either.*

She activated the shuttle's loudspeaker. "Calm down," she ordered. She could hear her voice echoing even through the shuttle's hull. Outside, the miners grabbed at their ears, falling back from the shuttle. "Other shuttles are coming with food supplies. I suggest that you clear the shuttlebay so they can land."

The miners didn't seem convinced. Several of them wanted to try to break into the shuttle and take her hostage, it seemed, others merely wanted to get off-world. Sameena couldn't help wondering how carefully they'd thought the entire scheme through; if they'd damaged the shuttle, it wouldn't be able to get them up into orbit. And the starships would know that the shuttle had been hijacked. Paddy would never let them board.

"This is pointless," she said, lowering the volume slightly. "There is no way that this shuttle can get you out of the system. You would do better to wait for the others to arrive with the food."

She turned off the loudspeaker and called Paddy, updating him on her situation. Paddy sounded unsurprised – he'd told her that miners could be brave and desperate, a dangerous combination – and offered to redirect the other shuttles. Sameena shook her head, then flickered another switch, powering up her own shuttle's engines. The miners started to fall back as they heard the sound.

"The hatch will have to be opened," Paddy said. "Have they taken control of the system?"

"Unknown," Sameena said. He was right. The shuttle was effectively trapped, unless she managed to blast the hatch open with her onboard weapons. And that would risk destroying her agreement with the colony. "Give me a moment."

She switched the loudspeaker back on. "The hatch is about to be opened so that the new shuttles can land," she said. "I strongly suggest that you vacate the shuttlebay, *now*!"

The miners hesitated, then started to walk back towards the airlock. Sameena let out a sigh of relief, even though their expressions promised ill for the future. They still felt abandoned by society. How could she blame them? They *had* been abandoned by the Empire.

"I'm dreadfully sorry about this," the Director's voice said, over the radio. "I didn't realise that they were on the verge of losing control."

"Glad to hear it," Sameena said. She wasn't in the mood to be diplomatic. "Open the hatch so that the shuttles can land, then start unloading. And I suggest that you provide all of your security officers to defend the crews. I will not put my people at risk."

She boosted the shuttle out of the shuttlebay as soon as the hatch opened, looking down on the handful of domes as the shuttle clawed its way upwards. Unlike Jannah – and almost every other Earth-like world – Marigold's Folly didn't spin, always presenting the same face to its parent star. She'd looked at the images from the light side and seen rivers of molten metal flowing across the landscape, while the dark hemisphere was cold – or at least as cold as the planet ever got. All of the human settlements had been established on the dark side of the planet.

"The shuttles are landing now," Paddy said. "I suggest that we bring heavier escorts next time."

"Sure," Jayne's voice said. "Like the entire 1st Marine Division, for one thing."

Sameena snorted. It was unlikely that the Empire, at the height of its power, would have spared an entire Marine division to distribute food to a mining colony. Now, thanks to Jamie, she knew that the Marines had been pulled out of the sector, along with most of the Imperial Army units. Paddy, retired as he was, might well be the only Marine for hundreds of light years. They'd have to bring some of Fox's men from Rosa or hire mercenaries. She wasn't keen on either idea.

She took the shuttle towards *Lead Pipe* and docked, then scrambled through the hatch and into her ship. The atmosphere definitely tasted better onboard ship. She'd grown up on a planet – unlike most of the traders – and yet she'd picked up their attitude towards planet-side life. But then, she *had* been comprehensively rejected by her homeworld. The other traders rarely stayed on any planet long enough to grow used to it.

"That could have gone better," Paddy said, as she walked into the galley. "Next time, take someone with you."

"I could take Jayne," Sameena pointed out. "What about that?"

Jayne snorted, patting her chest. Her pregnancy was only just starting to show. Sameena had wondered why she hadn't moved the child to an artificial womb, but when she'd asked Jayne had told her that every woman should have at least one child naturally. Paddy had – unsurprisingly – agreed with his wife, even though he was clearly worried about her. It wouldn't be long before Jayne would have to go on reduced duty or even transfer to an asteroid until she gave birth.

"Maybe not," Paddy said. "We have to take care of her."

Jayne elbowed him sharply. Sameena hid her amusement with an effort; Paddy seemed very solicitous of his wife, which appeared to irritate Jayne, even though she was pregnant. There were times when she seemed to relax into his care and times when she was annoyed that he felt the urge to wrap her in cotton wool and protect her from the universe outside. It made her wonder how Brad would have treated her if they had ever lived together as husband and wife, even though the thought no longer hurt so badly.

"I thought so," Sameena said. "And someone has to stay here to provide supervision."

"Just you wait until your next physical," Jayne muttered, darkly. "I can *really* make it uncomfortable."

Sameena shrugged and picked up the datapad. The unloading was, much to her relief, going quite well. Marigold's Folly *would* survive, at least for another few months.

"I wouldn't be so sure," Paddy predicted, when she said that out loud. "These colonies are always run very close to the margin. The slightest delay in shipping could cause major problems, maybe even push them over the edge."

"We'll have to ship in some algae-production facilities," Sameena agreed. "Help them to become a little more self-sufficient."

"Or start evacuating the miners," Paddy added. "Or even just the kids. Rosa might want to take some of them, if the scholarship program doesn't have room for them."

Sameena allowed herself a smile. The scholarship program was starting to pay off, even if the rewards – as she'd told herself earlier – didn't come in money. Some of the graduates could tutor new students, which allowed the entire program to expand rapidly. Given enough time, she was sure, she would have a small army of workers, starship crewmen and other educated personnel.

"Maybe," she said. She doubted that the miners would fit in on Rosa, although it was possible that they might be retrained to mine the asteroids or moons instead. The plan for producing a new cloudscoop for the system was still in its planning stage. "But that will have to wait."

The unloading was completed without further incident, allowing all of the shuttles to return to their ships. As soon as they docked, Sameena took the small flotilla out of orbit and headed directly for the Phase Limit. Paddy debriefed the shuttle crews, getting their impressions of Marigold's Folly, then passed their words to Sameena. They hadn't seen anything that contradicted her thoughts on the planet.

She kept a sharp eye on the sensors – pirate attacks had been increasing as the Imperial Navy withdrew from the sector – but nothing appeared as they crossed the Phase Limit. Sameena ran one final set of checks on the drive, then powered it up and jumped into Phase Space. It would be two weeks before they reached Madagascar. By then, she wanted to have the next stage of her plan carefully worked out.

"Steve will definitely be pleased," Paddy said, as he sat down beside her and passed her a datapad. "He was saying that he needed more raw materials."

Sameena nodded. They would have to ship the raw materials through interstellar space in any case. Using Marigold's Folly ensured that they wouldn't have to mine for themselves, although she had no intention of becoming dependent on any one source. It would have been lethal, particularly if the next riot actually destroyed the processing facilities on the planet's surface.

And becoming dependent on a handful of suppliers had crippled the Empire.

CHAPTER TWENTY-SEVEN

> This created a vicious cycle whereupon increased government demands would lead to collapsing businesses, more people out of work and ever-increasing numbers of people demanding access to the social safety network.
> - Professor Leo Caesius, *The Science That Isn't: Economics and the Decline and Fall of the Galactic Empire.*

The junkyard was a depressing sight. There were upwards of two hundred starships in various states of disrepair, thousands of pieces of debris and ancient equipment and countless items that had never been properly catalogued. Sameena stared out of the viewing port and wondered, absently, why so much had simply been abandoned. It could have been used until it collapsed into dust.

"Heartbreaking," Steve said, coming up behind her. His face was very grim. "You'd be surprised how much of the equipment is still workable."

Sameena wasn't. Space wasn't a planetary environment. Vacuum didn't really damage starship components, no matter what it did to living beings. The starships had effectively been frozen in stasis since they had been abandoned, once their former owners had seen no further use for them. And much of the equipment was in the same state.

"They cannibalised quite a bit over the years," Steve added. "Some of these ships will need a complete refitting before they can fly again. But it can be done. The real problem lies in some of the more sophisticated equipment. We haven't been able to crack the access codes."

"Blast," Sameena muttered, quietly. "What were they thinking?"

But she knew the answer. The corporations that had built the equipment had encoded protections into their systems, making it impossible to use them for anything other than their designated purpose – assuming that they could be used at all. Much of the older equipment didn't have such protections, or they could be easily broken, but they tended to be less efficient than the newer tools.

The Imperial Navy-issue military production equipment had the same problem. There had been quite a few pieces lying around the junkyards, which had puzzled Sameena until she'd discovered that it was effectively useless without the right codes. She'd given some thought to obtaining them, but she hadn't been able to think of a workable method that wouldn't be far too revealing.

But even without the codes, the production lines were coming online, she reminded herself. They *were* inefficient – and the spare parts would often need to be replaced quicker than the spare parts from the Core Worlds – but they were all the sector had, now that shipments from the Core Worlds had almost ground to a halt. Her supplies were all that stood between the sector and complete collapse.

She looked back towards the junkyard and remembered walking through one of the abandoned starships. Even in a heavy spacesuit, the sight had been chilling, a reminder of what might happen if the Empire collapsed completely. What if there were *no* more production facilities, ever? Interstellar trade would fall apart so completely that nothing would be left, but a handful of low-tech worlds. She told herself that was an exaggerated fear, but in truth she didn't know. Some of the whispered reports from the Core Worlds spoke of civil war and massive bloodshed, with the Empire in full retreat. There was no way to know for sure.

"The kids are doing very well," Steve added. "You did good."

Sameena had to smile. Training the refugee children had *definitely* been one of her better ideas. Steve now had an expanding workforce, which was paid the best wages in the sector if they didn't want shares in Sameena's corporation. And the more students it trained, the faster it could expand. Thanks to her, Professor Sorrel had opened up an entire training school.

"Thank you," she said, softly. "Have there been any unexpected problems?"

Steve shrugged. "We found a dead body in one of the ships," he said. "It had been dead for at least three hundred years. There was no record of the man's existence when we ran his prints through the database, so we gave him a funeral and launched his body into the sun."

He shrugged. "Other than that…there has been some interest in our operation from the Imperial Navy."

Sameena felt her eyes narrow. She hadn't expected the operation to remain secret indefinitely, particularly now that the sector was effectively cut off from Earth. The traders might sneer at the Imperial Navy, but it did have an excellent window into trader activities, merely by monitoring places like Madagascar and Tabasco. And she had a feeling that Jamie's superiors would be becoming desperate.

"Ah," she said, keeping her voice under firm control. "That's the sort of thing that should probably be mentioned first."

Steve shrugged, apologetically.

Sameena sighed. "What *sort* of interest?"

"Some of our people were questioned during their visit to Madagascar," Steve said. "And they've been running ships past the junkyard ever since we bought the place outright. I think they think we're up to more than simply striping the junked ships apart for cannibalised supplies."

"But no overt threats," Sameena mused. "Or attempts to seize our ships."

"I don't think they know about the mobile factory," Steve said. "But the more factories we set up on other worlds…"

Sameena cursed, inwardly. This might be the most dangerous moment, no matter how carefully she'd tried to plan for it. They'd been noticed…before the Empire was too weak to do more than irritate them. If the massed power of the Imperial Navy was brought to bear against her, it would smash her like a nut under a sledgehammer.

"I know," she said. "How many people have moved back from the factory?"

"None," Steve said. "Once we started providing entertainments, few people wanted to actually *leave*."

Sameena shook her head. How much did the Imperial Navy *know*?

She worked it out, slowly. They might well have slipped an agent in with the crews Steve had hired – and if that agent hadn't gone to the interstellar factory, he might well have managed to report in at some point. Or they might have tried to track one of the freighters that made up the distribution network…or they might just have seen the new supplies of spare parts and put two and two together. There was no way to be sure.

"Tell everyone to beware," she said, finally. The mobile factory could be moved, but the factories they'd set up in interstellar space couldn't be hidden so quickly. "We'll have to see what they want."

She was still mulling it over when she docked at Madagascar and strode onto the asteroid, keeping a sharp eye out for possible spies. As always, she drew some attention from the asteroid's denizens – she was famous, if not for the right reasons – but she couldn't help noticing at least two people watching her. Both of them looked like experienced spacers, but they were wearing civilian clothes as if they found them uncomfortable. Did they come from the Imperial Navy? There was no way to be sure.

Lamina greeted her as soon as she walked into the eatery, waving her over to the backroom and pointing to a chair. The restaurant was doing a roaring trade, thanks to the cheaper shipments of meat and vegetables from Rosa; Sameena was quietly delighted that it had worked out so well. She'd even heard that Lamina was considering trying to start a chain of eateries across the sector, although *that* would be tricky. Only a handful of big corporations had ever managed to make it work.

"The kids are doing fine," she said, taking the other seat. She'd definitely blossomed since coming to space, becoming a hard-nosed businesswoman rather than a helpless refugee. "I assume that you'll want to see Brad?"

Sameena nodded. Brad Junior was – technically – her child, but her feelings towards him were mixed, to say the least. He'd been born from an artificial womb, raised on processed milk and cared for on the asteroid by his grandparents. Sameena felt almost nothing towards him, something that bothered her more than she wanted to admit. Perhaps Jayne had a point, she told herself whenever the guilt gnawed at her soul. Carrying the child herself might have helped her to develop feelings for him.

Or perhaps I'm just not the motherly type, she told herself. It didn't make it any easier to bear.

"Barbara has been taking quite good care of him when the grandparents are busy," Lamina assured her. "She's still young, but her master says that she will probably qualify as a basic doctor within the year and then can go on to take specialised courses that will prepare her for her future career. I think she was planning to stay in space rather than go back to Rosa – she still has nightmares, the poor little mite."

"Still?" Sameena asked. She was no stranger to nightmares, but they tended to fade away over the years. Or at least hers had. It bothered her that there were days when she couldn't remember what her father or mother had even *looked* like. "I knew she had nightmares on the ship, but now?"

"I think she should have chosen another career," Lamina said. "This one reminds her of what she had to do on her homeworld."

Sameena scowled. "I'll make time to see her," she promised, although there wasn't much she could do. She'd held Barbara on the ship during their flight to Madagascar, but she had barely seen the girl since. "Can you take me to Brad?"

Lamina nodded and led her through a hidden door, into the next section. They'd taken several apartments in the asteroid and added new doors, turning it into one vast apartment. A couple of refugee women had found husbands on the asteroid, but they had merely moved in rather than finding their own home. Sameena wasn't sure what to make of it. On Jannah, a woman would go live in her husband's house rather than the other way around.

Brad Abdul Hussein-Hamilton had surprisingly pale skin, despite his mother's dark complexion. His father's genes had obviously been quite strong, Sameena thought, as she looked down at her son. But he definitely had her dark eyes. He was going to be very handsome when he grew up. And yet she still felt nothing as she picked the child up and cradled him in her arms.

"He's growing like a weed," Ethne's voice said. She was sitting in the corner, playing with one of the older children. "You'll be able to take him with you in a year or so."

Sameena hesitated, looking down at her child. How could she tell Ethne – her mother-in-law, to all intents and purposes – that she felt little for the boy? That her first thought upon realising that she could take the child onboard ship had been that he would be a nuisance? It was wrong, she knew, and yet it was true. Perhaps, if Brad had lived…

She pushed the thought aside, angrily. There was no way she could admit that to anyone, let alone Ethne. The woman wouldn't understand. Her maternal instincts had led her to adopt Sameena; she wouldn't understand Sameena's rejection of her own child. Or, maybe, she would try to have the child taken away from her. If it wouldn't have destroyed her reputation, she wouldn't have considered that a bad option.

"Maybe," she said, reluctantly. Perhaps if she spent more time with her child, love and tenderness would blossom in her heart. She'd intended to hire more crew; perhaps Jayne would agree to look after both children, once hers was born. "Thank you for taking care of him."

"It's a pleasure, dear," Ethne said. "We've been stuck here for the last two weeks anyway."

Sameena looked at her, surprised and alarmed. "Stuck here?"

"Contract negotiations," Ethne said. "They keep changing their minds about what they want from us. If they weren't paying us a steady retainer fee I'd advise Thomas to go look for a contract elsewhere. But there are fewer and fewer contracts to be found."

Sameena held Brad tightly, thinking hard. If the Imperial Navy was keeping her adopted parents on Madagascar…what did it mean? They weren't under arrest and their ship hadn't been seized, but they were still effectively trapped. It suggested that the Navy didn't intend to threaten her, at least not yet. Or maybe it was merely a coincidence.

"There's no such thing as a true coincidence," Paddy had said, years ago. "If you think that the timing is suspicious, you're probably right."

"That's bad," she said. It was on the tip of her tongue to suggest that they take the kids and leave anyway, but she didn't quite say it out loud. "What do they want from you?"

"Hauling freight, mainly," Ethne said. "They actually gave us an escort for another trip, two months ago. I still don't know what we were carrying."

"Weapons, probably," Sameena said. She put Brad down, silently damning herself for her lack of concern. Maybe she should have stayed on the asteroid after he was born, or taken him to the interstellar factory. It wasn't as if there had been a shortage of work to do. Steve had had to take decisions on his own because she hadn't been there. "Have they asked you any questions?"

"Nothing, apart from the usual round of questions about carrying capacity," Ethne admitted. "They ask the same question every time they hire us – how much can we carry and how far can we go?"

Sameena had to smile. The Imperial Navy might be weakening, but its bureaucracy was as strong as ever. There was no shortage of forms that had to be filled in every time she visited a heavily-populated planet, all designed to do little more than make the bureaucrats feel important. It wasn't as if they had any way of *checking* on her answers, she'd discovered. Besides, cataloguing where she'd been and when over the past five years would have been a nightmare.

"But nothing else," she mused. "Is there?"

"Nothing," Ethne said. Her eyes narrowed. "Should there be?"

Sameena silently cursed herself. Ethne had been the negotiator on *Logan*; she was smart, perhaps smarter than her husband. And, unlike a woman on Jannah, she'd grown up in an environment that encouraged her to *use* her brains. *And* she knew far more about how the Empire worked than Sameena.

"I don't know," she admitted, finally. She didn't want to say anything out loud. Paddy had told her that Imperial Intelligence could produce bugs that were so tiny they couldn't be seen with the naked eye. She used the hand-signal she'd been taught to indicate that they might be being watched and pressed on. "But you might want to look for another contract."

"We will," Ethne said, grimly. "And you be careful too."

Sameena nodded and left her with the children, walking back down into the eatery. Barbara was standing there, looking surprisingly adult in her uniform as she waited on tables. Sameena took a moment to say hello to the girl – it was strange to realise that she was growing up – and promised to speak to her later, then walked out of the eatery and into the stalls. The environment still bothered her, but for a very different reason.

The signs of economic decay were everywhere. Some of the stalls she remembered from her first visit were gone. Others were selling reduced stock, at prices that would have been laughed at years ago. The dressmaker she'd visited with Jayne – it felt like centuries ago – was having a final sale before she went out of business. On a whim, Sameena stepped inside and looked at the clothes. Many of the selections she remembered from last time were gone.

She shivered. The Empire was slowly winding down. And she knew that the end could not be long delayed.

Her wristcom buzzed, informing her that she had one message. She glanced at it and felt her eyes widening. Jamie knew that she was on the station, even though she hadn't sent him a message, and was inviting her to dine with him. She hesitated, knowing that it could be a trap, then accepted the invitation. Part of her wanted to get some straight answers for once, whatever the risk.

Jamie had selected another expensive restaurant, one that offered buffet food from Han and its colony worlds. She couldn't help noticing a large sign, written by the owner, that proclaimed that his great-grandparents had left Han centuries ago. The uprising on Han had made the news all across the sector, even if it was thousands of light years away. Jamie himself was seated in a small compartment, wearing civilian clothes. He rose to his feet as she approached.

"It's good to see you again," he said, smiling. He looked older than she remembered, although she would have been hard-pressed to say how. Like everyone else on the asteroid, his genetic makeup had been improved to the point where aging left few marks on his face. "Please, take a seat."

Sameena nodded and sat down. She wasn't quite sure why Jamie spent time with her – she had been too disturbed by Brad's death to consider a proper relationship – but part of her enjoyed having someone to meet who wasn't a trader or working for her. Besides, she told herself, it wasn't as if either of them were *committed*. He might find a girl tomorrow and leave her as nothing more than a friend.

"This isn't exactly a pleasure call," Jamie admitted, once the waiter had placed a jug of water on the table. "I'm sorry about that, really."

"I understand," Sameena said. At least the penny was about to drop, even if it might turn out to be a hammer. Jamie's superiors might have put pressure on him to speak to her in semi-privacy. It suggested that they might want to make a deal. "What did you call me for?"

Jamie looked – for a long moment – guilty. "It's a long story," he said. He lowered his voice. "But first things first. Do you know that you are being followed?"

CHAPTER
TWENTY-EIGHT

This rapidly proved unsustainable, often too late to prevent disaster. Those dependent on the networks often came to see them as an easier way to live than actually working for a living, particularly as government taxes often ensured that wages were cropped. This shouldn't have been surprising. The decision was in the best interests of the person involved, not necessarily in the best interests of society as a whole.
- Professor Leo Caesius, *The Science That Isn't: Economics and the Decline and Fall of the Galactic Empire.*

Sameena stared at him. She'd known she was being followed, but she'd assumed that they worked for the Imperial Navy. Who *else* would be following her?

"I knew, yes," she said. "Who are they?"

"Good question," Jamie said. He leaned back in his chair. "There are four of them, all men. They came onto the asteroid two weeks ago. Since then, they've been asking a great many questions and eventually settled on you. We don't know why. Do you?"

Sameena hesitated. "No," she said, finally. Not the Imperial Navy? Who did that leave? One of the corporations? "I don't know."

"My...superiors are none too happy about their presence," Jamie said. "But so far they haven't done anything actually illegal. They cannot be legally evicted from the asteroid."

"I suppose not," Sameena agreed, turning it over and over in her mind. Who would have a motive to send people out after her? "I don't know who they represent…"

She saw it suddenly and cursed her own mistake. They were working for the Cartel, they *had* to be. Somehow, they'd noticed that there were more bottles of Firewater Mead in the sector than there should be and they'd eventually traced most of them back to Madagascar. And if they knew where the Mead actually came from, they'd know who was selling it the moment they looked at the list of registered corporations. In hindsight, naming her corporation after the Prophet's first wife had been a dreadful error.

"I think they want to kidnap me," she said, thinking fast. They'd want to ask questions, she knew; if they'd aimed at simple assassination they could have shot her by now. "I have to get out of here."

Jamie reached over and touched her arm. "Relax," he said. "They can't kidnap you from here. And I can call a naval party to help deal with them."

"You'd need to catch them trying to take me," Sameena said. She grinned, suddenly. "Do you want me to serve as bait?"

"After we finish our dinner," Jamie said. He fiddled briefly with his wristcom. "And I have something else to discuss with you."

Sameena nodded, somehow unsurprised. Jamie wouldn't be calling in help from the naval station unless he expected his superiors to approve of it – and that would only happen if they wanted something from her. There would be a price tag attached to their help, she was sure – but what? Her thoughts kept returning to one simple question. How much did they know?

She took her plate, walked over to the buffet and piled it high with rice and various kinds of stir fry, then returned to the table and started to eat. Jamie returned a moment later, placing a privacy generator beside her as he sat down. Sameena lifted an eyebrow, but said nothing. He would tell her what he wanted in his own good time.

"We keep an eye on trading networks – official and unofficial," Jamie said, once he had taken a bite of his food. "I think you know that already, of course."

Sameena nodded, impatiently.

"We know that you are plugged into a network that has been supplying spare parts to the civilian shipping communities," he continued.

"Without that network, civilian shipping in this sector would have collapsed completely by now."

He didn't know that Sameena was *running* the network, she realised. They'd probably assumed that it was linked into the trader clans and the RockRats, with her as one of their representatives. If he'd known the truth…she pushed that thought aside and nodded, slowly.

"We need supplies ourselves," Jamie said. "The squadron is on the verge of collapse too."

"I hadn't realised that it was that bad," Sameena admitted. She'd always assumed – foolishly, she realised – that the Grand Senate would ensure that the Imperial Navy was always supplied. After all, the Navy was their enforcer. "I…"

"There are thirty ships officially assigned to this station," Jamie said, cutting her off. There was a quiet brooding anger in his voice that shocked her. "Twenty-one of them are effectively immobile because we've run out of spare parts to keep them functioning. The remaining nine are being held together with spit, baling wire and pieces cannibalised from the other ships. In a few more months, if that, the entire squadron will be stranded."

His scowl darkened. "Five of the ships are capable of sublight travel only," he added. "They can protect Madagascar, but they can't leave the system. The remainder aren't even capable of doing that. They're going to be sitting ducks if anyone turns up with a great deal of firepower and bad intentions."

Sameena blinked. "Is that going to happen?"

"There are odd reports – all denied, naturally – filtering through the Navy's grapevine," Jamie said. "Entire sectors in revolt, naval commanders declaring war on each other…the bottom line, Sameena, is that we will not be receiving any more supplies from the Core Worlds for a long time, if ever."

"And you want to draw supplies from the network," Sameena said, slowly. It was obvious where this was going. "You do realise that most of the components the network put together are low-grade stuff?"

"They can be adapted," Jamie said. "We're desperate."

Sameena considered it carefully, piece by piece. Helping the Navy wouldn't make her many friends among the traders, but she doubted that she was being offered an alternative. Besides, having them owing her a favour might come in handy. And they *did* have something she needed.

"I believe that we can come to an agreement," she said, slowly. She hesitated, then plunged ahead. "My superiors will want something from you."

"Mercenaries," Jamie muttered, although there was no heat in his words. "How much do you want?"

"Money isn't likely to be worth much in the very near future," Sameena said. "We want the access codes for military-grade production equipment. And high-level commercial equipment, if you happen to have them."

Jamie studied her for a long moment. "You seem very confident that they will want those codes," he said. "Are you *sure*?"

"It's something you can give them that will be worth more than money," Sameena said, keeping her voice level. Did he know that he was speaking directly to the leader of the network? Or did he genuinely believe that she was a subordinate? "I have standing orders to obtain the codes if an opportunity presents itself."

Jamie reached into his pocket and produced a datachip. "This is a list of components we desperately require," he said. "We will need shipments every five months, at the very least, just to keep the ships operational. In the long run, we might want to reactivate some of the cannibalised ships, but that will require additional shipments. If you make a commitment to supply us, I believe that my superiors would agree to hand over the codes."

Sameena slotted the datachip into her reader and skimmed it quickly, mentally comparing it to the lists Steve sent her. Some items would be fairly easy to produce, a handful required the codes to unlock the military production equipment. But it would consume a considerable portion of her productive capability. There would be shortfalls elsewhere.

"Tricky," she observed, finally. Steve would have to be consulted. "I'd have to get back to you on this one. There might be a few other aspects to the agreement to consider."

Jamie nodded, unsurprised. "We can meet again when you return," he said. "Do you have any idea what they'd want?"

Sameena did – but most of the list would be far too revealing. "Escorts, I suspect," she said. "and perhaps a few other things."

She put the datapad back in her pocket and took another bite of her food. "Just how bad is it over there?"

"We lost four crewmen five days ago to a blowout in the airlock," Jamie said, bitterly. "They should have been safe. Airlocks are the simplest pieces of technology in the damn ships. But something jammed and the airlock blew open, throwing all four of them out into space. Others have been injured, or killed…one of the destroyers didn't return from patrol a month ago. Was it lost somewhere in Phase Space? We don't know."

Sameena shivered. Brad had been fond of novels and films that showed the plucky crew of a damaged starship limping home across interstellar space, but real life suggested that such stories always ended badly. There were only a handful of confirmed reports; normally, all that happened was that a starship was noted as overdue and eventually listed as missing, presumed destroyed. The odds were astronomically against someone stumbling over the wreckage. On an interstellar scale, even a colonist-carrier or a battleship was smaller than a grain of sand on a beach.

But there was another possibility. There were rumours that the crews of Imperial Navy ships were mutinying, leaving the service and becoming pirates. Sameena knew just how badly corruption had infected the Navy, spearheaded by senior officers who owed their slots to political or family connections, rather than competence or even dedication. It wasn't something she wanted to discuss with him.

The rest of the dinner went smoothly, much to her relief. It wasn't until she was prepared to leave that Jamie stopped her. "Head down the South Walk," he said, seriously. "My team will be there to intercept the snatchers when they come after you."

Sameena scowled. She'd been targeted before, but she'd never made herself a target deliberately. But there was no other choice. If she was right, luring the watchers into a position where they could be legitimately arrested was extremely important. The longer she waited, the greater the chance they would jump her before she was ready to deal with them.

Jamie walked her to the exit, gave her a kiss on the cheek and then waved her goodbye. She resisted the temptation to look around for the watchers as she walked into the South Walk, a corridor that ran around the edge of the asteroid. Originally, she'd been told, the designers had intended to turn it into another shopping complex, but profits had never been high enough to justify it. Instead, it looked abandoned, almost completely isolated. Apart from a handful of squatters, no one lived there. It was the perfect place for a kidnap.

It was always harder to listen for unexpected sounds in an asteroid. Unlike a ship, parts of it were eerily silent – and parts of it were deafeningly loud. The air circulation flickered without warning, there were strange sounds that echoed through the air…she felt the hair rising on the back of her neck as she walked further down the corridor. They had to know that they wouldn't get a better opportunity to snatch her without being detected. So where were they?

There was a sound, right behind her. She half-turned, just as something slammed into her back. She felt an electric shock running through her body, sending her crashing to the ground. It took her a moment to realise that she'd lost all voluntary control over her own muscles. Her body might as well have been nothing more than a sack of potatoes.

"That's her," someone muttered. It took Sameena a moment to realise that he was speaking Arabic. She had barely used the language outside prayers since leaving Jannah. In fact, he was definitely speaking with a Jannah accent. "Get her into the box, quickly!"

"Treacherous bitch," another man grunted. "And carrying a gun too."

Sameena couldn't see either of them from where she had fallen, but she felt one of them frisk her and remove her weapons and wristcom, before lifting her upright. A moment later, there was a blinding flash of light and a series of Arabic curses. Her captor dropped her to the floor again as a shot rang out, followed by the buzzing of several stunners. Footsteps ran up behind her a moment later.

"See to her," a voice barked. "And secure these assholes."

"They're dead, Jim," another voice said. "Three of them, at least."

Sameena felt a hand rolling her over, allowing her to see a middle-aged man staring down at her. There was something in his face that she found herself liking instinctively, reminding her of one of the few religious teachers who had seemed to care for the girls. He pressed an injector against her arm and she heard a faint hiss.

"They hit you with a nerve jammer," he said, softly. "You would recover anyway, but the drug will ensure that you recover quickly. These things can cause unexpected complications, so I'd prefer to take you to sickbay for observation."

"Get the fourth into cuffs and then move him to a cell," a familiar voice ordered. Jamie knelt down beside her. "Are you all right?"

Sameena found feeling slowly inching its way back into her body. She ached from where she had hit the ground, twice; the nerve jammer had apparently prevented her from feeling a thing. The doctor helped her sit upright and pressed a flask of water against her lips. She sipped gratefully, then looked a question at Jamie. He hesitated, then answered.

"Three of them killed themselves," he said. "Suicide implants, I think; we didn't use lethal force. The fourth is in custody."

"Help me up," Sameena said. The doctor frowned, but helped her to her feet. Her legs felt weak, but they grew stronger as she forced herself onwards. "Who are they?"

The would-be kidnappers were clearly from Jannah, she knew – and she was surprised that the others hadn't realised it. They had the same dark skin genotype as Sameena herself. She laughed at herself a moment later. Jannah was hardly the only planet to have dark-skinned or Arabic-speaking inhabitants. They weren't likely to see a personal connection between Sameena and her kidnappers.

Unless they compare our DNA, she thought, grimly. *How close am I to them?*

She looked over at the fourth kidnapper, lying on the ground with a burly naval crewman sitting on his back and frowned. He *wasn't* from Jannah, not unless he'd had his genotype extensively remodelled – which was possible, but unlikely. Judging from his face, he might well be a hired mercenary rather than a fanatic. And he hadn't killed himself.

"You need to get to sickbay," the doctor said, firmly. "If you don't walk I'll have to ask the CPO to carry you."

"He's right," Jamie said, equally firmly. "This gentleman" – he glared at the captive – "will be escorted to a holding cell, where he will be interrogated. Their ship will be seized and held for investigation, followed by disposal. Unless you wish to register a claim, of course."

"I will," Sameena said, weakly.

Walking more than a few metres was a strain, but the more she walked the better she felt. By the time she reached the asteroid's sickbay, Jayne had been called and – despite her pregnancy – met Sameena as she stumbled into the room. The two doctors scowled at each other, then helped Sameena to a table and ran scanners over her body. Part of her felt so very tired…

She jerked awake, realising that something was wrong. The lights were dim and someone was in the room with her. For a moment, she was confused, unsure of where she was. If she was in her cabin on her ship, no one should have entered without her permission. And then she remembered that she was on Madagascar and that someone had tried to kidnap her. A figure bent over her, holding a weapon…she kicked out instinctively, knocking the weapon out of the figure's hand. The figure stumbled backwards, barely visible in the semidarkness then came at Sameena with murderous intent. Dizzy, Sameena rolled off the table and allowed herself to drop to the floor. The pain helped focus her mind.

Her pistol was gone; her other concealed weapons were gone. She saw the weapon the figure had dropped and scooped it up, pointing it at the figure's chest. There was a faint hiss, but the figure stumbled backwards, folded over and collapsed to the ground. Sameena looked down at the weapon, puzzled, then carefully put it down. She'd never seen anything like it in all of Paddy's lessons.

She stepped closer to the prone assassin and blinked in surprise as she saw the unmistakable shape of breasts. A woman? If the assassins had really come from Jannah, she asked herself, why would they bring a woman? She laughed at herself a moment later. She'd killed in self-defence. Why would another woman be unable to do the same?

The hatch burst open a moment later. "Good God," a voice said. "What happened here?"

"You missed one," Sameena said, turning to face the Imperial Navy doctor. "She tried to kill me."

"Commander Cook is going to be pissed," the doctor said. He examined the assassin for a long moment, then looked up. "How are *you* feeling?"

"Pissed," Sameena snapped. "How do we know that she's the last of them?"

"I don't know," the doctor said. "There's no way to be certain."

Sameena knew. There would be others. Even if they didn't know precisely who she was or how she'd obtained the berries, they would come looking for her. Maybe it was time to start giving the berries away. The cartel's source of wealth would be shattered if everyone started producing their own Firewater Mead. It wasn't as if she needed it any longer.

She smiled at the thought, then headed for the hatch. "I'm going back to my ship," she said, firmly. "I'll speak to the Commander in the morning."

"Take a guard," the doctor said. "As you say, we don't know that she's the last."

CHAPTER TWENTY-NINE

This too should not be judged too harshly. It is easy to speak of sacrifice when one's children are not starving, or at risk. A loner may choose to die rather than request – or demand - charity. A family man will go further – he may steal – to save his family.

- Professor Leo Caesius, The Science That Isn't: Economics and the Decline and Fall of the Galactic Empire.

"We missed the girl," Jamie admitted, the following morning. "The surveillance team didn't realise that she was one of them."

Sameena shrugged. She wouldn't have realised it if the girl hadn't attacked her either. "What happened to her?"

"She had a nasty little assassination weapon," Jamie said. "According to the Chief, it shot frozen particles of nerve poison. You shot her with her own weapon."

He scowled. "We interrogated the survivor pretty harshly," he added. "He said that he'd been hired to assist the other four in getting onto Madagascar and finding you, but he didn't know why. Would you care to explain?"

"It's a long story," Sameena muttered. She wasn't sure how much she wanted – or dared – to tell him. Who knew how he'd react? "Does it actually matter?"

Jamie hesitated. "Sameena, these…people attempted to kidnap you and take you off the asteroid," he said. "We found an interesting selection of weapons and equipment on their ship. They would have forced you to talk, eventually, and then disposed of you. And then there's their DNA."

Sameena winced, knowing what was coming.

"They had hackwork in their background that was identical to yours," Jamie said. "We need to know what is going on."

"I know," Sameena admitted.

She wasn't sure which way to jump. If Jamie knew the truth, what would he do? Obtaining a false ID was technically illegal, even though most of the population of the asteroid probably had a false ID or two. And then there was the question of what would happen if they knew where she had actually come from. Would they demand that she went back to Jannah? It seemed absurd and yet the fear nagged at her mind. But he did need answers.

The cartel hadn't known precisely who they were looking for, she suspected. If they had, they might have tried to contact her and use her birth family as leverage to get her to do whatever they wanted. Assuming, of course, that her birth family was still alive. The Guardians were not known for being gentle to heretics. A lifetime in the labour camps was considered too good for them. Sameena wouldn't have believed that her family was still alive unless she'd been given some *very* convincing proof.

"I don't come from the Lumpur Cluster," she admitted. "I..."

Jamie surprised her by laughing. "If everyone who claimed to come from the Lumpur Cluster actually *did* come from the Lumpur Cluster," he said, "they would have a population far greater than Earth's. We generally assume that anyone who claims to come from the cluster isn't actually being honest about their origins."

Sameena felt her cheeks flush, but she forced herself to go on.

"I was born on a world called Jannah," she said. He didn't recognise the name, unsurprisingly. Few worlds outside Earth were universally known. "And I had to flee when I was fifteen years old."

She ran through the whole story, starting with her brother's arrest and ending with her acceptance on Captain Hamilton's ship. Jamie seemed shocked by her words, to the point where she wondered if he didn't quite believe her. Jannah was hardly the only planet controlled by a religious tyranny.

"Imperial Law states that anyone who wants to leave must be allowed to leave," Jamie said, when she had finished. "You would not have had any difficulty requesting asylum."

"It's a little more complicated than that," Sameena admitted. "You see, Jannah is the source of Firewater Mead."

Jamie stared at her…then started to laugh. "And you gave the Admiral *fifty* bottles of the stuff," he said. "You're producing it for yourself, aren't you?"

Sameena nodded. "Yes," she said. "But not for much longer."

The Admiral had boasted about his acquisition, she suspected. Fifty bottles, effectively appearing out of nowhere, might have caught the Cartel's attention. But it wasn't as if she could have forced him to swear an oath to keep the bottles secret. Giving up so many might have been a mistake, in hindsight. And yet if she hadn't…

She pushed the thought aside. What was done was done.

"So they came after you to silence you," Jamie said. "Why?"

"It isn't hard to boost production," Sameena said. "If the source of the mead ever fell into outside hands, the Cartel's monopoly would be utterly destroyed within the year. I had no difficulty in speeding up the growing process. A corporation would find it easy to turn out the mead as if it were fruit juice. And that would be the end for the Cartel."

"Sounds like a plan," Jamie said. He cleared his throat. "Officially, the case will be closed in two days, unless more evidence comes to light. It would only confuse matters if the full truth was entered into the records. Their ship will be sold unless you want to make a claim on it."

"I do," Sameena said, quickly. Another starship would be very useful; besides, she wanted to see what else they'd brought from Jannah. "What will you use as motive?"

"You're a wealthy merchant," Jamie said. "Kidnap attempts are to be expected."

He scowled. "Speaking of which, I suggest that you hire a few bodyguards," he added. "One retired Marine, particularly one married to a pregnant woman, isn't going to cut it. The next team might have murder in mind from the start."

Sameena nodded. She didn't *need* to sell Firewater Mead any longer. Instead, she could simply give the berries away, along with an explanation of what they were and how to turn them into mead. With a little work, she could even make it seem that the assassination team had been the ones to tell the entire universe. In a year or two, the Cartel's source of funds would be completely destroyed. Even if they convinced the Grand Senate to ban outside production, which might be beyond their resources, it wouldn't stop others from growing their own berries.

But if the assassination team had sent a report back, the Cartel would definitely want to murder her after their comfortable perch was destroyed.

Jamie smiled at her. "I had a chance to speak to my superiors," he added. "They hemmed and hawed a little, then gave me this." He passed her a datachip. "Those are military and civilian override codes for production equipment. You should be able to unlock the equipment and use it freely."

Sameena sucked in a breath as she looked down at the datachip. They hadn't even *tried* to bargain further, which suggested…desperation?

"They'd prefer that you kept it to yourself," Jamie added. "If times get better, giving away those codes could have unpleasant consequences."

"I understand," Sameena admitted. The corporations that had built the equipment wouldn't want to see them being used for just *anything*. Nor would they be happy if their patents were being casually violated – and they would be, she knew. They couldn't afford to respect patents or legal rights if they were going to save part of the Empire. "I won't tell anyone where I found the codes."

"They'll want you to provide as many spare parts as possible," Jamie warned. "The squadron needs them, desperately."

"I'll do my best," Sameena promised. Meeting their requirements would be difficult, to say the least. Steve might have some ideas, but as she saw it they wouldn't be able to produce half as much as the Imperial Navy needed. "And thank you."

"Thank *you*," Jamie said. "Are you sure that you're all right?"

"I knew that the Cartel would find out about me, sooner or later," Sameena said. She was still kicking herself for making it *obvious*. "And I feel better than I have in years."

Jamie lifted an eyebrow. "Really?"

"Yes," Sameena insisted. "I feel *alive*."

"I've had that too, when I went into combat and survived," Jamie admitted. "Even when it's just pirates, there's a sense that you beat the odds once again."

Sameena had to smile. It was a rare pirate who would challenge an Imperial Navy ship, even if they had a bigger ship with more firepower. Even if they won, their ship would definitely take a battering – and the Imperial Navy never surrendered to pirates. Offhand, she couldn't recall any Imperial Navy ship surrendering at all for hundreds of years. But then, without a peer power to fight, there had never been any real wars, merely endless police actions.

"I was planning to visit the entertainment centre," Jamie added. "You should come with me."

"I have work to do," Sameena said, although she knew that she could be tempted. She hadn't liked the movies very much – they were either bad propaganda, bad romantic comedies or outright pornography – but some of the other activities had been fun. Bowling, archery and even puzzle games…she'd enjoyed herself more than she had expected. "And shouldn't I get a bodyguard?"

Jamie laughed. "Hoisted on my own petard," he said. "I'd suggest that you speak to your friend about finding someone suitable."

"I will," Sameena said. She paused as a thought struck her. "What's going to happen to the surviving kidnapper?"

"I'm not sure," Jamie admitted. "Normally, we would send him to a penal colony and drop him there, but it may be a long time before we send a ship out there. The Admiral may decide to assert his authority and execute him instead. Do you have a specific request?"

"He may know something that can be traded," Sameena mused. "He didn't have a *personal* reason to go after me, did he?"

"We can ask him if he wishes to turn state's evidence," Jamie said. "But he may refuse to talk, even with a short trip out of the airlock staring him in the face. And the Admiral may wish to dispose of the prisoner before the Cartel realises what happened and starts trying to pile political pressure on him."

Sameena nodded. Money brought power and influence; it hadn't taken her long to realise that those who had the money made the rules. The Cartel had probably paid out vast sums in bribes over the years, just to ensure that they maintained their monopoly. Given time, they might try to get to the Admiral…if the Empire lasted that long. It would be months before they realised that their assassination team had been killed or captured. The news about Sunflower Berries and Firewater Mead might be unstoppable before the Cartel quite realised what had happened.

"Maybe he knows something I might be able to use," she mused. "Or maybe I'm just wasting my time."

"We can ask, if you have a list of specific requirements," Jamie said. "but I doubt the Admiral would just be willing to turn him over to you. Unless, of course, he was insulted with a fairly…"

"Considerable bribe," Sameena concluded. Watching *The Mikado* had been brilliant, even if half of the verses had been rewritten to suit modern sensibilities. It wouldn't have been allowed on Jannah, naturally. "I could offer him another fifty bottles of Firewater Mead…"

Jamie snickered. "Why do I have the feeling that they wouldn't be worth more than a credit apiece?"

Sameena grinned. "You have a working brain?"

"Let us know when you can supply the first shipment of spare parts," Jamie said. "I'll walk you back to your ship, if you don't want to join me elsewhere."

"Next time," Sameena promised. She paused. "Can I ask a different question?"

Jamie quirked an eyebrow, inviting her to continue.

"My…adopted parents have been held at the asteroid," Sameena said. "Is there a reason for that?"

Jamie scowled. "The requirements for what we want from them – and the others who signed up to help us – keep changing," he admitted. "We haven't been able to settle on a final contract."

Sameena scowled openly as she stood up. It was yet another sign of decay.

People *glanced* at her as they walked back to the spaceport. She was used to attention by now, but there was a new edge to it that was faintly disconcerting. Paddy had reported that there were already exaggerated rumours flying through the asteroid, including one that she was closer to the Imperial Navy than any self-respecting trader would consider proper. The rumour was explicit enough to make her blush. And then there was the story that suggested she'd killed all of the assassins herself in single-combat.

Paddy met them at the airlock, wearing body armour and carrying an immense rifle slung over one shoulder. Sameena muttered her goodbyes to Jamie, painfully aware of Paddy's amused gaze, and then stepped into the airlock, relaxing slightly when the airlock closed behind them. She'd outfitted her ship with a handful of weapons that made her feel safe inside it, even though she knew better than to relax completely. A light freighter, no matter how heavily armed, was no match for a warship.

"He seems to like you," Paddy commented. "Should we be worried?"

Sameena hesitated, confused. The traders were so loose that it was sometimes hard to remember that they *had* morals, morals that were completely alien to her homeworld. By being friends – and perhaps more – with Jamie, was she betraying Brad? But Brad had died two years ago and traders had been known to marry again much sooner. Or was there something else involved?

"I don't think so," she said, finally. "He did suggest that I get bodyguards."

"And quite rightly too," Paddy said, as they stepped into the galley. "We can't expect the truce to last for much longer."

"It's already broken," Jayne pointed out. She was seated at the table, reading from a datapad and rubbing her swollen belly. "At this rate, Madagascar will be a war zone within the month."

Sameena scowled. She didn't quite understand the relationship between the Imperial Navy and Madagascar, but she did understand that the asteroid was generally viewed as neutral territory. As long as they didn't cause trouble, anyone was welcome to dock and take advantage of the facilities, even though there was an Imperial Navy base right next to the giant asteroid. People could bicker if they wanted, but outright warfare was discouraged and the asteroid's staff stomped on it whenever it cropped up. Now…that truce had been broken.

"I don't know how to judge bodyguards," Sameena said, as she poured herself a cup of tea. At least she'd learned how to delegate. "I want you to find a couple of good people, ones you would trust at your back."

"He'll go for Marines," Jayne predicted.

"If I could," Paddy agreed, without heat. "No shame in wanting the best, is there?"

Jayne snorted.

"But there may not be any to be found," Paddy added. "Most Marines who go into retirement tend to go to stage-one colony worlds. I might get lucky, but I wouldn't count on it."

"Let me know what you find," Sameena said. "But they have to be trustworthy."

"Everyone has a price," Paddy observed, gloomily. "But I'll do my best."

Sameena nodded. "We're going to have to go out to the factory," she said, changing the subject. The datachip Jamie had given her felt heavy in her pocket. "And then…I don't know where we will go."

"I was looking at possible contracts," Jayne admitted. "There's almost nothing suitable for us – and certainly nothing long term. Costs are skyrocketing, Captain. I have a feeling that most of the freighters out there" – she nodded to the hull – "are going to be stuck at Madagascar soon enough. There's even a suggestion flowing through the datanet that they should go to one of the abandoned colonies and just take over."

Sameena grimaced. *That* would certainly add to the chaos spreading through the sector – and the rest of the Rim. Worlds would drop out of contact entirely as interstellar shipping ground to a halt…she pushed the image aside, angrily. It was something else she would have to handle, somehow. The contingency plans would have to be updated yet again.

She smiled, suddenly. Perhaps she could point them towards Jannah. The planet had no defences, no starships…even a handful of freighters would be able to take control of the high orbitals and bombard the planet into submission. Such a disaster would shatter the Guardians and their grip on the planet. And then the influx of outsiders would change Jannah forever.

If nothing else, she thought, *they can't keep pretending that low-tech is a good idea when it left them utterly defenceless.*

But Jannah was *hers*. One day, she promised herself, she would return.

And then there would be a reckoning.

"I'll see if we can hire others," she said, flatly. Rosa was producing enough food to keep several mining colonies supplied. A few additional freighters might come in handy too. "But I don't know how long society will hold together."

"Not long," Paddy said. He paused. "All of the rumours are growing worse. Something is going to blow."

Sameena nodded, remembering just how quickly Jamie had given up the unlocking codes, even though it might destroy his career. The Imperial Navy – or at least the fraction of it that remained in the sector – was *definitely* desperate. Who knew what was in the classified communications they received from Earth?

"We'll leave this evening," she said, finishing her tea. "By then, I should have made arrangements for their starship to be handed over to Captain Hamilton. We might find a use for it."

"We can cannibalise it, if nothing else," Paddy grunted. "God help us."

CHAPTER THIRTY

> And when so many people are desperate, politicians will seek to redirect their desperation against others. Many societies fell into the trap of blaming unpopular minorities for economic problems. Small – and therefore powerless – groups of humans made excellent scapegoats. However, destroying them solved nothing.
> - Professor Leo Caesius, *The Science That Isn't: Economics and the Decline and Fall of the Galactic Empire.*

Space was...*immense*.

Out in the wastelands of interstellar space, there was no hiding from the truth. Humans were utterly *tiny* on a cosmic scale, hardly noticeable at all. The stars had been burning for millions of years before the human race had been born, Sameena knew, and they would be burning for millions of years after the human race was gone. And, as far as anyone knew, humanity was alone. It was easy to see why the Nihilists believed humanity to be a plague on the universe. Intelligence was very much the exception, not the rule.

Sameena couldn't agree with them. If God had created mankind, He had not created them to be a plague, but to bear witness to His works. Mankind added randomness to a universe otherwise run by clockwork, eyes to a universe that would never go appreciated by anyone other than its creator...humans were important, even if they seemed tiny. But then, germs were important and they were smaller still.

It was rare for anyone, even the RockRats, to establish bases light years from the nearest stars. Apart from the giant slowboats, generational starships that crossed the interstellar void slower than light, few humans could tolerate the aching emptiness for long. It was psychological, they knew, and yet they feared the void. *Anything* could be lurking out in the darkness between the stars.

But it had been the safest place to establish her factory. Hundreds of industrial nodes floated in place, taking in raw materials from Marigold's Folly and a dozen other mining colonies and reprocessing them into spare parts and duplicate factories. Freighters, some of them larger than the industrial nodes they served, nudged up beside them, unloading the ore and loading on the cargo. Given time, Sameena knew, her operation could grow into a full-sized shipyard, an industrial node to rival Earth's Halo or Terra Nova's Belt. But they might not have the time.

"The RockRats weren't too keen on trading with us," Steve admitted, coming up behind her. "I had the feeling that their leadership believes that hiding is the best option."

Sameena scowled. The RockRats kept themselves isolated from the Empire, refusing to have anything to do with it – and, in turn, the Imperial Navy treated them as criminals. She couldn't blame the RockRats for wanting to hide, even though their assistance would have been very helpful. They knew more about building a space-based industry from scratch than anyone else.

"They probably think they can just take over when the Empire destroys itself," he added, sourly. "Some of them are probably doing what they can to make it worse."

"No doubt," Sameena agreed, never taking her eyes off the void. She refused to allow it to get to her. "Did the codes work?"

"Yes," Steve said. "They work."

He'd taken four days to inspect the datachip *thoroughly* before agreeing to test it. It would have been easy, he'd argued, for the Imperial Navy to have added something else to the chip, perhaps a virus intended to copy all their files and then smuggle them back to Madagascar. But nothing had turned up after a brutal investigation that had left Sameena worrying that they might accidentally destroy the chip.

She smiled in relief. "So you unlocked the equipment?"

"*And* the classified technical specifications," Steve confirmed. "We can now produce just about anything that can be produced in the Empire, provided that we have the right raw materials. Give us a couple of months and we'll be drowning in spare parts, tools and weapons."

Sameena smiled. "Weapons?"

"We can produce as many as you like, given time," Steve said. "But it will be at least a year before we can start producing our own warships, unless you want us to drop everything and concentrate on the ships. Hullmetal alone is a bitch to produce."

"True," Sameena agreed. They had to make the machines to make the machines before they could turn out a shipyard – and producing starships took much longer than spare parts. "Can we start bolting weapons onto freighters and other ships?"

"Yes, but that won't make them warships," Steve warned. "If they go up against a real warship they'll be cut to ribbons."

"Pirates don't want to risk their lives or their profits," Sameena reminded him. "If a few freighters happened to be armed to the teeth, the pirates will go elsewhere rather than risk losing their ships."

"There will be legal problems," Steve said. "At least until the crunch finally comes."

Sameena nodded. The Imperial Navy frowned on armed merchantmen, although the official excuse – that armed merchantmen could easily turn into pirates – didn't hold water. It had taken her some research to discover that the real reason was that the Imperial Navy could and did charge fees for escort work, which might not have been so bad if the Navy had been able to provide half the escorts interstellar shipping *needed*. Instead, they ensured that most tramp freighters were unarmed and unable to deter pirates.

The bigger corporations also left their ships unarmed, even though they could have paid the colossal fees for the permits out of pocket change. She honestly wasn't sure what *they* were thinking. *Sameena* had paid the fees herself and it had cost her a sizable chunk of her fortune. Maybe they just didn't care about losing a handful of freighters. The insurance would pick up the bill.

"Under the circumstances, I think we can afford to pay for permits," Sameena said, dryly. "Besides, it won't be long now before permits become immaterial."

Steve nodded. "I've been following the reports from the network," he agreed. "Far too many planets are now outside Imperial Law, whatever the Empire says. Madagascar will be abandoned soon, I suspect. Are you going to recruit the people there?"

"Some of them," Sameena said. They'd hired hundreds of experienced workers from Madagascar, as well as training up new ones. The entire program would have to be expanded soon, she suspected. It would give the children of Marigold's Folly a chance to be more than miners – or dead before they reached their twenties. "I don't know about the others."

She caught sight of *Pleasure Palace* and scowled, feeling a twinge of disapproval – and guilt. The starship had been a luxury liner before it had been decommissioned and abandoned; Steve had had it towed to the shipyard and retrofitted into an entertainment complex. It was easy to accept movies, but harder to tolerate prostitutes, even though Steve had pointed out that their crewmen were going to be living and working on the complex for years, without a chance to leave. She'd insisted on selecting volunteers, paying proper wages and providing excellent medical care, but she still felt guilty. Could anyone truly be said to be a volunteer when it was a choice between prostitution and starvation?

A surprising number, she'd discovered, had been pleasure workers before accepting their new contracts. Sameena had talked to a few of them and had been astonished by how calmly they accepted their positions – and how hard they had worked to earn their qualifications. She had never thought of the arts of pleasure as a scholarly qualification, certainly not one that could be earned. The women had explained, quite seriously, that there was more to it that just sex.

"We're there to make people relax into pleasure," she'd said. "It isn't just a quick fuck, but a long session that can include a massage, a long soak in a bathtub and much else besides."

She dismissed the memories and looked over at Steve. "Can we meet the Navy's requirements?"

"We have a stockpile of spare parts now," Steve mused. "It wouldn't be hard to give them enough to keep some of their ships running. But I should warn you that providing *everything* in their list of requirements will take years, unless we devote everything we have to meeting their demands. This isn't the Halo. Not yet."

Sameena nodded, thinking wistfully of Earth's colossal network of orbiting industrial factories. At its height, Earth had been capable of supplying the entire Empire with everything from spare parts to mass-produced starships. Combined with a handful of other major industrial nodes, it had encouraged the other worlds not to develop their own industries. Now, the Empire's great success had turned into a disaster of the first order.

And the Grand Senate was *still* trying to discourage competition.

She scowled. "Robbing Peter to pay Paul," she muttered. "What can we *reasonably* give them?"

"We can give them half of our production of spare parts," Steve said. "That production line is fairly stable now. Combined with a few additions once we get the military-grade equipment up and running, they should have enough to keep them going. As we expand our facilities, we should be able to provide the rest of their requirements. But it may be some time before we can do so."

"It'll have to suffice, for the moment," Sameena said. She knew that Jamie wouldn't be happy, but she couldn't promise more than she could deliver. "Do you have any leads on more industrial gear?"

"Several," Steve said. "I've dispatched a team to inspect another junkyard, ninety light years away. But by now it could easily have been cannibalised. We won't know until they return."

"I know," Sameena nodded. "I don't suppose you have a working theory for an FTL radio?"

Steve laughed. "No," he said. "And there may not be one for a very long time."

Once, back when they'd started working together, he'd told her a secret belonging to the Engineer's Guild. They'd come to believe, he'd said, that the Grand Senate was *deliberately* impeding the process of scientific research and development. All of the discoveries over the last four hundred years, he'd claimed, were really improvements on technology that had gone before, rather than anything completely new. Theoretical science into new power sources, starship drives and other ways of breaking the light barrier had largely been discontinued. It was as if the Grand Senate believed that the human race no longer needed to advance.

"A starship with enough power reserves can project a gravity shield and rotate it around the hull to interdict incoming fire," he'd said. "In theory, one can link together generators and create a bubble that would shield the ship completely. The Imperial Navy would *love* such a development. But all research into it has been barred.

"And, in theory, you could produce just about *anything* from energy, with the right equipment," he added. "But research into that has been barred too."

Sameena understood, she thought. The Grand Senate was on top of the universe; directly or indirectly, they controlled the lives and destinies of *trillions* of people. And there was no threat outside the Empire to encourage technological advancement. Why would the Grand Senate want the universe to change? What might it do to the universe if Earth's population ever learned what the Grand Senate did to the colonies in their name? Or if a word of a rebellion spread faster than it could be suppressed?

Maybe it's for the best, right now, she thought. *An FTL radio would show everyone just how badly the Empire is falling. Panic alone would take down the rest of it before we were ready.*

She scowled. In the hope of turning out compliant peons who didn't even *want* to think for themselves, the Grand Senate had sabotaged the schools…which had had the unintended consequence of reducing the pool of trained manpower available to the Empire. This in turn had ensured that the Empire's infrastructure had begun to decay. It seemed like absolute madness, but if they'd believed that they would never have to face the consequences of their actions…it was the only explanation that made sense. They were simply too isolated from the universe to see the decay pervading through the Empire.

"Maybe we can invent one soon," she said, although she wasn't hopeful. If the stories of the old days were true, the genius engineers had been able to come up with a concept on Monday, produce a working model on Tuesday and start mass production on Wednesday...and then the whole cycle would begin again the following Monday. Real life had taught her that research and development could take years. "Or see what other developments we can produce."

"Having the kids actually *thinking* helps," Steve said. "I feel slow and stupid compared to some of them."

Sameena shook her head in awe. *Steve* felt slow and stupid? There had been times on *Logan* where *she* had felt stupid compared to Brad or Steve or the rest of their family. Ignorance was not stupidity – Ethne had reminded her of that, more than once – but bad habits could take a lifetime to erase. Ginny had been lucky, she knew. She hadn't been exposed to Earth's educational system for very long before she'd moved to Rosa.

"Oh yes," Steve confirmed. "They look at the technology, they actually *understand* it...and then they start asking questions. Given a few years, we might even be able to improve on the Phase Drive. I think that Professor Sorrel was talking about setting up a proper university...which I think is a terribly bad idea, by the way."

Sameena looked over at him in surprise. The naked hatred in his voice was very unlike him.

"You do?" She asked. "Do you hate him?"

"I've had to deal with one or two graduates of Imperial University," Steve admitted. "They had degrees in social anthropology or some such nonsense and they wanted to do research into the trader sub-community. It wouldn't have been too bad if they'd approached with an open mind, but they were already crammed full of ideas and preconceptions that had taken over their minds and refused to make room for anything else. Do you know they believed that traders effectively enslaved their own children?"

Sameena blinked. "Really?"

"Yes," Steve said. He sounded as if he was about to start ranting. "And that was minor, compared to some of the others. Apparently, we also exploit planets by charging them through the nose for minor deliveries, smuggle contraband whenever we can and generally exist on the seedy side of life. Oh, and that we buy and sell slaves and put them to work on our ships. And that we all worship Mammon."

"Oh," Sameena said. Mammon was the personification of wealth, she'd discovered after leaving Jannah. The Guardians frowned on great wealth, but there had been no attempt to link it to anything satanic. She suspected that the sin was in hoarding wealth, rather than using it to create more and improving the local economy. "What happened?"

"There was a fight; one of the boys, it seemed, believed that trader women were easy," Steve said. "They got sent home. I don't know what happened after that."

He shook his head. "I wouldn't place any credence in a university without a great deal of practical experience being included," he added. "And learning experiences that actually teach the kids to think for themselves."

"You can help design it," Sameena said. "But for the moment the scholarship program seems to be working fine."

"It will need to be expanded again," Steve admitted. "There will always be shortages of trained manpower."

Sameena nodded. "Something else to do," she said. "It never ends, does it?"

Steve shook his head.

She allowed him to take her on a tour of the growing complex, admiring his work. They'd come a long way, she knew; the crews were delighted to have a chance to meet her. Sameena couldn't help feeling crowded as they surrounded her, but somehow she managed to shake hands and share a few words with them. They seemed to appreciate it.

"They appreciate *you*," Steve muttered, when she said that out loud. "If you hadn't started all this, they would be lucky to have gainful employment *anywhere*."

Sameena saw the way some of them were looking at her and nodded. It was almost worshipful, something that bothered her on a very primal level. And yet part of her welcomed it, considering it nothing less than her due. The conflict gnawed at her as she walked onwards, pressing the flesh, and finally reached Steve's personal quarters. She sagged the moment the airlock hissed closed behind them.

"It can be overwhelming," Steve said. "But you did fine."

"Maybe," Sameena said. "But it was also terrifying."

The storm of emotion surrounding her had been almost physical in its intensity, threatening to overwhelm her. She hadn't felt anything like it since she'd prayed with the other women on Jannah, where the emotion had been more focused. Here, it had been utterly uncontrolled. She'd wondered why mobs went crazy and did things that they would never do as individuals. Now she knew.

"They wanted to meet you," Steve said. "There isn't a person on the platforms who wouldn't die for you, for what you offered them. That's something you have to bear in mind."

"I'd rather they lived for me," Sameena said, remembering the would-be kidnappers. They'd been fanatics, prepared to die rather than surrender. "And I want you to live too."

"I will," Steve promised. "You've given me one hell of a challenge."

He scowled as an alarm chimed. "An unscheduled starship?"

Sameena leaned forward. "Who?"

"One of the courier ships," Steve said, looking down at the datapad. "They're transmitting an urgent message."

He scanned the message and turned pale, then passed the datapad to her. "They came directly from Madagascar," he said. He sounded utterly stunned. "The Empire has abandoned us. They've abandoned the entire sector!"

Chapter Thirty-One

> It was this process that destroyed the Empire. Having achieved supreme power, the Grand Senate set about ensuring that their power would never be challenged. They wrote the laws in their own favour, making it harder for competitors to arise, and taxed the politically-weak outer worlds mercilessly. This not only supplied the Empire with raw materials, it also ensured that the outer worlds would not be able to establish their own economies.
>
> - Professor Leo Caesius, *The Science That Isn't: Economics and the Decline and Fall of the Galactic Empire.*

Sameena wasn't sure what she expected to see as *Lead Pipe* returned to Madagascar. She'd worked out dozens of contingencies over the years, but there had been no way to tell which way people would jump. It was possible, she knew, that the asteroid's population might have torn itself apart – or that it was trying to come to grips with the new situation. There was no way to know until she actually made contact with the asteroid.

"The Imperial Navy ships are still there," Paddy said. "All of them."

"Curious," Sameena said. The message hadn't been very detailed, merely stating that the Grand Senate had ordered the remainder of the Empire's personnel to head back to the Core Worlds, abandoning the entire sector. It probably wasn't the only one either. The entire Rim might have been abandoned. "Are there any power readings?"

"I can't tell at this distance," Paddy admitted.

"I've got in touch with mum and dad," Jayne said, from her console. "They're safe!"

Sameena allowed herself a sigh of relief as she turned to stand behind Jayne. Captain Hamilton looked older and greyer than she remembered, but he was alive! She smiled at him and relaxed as he smiled back. No one was dead, then. Yet.

"Everyone seems to be stunned," Captain Hamilton said. "We've moved the kids and their parents to *Logan*, but we're unsure of what to do next."

"Take them to the base," Sameena said, decisively. Rosa might be a better choice, but it was hopelessly vulnerable if pirates or secessionists came knocking. "What's the Imperial Navy saying?"

"Very little," Captain Hamilton said. "All personnel were recalled shortly after a light cruiser arrived and passed on the message. Since then…nothing, apart from the light cruiser departing several hours later. There's even some speculation on the datanet that the entire base has been abandoned."

"Unlikely," Paddy said, turning to look at them. "The ships could be taken back to Earth, if nothing else. They wouldn't be likely to leave them drifting in space for someone to recover."

If that were possible, Sameena thought. Jamie had told her that five ships weren't capable of going FTL any longer. They'd be stuck in the Madagascar System unless they managed to rebuild their drives. But it looked as if almost all of the squadron had been left behind.

Paddy had a more pertinent question. "How is the fine population of Madagascar taking the fact they've been abandoned?"

"Stunned, as I said," Captain Hamilton said. "Everyone seems to have battened down the hatches and prepared for trouble, but so far no one's started anything. God knows how long that will last; the asteroid's administrators haven't said *anything* since the official announcement. Several ships have left for undisclosed destinations."

Sameena scowled. The economy was doomed, unless her contingency plan worked – and if the economy of the sector went down, civilisation would go with it.

Her lips quirked in a bitter smile. If nothing else, the cartel would be gone too.

"We're going to dock as soon as possible," she said. How would the asteroid react to new starships, now that the Empire was gone? "Is that likely to be safe?"

"I honestly don't know," Captain Hamilton said. "But you might be better advised to wait and see what happens."

"No time for that," Sameena said. She'd learned enough to know that either she sought to take control of the situation or the situation would take control of her. "And I need you to call a Meet."

"One has already been called," Captain Hamilton said. "It's going to be held in two weeks, but I have a feeling that not everyone will be available to attend."

Sameena felt her scowl deepen. The traders weren't precisely a democracy or a dictatorship, but some strange combination of the two. What was agreed on at the Meet was binding on the attendees, everyone agreed, yet it didn't apply to those who hadn't attended. And she needed most of the traders assisting her or, at the very least, staying out of the way. A few more years to lay the groundwork would have been very welcome.

Not going to happen, she told herself, crossly. *Concentrate on what you know to be true.*

"I'm going to have to discuss matters with the Imperial Navy," she said. "I'll speak to you afterwards, I hope."

"Good luck," Captain Hamilton said. He knew enough about her plans to try to help, even though he'd been doubtful that she could succeed. "And I'll ensure that Brad is safe."

Sameena felt a twinge of guilt as the channel closed, silently resolving to spend more time with her son if they survived the crisis. Pushing the feeling to one side, she sent a brief message to Jamie's communicator, silently praying that he hadn't gone back to Earth. He was the only Imperial Navy officer she knew well.

A response came seventeen minutes later, asking for an immediate meeting.

"He'll probably want you to come onboard his ship," Paddy said. "It's a fairly typical tactic for placing you at a disadvantage, as by coming to him you appear a supplicant. Invite him here instead."

"I prefer not to have him exploring this ship," Sameena said. She considered it briefly, realising that Paddy was right. "I won't forget what I have at my disposal."

The Imperial Navy destroyer *Pinafore* was a blunt hammerhead of a ship, bristling with weapons and sensor blisters that tracked *Lead Pipe* as the two ships rendezvoused. It was a gesture of trust, she knew, one that was almost completely unprecedented. Normally, the Imperial Navy preferred to shuttle freighter commanders over into their ships, rather than linking docking tubes. If Sameena had been carrying a nuke she could have vaporised both ships before they could hope to react.

She left Paddy behind at the airlock and stepped into the Imperial Navy starship, looking around with interest. It looked cruder than her freighter, somehow; the bulkheads were cold grey metal, rather than the colours freighter crews added as a matter of course. There were no paintings, no photographs, nothing to personalise the ship. The crew seemed competent enough, she decided, but by the way they held themselves she could tell that they were nervous. They'd been abandoned too.

"Welcome onboard," Jamie said. He looked immensely relieved to see her, something else that was largely unprecedented. Outside friendships like the one they shared, Imperial Navy officers tended to sneer at freighter crews and freighter crews thought the Navy snobbish and stuck up. "It's good to see you again."

He didn't say anything else until they were in his cabin, with the airlock firmly shut. Sameena had ample opportunity to inspect the ship as they walked through the passageways, catching sight of hundreds of places where maintenance had been trimmed down to the bone. *Pinafore* wasn't quite a death trap yet, she decided, but it was getting there. Jamie poured himself a glass of something that smelled like pipe cleaner and took a swig.

"Rotgut?" He asked. "Or water?"

"Water would be fine," Sameena said. It was hard to be sure, but Jamie seemed to be on the verge of collapse. His face was lined and gray with stubble, as if he hadn't even been able to muster the will to run a shaver across his chin. And she didn't like the signs of him drinking, even if he didn't seem to be completely drunk. "What happened since I left."

Jamie barked a harsh laugh. "The Admiral fled," he said. "Took his aide, a couple of his staffers, a handful of other officers and flew off back to the Empire. And the Commodore had a heart attack when he heard the news. I am the last commander of this sector."

Sameena stared at him. "But you're a *Commander*."

"Admiral promoted me before he left, stuck me in the Commodore's slot," Jamie sneered. "You're talking to Commodore Cook."

He snickered, darkly. "And I'm here to watch helplessly as the lights go out," he added. "My crews are on the verge of mutiny, half of my officers think they should have my post…hell, legally they'd probably be right. Jumping me up three whole grades isn't exactly kosher, even if the Admiral did have broad authority. The bastard just fled. Didn't even bother to try to take the remaining ships."

And thank God for that, Sameena thought. She didn't say it out loud.

"We're doomed," Jamie said. He picked up the bottle and took a long swig. "We're going to float here forever and die when the atmosphere runs out."

Sameena stood up and walked over to the drinks cabinet on the bulkhead. By law, there should be a selection of sober-up tabs there for her to use. Finding one, she carried it back to Jamie and pressed it against his neck. He let out a yelp as she shot the drug into his system, then scurried over to the washroom. Sameena gave him what privacy she could as his system violently expelled the alcohol.

"You…you…"

She had to smile as Jamie stepped back into the cabin, leaving his jacket behind. "I think we'd be better off talking if you weren't on the verge of drunkenness," she said. She'd learned to recognise the symptoms from Jayne, who had told her that alcohol was a persistent menace on tramp freighters. Jamie hadn't been a heavy drinker and that much rotgut would have hit him hard. "Now, what is the current situation?"

Jamie scowled at her, then picked up a glass of water and washed his mouth out before speaking. "Assuming that there are absolutely *no* more supplies from the Core Worlds, and that is what I was told, we will be able to maintain the current level of operations for around three months before our equipment falls below our ability to maintain it," he said, bluntly. "We might be able to eke out another couple of months through cannibalising equipment and supplies, but we will be completely worn down then. That will be the end.

"There are four thousand crewmen on the station or ships, all convinced that they've been abandoned and the only thing to do is wait for death," he continued. "Several commanders have been making noises about relieving me, or taking off on their own along with their ships. Discipline is in the pits, drunkenness is on the rise…and we're thoroughly screwed."

He smiled at her, wanly. "There doesn't seem to be any way to save ourselves," he concluded. "I just…"

"Started crawling into a bottle," Sameena said, tartly. "I don't think that was very helpful."

She looked him in the eye. "Answer me a question," she said. "What do you want to do with yourself? And your people?"

Jamie did her the honour of considering his words before he spoke. "Most of us don't have any family, but the Navy," he said. "We spend so long away from our biological families that we eventually lose touch with them. But right now, we've been betrayed by the Navy we trusted. That family has been shattered."

He shrugged. "Ideally, I would like to remain in space and continue to work on a starship," he said. "Right now, it's looking like the best option is round up a couple of freighters and head for a colony world. We might be able to settle down before our tech fails spectacularly."

"I brought you supplies," Sameena said, quietly. "You don't *have* to surrender to entropy."

Jamie laughed, harshly. "You might as well keep them," he said. "What are *we* without the Imperial Navy?"

Sameena leaned forward. "Remind me," she said. "What oath did you take when you entered the Academy?"

"To serve and protect the Empire," Jamie said. "But the Empire is gone."

He snorted. "There were all sorts of joke oaths going around," he added. "The joke was that you had your chance at a slot if you actually read the oaths first before making them and realised that they weren't serious."

"Civilisation exists in us," Sameena said. "If you don't uphold civilisation, all that is left is barbarism. That's what is going to fall over the sector now, unless you help us. You're in command of the last remaining bastion of military power in the entire sector."

"Not the last," Jamie said. "There are other starships out there. We'll have to tell them the truth when they check in. I don't know how they will take it."

Sameena winced. News spread oddly throughout the galaxy, moving from worlds on the trade routes to worlds that had only limited contact with the Empire. Jannah might never even realise that the Empire had fallen until the first pirate band turned up to demand money with menaces. Or it wouldn't have realised, she knew, if they weren't linked to the Cartel. Their profits would vanish even without her sharing the secret of the Sunflower Berries with the entire universe.

"You'll get supplies from me," she said, firmly. "And pay too."

Jamie stared at her. When he spoke, he sounded shocked. "Are you planning to hire us like we're mercenaries?"

"You got paid for serving the Empire," Sameena pointed out. Madagascar might not have been so profitable if the Imperial Navy crewmen hadn't spent most of their salaries on the rock. "You will be paid by me for upholding civilisation."

She pushed onwards before he could think about it too much. The traders did tend to call the Imperial Navy mercenaries, precisely because they *did* get paid to enforce the Grand Senate's whims. But they also hunted down pirates and protected convoys. Sameena had a feeling that countless worlds were going to wish that the Imperial Navy was still there, soon enough. Only a handful of worlds in the sector had *any* form of planetary defence network.

"Your duties will be to escort convoys and engage pirates," she continued. "You will also protect worlds that sign up with us. Given time, we can repair your cannibalised ships and produce new ones. You will be able to recruit new officers and men from the traders, the asteroids or even the colony worlds."

"You're setting up an empire of your own," Jamie said, wonderingly. "Or is it a giant protection racket?"

"I'm trying to preserve civilisation," Sameena said. "And as for it being a protection racket...tell me, what is the difference between one such gang and the Grand Senate? I won't force anyone to join."

"I believe you mean well," Jamie said, "but are you sure that it will work?"

"I think there's no choice, but to try," Sameena said. There would be quite a few disparate factions left behind by the Empire. Pulling them together would be a real challenge, but the rewards would be immense. Brad would have a *real* Empire to inherit. "Will you join me?"

"It will be hard to convince the other officers," Jamie said. He stood up. "But I can try."

"I'll hand the supplies over to you," Sameena said. It was a calculated risk; she knew Jamie wouldn't try to steal from her, but she wasn't so sure about the other officers. Besides, she did owe the Imperial Navy a considerable debt. "That should give you some bargaining power."

Jamie reached for her and wrapped his arms around her as she stood up, hugging her tightly. "Thank you," he said, softly. "And I'm sorry about…"

He waved a hand at the bottles. "Don't worry about it," Sameena said. Ethne had taught her, in one of her motherly moods, that there was nothing to be gained from humiliating a man time and time again. They tended to resent it, which led to eventual separation – or violence. "Just don't turn up drunk while you're working for me."

She allowed him to lead her back to her ship, then waved goodbye as she stepped through the airlock. Paddy gave her a concerned look, so she filled him in as they separated from the destroyer and headed towards Madagascar. There was no trouble about receiving permission to dock, although there was an unusual warning that weapons would not be permitted onboard the asteroid. A check with Captain Hamilton revealed that several arguments in bars had turned into brawls when the magnitude of the Empire's betrayal had been revealed and several people had been killed.

Madagascar felt *weird* when she stepped through the airlock and into the asteroid. The market place was almost completely deserted, save for a handful of unlucky souls who had nowhere else to go. Everyone else was holed up in their apartments or starships, only venturing out when they needed something. Sameena remembered how noisy it had been when she'd first visited, how many different cultures had blurred together in front of her. Now, it was almost dead…

The stalls were boarded up, the shops locked; the great chamber was almost painfully silent. Her footsteps seemed deafeningly loud in her own ears as she walked down the middle of the aisle, feeling tears prickling at the corner of her eyes. It was easy to believe that Madagascar was dead, as dead as the starships they'd pulled from the junkyard. There was no fertile soil that might give birth to new life. Sometime in the future, the morbid part of her mind remarked, archaeologists might stumble across the asteroid and wonder just what brought such a powerful civilisation to its knees.

It felt like the end of the world.

CHAPTER THIRTY-TWO

> The Grand Senate looked upon this and considered it good. From their point of view, it worked splendidly - and, when the colonists objected, the military could be sent in to break a few heads. However, it actually ensured that the Grand Senate-backed corporations no longer tested themselves against peer powers. Of course, had the Empire faced a peer power as a whole, things might have been different.
> — Professor Leo Caesius, *The Science That Isn't: Economics and the Decline and Fall of the Galactic Empire.*

Sameena had attended three Meets in her life. As the owner of a trader starship – and a blood tie to a very well established trader clan – she had the right to vote and speak. It was something she hadn't really understood until her marriage to Brad – and Brad Junior's birth – when Captain Hamilton had explained it to her. Brad had had ambitions, he'd admitted, reluctantly. A captaincy of his own would have allowed him to step out from under his father's shadow.

The Meet itself took place inside a giant bubble of air that had been designed and built for that purpose. It gave the impression that they were floating in space itself, wearing nothing more than shipsuits. Sameena suspected that it was intended as a subtle challenge to the Captains. Those who couldn't endure the experience were not considered worthy of attending the Meet. She still had nightmares, sometimes, about falling into space, but she kept her emotions under strict control. They couldn't be given any reason to disregard her.

Only Captains attended the Meet physically, but everyone on the two hundred starships that had entered the system would be able to watch proceedings through the jury-rigged datanet. They had no formal vote, she knew, yet the wiser Captains would listen to their subordinates before casting a vote in the Meet. It was a very open system of government, even if it wasn't entirely a democracy. But then, a democracy would be a dangerous way to run a starship.

She caught her breath as the Mistress of Ceremonies – selected at random from the Captains – called the Meet to order. The Captains, who had been chatting softly to one another, settled down, floating in the zero-gravity field. It made her think of being at prayer, even if the Captains seemed to be scattered around at random. And yet there was a certain elegance to the whole system.

"Captain Hussein-Hamilton wishes to bring a proposal before the Meet," the Mistress said. Her voice echoed through the chamber. "Who will second her proposal?"

"I will," Captain Hamilton said.

"As will I," Captain Barker added.

Sameena smiled, inwardly. The Meet rules stated that all proposals had to be supported by at least one Captain, preferably one unrelated to the proposer. Captain Hamilton was her father-in-law, technically; Captain Barker was a friend. Between them, they would ensure that the Meet would *listen* to her. But that didn't mean that they would *agree*.

"The proposal has been seconded," the Mistress said. "Captain Hussein-Hamilton; you may speak."

The Captains looked at her, waiting for her to speak. Sameena felt a flicker of nervousness, which she ruthlessly squashed. She couldn't afford to show any doubt or uncertainty, not now. They had to believe that she believed every word she said – and that she was confident enough to see matters through to the end. The fact she was so new to the traders didn't help, she knew. She was a very minor member of the Hamilton Family – and only by marriage.

But she had earned some respect.

"We are those who are truly free," she said.

A low rustle ran through the chamber as she quoted the funeral oration. The traders considered themselves truly free, not bound by the conventions of the Empire or the strange semi-religious society of the RockRats. They were a diverse group bound together by a common interest in profit and mutual support. The traders prided themselves on their flexibility – but were they flexible enough to adapt to the new order?

"We tell ourselves that, from the moment we are born to the moment we die," she said, ignoring the fact that she hadn't been a trader five years ago. "We move from star system to star system, picking up a cargo here, passengers there, and keep ourselves as separate as we can from the stifling presence of the Empire. If times get too hard, we tell ourselves, we can leave and go elsewhere.

"That is self-delusion. We were dependent on the Empire. We took cargoes from the Empire's worlds, we used the Empire's facilities, we even made a profit from quietly ignoring some of the Empire's laws. And now the Empire is gone. What interstellar trade hasn't dried up already will soon be gone. Supplies from the Core Worlds have come to an end. They will be followed by the complete breakdown of law and order across the spaceways."

She paused, trying to gauge their reaction. Some of them had definitely been amused by her sly reference to evading laws – smugglers could only turn a profit if their cargos were illegal – while others were angry at her unconcealed disregard for one of their most stubbornly-held beliefs. If the rules governing the Meet hadn't been so strict, some of them would probably have stormed out or challenged her to a fight. But they had to let her finish before they could speak themselves.

"Right now, the Empire is gone," she continued. "There is a power vacuum. And nature abhors a vacuum. Sooner or later, someone will try to fill it."

She ran through some of the possible scenarios she'd worked out over the years. Pirates, seeking a chance to create their own Empires. Former Imperial Navy officers, carving out their own little empires in the ruins of *the* Empire. Newly-independent planets dragging up grudges from before the Unification Wars and starting a new series of interstellar wars. The Empire had been brutal, oppressive and run for the greater good of the

Grand Senate, not humanity as a whole. It was terrifying to realise that the chaos caused by its fall might easily be worse.

"We have a window of opportunity here," she said. "I propose that *we* seek to fill the power vacuum."

There was a long moment of absolute silence, then everyone started talking at once. The Mistress blew her whistle angrily, glaring around her until she had achieved some semblance of order. They had to be deeply shocked, Sameena realised, with some amusement. Nothing else could convince them to break the Meet's most sacred laws.

"I have been gathering pieces of industrial production equipment for years," she said. A handful of others had copied her idea, but she was light years ahead of them. "We would have the basic building blocks of an industrial base. I propose that we leverage those into creating a government, one that will replace the Empire in this sector."

She keyed her datapad, sending them all a copy of the proposal. "We will not seek to control worlds directly," she continued. "Instead, we will merely provide a framework for interstellar law and common defence. We will encourage the behaviour we want rather than force it at gunpoint. In the long term, we will build a society that combines the best of the Empire with the best of ourselves.

"I have already hired the remains of the Imperial Navy in this sector. We can build more warships, given time, to provide protection to our ships as they move from world to world – and to hunt down and eradicate pirates. Our industrial base can be expanded and used to support our position. We would no longer have to fear the government's whims. We would *be* the government."

She nodded to the Mistress and waited, as calmly as she could, for the first question. The Captains were studying the document she'd sent them, looking for possible loopholes and potential problems. Unlike the Imperial Charter – which was hundreds of thousands of words long – it was simple and straight to the point. There would be little room for the kind of creative interpretation that made money for lawyers. Ethne had helped her to write and revise it until the document was as close to perfect as she could make it.

A chime rang through the chamber. One of the Captains had a question. "You intend to hire the remains of the Imperial Navy," he said, bluntly. "How do you know that you can trust the mercenaries?"

Sameena decided not to point out that she had *already* hired them. "Because they need supplies and payment," she said. "They cannot survive on their own for more than a few months. And because they have nowhere else to go."

She scowled, inwardly. Some of the traders had had bad experiences with Imperial Navy officers, particularly the ones who looked down on traders. *They* would welcome the Navy's disappearance, at least until the pirate attacks really began to bite. By then, it would be too late. The new government – assuming they accepted it – would not have any laws banning weapons at all, but freighters would *still* never be warships. Pirates might be deterred…

…But an Imperial Navy officer turned warlord wouldn't consider the armed freighters any kind of threat.

The last Meet she'd attended had lasted for nearly two hours before the decision had been taken. This one seemed to go on for far longer, with questions being thrown at her from all sides and arguments popping up between Captains as they debated the merits of her proposal. It was difficult to keep track of who was on her side and who wasn't; several Captains went off on tangents and asked about funds that should have been saved in Imperial banks. The new government couldn't start by reimbursing them. Hell, the new government didn't even have a financial policy yet.

A glance at her datapad showed her that data traffic between the starships was at an all-time high. *Everyone* seemed to be debating her proposal. The Mistress was having a hard time coping with the different speakers, despite the strict rules that should have supported her. It might be *days*, Sameena realised, before they came to an agreement. Her proposal was far more complex than a boycott of an inhabited star system or whatever else might affect the traders as a whole.

"This issue remains one of trust," one of the proposal's strongest opponents said, finally. "How can we trust the Imperial Navy? We would be revealing far too much about ourselves to those we…hired."

Sameena scowled, inwardly. She *did* have a solution that she thought would satisfy them – she was mildly surprised that it hadn't already been proposed – but it wasn't one she really *wanted* to use. But at least it would be her idea.

"The current commander of the Imperial Navy's Madagascar squadron is Commodore James Cook," she said. "I propose to marry him."

That brought absolute silence. Ever since Brad had died – and they'd realised the size of her growing empire - there had been a string of marriage proposals from various traders. She'd turned them all down, knowing that there was nothing to gain from such marriages. It wasn't as if she'd needed to bind someone firmly to her crew. Marriage was serious business. The traders had understood her reluctance to commit herself.

But if she was prepared to put herself on the table, she had to be serious.

She would have felt amused at their reactions, if she hadn't known that she was committing herself. It was possible that Jamie would turn her down…which would discredit her in front of the traders. Or that he would accept. Trader society might make or break marriages when it suited them, but they took them seriously. She would be unable to merely be married in name only.

I will be expected to sleep with him, she thought. Cold ice seemed to flood through her veins. *We will be husband and wife.*

She hadn't known much about sex on Jannah. Young girls were taught everything about children, save how they were produced. She'd picked up more from some of the movies she'd watched on *Logan*, once she'd realised that steamy sex scenes were almost always included in the Empire's entertainments. And she'd read a handful of books that Jayne had given her, back when she'd moved to join Brad. It was strange to realise that Jayne had known that Brad had hoped to marry her…

The thought of sharing herself was scary – and the thought of sharing her life was terrifying. On Jannah, everything a wife owned automatically belonged to the husband. It had been one of the reasons she'd been so reluctant to marry in the first place. The traders expected husband and wife to share everything, including political power. She would be bringing an outsider into the heart of the trader community…just for a moment, she understood how Captain Hamilton must have felt, when he'd adopted her. And *she* had been a powerless stowaway.

I chose this, she reminded herself. *I can deal with it.*

Captain Hamilton caught her arm. "They'll be arguing for hours," he said. "You're shaking like a leaf. Come and get some rest."

Sameena half-expected him to berate her for betraying Brad, but that wasn't the trader way. Marriages came to an end, either through death or separation…and it happened. As long as the separation was amiable and the children were cared for, there would be no outside recrimination. No one would expect Sameena to remain single after Brad's death.

It took two days for the Meet to come to a consensus, a surprisingly long time. "The votes have been tallied," the Mistress said. "We will support the plan, provided that the marriage between Captain Hussein-Hamilton and Commodore Cook goes ahead."

"Blood ties," Captain Hamilton muttered in her ear. "Always the most reliable for us."

"I will return to Madagascar and propose to him," Sameena said.

She flushed at their amusement, although it was in good humour. On Jannah, a woman wasn't expected to propose to a man. And it was rare for a man to propose, certainly not without asking the girl's father first. Normally, both husband and wife would be told who they would be marrying by their parents.

"Good luck," Captain Hamilton said. "I will be happy to stand as your father during the ceremony."

"Thank you," Sameena said. "I'll head back to Madagascar this afternoon."

It took two days to return to the asteroid, which she used to catch up on her sleep and do a little research. Jayne was happy to chat with her, offering her blunt advice that had Sameena giggling and blushing. She suspected that her mother would have given similar advice once her marriage had been organised, although there hadn't been time for a mother-daughter chat after her father had engaged her to the judge. The thought made her scowl, inwardly. Her mother might not have approved of her choice of husband, but she would have liked her parents to be there.

Jamie looked better, she noted with some relief, as he joined her on her ship. He wore a Commodore's uniform, along with the golden star that designated command of a starship – and, she couldn't help noticing, a pistol at his belt. The spare parts and food Sameena had provided had gone a long way towards solidifying his position, but it wasn't secure yet. That was about to change.

"I have a proposal for you," she said, fighting down the urge to giggle. How *did* one propose to a man? God knew she'd never even considered it a possibility before she'd fled to space. "But you need to listen to me first."

She outlined everything, from her proposal to the Meet to what she was prepared to do to uphold it. Jamie listened, his face twisting with conflicting emotions, as she revealed that she had volunteered to marry him, bringing – by proxy – the Imperial Navy squadron into the trader clans. Perhaps it would have been better to have asked him to marry her first, the colder part of her mind noted, but she knew that wouldn't have been fair. He had to make an informed choice.

"I…you're serious about this?" He asked. "About marrying me for my ships?"

"In a manner of speaking," Sameena said. She'd worried that he might marry her for her fortune and industrial production facilities; it honestly hadn't occurred to her that he might have the same worries. "The traders want blood ties between us and you."

"As far as I know," Jamie pointed out, "I have no blood relative with the squadron."

"Details, details," Sameena said, waving them away. "Besides, not everyone in the trader clans is a blood relation either. Trying to track who is related to whom requires a computer and plenty of free time."

She met his eyes. "I'm sorry to spring this on you," she said. She swallowed. The coldness that had served her well in the past had deserted her. "And I don't know what sort of wife I will be. But this is our best chance to salvage something from the ruins of the Empire."

"I understand," Jamie said. He smiled, suddenly. "No pressure, then?"

"None," Sameena said. She'd cursed men who had forced girls into marriage before, but now…just what was the difference between her and them? Did it make a difference if it was the boy who was forced into marriage? "If you turn me down, I will understand."

Jamie was a decent person, she knew. He struggled with the concept; he did want her – she had no doubt of that – but he didn't want her forced into anything. And yet it had been her idea in the first place.

"I accept," Jamie said, finally. "I do like you. I…"

Sameena surprised herself. She leaned forward and kissed him.

After a long second, he kissed her back.

CHAPTER
THIRTY-THREE

> Instead of developing new products, interstellar corporations concentrated on ensuring that there was no hope of any outsider managing to take power. The colonies were either prevented from developing their own industrial bases or brought firmly under outside control before the bases could be brought online. Production of spare parts, for example, was based in the Core Worlds, increasing the price quite significantly by the time they reached the Rim.
> - Professor Leo Caesius, *The Science That Isn't: Economics and the Decline and Fall of the Galactic Empire.*

Sameena stood alone in her room and stared at her reflection in the mirror. Vanity had never been one of her failings, despite Jayne's best attempts to corrupt her, and she hadn't just *looked* at herself for years. Now, the face looking back at her was almost a stranger. Thanks to Paddy's physical training and carefully-tailored food supplements, she looked stronger than she'd ever been on Jannah. Her long dark hair fell around a face that was fuller than she recalled, with soft brown eyes and flawless brown skin.

Her dress was white, setting off her skin colour. Jayne had convinced her to buy something completely new on Madagascar, although the dressmaker had had to adapt something she'd had in stock to fit Sameena, rather than making something completely new. It fitted her like a glove, clinging to her skin in all the right places. It was funny how that no longer bothered her. At least it covered up her skin below the neckline.

Jamie will see everything tonight, she thought. She shivered, half in fear and half in anticipation. The two days it had taken to arrange the wedding ceremony had been filled with kisses, convincing her that it might not be so bad. But the thought still nagged at her.

There was a knock at the door. Sameena opened it with the touch of a button, revealing Ethne and Jayne. "You look lovely," Ethne said, inspecting Sameena minutely. "I just wish that it could have been a bigger ceremony. The first one is always important."

Sameena wondered, suddenly, if Ethne had been married before she'd married Captain Hamilton. It had never occurred to her to ask. Did she have other children? No, *that* was unlikely. Ethne wasn't the type of person to leave her children behind while she sailed off with her new husband.

"Thank you," she said. "And I *really* don't need any more advice."

Jayne giggled. "I think I told her everything she needs to know," she said.

"Oh," Ethne said. She looked up at Sameena. "I'm very sorry, my dear."

"*Mum*," Jayne protested. "I was quite open with her."

Ethne shot her daughter a look that made her shut up instantly. "I know that marriage can be difficult," she said to Sameena. "It can be harder when husband and wife go off on their ship, away from both sets of parents. Even with the best will in the universe, things can go wrong."

"I know," Sameena admitted. And she knew what would have happened on Jannah too. The wife would be expected to put up and shut up. "But I…"

"If you need any advice, or even a friendly ear, you know where to find me," Ethne said, interrupting her. "Men are…strange creatures at times. It's usually good to compare notes with someone else."

"You can probably talk to James about men," Jayne put in. "Just don't listen to a word Paddy says."

She walked over and stood in front of the mirror, inspecting herself. Both women wore green dresses, but Ethne's was relatively decent while Jayne's exposed far too much of her breasts and legs. Sameena couldn't help wondering if Jayne was trying to draw attention away from her – and if that was actually a good thing or not. It could be argued both ways, she decided.

"It's time," Ethne said, quietly. "Shall we go?"

Sameena sucked in a breath as they walked into Madagascar's great hall. It occupied an entire blister on the asteroid's surface, allowing the wedding to take place under the stars, which – according to the RockRats – gave their blessing to happy events. Jamie and his best man entered from the other side of the chamber at the exact same moment, walking with long steps towards the centre of the room. The watching crowd fell silent.

In the centre of the chamber, there was a simple circle drawn on the floor. Sameena, at Ethne's touch, halted just outside it, waiting. She caught Jamie's eye and realised that he was as nervous as herself. And yet he looked dashing in his dress uniform. His best man gave her a smile, then elbowed Jamie. Sameena bit her lip to hide a smile.

Director Yang, the asteroid's supervisor, stepped forward. "We are gathered together to perform the binding of blood," she said. It had taken almost a day to settle on a person to carry out the wedding. Yang had the great advantage of not being linked to either the traders or the Imperial Navy. "Before witnesses, Jamie Cook and Sameena Hussein-Hamilton will pledge to share their lives, to be husband and wife as long as they choose."

She looked over at Sameena. "Do you come, freely and without ties, to this ceremony?"

"I do," Sameena said.

"If there is anyone who wishes to dispute her claim," Yang said, raising her voice, "let him speak now or forever hold his peace."

There was a long nerve-racking pause. Sameena knew no one who could raise a legal objection, but if someone hated her enough…

Yang looked over at Jamie. "Do you come, freely and without ties, to this ceremony?"

"I do," Jamie said.

It would be easy, Sameena knew, for a trader to dispute Jamie's claim. He was – or he had been - part of the Imperial Navy, a tie that would never have been tolerated by the traders in the days of the Empire. Someone *could* make an issue of it…

No one spoke.

"Step into the circle," Yang ordered.

Sameena had to force her legs to move before she could step into the circle. There was no physical barrier, yet she was sure she felt something testing her as she moved, resisting her just long enough for her to prove that she was serious. Perhaps it was her imagination…none of her mother's stories about her wedding had suggested anything of the sort. But then, it was a very different ceremony. And one that would never have been tolerated on Jannah.

What would her father have said, she wondered, if he'd been there? He would have had to approve the marriage on Jannah, as if a young woman couldn't make up her mind who to marry herself. Would he have approved of Jamie, or would he have thrown a fit because he wasn't a Muslim? The Guardians certainly would, she knew. Heaven forbid that young Muslim women married outside the faith! And yet there was a story of kidnapped Muslim brides who had converted their new husbands…

But it was hard to know, looking back across thousands of years, what to believe.

She faced Jamie, who gave her a shy smile. Yang stepped forward, carrying a golden cord in one hand. She looked from one to the other, then nodded in approval.

"Take hands," she ordered.

Sameena reached out with her right hand, taking Jamie's hand in hers. His skin felt warm to the touch and unstable, as if he were shaking slightly. Yang reached out and gently wrapped the cord around their hands, binding them together. It felt both fragile and very strong, as if it was both breakable and unbreakable. Like so many other religious practices, she knew, it was largely symbolic. They were tied together now – and, no matter what happened, they would always be linked together.

"The bonds of blood are formed when two people decide, of their own free will, to share their lives," Yang said. She looked up at Sameena, then over at Jamie. "Do you both still wish to continue."

"I do," Sameena said. Jamie echoed her a moment later.

"Then I proclaim that the bonds of blood are formed," Yang said, formally. She stepped out of the circle, leaving them both alone. "You may now kiss."

Jamie leaned forward. Sameena hesitated for a fraction of a second – she didn't *want* to do anything like that in front of the public gaze – and then kissed him. She heard the sound of people cheering dimly, as if they were miles away, as she caught him up in a hug.

"You have to remain bound until the end of the day," Yang informed them, as they separated. "It helps the bonds of blood to form."

Jamie bent down to whisper in her ear. "And provides no end of amusement for everyone else."

Sameena giggled.

"Congratulations," Jayne said, throwing her arms around Sameena and hugging her tightly. "I hope that the two of you will be very happy together!"

"Thank you," Sameena said, hugging her back. "And thank you for your help."

Captain Hamilton gave her a brief hug, then shook Jamie's hand firmly. "You deserve some happy time together," he said. Sameena felt herself blushing and, looking over at Jamie, realised that he was blushing too. "I think you can forget about the rest of the universe for at least two days."

Sameena scowled. The traders had a tradition of honeymoons, where the new husband and wife would go away to spend time together away from their families, but she didn't have the time. Captain Hamilton and a handful of others could make most of the decisions, yet others would need her presence. Jamie and her would only have a few days before they were called back to duty. There was no way they could go to another star system.

"Don't worry about it," Jayne advised. "I prepared the ship personally. Look in the hold."

"I think we all owe you thanks," a gruff voice said. It took Sameena several moments to realise that the speaker was the CPO who'd helped catch her would-be kidnappers. "If you hadn't come along, we would have wasted away out here."

"Damn right," Jamie's best man said. "We owe you our lives."

He already had a glass of Firewater Mead in his hand, much to Sameena's quiet amusement. Everyone thought that she'd spent billions of credits amassing the bottles of mead on the tables. Or maybe not. They knew that she didn't waste money in pointless displays of conspicuous consumption. Quite a few people might work out the truth.

Not that it matters any longer, she thought. *The Cartel might not survive the fall of the Empire.*

The rest of the ceremony passed in a blur. There was food as well as drink, a mixture of supplies from Rosa and various dainties that had been imported from the Core Worlds and stored in stasis pods until they were needed. Sameena discovered that she didn't like most of them, particularly the more expensive ones. She couldn't help wondering if someone had created a cunning marketing plan to convince the very wealthy that only *they* could afford to eat disgusting foods. It was the only explanation she could think of for their success.

There was music and dancing, followed by long speeches from Captain Hamilton and a handful of others. Sameena rolled her eyes when she saw Yang take the stand long enough to speak about the asteroid's future, silently wondering why Captain Hamilton – who had organised the ceremony – had allowed her to speak. But maybe he did have a point. Yang was in charge of Madagascar, which would be serving as the sector's capital. It was effectively neutral territory.

And the home of the Imperial Navy squadron, she thought. *And where outsiders will go first, just to find out what is happening here.*

It was a relief when, after a final round of toasts, they were allowed to depart the great hall. Jayne, Ethne, Paddy and Captain Hamilton escorted them down to the airlock where *Lead Pipe* had docked; Sameena wondered, briefly, just what Jayne had done to the ship to prepare it for them. The escort stopped at the airlock, allowing them to board the ship alone.

"Husband and wife," Jamie said, wonderingly.

Sameena looked over at him, feeling a smile creeping across her face. He smiled back at her, then followed her onto the bridge. Jayne had already programmed in a course that would take them away from the asteroid, but not too far away, just in case pirates raided the system. Sameena checked it anyway, remembering the stern lecture she'd received from Captain Hamilton after not checking someone else's work, then disengaged the starship from the airlock.

Jamie started to laugh. "Look," he said, pointing to one of the viewscreens. It showed the live feed from the airlock's sensors. "Who did that?"

Sameena followed his gaze, then burst out laughing herself. Jayne had hung a sign over the starship's airlock, somehow. It read JUST MARRIED. Or maybe it had been Paddy's idea of a joke. There was no way to know.

"One of my crew, I guess," she said. She engaged the autopilot once the ship was away from the normal shipping lanes, then stood up. "She said we should look in the hold."

She couldn't help feeling nervous as they walked, hand in hand, down to the hatch leading into the hold. Jayne was her sister, in every way that mattered, yet they were very different people. Something she would have enjoyed might only embarrass Sameena. The hatch hissed open, revealing a pile of blankets and cushions neatly placed on the deck. A handful of simulation candles had been hung from overhead, while a large stasis pod occupied the rear of the hold.

There was a piece of paper stuck to the deck. Sameena picked it up and read it quickly, then started to laugh. Trust Jayne to come up with something to break the ice.

"You don't need to wear your shipsuit for this," Jamie read out loud, his tone suggesting that he was trying not to laugh. "In fact, it quite spoils the mood."

"We were told to wear shipsuits at all times," Sameena admitted, shaking her head in droll amusement. If this was how Jayne had prepared the hold, it was a relief that she hadn't accepted Jayne's offer of a hen night. "I suppose it *would* get in the way."

Jamie laughed. "Us too," he said. "When I was a cadet, they used to say that anyone caught out of a shipsuit would be doing exercise for hours, even when we were on an Earth-compatible planet."

Sameena glanced at him, realised that he was just as nervous as herself, then peered down into the stasis pod. The eerie blue glow of the stasis field illuminated a handful of boxes of chocolates, several bottles of unfamiliar drinks and a small selection of pre-prepared meals and puddings. They would eat well for their short honeymoon.

"I think your sister did a very good job," Jamie said, finally.

"She did," Sameena agreed. She turned to face him, then giggled to cover her nerves. "I think you're meant to kiss me now."

Jamie took her in his arms and kissed her. Sameena tensed as she felt his hands running over her back, then down to cup her buttocks. She forced herself to relax as the kiss deepened, trying to remember Jayne's advice. His hands found the fastening of her dress and undid it, allowing it to fall off her body and crumple to the deck. The shipsuit followed a moment later, peeling away to reveal her bare skin.

"You're beautiful," he whispered, as he started to kiss his way down to her breasts. "You really are."

Part of Sameena wanted to squirm away as his tongue flicked at a nipple, the rest of her wanted him to keep going. Her hands, seemingly of their own accord, pulled at his uniform tab until it joined her dress on the deck. She couldn't help noticing that his shipsuit was tighter than hers, with a hard bulge over his groin. It came off as he pulled her towards the blankets, revealing his naked body.

She'd seen Brad naked a few times, back when they'd been on the same ship, but this was different. This was her husband. Suddenly, some of the whispers she'd heard on Jannah made sense. He was going to penetrate her, to enter her body, to…the thought overwhelmed her, her body stiffening against his. For a moment, she was frozen, unable to move, as memories of Rosa flickered through her mind. They hadn't raped her, but she had still felt violated. And the judge…whatever he had told her father, he would have seen her as nothing more than a pleasurable diversion. A powerless girl who could never escape his clutches. She would have been his slave.

And then the feel of Jamie's mouth on her body melted the ice.

"Be gentle," she whispered, as his mouth moved down to the space between her legs. "It's my first time."

It wouldn't be his, she knew. The Imperial Navy crewmen used the brothels on Madagascar as often as the traders, particularly as there were strong regulations against relationships with someone else on the same crew. Jamie might not even have been sixteen by the time he'd lost his virginity, perhaps to a girlfriend…or a whore. She had carefully refrained from asking, if only because she didn't want to know. It would bother her for no logical reason.

There was a brief pause, so brief that she couldn't help wondering if she had imagined it, then his lips kept working their magic. The universe melted away in a flurry of strange new sensations, until they were completely alone. For the moment, she thought as she gave in to the feelings, everything was well with the universe.

INTERLUDE THREE

The attack came out of nowhere.

Captain Cassie Horsham was blown out of her chair when the first missile slammed into the rear of her freighter. The gravity failed a second later, sending her flying across the compartment and into the bulkhead with stunning force. Alarms rang – too late – throughout the hull, seconds before half of the consoles simply failed. The lights flickered, then dimmed as emergency power came online.

"Enemy starship, right on top of us," Hart snapped. Her co-husband sounded cold, but she heard the undertone of rage in his voice. "It was lying doggo!"

Cassie caught hold of the handles on the bulkhead and used them to pull herself back down to stare at his console. The enemy, whoever they were, had taken no chances. Instead of trying to negotiate, or simply demanding her surrender at gunpoint, it had fired as soon as the freighter entered point-blank range. She had to admire their dedication; they could have been *certain* of an intercept if they'd used their main drives. Instead, they had to have used gas thrusters to inch their way into attack position.

"The entire aft section is *gone*," Jazz said. The youngest co-wife looked terrified, but her voice was steady. "Dear God; the kids!"

Her words hit like a kick to the belly. Nellie and Penelope, James and Lucas; they'd been in the aft section, learning from another of Cassie's co-husbands. The entire family was a tangled mass of relationships and they liked it that way. But now the kids were dead, along with her husband and perhaps a co-wife. The oldest had been merely ten years old.

"They're launching shuttles," Hart reported. "Two of them, both military-grade."

Cassie stared at the display. She'd heard the reports, she'd known that some Imperial Navy ships had gone renegade…but she hadn't quite believed them. Not that the shuttles proved anything, she had to admit. There was more second-hand or junked Imperial Navy equipment pressed into service along the Rim than anyone was prepared to admit. She thought desperately, trying to think of a way to turn the situation around, but there was nothing. Their main drive had been smashed. Escape was impossible.

She wanted to destroy the ship, but she couldn't even do that any longer. The missile had been *very* precise.

"I'm sorry," she said, to her remaining crew. "I'm so sorry."

On the display, the pirate shuttles continued their advance towards the drifting hulk.

CHAPTER THIRTY-FOUR

That is, but just one example. Independent freighters were largely forced out of the Core Worlds by cartels controlled by the interstellar shipping lines, who effectively set the prices for all interstellar shipping. One might expect the independents to help force the cartels to keep prices low. Instead, the cartels manipulated shipping authorities to levy fines on freighter operators who made small mistakes. These fines, at the very least, ensured that prices remained high.

- Professor Leo Caesius, *The Science That Isn't: Economics and the Decline and Fall of the Galactic Empire.*

"That's the latest report from Maxwell," Commander Sidney Peterson said. "Pirate raids are definitely increasing."

Sameena stared down at the display, nodding slowly. The pirates had been slow to realise that the Empire was definitely gone, but when word had finally reached their lairs attacks had skyrocketed. A dozen freighters had been reported destroyed in the last two weeks, as well as three worlds attacked and pillaged by pirate ships. And she didn't have the resources to cover *all* of the possible targets.

"And famine is striking Dueller," she muttered. "What sort of idiot puts a couple of million settlers on such a world?"

"They didn't actually realise that a native crop-eating bug could make the jump from one biological system to another," Peterson said. He'd been the squadron's junior intelligence officer before his superiors had fled, leaving him behind. Since then, he'd shaped up nicely as her intelligence officer. "It isn't actually common."

Sameena scowled. Six months had passed since she'd convinced the traders to back her plan – and she'd married Jamie – and the sector's decline was becoming alarmingly evident. It was simple enough to keep Rosa afloat – it could feed itself, if nothing else – but other worlds had been dependent on the Empire for supplies. As the decline picked up speed, failures she had never even imagined were starting to take place. And now two million colonists were on the verge of starvation.

The Empire could have handled it, she thought sourly. *A team of biochemists and genetic engineers could have hammered out a disease-resistant strain for that particular world...*

It was absurd, she had thought, to think of disease as something that spread between star systems. But if rats and cockroaches could make it from world to world, why couldn't a disease? Most humans had some manner of improved disease resistance engineered into their bodies, but the same couldn't be said of their crops. If the disease on Dueller reached Rosa, it would wipe out their entire farming sector. And Dueller was begging for help.

There were times when she wondered if the Grand Senate had deliberately intended to leave the sector to wither on the vine, now that they had been separated from the Empire. For every world like Rosa, there were three or four colonies that couldn't even feed themselves, let alone sell their products. Marigold's Folly had narrowly escaped catastrophe only a month ago, when two air processors had failed simultaneously. It was easy to believe that the Grand Senate had been guided by malice.

"We can gather enough supplies to keep Dueller ticking over until they set up algae farms," she said. Naturally, the colony's founding corporation hadn't bothered to set up algae farms of their own, no matter what Imperial Law said. They'd probably seen it as a needless expense. "But getting them there is going to be a pain."

"Pirates might see what we're doing and come after us," Peterson agreed. "Maybe we could use it to set a trap."

Sameena was still considering it when she went home, back to the quarters she shared with Jamie. She hadn't realised, somehow, that taking on the job of coordinator for the new government would mean that she would have to stay at Madagascar. There were plenty of jobs she could hand down to someone else, but that still left her with hundreds of issues that required her personal attention. In hindsight, perhaps she should have offered the post to Captain Hamilton instead.

Madagascar, thankfully, was blossoming again after a month of difficulties. Interstellar trade was picking up; with most of the convoys rotated through the asteroid's system its denizens had a chance to make money. And then there were the vastly-expanded training programs to produce new starship crews, engineers, doctors and everything else the new government might need. Given time, the system might well be able to stand on its own two feet.

She stepped through the hatch and smiled as she saw Jamie sitting on the sofa, reading a datapad. Neither of them had much time to relax, even when they were technically off-duty; the squadron required as much of Jamie's attention as the rest of the government did from her. Six months of frantic activity had put five of the older craft back into commission, but it wasn't enough to cover the entire sector. They'd been reduced to bolting weapons onto freighters and hoping for the best.

"Good to see you again," Jamie said, as if they hadn't last seen each other in the morning. "I brought home dinner."

Sameena nodded and sat down next to him, taking his hand in hers. "The people on Dueller are starving," she said, softly. "We're going to have to send food stocks from here to there."

Jamie took a moment to consider it. "Gathering so many freighters in one place would be a tempting target," he pointed out. "The pirates will definitely hear of it."

"I know," Sameena said. "There's no way to keep it hidden."

She scowled. Most of the traders might have agreed to go along with the new government, at least for the moment, but there were plenty who hadn't been involved with the decision and saw no reason to be bound by it. And then there were true independents, and grey colonies, and…she knew that there were plenty of links between the pirates and her growing economy. They would definitely hear of the planned shipment.

"And we will tie up at least six of our destroyers escorting it," Jamie said. "That means that they won't be available elsewhere."

"I know," Sameena admitted. The pirates might go somewhere else, convinced that the chances of interception would be lower. And they'd be right. "Is there any way we can do both?"

Jamie scowled. "Steve has been working on a possible solution," he said. "He turned a couple of medium freighters into q-ships. They're not exactly warships, but they wouldn't have to be."

Sameena lifted an eyebrow.

"They don't need to move any faster than the average freighter," Jamie explained. "It isn't uncommon for freighters to have military-grade sensors, so the pirates won't see anything odd about them until they get into firing range. And then we blow them away."

"Or try to take them alive," Sameena said. "If we could hunt down their bases, we might be able to put a crimp in their operations."

She scowled. "But will they take the bait?"

"We would only send two destroyers with the convoy," Jamie said. "If nothing else, we would have four more available for duties elsewhere. The pirates might even consider that they could *take* two destroyers. It wouldn't be impossible."

"It would be a stupid pirate who tried," Sameena muttered. "How long until the ships are ready?"

"A week, from what Steve said," Jamie admitted. "How long will it take to load up the other freighters?"

"At least that long," Sameena said. She thought about it, briefly. "We do have a pirate problem out at Maxwell too. Maybe we can use that attack as an excuse to cut down on the convoy escorts."

"Then have the destroyers called away as soon as they reach Dueller," Jamie suggested. "That would leave the field clear for the pirates to engage the convoy."

Sameena considered it. If they got a clear shot at the pirate ships, it was worth a little risk…but losing the convoy would be disastrous if the operation went wrong. Dueller couldn't be left to starve. And the pirates would know that too. Leaving the convoy uncovered would look very suspicious to their eyes.

"We could have the destroyers race ahead," Jamie said. "They desperately need the food production equipment, if nothing else."

"I know," she said. That would at least look *plausible*. She made her mind up. "I'll go with the freighters."

Jamie stared at her. "You'll go with them?"

"I have to show my confidence in the scheme," Sameena pointed out. "Besides, I should be there to show the people of Dueller that we haven't forgotten them."

"It isn't the only planet that needs help," Jamie said, with the air of a man who knows that he has already lost the argument. "But if you go, I should command the destroyers."

"You can't," Sameena said. "One of us definitely has to remain here."

Jamie sighed. It was funny, but the only times they really argued was when they were on the verge of separation, even for a few days. Each of their trips out to the interstellar factory had been punctuated by arguments. Maybe it would get worse as they grew older, Sameena had wondered. Jayne and Paddy had had some arguments that had been audible even outside the locked hatch.

"Just take care of yourself," he said, firmly. "It's *you* that's holding this mess together, you know. Not me."

Sameena gave him a hug, then stood up and walked over to the kitchen. The pleasure of cooking her own food was something else she'd had to give up; now, they could only take food from the Navy kitchens and reheat it in the microwave. Jamie swore that the Imperial Navy's cooking course was the hardest in the Empire, if only because no one had ever passed it. Sameena had needed several minutes to get the joke.

"This mess will endure, I hope," she said. Fifty-seven planets, thirty of them Earth-compatible, had signed up with her government. Compared to the Empire, her yoke was very light – and almost non-existent groundside. The only restrictions were certain limits on how planets could treat visitors from off-world. "We just have to hang on until we start producing new warships."

She scowled. Steve had been doing his best, but production of planetary defence systems was an immensely slow project. The Imperial Navy, he'd commented when they'd last met, had designed defensive systems that were hard to construct, if only to deter planets from producing their own. They'd prefer that planets were defenceless if they ever alienated the Grand Senate. He'd started designing cheaper platforms, but they tended to be easier for the enemy to take out.

The microwave *dinged*. She removed the tray of food, separated it out onto two plates and then passed one to Jamie. He took it and smiled gratefully, picking up a fork and using it to eat with gusto. Sameena eyed her food – a mix of watery potatoes and stringy meat – and reminded herself that beggars couldn't be choosers. Besides, she shouldn't be dining out in style when too many people were forced to eat ration bars. It would leave a bad impression.

"I'll organise the convoy tomorrow," she said, distracting herself from the taste. Jamie was right. *Clearly*, the catering course *was* too hard for anyone to master. "Can you assign two destroyers to the escort force?"

"There are six in the system at the moment," Jamie said. "I can have two of them assigned to you and send a further two out to Maxwell. That should suffice for the deception plan."

Sameena nodded. They'd publically determined that they would keep at least two destroyers in the Madagascar System at all times, just to ensure that the universe knew that Madagascar was safe. No one would see anything suspicious if they only sent two destroyers with the convoy.

"Good," she said. She put the plate aside with a grimace. "How can you eat that crap?"

Jamie chuckled. "It's amazing what someone will eat if they're starving," he said. He sobered, his face turning grim. "They'll be eating themselves on Dueller soon enough."

Sameena shuddered. One mining colony, not too different from Marigold's Folly, had gone silent. When a starship had finally investigated, they'd discovered that the food production system had failed and the inhabitants had resorted to cannibalism. The handful of survivors had reported that they'd drawn lots and the chosen sacrifices had accepted their fate, but Sameena suspected that the truth was far darker. No one really wanted to think about having to go the same route.

"Cheerful thought," she said, sarcastically. "Is there any better news?"

"We came across a stranded mercenary company on Sungai Buloh," Jamie said, "After some negotiation, they agreed to join us rather than remain there indefinitely."

"Good thinking," Sameena said. "Why were they there?"

"There was a civil war on the planet," Jamie reminded her. He smiled with some private amusement. "They moved in and joined up with one side as soon as the Imperial Navy pulled out and helped them win the war, just in time for the Empire to collapse. Evidently, there was a second round of civil war and their transports were destroyed."

"Careless," Sameena said. Most mercenary outfits had their own transports, although the Empire had tried to prevent them from obtaining any actual *warships*. That restriction had been destroyed now, along with the Empire itself. "Can we trust them?"

"I believe that they will be interrogated thoroughly by Paddy," Jamie said. There might be a good-natured rivalry between the Navy and the Marines, but there was a great deal of respect too. "He'll make the final decision."

Sameena nodded. The negotiations that had produced her government had resulted in an agreement to establish a space infantry force – they'd shied away from using the term Marine – but an absolute ban on a force capable of occupying an entire planet. Sameena had agreed, once the treaty had been revised to ensure that the signatory planets would provide ground troops if necessary. Besides, once someone took the high orbitals, a planet was effectively defenceless anyway. She didn't *need* a ground occupation force to make her mark.

But there was a considerable shortage of equipment for her not-Marines. Most of the Marine supply depots had been emptied when the Marines had been called back to the Core Worlds - and Paddy had warned her that most of the remaining gear wouldn't be usable. They would have to build up their own sets of powered combat armour or protection suits from scratch, once the handful of untailored suits on the naval base ran out. Oddly, the suits were actually more complex than a destroyer and the more advanced versions were more expensive than a planetary defence gunboat.

"The other odd point comes from Intelligence," Jamie admitted. "Our networks were fragmented when the Empire withdrew, but the intelligence staffers have been putting together an odd report. Someone was buying up quite a few warships over the last three to four years."

Sameena scowled. "Pirates?"

"Perhaps," Jamie said. "But some of their purchases were for heavier ships than destroyers or light cruisers. It would be a rare pirate crew that could handle them. I think it's more likely that they were purchased by a planetary liberation force, although such big ships would still be difficult for them to handle."

He shook his head. "It's possible that Intelligence was seeing something that isn't really there," he warned. "They've seen patterns before that were really nothing more than coincidence. But it's still odd."

Sameena nodded. One of the things she'd picked up quickly was that Imperial Navy starships required immense crews. They could have cut their crewmen by an order of magnitude, she knew, but if the ship ran into trouble they'd need the extra manpower to carry out repairs. Apart from a handful of planetary defence forces in the Core Worlds, the only force that could generate such manpower was the Imperial Navy. A pirate gang would have real trouble maintaining just one heavy cruiser.

"They might have been buying them while training the crews," she said. "It was what I did, in a sense. The ships could have been kept in cold storage…"

"I'd hate to have to rely on that," Jamie said. He shook his head. "If someone in the sector had purchased so much firepower, I would have expected to see it by now."

"Pointed at us," Sameena said, reluctantly. There were several worlds in the sector that might have tried to build their own empires, if they'd had a chance. "Or they could have offered us the ships."

"It would be years before we could absorb them, let alone bring them back up to full operational status," Jamie admitted. He sounded rather doubtful. "Our manpower needs to be built up too."

Sameena nodded. The educational system needed trained manpower – and there were too many demands on their manpower elsewhere. Given time, she knew, they would overcome the bottlenecks. But it would still take years. Who knew what could happen in that time?

She looked down at the datapad, then put it aside and reached for her husband. It was funny how she'd gone from being a little nervous of sex to demanding it all the time, but Jayne had assured her that was perfectly normal. It was when the ardour cooled, she'd admitted, that couples had to be careful of themselves. They needed to lay the foundations for real love or their relationship would break apart.

And Jayne has a happy life with Paddy, she reminded herself. *Perhaps I should listen to her.*

"I'll be leaving to see Steve tomorrow," Sameena said, firmly. Captain Hamilton could handle everything that was likely to crop up in the next few days. "And I'll miss you dreadfully. I think I can think of better ways to spend the evening."

Jamie grinned at her. "Me too," he said, as his hands started to work on her shipsuit. "I can definitely think of a better way."

CHAPTER THIRTY-FIVE

Another example lay in food and entertainment production. The Empire could (and did) produce vast amounts of algae-based products to feed its population and even more entertainment to keep the population distracted. This caused a population boom – the cost of raising a child had fallen – that placed colossal stress on the social network.
- Professor Leo Caesius, *The Science That Isn't: Economics and the Decline and Fall of the Galactic Empire.*

"Welcome aboard, Captain."

Sameena smiled, accepting a somewhat sloppy salute from Commander Foxglove. He seemed absurdly young for such a position, but trained manpower *was* very limited. Besides, as Jamie had pointed out, Foxglove wouldn't be the senior officer on the convoy. Sameena outranked him in at least two different ways.

"Thank you," she said.

Foxglove's enthusiasm was infectious, she realised, as he showed her around the Q-Ship. The small crew – mostly former Imperial Navy crewmen who had settled on various worlds, only to be called back into service – seemed to like him, despite his youth. Sameena had feared that there would be some doubt about serving under such a young officer, but it didn't seem to be a problem. Proven competence went further than age.

Sneaky Bastard had been a standard medium freighter before Steve's crews had torn out the cargo holds and replaced them with missile launchers and energy weapons. According to Foxglove, who chatted happily about the destructive power under their command, they could give anyone who came too close a very bloody nose, although he reluctantly admitted that there were some flaws in the design. The starship just wasn't designed for a long engagement with an enemy ship.

"The internal transport system is inefficient compared to a standard warship," he explained, seriously. "It actually takes us longer to reload the missile tubes than I'd prefer, which reduces our rate of fire after we shoot the tubes dry. Unfortunately, rebuilding the hull to include a properly automated system for missile transfer would have taken far too long."

"So short engagements only," Sameena said, slowly. She'd never commanded a real engagement before, outside simulations. And Jamie had warned her that simulations were rarely as complicated as the real universe. "What about damage control?"

"We have little more armour than the average freighter," Foxglove confessed. "If we happened to take serious damage, Captain, we would be in real trouble."

He went off into a long stream of technobabble that Sameena had difficulty following, but the basic idea was simple enough. Battleships were built to soak up damage and keep going; freighters, as a general rule, were built as close to the margin as possible. Adding additional armour might have tipped off the pirates, if they happened to watch the convoy carefully before revealing their presence, as well as putting additional demands on an already overworked power plant. She would have given anything for Earth's vast industrial base.

And while I'm wishing, she thought sourly, *I'd like the entire Imperial Navy too.*

The bridge had been extensively redesigned, she discovered as Foxglove led her into the compartment. Instead of the comfortable shambles of a trader bridge, there were nine consoles arranged in front of the command chair and a single massive holographic display. It looked very neat and precise; the consoles, Foxglove explained, would be manned at all times, even in Phase Space. If nothing else, Sameena told herself, it would provide time for training. Half the crew was rusty and the other half was composed of volunteers from the trader community.

"The convoy is ready to depart," Foxglove said, as Sameena took the command chair. It was surprisingly comfortable, but it was designed to prevent slouching. The Captain, it seemed, always had to look as if he were in charge. "All it needs is your command."

Sameena allowed herself a smile. It felt *good* to be out in space again, even if she was leaving her husband and son behind at Madagascar. And it would ensure that she remained in practice, rather than watching her skills degenerate and her perceptions warp to the point where she started demanding the impossible. The Grand Senate's distance from the rest of the population had distorted its perception of reality, she knew. It was something she didn't want to happen to her.

The Grand Senate had plenty of margin for error, she thought. *It took them thousands of years to grind the Empire into rubble. I don't have that kind of time.*

"Set our course," she ordered, "and then take us out."

Her smile widened as *Sneaky Bastard* shuddered into life, following the first destroyer as she led the way towards the Phase Limit. The freighter handled very poorly, she couldn't help noticing; Steve's engineers had crammed weapons and sensors into the hull, but they hadn't been able to upgrade the engines without revealing far too much. She was silently grateful that *this* freighter wouldn't have to dock at an orbiting station, let alone land on a planet's surface. It would be an immensely tricky task.

She glanced down at her console as a private message popped up. Jamie wished her good luck and good hunting – and told her that he loved her. Sameena felt an odd sense of loss, finally understanding why so many Imperial Navy officers considered themselves married to the service, rather than to their husbands or wives. They might not see their families for months or years after they departed. Part of her wanted to turn the convoy over to the next senior officer and go back to Madagascar…she pushed the thought aside, bitterly. She couldn't do that, any more than she could call Jamie's ship to escort them.

Command has a price, she thought, remembering Captain Hamilton's words. He'd been lucky; he'd been able to take his wife with him. The Imperial Navy wasn't so tolerant; she'd discovered, to her amusement, that there was an entire series of regulations on intimate relationships between officers and crew. On paper, at least, relationships were either banned or hedged around with practical restrictions. Jamie had admitted, reluctantly, that well-connected officers were free to ignore the rules. And frequently did so.

She wrote a quick reply, telling him that she loved him too, then sat back in her chair as the convoy crossed the Phase Limit. As always, the destroyers seemed impatient to zip into Phase Space, but the convoy waited until they were some distance from the limit before powering up their drives. Sameena – for the first time – felt uncomfortable as the freighter heaved and moaned its way into Phase Space. The drive, she realised grimly, wasn't properly tuned.

"It's a refurbished piece of junk," Foxglove explained, when she asked. "The engineers swear that it's reliable, but they haven't been able to eliminate the uneven harmonics in the drive field."

Sameena scowled, feeling an unpleasant sensation in her chest. She'd always seen her complete lack of reaction to the transit into Phase Space as a sign that she was truly where she belonged; feeling a reaction now bothered her, even though there was a technical reason for it. Making a mental note to have the drive replaced completely at the next available opportunity, she stood up, passed command of the bridge over to Foxglove and headed out to find her cabin. It was only a short distance from the bridge.

She had to smile as she stepped inside. Imperial Navy warships had large cabins for their senior officers – battleships, she'd been told, gave their commanders virtual palaces – but Steve and his design crew had largely been composed of civilians. The cabin was the largest she'd ever owned, yet it was smaller than her bedroom on Jannah or the rooms she shared with Jamie on Madagascar. She had no doubt that an Imperial Navy Captain would have complained loudly if he'd been given a space more suited to a Lieutenant. They probably thought that they'd earned more space, by the time they'd worked their way up from the shared quarters used by ensigns or crewmen.

Idiots, she thought, as she sat down on the bed. Captain Hamilton had shared a cabin with his wife…and she'd never heard either of them complaining about the space. Nor had Brad, come to think of it, or Sameena herself. *No wonder the Imperial Navy ran into trouble.*

She picked up a datapad Jamie had given her and flicked through to the first page. He'd explained, reluctantly, that she had very little tactical experience – and she had to learn what her forces were capable of, before she sent them into battle. Paddy had seconded his words, pointing out that the Grand Senate's more absurd orders had come from ignorance rather than malice or stupidity. They simply hadn't known what they were doing.

The first set of tactical exercises seemed relatively simple, on paper. Sameena puzzled out the problems involved in running down another starship, attacking a planet and protecting a convoy, then read the next set of explanations and realised that they were actually quite complicated. Attacking a planet, according to the Imperial Navy's tactical manual, actually offered an opportunity to bring the enemy's fleet to battle. Their homeworld couldn't run away from combat.

But if the enemy had even a short lead, avoiding engagement would be simple, she realised, grimly. So many of the Imperial Navy's tactics were geared around forcing the enemy to fight that she had no difficulty in grasping *that* factor. *Cutting them off from their supplies makes it impossible for them to keep going.*

She finished the first set of paper exercises, promising herself time in the simulator over the next two weeks, then headed down to the galley to eat. Unlike a trader starship, there was a single table at the head of the compartment for the Captain, even though the freighter wasn't a proper warship. Sameena couldn't help feeling isolated as she sat down and ate a small meal, prepared from food stocks imported from Rosa. Everything on the ship, she realised sourly, was designed to both isolate the Captain and promote his superiority. The traders agreed that each starship had precisely one commander, but they didn't grant their commanders anything like the absolute power of the Imperial Navy. It would be devilishly easy to abuse it.

And it has been abused, she thought, as she finished her meal. She'd encountered a handful of Imperial Navy commanding officers who had acted like little tin gods, while the former CO of Madagascar had required a huge bribe to make sure that justice was done. *It won't be abused on my watch.*

She stood up and walked back to her cabin, shaking her head inwardly at how many salutes came her way. Outside the rank-less compartments – the bridge, galley and engineering – everyone who saw her was legally required to salute her, unless they happened to be carrying something that required both hands to hold it steady. Jamie had told her, mischievously, that every cadet at the Academy had looked for excuses to do just that. Compared to the traders, the Imperial Navy was ridiculously formal.

Her cabin felt empty when she entered and turned down the lights. It took her a moment to realise that she missed Jamie, so badly that it was almost a physical pain. They'd been separated before – when one of them had gone to the factory complex, or out with the destroyers on training exercises – but this was different. She wouldn't see him for nearly a month, if that. They might well be held up, delaying their return to Madagascar. Her bed felt cold and empty as she pulled the sheets over her head and tried to sleep.

The next two weeks fell into a routine. She would stand watch on the bridge in the morning, then run simulations or explore the ship in the afternoon. It felt odd to have so many people around her – both of her previous ships had been minimalist – but she could see why some people would take comfort in it. Besides, if they *did* run into trouble, there would be more hands to help with the repairs. They ran through emergency damage control drills, practicing endlessly until they knew what they were doing. Sameena just hoped that it would work so well in real life.

"It probably won't," Foxglove admitted, when she broached the topic with him. "Back when we were doing tactical exercises at the Academy, there was always *something* screwy about the instructions we were given. If we followed them blindly, we generally ended up dead – or worse. There was always an element of unpredictability in the simulations."

He smiled, enjoying the chance to lecture. "A standard *Flower*-class destroyer can have several different weapons loads," he added. "If you thought you were facing a missile-heavy design, you'd hang back and engage at long range, while an energy-heavy design would allow you to move closer before you entered their firing range. But if you picked the wrong tactics…you might have your head handed to you. And pirate ships tended to have even *weirder* weapons loads. I recall an exercise where the pirate ship had crammed external racks onto the hull, giving them a crushing opening barrage."

Sameena blinked in surprise. "But a single direct hit might cripple them," she protested. It was unlikely that any of the missiles would actually be *detonated* by enemy fire, but a direct hit would certainly smash the external racks. They were fragile, designed for immediate jettisoning as soon as they'd launched their deadly cargo. "What sort of idiot would do that?"

"An idiot looking for a brief advantage," Foxglove said. "And, according to the report I read, it worked – once."

Sameena mulled it over as she worked through the next set of combat simulations. Foxglove was right, she realised; the pre-operation briefings tended to miss out certain vital details, or deliberately misinterpret certain pieces of intelligence. She felt a new respect for Jamie and the others who had gone through the Academy's program, even though it hadn't taught them much about the real universe. They'd mastered combat tactics that hadn't been required for hundreds of years.

But they will be required now, she thought, thinking of all the Imperial Navy officers who might have gone rogue. The Core Worlds might as well be millions of light years away for all they'd heard from them, after the brief announcement that the Empire was pulling out. It was possible that they were stable…no, the decay had gone too far to be stopped by Imperial Edict. The whole system would collapse, leaving only rubble and a handful of successor states. Sooner or later, those states would come to find out what had happened in her sector.

And start fighting each other, she thought. Somehow, she doubted that multiple interstellar powers could co-exist peacefully for very long. The Unification Wars had come in the wake of massive interstellar conflicts that had killed billions of people and sterilised a few dozen worlds. Professor Sorrel had admitted that there was a great deal they didn't know about that time – the Empire had written the history books – but he had agreed that the pre-unification era had been one of massive bloodshed. The post-Empire era was likely to be the same.

It made her wonder if anyone else had seen the disaster coming. She'd had the advantage of not being immersed in the trader community from birth, but surely she wasn't unique. There were – or had been – trillions of humans in the Empire. It seemed impossible that she could have been the *only* person to see disaster looming and take precautions. What if some of the planetary governments had made their own preparations?

She shook her head. There was no way to know.

It was a relief when they finally dropped back into normal space, just outside Dueller's Phase Limit. There was a long pause as the destroyers checked for enemy contacts, then escorted the freighters across the Phase Limit before broadcasting a message stating that they were going to take emergency supplies to the planet. Dueller *needed* the algae-production facilities, Sameena knew; it was the most convincing excuse they'd been able to devise for the destroyers to leave the convoy. She watched them go, unsure if she really wanted to encounter pirates or not. Giving them a bloody nose was important, but so was saving Dueller.

"Picking up a greeting broadcast from Dueller," the communications officer said, as the convoy crawled towards the planet. It would be hours before they could enter orbit and start unloading. "The situation seems to have grown worse."

Sameena gritted her teeth, feeling powerless. There was nothing they could do, apart from pray that the supplies on the convoy were enough to see the planet's population through a very bad time. Jamie had wondered out loud, the last time they'd seen each other, if the disease striking Dueller was wholly natural. It really was astonishingly rare, he'd pointed out, for something to jump from one biosphere to another. Jayne had agreed when Sameena had checked with her.

"It would be easier for us to get pregnant off snakes and elephants than something from one biosphere affecting others," she'd said. She'd winked at Paddy and made a remark about a gorilla having made her pregnant before returning to the topic at hand. "It is quite possible that someone gave it a little push."

The thought made Sameena scowl. Whatever else could be said about the Empire, it had been careful to preserve and protect planetary biospheres. If someone had created a biological weapon to wipe one biosphere clean, it was easy to imagine it spreading to other worlds. Who would be so damn irresponsible? There were easier ways, she knew, to eradicate an entire planetary population, if someone happened to be so depraved that they wanted to try. Surely the population would be more useful alive.

There was a chime from the sensor console. "Captain," the sensor officer said, "I think we have company."

CHAPTER THIRTY-SIX

Unsurprisingly, economic growth staggered and started to fall. This had disastrous knock-on effects. An empire that included trillions of human beings – with eighty billion on Earth alone – found it harder to find enough educated people to maintain its society. What newly-educated people there were found themselves being pushed into trying to keep the society running, rather than making new developments.
- Professor Leo Caesius, *The Science That Isn't: Economics and the Decline and Fall of the Galactic Empire.*

"Show me," Sameena ordered, pushing her morbid thoughts aside.

"Two contacts, possibly more," the sensor officer said. "Both advancing towards us on intercept vector."

Sameena peered over his shoulder, scowling inwardly. It was difficult to acquire accurate readings at such a distance, but there were definitely at least two starships heading towards the convoy. She worked it out in her head, then glanced at the main display to confirm her thoughts. The unknown ships would enter missile range in thirty minutes.

"They're crawling," Foxglove observed, thoughtfully. "They could be on us in less than five minutes if they pushed their drives a little harder."

"Perhaps they can't," the sensor officer suggested. "Pirate ships aren't always the best maintained in the galaxy."

"We dare not assume that to be true," Sameena said. It would be a very rare pirate crew that chose to operate such a ship. The freighters might be able to outrun them even without much of a head start. And an Imperial Navy warship would have no difficulty chasing them down. "I think they're being careful."

She sat back down in the command chair and studied the main display. Assuming that her convoy had had only civilian-grade sensors, they wouldn't see the pirates for at least another twenty minutes…did the pirates *know* that they had military-grade passive sensors? But if they had known, they would surely have assumed that they had already been detected…she scowled, realising just what the tactical manuals had meant when they'd talked about the burden of command. A wrong decision or a badly flawed assumption might get them all killed.

"One of them is definitely a light cruiser, judging by the power curves," the sensor officer said, seven minutes later. "The other is smaller. I think it's probably a destroyer, but one that has been heavily modified at one point. The power signature doesn't fit anything in the databanks."

Sameena nodded. The Imperial Navy designed its ships for easy repairs and upgrades, something that had come in very handy as the Empire's education and technical base had started to decline. They might be facing an old hull crammed with modern weapons, such as they were. Steve's complaints about technological stagnation applied just as much to the Imperial Navy as they did to the Empire as a whole. There hadn't really been *that* many improvements since the first battleship had been launched into space, thousands of years ago.

"Looks like a vanity project ship," Foxglove observed. He pressed on when Sameena shot him a questioning look. "Every so often, one of the richer worlds starts its own building project, rather than borrowing designs from the Imperial Navy. Those ships are sometimes superior designs, but it's more common to end up with a useless hodgepodge. They tend to be right buggers to maintain too."

Sameena frowned. "How many have you seen?"

"There were a handful stored at the Academy," Foxglove admitted. "Mostly used to show us precisely what we should *not* do, if we ever went into starship design."

"Sensor sweep," the sensor officer snapped. "They just pinged us."

And now we're allowed to know they're there, Sameena thought. "Bring up our civilian active sensors," she ordered. Even primitive equipment wouldn't have missed the pirate sensor sweep. "Scan them back."

She scowled as the display sharpened. "One light cruiser, confirmed," the sensor officer said. "One frigate…I can't identify the class. Both picking up speed now and sweeping us regularly."

"General signal," Sameena ordered. "Alter course to head away from the incoming ships, then accelerate to maximum speed."

They'd drilled endlessly in simulations, but she couldn't help feeling nervous as they tried it for the first time. The convoy was hardly uniform; the two q-ships had a lower maximum speed than the other ships in the flotilla. If the pirates came after them, they should run the q-ships down first. If…she scowled, remembering all the times the simulations had gone wrong. The pirates might be trying to herd them into a trap.

"And send a general distress call," she added. "They'll expect us to call back the destroyers."

"It will be an hour before they can get here," Foxglove said, darkly.

Sameena nodded. The pirates would have an hour to capture the ships, get them back across the Phase Limit and escape into interstellar space, where the freighters could be looted at leisure. If the q-ships hadn't been there, it wouldn't have been too difficult for them, even if the freighter crews wanted to fight. Resistance would have been largely futile. Besides, everyone knew what happened to people who were captured by pirates.

The range slowly narrowed as the pirate ships came after them. Sameena frowned; there was something odd about their motions, but she couldn't quite put her finger on it. And yet it looked oddly familiar…

"They're new to their ship," the sensor officer said. "I don't think they quite know what they are doing."

Sameena grinned. *That* was what she'd been missing.

Foxglove was more sceptical. "How can you be sure?"

"There are dozens of tiny little details," the sensor officer reported. He sounded pleased with his deduction. "The drive field is baseline; they're not even trying to squeeze additional power out of it. They're not trying to massage their sensors to pull out more data, or even spoof *our* sensors.

And their targeting is straight out of the manual. We could break their locks if we didn't care about revealing ourselves."

His smile dimmed. "They don't even understand the basics cadets are taught," he added. "I don't think they really know what they are doing."

There's a lot of that about, Sameena thought, remembering just how hard it was to turn ignorant teenagers into mechanics and engineers. *She'd* had problems and she'd had much less to unlearn than the average child born in the Empire. But it was heartening, in a way. The pirates might have more firepower, yet her crews had more experience and understanding of their own equipment.

"Let us hope that you are right," she said, out loud. "Time to intercept?"

"Seventeen minutes, unless they accelerate," the helmsman said. "I…"

"Missile separation," the sensor officer barked.

"Warning shot," Foxglove said, from the tactical console. "They aimed to miss us by a comfortable margin."

Sameena nodded, but she couldn't help tensing as the missile detonated. A direct hit would cause considerable damage.

"Standard penetrator warhead," the sensor officer reported. "Not a nuke or laser head."

"They wouldn't want to waste those on warning shots," Sameena said. Obtaining nuclear warheads was depressingly easy. Laser heads were trickier, but pirates always seemed to have few problems obtaining what they needed. It had puzzled her – the Empire seemed to take a dim view of weapons in private hands – until she'd realised that a pirate ship could easily bombard a planet with rocks rather than nukes. "I imagine that they will be hailing us in a few minutes."

"Picking up a laser message," the sensor officer said. "It's audio only."

"Put it on," Sameena ordered.

The voice was utterly atonal, almost certainly produced by a computer and scrubbed clean of anything that might identify its origins. Not, Sameena suspected, that it would have mattered if they pulled a perfect voiceprint out of the signal. It was easy to fake someone's voice, creating reasonable doubt in a courtroom. But then, few pirates ever saw a courtroom anyway. If they were caught, they were generally interrogated and then pushed out the nearest airlock.

"You are under the guns of a warship," it said. "You will cut your drives and surrender immediately or we will fire into your hull."

Sameena suspected that the pirate was bluffing. *Sneaky Bastard* wouldn't look like a warship, or anything other than a doddering old tramp freighter. Firing into her hull might cripple the drives, leaving her utterly helpless…or it might destroy the ship completely. The pirate crews were held together by fear and the spoils of their raids. Wantonly destroying a possible prize wouldn't endear the pirate commander to his subordinates.

"Keep us on our current course," she ordered. "And send another transmission to the destroyers. Make it sound more panicky than the last one."

"They're firing a second missile," Foxglove reported. "This one is going to come far too close to our hull."

Sameena watched as the missile flashed past them and detonated. "I think they're getting more serious now," she said. "Order the *Lying Bastard* to cut engines with us."

She was tempted to broadcast their surrender, hoping to lull the pirates into overconfidence, but Jamie had been horrified when she'd mentioned it to him. If they used surrender as a ruse of war, he'd pointed out, no one would accept their surrenders. Her crews might one day face a honourable opponent, rather than pirates, and they might have no choice, but to surrender. But if the enemy believed the surrender to be a trick…

"Cut engines," she ordered. "Now."

The pirates came on rapidly, altering course slightly to close in on the q-ships. Sameena ran through it again and again in her mind; timing was everything. If they fired too soon, the pirates might have a chance to escape or engage her in a long-range missile duel, while if they fired too late the pirates might be able to destroy her ships too. There would be a very brief window of opportunity to use the advantage of surprise ruthlessly. If she missed it…

"They're launching shuttles," the sensor officer reported.

"Target them with lasers," Sameena ordered. Her crew was armed, but she didn't dare risk allowing the pirates to board. "Fire as soon as we engage the enemy starships."

She couldn't fault the pirate tactics, she decided, ruefully. The pirate commander evidently intended to scoop up as much of the convoy as possible; now that he'd cowed the two slowest freighters, he could go after the other freighters while his shuttle crews secured their targets. It actually opened up a new danger, she realised; they might accidentally evade her best window of opportunity without even noticing what they'd done. *That* would be ironic. The same luck that had kept them alive, if they really knew nothing about operating and maintaining their ships, would save them from destruction.

They could adjust their own course slightly, she considered, but it might seem like they were trying to flee…or, if the pirate commander was feeling paranoid, get into firing position. He might flee himself or he might open fire on the entire convoy. She didn't dare allow him too much time to think. Her eyes tracked the display as the four starships converged…

"Load up the firing patterns," she ordered. "If you can take advantage of their poor sensor controls, do so."

"Understood," Foxglove said. "I'm programming the missiles for random evasive patterns. If they are actually trying to run their fire control manually…"

Sameena smiled. No human brain could hope to keep up with the split-second decisions that were needed to handle a starship's point defence. Even the Imperial Navy allowed the computers to control their point defence, rather than risk disaster. But the pirates might not have even realised that was possible. It was a curious oversight, one that made little sense.

Perhaps their tactical officer is trying to make himself indispensable, she thought. If *she* had been stuck on a pirate ship, she would certainly have sought some protection to keep her skin intact. *Or maybe they're just idiots.*

"Entering firing range now," Foxglove said. "Captain?"

Sameena braced herself. "Fire."

Sneaky Bastard rocked violently as she unleashed her first barrage of missiles, followed rapidly by her second. The pirate ships were caught completely by surprise, unsure of what to do; she saw their crews hastily trying to reconfigure their point defence before it was too late. Their shuttles didn't even realise that they were under attack before they were blown into dust.

"Shuttles destroyed," Foxglove said, with heavy satisfaction. "Cycling third barrage now."

Sameena scowled. They'd drilled and drilled until the entire crew was thoroughly sick of it, but it still took five minutes to transport the missiles from the hold into the weapons pods and launch them out into space. In a real battle, she knew, they'd be in deep trouble. She looked over at the pirate cruiser and watched as its crew struggled desperately to survive. Their point defence fire was hesitant and largely ineffective. Five laser heads detonated near the ship, burning through the hullmetal and wreaking havoc inside the hull. Moments later, the entire starship exploded into a ball of superheated plasma.

"Target destroyed," Foxglove said.

The pirate frigate had been luckier – and helped by the fact that they'd had to throw most of their first barrage at the cruiser. Her crew were clearly better trained, Sameena decided; they managed to sheer off and even launch a handful of missiles back towards the q-ships before the second barrage caught up with them. A nuke struck their drive section, crippling the ship. Sameena was mildly impressed that it had survived.

She winced as the enemy missiles closed in on her ship, but she should have had more faith. Foxglove's computers tracked and targeted them all, then systematically wiped them out of space. They hadn't even *tried* any trickery, not even basic ECM. The sensor officer had been right, she decided. They didn't know the capabilities of their own systems.

"Launch shuttles," she ordered, leaving the thought for later consideration. The pirate ship was effectively powerless. It was time to deal with it before the crew could perish – or try to escape. "And transmit our own surrender demand."

She'd pre-recorded the message when they'd worked through possible scenarios for intercepting the pirates. Unlike the Imperial Navy, she'd decided to offer the pirates a chance at life on a penal world, if they surrendered without further resistance. It hadn't made her many friends – one of the few things that the traders and the Imperial Navy agreed upon was that the only good pirate was a dead pirate – but it might help save lives. Even a cornered rat could put up a fight against a cat or dog.

"No response," the sensor officer said. "They may well be completely powerless."

"Very bad maintenance," Foxglove commented.

Sameena couldn't disagree. Steve had spent months showing her how the power distribution network on *Logan* actually worked – and the Imperial Navy had built far more redundancy into its ships. It was actually quite difficult to render the ships completely powerless without practically battering the ship into a hulk. On the other hand, if someone allowed the nodes to decay, the network might fail quicker.

"Shuttles away," the helmsman reported.

Paddy would have loved this, Sameena thought, remembering some of his stories about boarding enemy ships. They were always nerve-wracking; one never knew if the crew would offer resistance, try to destroy their ship with the boarding party on it…or if the ship would simply come apart, dumping them all into space. But Paddy had made it sound like an adventure. His wife had commented that insanity was part of the job description for a Marine.

"Signal the convoy to hold position," she ordered. The destroyers would be back with them in twenty minutes. She could order one of them to wait with the pirate ship while the other escorted the convoy to Dueller. "Is there anything from the boarding party?"

"They've had to go through a gash in the hull," Foxglove reported. "So far, they've not located any live crewmen, just bodies. Their life support appears to have failed spectacularly. As far as they can tell, the ship is completely depressurised."

Sameena shivered. *Logan* had been honey-combed with compartments that could be isolated from the rest of the ship at the touch of a button, as was a standard warship. Even a major hull breach shouldn't have been enough to depressurise the entire ship. Yet another sign of bad maintenance or something more sinister? She could understand the pirates having backers who would not wish to be identified.

"Have their report sent to me as soon as possible," she ordered. If the pirates were all dead, she could wait to find out what they could pull from the ship's remains. "The convoy will resume course for Dueller, maximum speed."

"Aye, Captain," the helmsman said.

Sameena looked around the bridge and saw the same expression on everyone's face; relief, combined with the exhilaration of surviving their first engagement. It hadn't been fair – they'd lured the pirates in, rather than revealing themselves from the start – but it hardly mattered. They'd won! And they were alive!

"Well done, all of you," she said, calmly. She wished that Jamie had come with them, just so he could be with her. If he'd been there, they could have celebrated…she pushed that thought aside, angrily. Wishful thinking was never helpful. "Our first engagement was a smashing success."

"Our training was far superior," Foxglove said. "With your permission, I would like to analyse the sensor readings closely. There may be clues as to their origins in there."

"Granted," Sameena said. She had her doubts, but one of the things she had learned from Steve was never to get in the way of enthusiasm. Foxglove would be more driven by his own determination than by any orders. "Let me know what you can deduce."

Seven hours later, they arrived in orbit around Dueller.

Chapter Thirty-Seven

Two hundred years before I left Earth, it was becoming alarmingly clear that the task was beyond their ability to complete. Infrastructure that had been built up over centuries was wearing away faster than they could repair it. This crippled the Empire's ability to produce spare parts, which drove prices up and ruined businesses.

- Professor Leo Caesius, *The Science That Isn't: Economics and the Decline and Fall of the Galactic Empire.*

"I don't know what we would have done without you," Governor Higgins said, as they stood together in Government House. "My world was about to die."

Sameena nodded. She'd seen traces of the crop blight as her shuttle dropped through the planet's atmosphere and came in to land. The crops had been darkened, rotting away into mush…and becoming poisonous, rendering them completely useless. Even pigs, she'd been shocked and amused to discover, had been unable to eat the blighted food. Without algae-production plants, she knew, the entire planet would rapidly starve.

"We promised to assist any world that fell into trouble," she said, remembering how hard it had been to work out a charter that everyone could support. "It might be another world tomorrow that needs your help."

"And my people are grateful," Higgins assured her. "I believe that many of them have already expressed a wish to meet you."

"If I have time, I would be delighted," Sameena assured him, although it wasn't entirely true. It was still hard to face crowds, even with Jamie's quiet encouragement. "However, I cannot stay here indefinitely."

"I quite understand," Higgins said.

Sameena smiled as he turned to stare out over Landing City. It was older than Rosa's capital city, built out of stone quarried on the planet's surface – and yet they hadn't bothered to rename it. There were *thousands* of Landing Cities scattered across the Empire, which suggested a lack of original thinking to her mind. Or, perhaps, bureaucratic indifference. Even so, the planet had done very well until the blight had arrived. Sixty or seventy years might have seen the birth of an industrial economy.

Higgins, according to Intelligence, was surprisingly popular for an Imperial-appointed Governor. There were several worlds that had taken advantage of the Empire's departure to appoint their own political leaders, but Dueller had stayed with Higgins. The cynical part of Sameena's mind wondered if the blight had ensured that no one else actually wanted the job, although she had to admit that it was unlikely. There was *always* someone who wanted power, someone prepared to do whatever it took to get it.

"I understand that you are also working on setting up industrial nodes," Higgins continued. "We would be quite interested in having one here."

Sameena smiled. *Appleseed* – the converted colonist-carrier – had been moving from system to system, helping to set up the building blocks of a network of industrial stations. It would take time to build up the network, but her projections suggested that in ten to twenty years she would have a superb industrial base…and one decentralised enough to make it hard for anyone to cripple. Dueller would have to agree to the standard contract she'd written – forbidding political interference, among other things – but it was definitely a good idea. Assuming, of course, that they could defeat the blight.

She looked over at his back. "Have you found any way to challenge the blight?"

"We've got biochemists working on finding solutions," Higgins admitted. "They think they can grow crop strains that would be completely resistant to the blight, but it will take three to five years to replace the destroyed fields. So far, the blight hasn't shown any inclination to actually *attack* humans directly, but everyone who eats infected crops gets ill. Something must have been missed on the planetary survey."

Sameena scowled. Imperial Law demanded that a planet be thoroughly investigated before settlement began, a law that had started out as common sense and mutated into yet another nail in the Empire's coffin. Only the interstellar corporations could afford to pay for the inspections, which meant that independent survey teams had to sell their findings to the corporations, rather than independent settler groups. Often, it didn't really hurt if the law was ignored. But when it did, the results were always spectacular – and disastrous.

And yet it was rare, she had to admit, for a full investigation to miss something.

"It might not have been natural," she said, softly. "Someone might have decided to kill your entire population without showing themselves."

"A handful of rocks would have achieved the same result," the Governor pointed out. "And besides, they'd have to tailor something specifically to this world. Why bother?"

It *could* be a coincidence, Sameena knew. "The timing seems odd," she said. "Your famine starts bare months after the Empire withdraws. I could understand a life support failure on a rocky airless world, but here? It's just a suspicious coincidence."

"I don't have any evidence, one way or the other," the Governor said. "But if you were right, surely the blight would appear on other worlds."

"I've passed on a warning," Sameena said. "But I don't know how well it's been heeded."

For a moment, she felt a twinge of sympathy for the Grand Senate. It took six months for orders to reach the Rim from Earth, which meant that the situation might well have moved on before the orders actually arrived. They would always have to wait and see what happened, knowing that the people on the spot would have to make the real decisions. If *she* had problems handling a small sector, managing the entire Empire would be impossible.

But that had been their mistake, she knew. They'd sought to centralise the Empire, never realising that it was simply impossible. Instead, their orders always had been outdated, never taking the true situation into account. Maybe that was why they'd worked to limit the potential of the colonies along the Rim. A revolution could become quite serious before the Grand Senate heard the first rumblings of trouble.

Her own plan was to decentralise as much as possible, even though she knew it limited her own power. But there was no choice.

"Father," a voice said. "This is the Captain?"

Sameena turned to see a pale-skinned girl with long green hair, barely on the verge of becoming a teenager. She felt a sudden stab of guilt as she remembered that she had neglected Brad, leaving him behind on the asteroid for a month. She'd tried to play with him each day, but there were just so many demands on her time. And then she hadn't really spoken to Barbara at all.

He's your child, she told herself, sternly. *You need to take him with you when you go.*

But he's still a baby, her thoughts answered her.

"This is the Captain, Gretel," Higgins said. He picked his daughter up and held her in his arms. "Captain Hussein, this is Gretel."

"Hi," Gretel said, shyly.

"Hi," Sameena answered - and smiled. The girl was sweet, although her hair colour wasn't natural. "Your father is welcoming me to your world."

"I love it," Gretel said. "I'm going to be a farmer when I grow up. I love the land and growing things and…"

Sameena felt her smile widening as the child prattled on. "I hope you get the chance," she said, gravely. Talking to children was definitely not her strong point. "We're doing our best to see to it."

"You are," Higgins agreed. He put his daughter down and motioned for her to go back to her quarters. "Captain, I honestly can't thank you enough."

"It isn't necessary," Sameena said. Her wristcom chimed. "Excuse me."

She keyed the wristcom. "Captain, this is Foxglove," Foxglove said. He wouldn't have interrupted her unless it was important. "I have the complete report from the boarding party. They found quite a few odd things."

"Understood," Sameena said. "I'll be back on the shuttle in twenty minutes."

"I don't know why they were prowling the edge of this star system," the governor said, as she closed the channel. "But I am very relieved that you beat them."

Sameena nodded and accepted his offer of a car back to the spaceport. The complex was bustling with life, shuttles dropping down from high overhead and unloading their cargo of food and algae-production equipment. Given enough time, Sameena knew, they would be able to feed themselves once again, perhaps long enough to beat the blight and re-establish their farming industry. The governor had mentioned that they might be setting up on the uninhabited continent, although Sameena doubted that would work in the long run. It was quite likely that the blight – if it was natural – would be there too.

She couldn't help noticing the open relief on faces as they helped unload the shuttle. The population had gone on rations as soon as the Governor had realised the scale of the problem, but they'd known that they were on the verge of starving to death. And they'd also known that the Empire had abandoned them. Governor Higgins had to be *very* popular, or he wouldn't have survived. She couldn't help wondering what his long-terms plans were as she climbed out of the car and walked over to her shuttle, then pushed the thought aside. It wasn't her concern.

Inside, she breathed in the processed air and sat down, activating one of the consoles. The full report had already been transmitted to her shuttle, even though it was technically against Imperial Navy regulations. Jamie had spent a few days trying to revise the regulations to cope with their new situation, before admitting that they might as well start from scratch. It would probably take years, he'd warned, before everyone was following the same rules. She downloaded it to a datapad and settled down to read.

The first part of the report was simple; the enemy ship had been poorly maintained, as she'd suspected, and the battering it had taken had simply been too much for the abused system to take. One of the engineers on the boarding party had reported that they'd somehow obtained new spare parts – it was quite possible that Sameena's industries had supplied them – yet they hadn't known precisely how to use them. He'd cited a few examples – datachips stuffed in the wrong way around, computer nodes not connected to the network – that would have made her laugh, if it hadn't been so serious. It was a testament to the Imperial Navy's design skills, she decided, that the ships had even continued to function.

But the second part was downright alarming.

Seventy bodies had been pulled from the wreckage, all mangled beyond repair. Their DNA had been hopelessly scrambled, the medics had discovered; there was little hope of identifying their homeworld, or even comparing them to the Imperial Criminal Database. And their brains had been completely liquefied…it was, the medics had concluded, an extremely unusual form of suicide implant. It looked to Sameena as if someone had wanted to bury their tracks *thoroughly*.

That was unusual, she knew. It wasn't like pirates to give a damn if anyone identified them; they were rare visitors to places where their DNA might be tested and checked against wanted lists. And they wouldn't even care if someone identified their homeworld, if that was even possible. Relatively few worlds were so isolated that a native could be pin-pointed through his DNA. It was far more common for pirates to leave DNA evidence all over the place. Some of Paddy's stories had been so horrifying that they'd given her nightmares.

They want to remain unidentified, she thought. *But why?*

Jamie and Brad had both sneered at entertainment programs that had branded pirates as nothing more than misfits, misunderstood members of society. In truth, they ranged from simple thieves and robbers to rapists, mass murderers and outright sociopaths. It was rare for a pirate crew to do something that horrified the rest of the underground community; in fact, it was difficult to imagine what *could* horrify those hardened men, let alone convince them to tip off the Imperial Navy. Even if the worst of the scum were responsible for destroying entire asteroid settlements, after raping and murdering every last man, woman and child, betraying them would have consequences. The Imperial Navy didn't share the belief that pirates were *misunderstood*. They understood them far too well.

The third part of the report puzzled her. Every recovered body was male. It was rare, Sameena knew, to have a female pirate – they tended to be far more sociopathic than the males – but most pirates kept sex slaves on their ships. This crew…hadn't. Pirates weren't the Imperial Navy, or even a trader crew; she found it hard to imagine a pirate commander telling his men that they couldn't have their pet whores. So where were they?

She shook her head and looked at the final part of the report. Annoyingly, the only part of the enemy ship's systems that had worked was the computer self-destruct. The starship's main computer core had been reduced to dust, while the distributed nodes had been wiped clean. It was possible, the engineers had concluded, that *something* might be drawn from the nodes, but they didn't seem hopeful. The ship was completely beyond repair.

At least we can use it as a source of raw materials, she told herself, as she put the datapad down. The mystery would be solved in time. *Maybe someone just wanted to earn money through backing pirates and took excessive precautions to ensure that they weren't tracked down.*

"Have the hulk towed into orbit," she ordered, keying her wristcom. "The engineers can go over her and pull out anything we might be able to use, then we can have it picked up and transferred elsewhere."

"Understood," Foxglove said. There was a pause. "Captain, the loadmaster reports that it will take at least four more days to finish unloading all the freighters."

"That shouldn't be a problem," Sameena assured him, wryly. At least Dueller had an orbital station, but she wouldn't want to leave any of their cargo in orbit. If there were other pirates sniffing around, they might be tempted to try a smash and grab. The station carried some weapons, but it was also a sitting duck. A pirate ship could sit outside weapons range and hurl rocks at it until one hit. "We have time."

Governor Higgins had plans for her, she discovered over the next two days. There was a brief meal with the planet's government – thankfully, they only ate soup and bread, rather than a big feast – where they talked about the future of the union. They were rather surprised to discover that there was no real agreement on a *name*, which they seemed to think should come first. Sameena, who had been leaning towards Trade Federation, found it rather amusing that they could agree on the broad strokes without argument, but bogged down when it came to discussing the *name*.

The following day, they took her to see the blight. Sameena had never liked the countryside, even when she'd been on Rosa, but it was still depressing to watch cornfields decaying into a putrid sludge. Most of them had been abandoned, she'd been told; they'd actually been trying to burn fields to the ground in the hopes of eradicating the blight. Unfortunately, they'd established very quickly that a strong gust of wind could pick up tiny fragments of the blight and deposit them on untouched fields. Nowhere remained safe for very long.

"The few untouched fields are protected with everything we can muster," Higgins told her. They'd already inspected the isolated fields, placed on islands well away from the mainland. "But we don't have the facilities to shield them completely."

Sameena nodded. "You'll have to watch the algae farms too," she warned. Losing them would be disastrous, all the more so as they had brought hope. "I don't know what the blight would do if exposed to the chemicals there, but it might become a great deal more dangerous. Or it might die out."

"We can hope," the Governor said. He looked over at her, then back at the abandoned farmhouse in the distance. "Did you see the refugee camp?"

"Yes," Sameena said. It had reminded her far too much of Sungai Buloh, although it definitely seemed to be more under control on Dueller. The refugees seemed grim and bitter, but so far they hadn't collapsed into barbarity or riots. "It's going to get worse before it gets better."

"I fear so," Higgins said. "Without your promise of assistance, we might well have suffered a complete social collapse by now."

Sameena mulled it over as they drove back to Landing City. The Empire had simply abandoned the sector – and, if it hadn't been for her, millions would already be dead. Others were *already* dead, despite the best she could do. She couldn't help feeling as if she'd failed, even though cold logic told her otherwise. They were still going to die.

The cold equations, she thought, remembering Steve's favourite curse. *They always catch up with you.*

Her wristcom chimed. "Captain," Foxglove said, "a freighter just entered the system from Maxwell. It reports that the system was attacked and invaded by an unknown force."

Sameena sucked in her breath. "Have them make a full report," she ordered. "I'm on my way back to the ships. And tell all senior officers that I will issue a conference call as soon as I am back onboard."

She thought fast as she closed the channel. An unknown force... who? Pirates, renegade Imperial Navy ships, secessionists...there were too many possibilities for her to take a guess. But she knew that they had to respond. If they didn't, the promise of protection she'd made would be exposed as hollow.

And her house of cards would collapse in its wake.

CHAPTER THIRTY-EIGHT

> In turn, this further crippled the Empire's tax base. The result was inflation on a colossal scale. In real terms, the value of the Imperial Credit was falling, even as the numbers grew higher. A billion credits in the final days of Empire was, in real terms, worth barely as much as a thousand credits from even two hundred years previously.
>
> - Professor Leo Caesius, *The Science That Isn't: Economics and the Decline and Fall of the Galactic Empire.*

"We need to respond," Sameena said. "There is no choice."

The holographic faces of the convoy's senior officers looked back at her. None of them seemed to disagree with her, although several of them looked sceptical that they *could* deal with the mystery invasion force. Sameena had reviewed the files downloaded from the freighter, but they hadn't been too detailed. The unknown attackers had a heavy cruiser, two destroyers and a handful of freighters. That was far too much firepower for a planet like Maxwell.

But the system was actually quite valuable. Even before Sameena had placed one of her industrial nodes at Maxwell, there had been a small asteroid-mining complex and plans for considerable expansion in the future, plans that had only been marginally derailed by the collapse of the Empire. She could see why the attackers would want the planet – and why they couldn't be allowed to keep it. Besides, if they failed to respond, the credibility of her new government would be shot to hell.

"A heavy cruiser represents more firepower than we can handle," Captain Yew pointed out. He wasn't one of Jamie's bigger supporters – and Sameena privately suspected that he thought *he* should be Commodore. "Even if we amassed most of the squadron, it would be difficult to tackle."

"So we cheat, sir," Foxglove said. "We have two q-ships. We get into range, pretending to be two freighters, and blast their hull at point-blank range. Even a battleship would be crippled by the impact."

"That assumes that they will *allow* us to get into range," Yew said. "If they chose to keep us at a distance…"

"Nothing ventured, nothing gained," Sameena said, before the two naval officers could start arguing. "We take our small squadron to the edge of the Maxwell System and carry out reconnaissance, then the q-ships can head in-system to engage the enemy."

"That leaves us with another question," Captain Geoffrey said. "We have no Marine detachments. How do we secure the planet?"

"Maxwell didn't have any pansy ideas about banning weapons," one of the freighter Captains pointed out. "We could just drop KEWs in their support."

"It'll take them time to get organised," Geoffrey countered. "We really need to land troops."

"I intend to ask Governor Higgins for the loan of some troops," Sameena said. She looked down at her datapad, running through the requirements for transporting vast numbers of men from star to star. "Dueller has the men, the equipment and owes us a favour. They can provide whatever ground support we need."

"That's going to be a great deal," Geoffrey said. "I was involved in the liberation of a much smaller colony world, four years ago. Even with four companies of Marines and plenty of fire support it was still a damned bloodbath. Maxwell might make or break our government."

"We should at least send for reinforcements from Madagascar," Captain Yew said. "If we head off on our own…"

Sameena nodded towards the starchart. "It's two weeks for our fastest ship from here to Madagascar," she said. "It will be a month before any reinforcements can arrive, assuming that Jamie – Commodore Cook – has them on hand and can dispatch them at once. During that time, the mystery attackers will still be in possession of Maxwell. Do you know what they will be doing there?"

She'd reviewed the Imperial Navy's files. Pirate occupations of colony worlds tended to devolve into orgies of rape and looting, with the pirates stripping the colonies bare and taking every young and attractive woman with them when they left. Maxwell was too large to be easily looted, but the pirates – if they *were* pirates – could do a hell of a lot of damage before the planet was liberated.

"Yes," Captain Yew said, slowly. "I understand your feelings, Captain. But I also know that a half-baked liberation plan may leave us in a worse position than we already are."

Sameena couldn't disagree. Given a year or two, the new government would have started production of its own warships, allowing it to patrol the spaceways aggressively. Now, every loss *hurt*. It was unlikely that any outside government could destroy her industrial base – the interstellar factory was well-hidden, while *Appleseed* could just run if necessary – but it could certainly tear her worlds apart.

Who *were* the attackers? It was hard to imagine a pirate crew successfully operating a heavy cruiser, which meant…what? The closest world that might be able to deploy one was several hundred light years away. As far as she could tell, the only explanation that made sense was that the pirates were actually rogue Imperial Navy elements, although even *that* was odd. Surely an ambitious Imperial Navy officer could have found a better target for his ships?

"We go there, we recon the system and then we plan," she said, firmly. "If the system is too heavily defended for us to take, we withdraw and summon reinforcements. But we do have to try to get there as soon as possible."

She looked over at one of the freighter commanders. "I'm sending you straight back to Madagascar," she said. "You'll carry a message for Commodore Cook, asking for reinforcements. The other freighters will assist in transporting troops from Dueller to Maxwell."

"Understood, Captain," the freighter commander said.

Sameena looked from face to face. "I know that this is risky, but we are sworn to protect the planets that signed up with us," she said. "We have no choice. We have to respond."

Their faces winked out as the meeting came to an end. Sameena allowed herself a tight smile; the Imperial Navy might like face-to-face meetings, but the traders saw no logic in meeting personally when people could attend electronically. It was far more efficient – and besides, she could bring the meeting to an end without small talk. And if the ships were attacked, the commanders would still be present on their own vessels.

She tapped a switch, opening a channel to Government House on Dueller. Unsurprisingly, Governor Higgins answered immediately. Sameena explained what had happened, then requested troops. Much to her relief, the Governor agreed at once and promised to make arrangements to ship a full regiment of Civil Guardsmen to orbit.

"They're not bad at all, not compared to others," he assured her. "I ensured that they had a hard cadre of Imperial Army officers to lead them, but they have a shortage of actual experience. Their CO has the most experience and he only fought a handful of engagements with enemy forces."

Sameena scowled, but nodded. "We can run through landing and assault drills on the ships," she said, although her small squadron wouldn't have any simulators capable of handling the soldiers. She would have given her back teeth for Paddy, someone who actually *did* have experience in hostile landings on occupied worlds. "But right now we're short of options."

Higgins frowned. "Are they likely to come here?"

"I don't know," Sameena admitted, tartly. "We don't know who they are, or what they want; we certainly can't guess at their criteria for choosing targets. All I know is that if we don't nip this in the bud it's going to turn into a major problem and countless innocent people are going to suffer and die."

She wondered, absently, if Higgins would insist on retaining his troops for home defence, but he merely nodded and promised that the troops would be ready for embarking within the day, before inviting her to another function on the planet's surface. Sameena shook her head, dismissing the idea; she needed to do some tactical planning. Mercifully, Higgins didn't push. He cut the connection without further ado.

"Record," she ordered, tapping her console. "Jamie; I intend to respond to the occupation of Maxwell, at least to the point of checking out the system to see just what the enemy is doing there. I know this is risky, but we're the closest force that can react. Please send what reinforcements you can muster and meet us at the RV point, two light years from Maxwell.

"Whatever this is, we can't let it go past," she continued. "If I die, remember that I love you – and don't let them tear our new government apart."

She blew him a kiss, then terminated the recording, feeling an unaccustomed lump in her throat. It *was* risky, not least because she was – to all intents and purposes – a Head of State. Her capture or death might be disastrous. It wasn't just *her* holding the new government together – she'd called the Meet to ensure that the traders held it together, rather than one person – but without her the various factions might start pulling the government in different directions. The results would *definitely* be disastrous.

Cold logic told her that she shouldn't go with the squadron, but she knew that she couldn't remain behind, even on the edge of the occupied star system. She couldn't send men and women into danger without sharing the risk herself.

It took nearly two days to load up the freighters with troops, then head out of the Dueller System and back into Phase Space. Sameena spent the time working through tactical simulations with Foxglove or reviewing everything that had been pulled out of the pirate ship's wreckage, although that seemed to be largely a waste of time. The pirates hadn't bothered with maintenance, the engineers reported, and it had paid off for them. A dozen systems that should have stored data for analysis had been utterly useless.

On the plus side, we did manage to pull dozens of components for recycling, she thought, with some amusement. They would all have to be checked carefully first, but the pirates would still make a valuable contribution to society. The bodies, after a cursory final inspection, had been launched towards the local star. There had been no ceremony for the pirate dead. Sameena hadn't even bothered to watch.

The only piece of good news was that the algae farms on Dueller had begun production without any significant problems. Man could live on algae alone, even though Sameena knew no one who admitted to actually *liking* the ration bars; Dueller's population would survive long enough for a blight-resistant strain of crops to be developed. She'd still ordered maximum biological precautions for crewmen returning to the ships, however, just in case. It would be disastrous if the blight spread to another world.

There had only been two epidemics in the Empire's long history. The improved disease resistance engineered into the vast majority of the human race had countered most diseases without the human population quite being aware of it. Only a handful of diseases had managed to infect dozens of worlds before the Empire handled them – and only two of them had threatened the entire Empire. But now, with the Empire's health system utterly demolished, it was possible that an epidemic might spread rapidly.

Or maybe not, she thought. *If interstellar trade came to a halt, there would be nothing spreading the disease.*

She mulled it over as the small squadron sped through Phase Space. It was only a week to Maxwell, thankfully; long enough for her to simulate the most likely battles, but not long enough for her to drive herself frantic worrying over the possible outcomes. She honestly didn't understand how the Imperial Navy officers could be so calm. Didn't they realise, she asked herself, just how disastrous a single lost battle could be? But then, there was nothing she could do to make the battle come sooner. The Imperial Navy would have thoroughly drilled its officers on the value of patience.

"We don't know enough to be *sure* of what we're facing," Foxglove reminded her, one afternoon. "The freighter that took these recordings didn't go *too* close to the planet. They might well have missed something, for all the will in the world. If there's a second cruiser out there…"

Sameena gritted her teeth. If there was, they'd have to pull back and wait for Jamie at the RV point. Even with him, it would be tricky to defeat those two ships, at least until they started producing cruisers of their own. The modified freighters simply couldn't hope to face warships in even combat. She shook her head, tiredly. A few more years before the Empire fell and she would have had a squadron of heavy warships under her personal command.

"We'll try to find out what we're facing before we get in too deep," she said, shortly. "Can we recon the system without being detected?"

"Easily," Foxglove said. He grinned at her, his face illuminated by the holographic display. "A single starship can use a cloaking device to remain undetected unless it tries to enter orbit. I've known some crews capable of slipping *into* orbit with a cloak, but it is hellishly dangerous if detected."

Sameena nodded. A cloaked ship couldn't bring its drives up to full power – or open fire – without revealing its location. If the enemy caught a sniff of the ship's location, they might be able to fire on her before she dropped the cloak and prepared to fire back. Foxglove's tales of playing hide and seek at the Imperial Academy had chilled her, although he had admitted that it was impossible to search an entire star system. A skilled CO could easily remain undetected simply by keeping his distance.

She made sure to get plenty of rest the night before they reached Maxwell, dropping out of Phase Space some distance from the Phase Limit. Maxwell did have monitoring systems in orbit, assuming they remained intact, but they shouldn't have been able to detect their arrival at such a distance. The real question was just what sort of sensors were mounted on the enemy warships. If they had a military-grade sensor suite, they might well have picked up *something*.

"No enemy contacts detected," the sensor officer said. "Picking up limited data traffic from Maxwell itself, plus beacons in the asteroid field."

Sameena nodded. "Move us to the first planned waypoint," she ordered. One of the destroyers would slip in-system; the remainder of the tiny squadron would wait on the edge of the Phase Limit, allowing them to flee at a moment's notice if the shit hit the fan. She keyed her console, opening a laser link to Captain Yew."

"Captain," she said, "you are cleared to separate from the squadron."

"Understood," Yew said. Despite his expressed doubts, he didn't seem to be inclined to disagree any longer. "We'll be back before you know it."

Sameena scowled, inwardly, as the destroyer headed off towards the inner system. She didn't really *trust* Yew. It was easy to imagine him taking his ship and vanishing into Phase Space, although it would be difficult for him to find supplies along the Rim. Maybe he'd turn pirate…or try to head back towards the Core Worlds to see what had become of the Empire. No wonder the Imperial Navy worked so hard to develop a sense of brotherhood in its crewmen, she told herself. The shared loyalty kept them from deserting one another when they were under fire.

But that loyalty had been shattered, she knew, when the Admiral had deserted the rest of his squadron at Madagascar. How could she blame Yew for looking out for himself? He didn't have a relationship with Sameena, not like Jamie.

I should have put more crew on his ship, she thought, sourly. It was harder for a CO to take his ship and run if the crew might object to mutiny or outright treachery. But Jamie hadn't suggested it and Sameena had already agreed not to interfere with his command. Jamie was just too innocent to consider the possibility of treason.

Long hours ticked by. Sameena waited, studying the files on Maxwell and trying to make sense of the latest set of unprocessed data from Intelligence. There was nothing from the inner system, apart from brief chatter from the planet itself. The sensor officer analysed it and concluded that Maxwell's planetary broadcasting network had been effectively shut down.

"They should be saying more, Captain," he said. "But there are only a handful of brief messages."

Sameena wasn't surprised. The pirates – or whoever they were – wouldn't have wanted the locals actually *talking* to one another.

"Contact," the sensor officer snapped, as his console pinged an alarm. "One starship…it's Captain Yew!"

Sameena let out a breath she hadn't realised that she'd been holding. "Very good," she said. "Have him download his take to the command datanet."

She smiled as she left the bridge and stepped into the conference room. "Well done, Captain," she said, as Yew's image appeared in front of her. "What did you find?"

"One heavy cruiser and one destroyer," Yew said, bluntly. "The second destroyer appears to be missing."

Sameena nodded. That was better, she supposed, than thinking that they could see *all* the enemy's ships and then being caught because of their own overconfidence.

"We can take her," she decided. "We'll go with tactical plan five."

"Understood," Yew said. He hesitated. "I should note that the destroyer was apparently bombarding the planet. There's resistance going on down there."

"All the more reason to intervene now," Sameena said. The resistance would have nothing capable of stopping the destroyer from bombarding their positions at will. Their defeat was certain unless outsiders intervened. "The destroyers will accompany us under cloak. If worst comes to worst, we'll need their firepower."

She scowled, baring her teeth. "This has to be done," she concluded. "Good luck to us all."

CHAPTER
THIRTY-NINE

The Grand Senate refused to acknowledge this simple truth. Realistically, trying to fix the problems facing the Empire would have been an extremely difficult task. Instead, they struggled over portions of a pie that was steadily shrinking, while suppressing anyone who might attempt to reveal the truth. Such as your humble scholar.

- Professor Leo Caesius, *The Science That Isn't: Economics and the Decline and Fall of the Galactic Empire.*

Sameena couldn't help feeling naked as the two q-ships made their way into the inner system, even though it was part of the plan. They were hellishly exposed; if they failed to damage the heavy cruiser in the first salvo, they would be trading blows with a tougher and more capable opponent than themselves. The tension on the bridge slowly rose, to the point where Sameena was tempted to send half her crew off for a nap. Instead, she just waited as patiently as she could until the heavy cruiser broke orbit and headed out towards them.

"One heavy cruiser on intercept vector," the sensor officer said, unnecessarily. His eyes narrowed. "Captain, I think this ship is connected to the pirates we encountered in the Dueller System."

"That's odd," Foxglove said. "How can you be sure?"

"Their sensors and drives are giving me the impression that they really don't know quite what they're doing," the sensor officer said, studying the readings. "Again, they're not squeezing the most out of their systems. I don't think they even bothered to read the manual."

Foxglove smiled. "Who does?"

Steve, Sameena thought. He'd ranted endlessly about people who bought equipment without bothering to read the manual, or at least find out what it could and couldn't do. When they didn't, he'd said, he'd often had to repair the equipment and it could be a major headache. On the other hand, half of the equipment they'd brought out of junkyards wouldn't have been junked if the owners had known more about it.

"And I think that at least one of their drive compartments is completely out of service," the sensor officer added. "It isn't cutting into their speed, but they don't seem to have the power reserves they should have. Either that or they simply haven't turned the engines on completely."

Sameena smiled at the thought. Imperial Navy warships had multiple drive compartments and fusion cores, just to ensure that there was redundancy. But all the redundancy built into the starships wouldn't matter if the crews didn't know what they were doing. It was possible, she supposed, that someone might have cannibalised part of the cruiser to keep another ship going, but that would be risky. There would be no way to know when the ship might need to go to full military power.

"Any competent commanding officer would object strongly," Foxglove said, when she suggested the possibility. "Even if they were overruled, removing the fusion core alone would be an absolute nightmare. They'd have to cut through the hullmetal, then repair it afterwards. And then they'd have to replace all of the control systems, which would be configured for one particular ship."

Sameena nodded, looking at the heavy cruiser. It was clearly ex-Imperial Navy; a blocky hammerhead of a starship, bristling with weapons and sensor blisters. In some ways, it reminded her of Jamie's destroyer, only scaled up and armed with more weapons. But then, few Imperial Navy starships would win design awards. Only luxury liners and a handful of RockRat starships were designed with aesthetics in mind.

"I'd suggest configuring the missile strike to target their drive section," the sensor officer said. "Unless their damage control crews are absolute wizards, they won't be able to recover after we hammer them."

Foxglove scowled, but nodded. "I'll have to divert some firepower to target their missile tubes," he warned. "We don't want to let them have more than one free shot at us."

Sameena left it in their hands as she contemplated the heavy cruiser. The sensor officer was right, she decided; whoever was in command of the ship didn't know precisely what they were doing. It was a frustrating mystery, all the more so because even the Imperial Navy had ways and means to cope with incompetent officers. Why would pirates capture the ship and then not learn how to master its systems?

She pulled up the report from Dueller and scowled at it. The survey teams had highlighted several facts, oddities that had caught their attention. One of them nagged at her mind; pirates weren't known for basic hygiene, but *this* crew had been almost as clean as an Imperial Navy crew. There hadn't been any urine on the deck or shit in the tubes. Sameena hadn't understood – she knew precisely how Captain Hamilton would have reacted to someone who pissed on his deck – until Foxglove had pointed out that pirate ships normally stank dreadfully. Their commanders kept their men on a very loose leash indeed.

One of the books she'd read for her exams had gone into some detail on pirate society. Apparently, those who entered the pirate world rapidly lost all socialisation, forgetting the laws and customs of civilisation. It had explained that the pirates, when faced with a new recruit, would force him to stain his hands with blood, ensuring that he could never go back to the Empire. And once broken, the new pirate would swiftly wallow in his own filth until he was no better than any of the others. It was chilling to realise that she might have ended up like that, if she had been captured by the pirates.

Or sold to them, if Captain Hamilton had been any less decent, she reminded herself. And shivered.

"We're picking up a message now," the sensor officer said. There was a hint of nervousness in his tone. "They want us to prepare to be boarded."

"Surprise, surprise," Sameena said. The message they'd sent to Maxwell had claimed that they were carrying spare parts, something the pirates would want desperately. It might cause them to hesitate if they suspected that something was wrong. "Send back a whiny message explaining that we have urgent business on Maxwell."

There was a long pause. "They repeated their message," the sensor officer said finally, as the display lit up with bright red light. "And they've locked onto us with weapons sensors."

"Charming," Sameena muttered. Interstellar etiquette frowned on locking onto someone's hull unless one had bad intentions. It had started at least one war prior to the Unification Wars, when one side had thought the other intended to open fire and launched a pre-emptive strike. "Send them a cringing message demanding to know what's going on."

"They're ordering us to cut drives," the sensor officer said. "And they're launching shuttles."

Sameena nodded. "Have you targeted our weapons?"

"Yes, Captain," Foxglove said. "I will coordinate our first strike with *Lying Bastard*."

"Good," Sameena said. She gritted her teeth. She'd hoped that the heavy cruiser would come closer before she had to open fire, but luck clearly wasn't on her side. As it was, the heavy cruiser might be able to get two or three barrages off before her first strike slammed into its hull. And it would have plenty of time to get its point defence up and running. "Deploy all of our drones and decoys as soon as you open fire."

She hesitated, studying the display. The shuttles were separating themselves from the looming bulk of the heavy cruiser and zooming closer, just like the previous set of shuttles from the last pirate ship. She felt a flash of *Déjà Vu*, then pushed it aside. She couldn't afford distractions, not now.

"Target the shuttles with point defence," she added. "And…*fire!*"

Sneaky Bastard rocked as she unleashed her first missile salvo. The point defence opened fire in the same instant, vaporising the incoming shuttles. She could have sworn that she saw the heavy cruiser *flinch* on the display, although it was almost certainly her imagination. Even so, it took longer than it should have for the heavy cruiser to return fire. It spat out a wave of missiles towards her ships.

"ECM and decoys deployed," Foxglove said. "Standard deception patterns activated."

Sameena sucked in a breath as her missiles roared into the heavy cruiser's engagement range. Her point defence opened fire at once, wiping out a handful of missiles, but it seemed to be having problems coping with two separate barrages of missiles. *Lying Bastard's* shots were coming in from a slightly different vector and it seemed to be confusing the enemy ship. The sensor officer was right, she realised grimly; the enemy really *didn't* know how their ships worked. A computer wouldn't have been too shocked to coordinate a proper defensive pattern.

"They're launching a second barrage," the sensor officer reported. "Missile impact in…"

Sameena watched, grimly, as her missiles slammed into the heavy cruiser's hull. The ship's point defence seemed to have gotten better in the last few seconds, but not good enough to prevent four laser heads burning into its drive section. The ship's power curves flat-lined abruptly, leaving it drifting in space. A moment later, a series of internal explosions tore the ship apart.

"Incoming," Foxglove snapped.

Sameena hit the key on her command chair. "All hands, brace for impact," she snapped. "I say again, all hands…"

Sneaky Bastard shuddered, as if an angry god had hit her with a hammer. Sameena hung onto her chair as the gravity failed, several consoles going dark as parts of the ship's control network failed. Moments later, the gravity field reasserted itself, pulling at the crew so hard it was a wonder that none of them fell out of their seats. Sameena twisted her head and peered over at the live feed from damage control. They'd taken at least four direct hits and the missile launchers were completely out of action.

Did they aim at them deliberately, she asked herself, *or did the seeker warheads choose their targets for themselves?*

She pushed the thought to one side as the gravity slowly returned to Earth-normal. "Damage report," she snapped. "How badly are we hit?"

Foxglove scowled. "We've lost our missile launchers, our power distribution network is crippled and we're venting air," he snapped. "The ship is on the verge of breaking apart."

Sameena winced. *Sneaky Bastard* had never been intended as her permanent command, but losing her still hurt. "Tell the crews to prepare to evacuate," she ordered. "What about *Lying Bastard*?"

"Took one minor hit to the rear section," the sensor officer reported. "The damage control parties report that it is under control, but they'll need at least two weeks to carry out repairs."

Assuming that we can find the parts, Sameena thought, ruefully. They might just have to tow both ships back to Madagascar.

She looked over at the main display. "What happened to the other enemy destroyer?"

"High-tailing it out of the system," the sensor officer said. "They started to run as soon as they saw the heavy cruiser explode."

"Smart guys," Sameena muttered. She raised her voice as she keyed her console. "Captain Yew, advance to the planet and attempt to determine enemy positions. Then bring in the troops."

"Understood," Yew said. "Will you be transferring your flag?"

Sameena hesitated. She didn't want to leave her crew, not when their ship had to be evacuated, but she did want to keep an eye on Captain Yew. "Once I've supervised the evacuation," she said, finally. "I trust you to make contact with what remains of the planet's government."

There had been one hundred crewmen on the q-ship, far more than any trader ship would consider necessary. Thirty-two of them were dead or seriously wounded – and Sameena knew that she'd been lucky. If the enemy had been more competent, *Sneaky Bastard* might have been blown completely out of space. But they'd won – and their enemy was nothing more than a drifting hulk. She watched as the bodies were bagged up for the funeral and the wounded were moved to *Lying Bastard*, then insisted on being the last one to board the shuttle that left her ship. *Sneaky Bastard* would be nothing more than a drifting hulk too, at least until she was repaired. The enemy ship was well beyond being useful for anything, but scrap metal.

"It could have been worse," Foxglove said, as they watched the ship fade into the distance. "And we killed a much bigger ship in the process."

Sameena nodded. By the Imperial Navy's standards, they'd come out ahead – but if they'd had the Imperial Navy's sheer weight of numbers, she would never have had to send a pair of q-ships up against a heavy cruiser. What if there were *more* of them? God knew that the Imperial Navy's disposal procedures were careless to the point of recklessness. A cruiser that had been listed as being sent to the breakers might have been sent to pirates instead. Or an independence-seeking movement. Or a faction beyond the Rim, seeking to prepare for the fall of the Empire. Given the time to build up her own finances, *Sameena* might have started buying old ships too.

"Take us to link up with the destroyers," she ordered. The remainder of the crew could stay with the *Lying Bastard*, but she needed to keep an eye on Captain Yew. "And see if you can get me a report from the planet."

The resistance seemed to have launched a major attack as soon as they realised what was going on, she discovered. Apparently, the occupation force hadn't bothered to remove or execute the crew on the orbital station, who had remained in touch with their allies on the ground. The resistance had been alerted the moment the heavy cruiser was blown to atoms.

"The enemy dropped a large number of troops around Landing City," Yew reported, as she stepped onto his bridge. It was smaller than she had expected, although she was gratified to discover that the crew looked thoroughly professional. "They're also still in firm possession of the spaceport. However, the resistance has secured a handful of smaller landing strips and airports and would like us to deploy troops there."

Sameena scowled, remembering Rosa. "Drop the advance teams first to check the situation, then we can land the rest of the troops," she ordered. "Are they supplying targeting coordinates for KEWs?"

And another Landing City, she thought, inwardly. *Sooner or later, someone is going to go to the wrong one.*

"We've hammered all of the listed targets outside the cities," Yew informed her. "However, I have been reluctant to actually fire *into* the cities. The prospect of civilian casualties is simply too high."

Sameena couldn't disagree. KEWs were relatively precise, but a single mistake could cost lives. Far better to deploy her troops, get the enemy isolated and *then* hammer them from orbit, if they refused to surrender. But there was something about the enemy deployment that puzzled her. It was almost as if they had had more in mind than looting, rape and mass murder before vanishing back into space.

Foxglove put it into words. "They intended to hold the planet indefinitely," he said, softly. "Look at their deployments."

"I don't know much about deployments on the ground," Sameena admitted, reluctantly. "Why do you think they meant to stay?"

"Most of their positions are designed for population control," Foxglove said. "They've occupied the outskirts of the main cities, crossroads and bridges, the spaceport and most of the airports…everywhere they need to occupy to keep the population from moving around freely. I'd be surprised if they hadn't started registering the population by now. And I really don't like the implications of us not being able to contact any of the former planetary government."

Sameena followed his logic. "You think they've been killed?"

"It was standard procedure during the Unification Wars," Foxglove admitted. "You land a sizable force, keep bombardment platforms in orbit to hammer anything too big for your groundpounders to handle…and you arrest or execute everyone who might have the reputation to organise resistance. The Empire had plenty of penal colonies where former political leaders could be dumped; these people, I suspect, will simply have killed the planet's leaders."

Captain Yew motioned for Sameena's attention. "The first landing elements report that the resistance is very pleased to see them," he said. "They're calling down the rest of the troops now."

Sameena had seen enough problems with unloading a simple freighter to know that there would be problems unloading three giant freighters full of troops and their equipment. Somewhat to her surprise, the unloading proceeded with minimal delay, allowing Dueller's troops to start advancing on the enemy positions. Guided by the resistance and supported by precise orbital bombardment, resistance rapidly became futile. One by one – and then in droves – the enemy troops began to surrender.

"The resistance isn't too keen on taking prisoners," Foxglove said. "Most of the enemy soldiers who try to surrender are simply shot out of hand." His face twisted into a grimace. "And they want our prisoners handed over to them for execution."

"Tell them we need to interrogate them," Sameena said, firmly. She understood the need for vengeance, but they needed to know just who had attacked Maxwell – and why. Revenge could come later. Ideally, the guilty would be tried and then punished. "Have we captured any senior officers?"

"Only the planetary administrator," Captain Yew reported. He sounded rather pleased, unsurprisingly. With the senior officer in custody, the rest of the enemy force should surrender soon enough. "The resistance has him in their clutches."

He showed her a datapad. Sameena looked at the picture…and then froze. For a long moment, she was so shocked that her mind refused to process what she was seeing. It couldn't be true. It simply couldn't be possible. But it was. There was no mistaking a very familiar face, one she hadn't seen in five years.

Uncle Muhammad?

CHAPTER FORTY

> The net result was that the Empire was rushing blindly towards disaster, with only a relative handful of people aware of the coming catastrophe. And it was the colonies along the Rim that saw the first signs of trouble.
> - Professor Leo Caesius, *The Science That Isn't: Economics and the Decline and Fall of the Galactic Empire.*

Sameena still felt shocked as her shuttle descended towards Landing City, even though part of her had known that the attackers were no ordinary pirates. They acted more like a military force, complete with actual *hygiene* and basic organisation. And if they'd all come from Jannah, they would be starting from scratch when it came to understanding their technology. But how had they even obtained the ships?

The Cartel, she thought, grimly. If *she* could leverage the sales of Firewater Mead into a trading empire, there was no reason why the Cartel couldn't do the same. It hadn't diversified; it had simply concentrated on obtaining ships and weapons for…what? Taking advantage of the collapse of the Empire?

Her blood ran cold as she remembered what the clerics had said, time and time again. There would come a time when the citizens of Jannah, if they placed their faith in God, would return to Earth and purge God's finest creation of the unbelievers who had driven the faithful from their homes. Maybe it had seemed like nothing more than bravado, back when Jannah had been founded, but now…they'd started building their own empire already. If it wasn't nipped in the bud, it might rip the sector apart.

They couldn't match the rest of the Empire, she told herself. But if the Core Worlds fell into civil war…she scowled at the mental image of the Empire's diversity, swept away and replaced by the intolerance and stagnation of Jannah. It would merely be the prelude to war on a scale unseen in three thousand years.

She tensed as the shuttle came in to land at the spaceport. Landing City seemed largely intact, but there were a handful of blackened ruins that had once been buildings scattered throughout the city. It wasn't hard to guess that they'd once been churches – or mosques, or synagogues, or something founded by another religion. The Guardians wouldn't hesitate to kill someone who diverted from their view by even a tiny percentage. Why would they be reluctant to smash all other religions?

"Captain Hussein," a man said, as she stepped out of the shuttle. "I am General Jarvis, formerly of the Maxwell Militia. Welcome to my world."

"Thank you, General," Sameena said. He looked tough, but determined – and very relieved to see her. Without Sameena's ships, Maxwell would have eventually been beaten into submission. "I need to speak with the prisoner."

"So I was given to understand," the General said. "What do you intend to do with him?"

Sameena hesitated. "Interrogate him first," she said, finally. "He might be needed alive, General. This world isn't the only one at risk."

The General grunted. "So I have been told," he said. "Very well. You may take him."

He pointed to an old office block at the edge of the spaceport. "He's in there, under guard," he said. "Do you wish to speak with him now?"

Sameena nodded and allowed him to escort her towards the office. As they walked, he told her about how the newcomers had treated the civilian population, imposing strange new restrictions and curfews on them. As Sameena had anticipated, the invaders had executed most of the planetary leaders – and then gone on to execute priests, teachers and anyone with military experience. She had a feeling that the occupation force had assumed that without any of them left alive the population would be utterly biddable. The General and his men had been proving them wrong.

"He's cuffed to the chair," General Jarvis explained, as they entered the building. "Would you like someone with you in the room?"

"No," Sameena said, flatly. She'd never *considered* running into Uncle Muhammad again, not until she returned to Jannah. Which, she suspected, was going to be sooner than she had planned. "I will talk to him, then you can transfer him to my shuttle."

The General gave her an odd look, but nodded in agreement, motioning for her to enter the cell. It was nicer, she couldn't help noticing, than the cell she'd been held in on Rosa – or, for that matter, an Imperial Navy brig. The walls were solid stone, painted blue and white, but her attention was drawn to the man in the centre of the room. Time had not been kind to Uncle Muhammad.

He glared up at her, his face twisting as if he'd seen something unpleasant. One of his eyes had been blackened by his captors, while blood stained his white robes. Sameena felt an odd twinge of concern which she pushed down ruthlessly. Either through ignorance or deliberate malice, Uncle Muhammad had placed her in a position where only sheer luck had saved her life. Ethne's lectures ran through her mind and she shivered. She could easily have died if God hadn't been with her that day.

She felt almost insulted at his disdainful stare, before realising that he simply didn't recognise her. Her dress was so different from what she'd worn the last time they'd met – five years ago – that he probably hadn't realised that they shared the same homeworld. The uniform she'd donned for the q-ship was tighter than anything that would have been tolerated on Jannah, even though it was quite modest by the Empire's standards.

His mouth lolled open. "I have nothing to say to you, infidel bitch," he said, in passable Imperial Standard. "Kill me already and stop wasting time."

Sameena snorted. "Tell me," she said, in Arabic. "Don't you recognise me?"

His eyes went very wide. Outside the Islamic worlds, Arabic speakers were few and far between – and she'd never quite lost the Jannah accent that flavoured her words. The only real question was if he'd meant to try to kill her or if it had been simple ignorance. She would have thought the latter, if she hadn't known about the Cartel.

It took him several tries to speak. "*Sameena*?"

"In the flesh, as it happens," Sameena said. She allowed herself a tight smile. "Or didn't you *realise* that I was still alive when you discovered that someone was producing Firewater Mead?"

Her eyes narrowed. "Or didn't you *know* about that?"

Uncle Muhammad stared at her. "What are you *wearing*?"

Sameena couldn't help it. She burst out laughing.

"Let's see now," she said. "You're in deep trouble, everyone on this planet wants to kill you in all kinds of horrible ways…and *that's* your first question?"

She knelt down facing him. "I am wearing my uniform," she said, snidely. "Tell me; when you sent me out into space, did you expect me to die?"

"I never expected to see you again," he said. "But I never meant for you to die."

"That's interesting," Sameena said. "Because I really don't believe you."

She straightened up and started to pace around his chair. "I believed that our homeworld was almost completely isolated from the universe," she said. "I believed that only a handful of freighters ever visited each year. It honestly never occurred to me that our homeworld might be building up a space fleet. So tell me…are you really as ignorant about the outside universe as you seem?"

He cringed back as she swung around to glare into his eyes. "And if you are," she added, "why did they put you in command of a whole planet?"

"The Guardians came for me two days after you left," Uncle Muhammad said. "They told me…they told me that I put my contacts with off-worlders to good use and work for them or I could go into one of the work camps, along with my family. I had no choice. They…some of them were determined to eventually move out into the universe and reclaim it for us. All the profits they obtained from selling mead went into buying starships and personnel to train our young men. They wanted me to help."

Sameena hesitated, then asked the question that had been bothering her ever since she'd realised who she was facing. "What happened to my family?"

"They took them all away," Uncle Muhammad said. "I never dared ask what had become of them."

He snorted. "You'd have to ask them," he added. "Maybe if you offered them your help…"

"Never," Sameena said, flatly. "What else did they have you doing?"

"They wanted this world," Uncle Muhammad said. "I was meant to prepare it for becoming part of the new empire…"

"By slaughtering everyone who might have been *productive*," Sameena sneered. A nasty thought crossed her mind. "Did you create the blight on Dueller?"

The expression on his face told her the answer. "Are you mad? Are *they* mad? What would the blight have done to *Jannah* if it had escaped into the wild?"

"They don't care about the dangers," Uncle Muhammad said. "I heard that they planned to unleash it on Salaam."

Sameena shuddered. Salaam was the oldest surviving Islamic planet in the galaxy, its foundation predating the Empire by at least seven hundred years. The founders had learned hard lessons from the wars on Earth, prior to the discovery of FTL; they'd learned the value of tolerance, disagreement and debate. Sameena had thought about going there once or twice, but she'd always known that she preferred the life of a trader. For the Guardians to sentence the entire planet to death…

"There can be only one, can't there?" She said. "They will only accept one version of Islam – theirs. Everyone else can join them or die."

The blight would spread rapidly in the Core Worlds, destroying food production facilities across countless inhabited planets. Unlike Dueller, the Core Worlds *did* have algae-production facilities, which should prevent starvation, but there would be riots. No one ate algae-based foodstuffs if there was any other choice.

She gritted her teeth as she saw the full awfulness of the plan. If Jannah's role was ever discovered, there would be a pogrom against Muslims that would exceed the mass slaughters of the pre-Unification

Wars era. Muslims across the galaxy would have no choice, but to fight to defend themselves, which would force them to work with the Guardians. But even so…she couldn't see any way the plan would end, but in total defeat and extermination. The Empire might be crippled, yet it was still vastly more powerful than Jannah – or, for that matter, every Islamic world put together.

"The Empire outnumbers you billions to one," she said, stunned. "You must be out of your minds!"

"There are billions only in theory," Uncle Muhammad pointed out. "In practice, the Empire is slowly coming apart, shattering into its component pieces. The Guardians decided to move now to establish a new power in the sector, accelerating their plan. It will give them some room to manoeuvre later on."

The plan was doomed, Sameena was sure. Given time, the Empire's stagnation would merely be replaced by *Jannah's* stagnation. All the factors that had encouraged the Grand Senate to limit education worked against Jannah too. They'd already shot most of the people on Maxwell they'd need to maintain their little empire, let alone make it stronger. And it would simply collapse under its own weight.

Just like the Empire, she thought.

"This scheme isn't going to succeed," she said.

Uncle Muhammad snorted. "The Empire is gone," he said. "Who is going to stop us?"

"Me," Sameena said. "*I* will stop it."

"You're just a girl," Uncle Muhammad said. "You won't be stopping anything."

"I never believed that, even when I was stuck on Jannah," Sameena said, in a tone her mother would have slapped her for using to speak to a male relative. "Right now, I put together the force that destroyed one of your ships and sent the other one fleeing for its life. I can and I will stop you."

"You have a duty to your homeworld," Uncle Muhammad said. "You should join us…"

"My homeworld saw fit to reject me because of my brother's big mouth," Sameena said, dryly. "And even before then" – she pressed her fingers between her breasts – "it saw fit to treat me as dirt merely for being born female. Why should I not show them the same kind of loyalty they showed me?"

She met his eyes, something she would never have dared before she'd left Jannah. "Why should I not avenge my family by bombarding Jannah into rubble?"

"Millions would die," Uncle Muhammad objected. "Sameena, I…"

"Millions would die if their insane plan was allowed to succeed," Sameena snapped. "Maybe more, maybe *billions*. Or maybe the Empire would forget its woes long enough to put together a task force and scorch Jannah down to bedrock. Or maybe they would just blow the entire planet out of orbit and into the sun. And even if they succeeded, in a few generations we'd all be grubbing in the dirt again."

She slapped him across the face. "Listen to yourself," she ordered. "This *cannot* end well!"

The slap wasn't very hard, but seemed to stun him. He would never have been hit – or even threatened – by a woman in his entire life. Jannah didn't teach its women to use violence, merely to submit to their treatment. In hindsight, Sameena could see how the Guardians had handled their inadequacy issues. They'd merely ensured that they always had an entire sex to look down on.

"You will be interrogated by my officers," Sameena continued. "They will drag out everything you know about the Guardians and their plans. I suggest you don't try to lie – or to hide anything. You won't enjoy the experience."

"I can tell them about you," Uncle Muhammad said. "Will they trust you after they find out where you're from?"

"My husband already knows," Sameena said. She smiled at his shocked expression. It was forbidden on Jannah to marry without the consent of a male guardian. If there was no biological guardian, *the* Guardians would take on the role. It was easy to see how such a system can be abused. "And *he* doesn't care."

Uncle Muhammad looked around, as if he expected to see Jamie standing behind her. "He lets you out on your own?"

His eyes sharpened. "I wish to speak with him at once," he said, imperiously. "I am *most displeased* with your behaviour."

Sameena slapped him a second time. His head snapped backwards, blood trickling down from his lip. On Jannah, a husband was responsible for his wife's behaviour…but she'd left that attitude behind a long time ago. Jamie wasn't going to beat her for being rude to her Uncle.

"This isn't your homeworld," she said. "And soon enough, your homeworld will be changed too."

She looked down at him for a long moment, unable to escape understanding just how pathetic he really was. Once, he had been important… but the price of his survival was submission to a very old evil, an evil that had infested her homeworld for hundreds of years. Now, he was a helpless prisoner, a man responsible for meting out all kinds of torments to the planet's population.

There were girls on Jannah who had admired the Guardians, who had cast longing glances at them from beneath their veils. How much of that, Sameena asked herself, had been foolishness – and how much had been Stockholm Syndrome? *She* had always been a little afraid of the men in black, even though she'd never spoken to one of them. And then they'd come for her brother and his entire family.

And now her family was gone.

"I don't believe that we will talk again," she said, softly. She refused to acknowledge him as her Uncle any longer. "Goodbye."

She walked out of the cell without looking back. "General," she said. "Please can you have him transferred to orbit now?"

"Of course," Jarvis said. "Do you want him drugged for the flight?"

"Please do," Sameena said. She hesitated. "How much longer do you need the troops?"

"Maybe a week or two," Jarvis said. He gave her an odd look. "Do you want to take them back home?"

"I may need them elsewhere," Sameena admitted. She'd have to talk to Jamie and plan the operation carefully. One of the destroyers could go to Jannah now and sneak around the system to see what they were hiding. Somehow, she doubted that the Guardians would have left their homeworld defenceless. "But it won't be a problem until then, I hope."

She watched grimly as a drugged Uncle Muhammad was manhandled out of the office block and carried over towards the shuttle, then looked back towards the clear blue sky. Maxwell was far better developed than Rosa or Dueller, but there was relatively little hint of industrial pollution in the air. That might change, given time.

"I have to get back to Government House," Jarvis said. In the distance, there was a brief rattle of gunfire as one of the holdouts was summarily exterminated. "It may take some time to establish a working government. Everyone with any experience was targeted for death and not all of the survivors have come out of hiding."

"I understand," Sameena said. She briefly considered asking him for troops, then dropped the idea. Maxwell needed everyone it could get. Besides, they had too many reasons to mistreat people on Jannah. "I can wait to deal with the government when you form it."

She looked towards a pillar of smoke, rising into the sky, and shuddered. It was less dramatic than fighting in space, or the blight wiping out an entire planet's agriculture, but somehow it affected her deeply. No matter what she did, people were going to suffer and die.

I'll just have to deal with them quickly, she told herself.

But how?

INTERLUDE FOUR

Everything was going as the Founders had planned.

Grand Mufti Mahmud Shaltut al-Zarqawi sipped coffee in his office and contemplated, once again, the wisdom of those who had founded Jannah. They'd known that the universe was against them, that they would have to hide and prepare for the day that the Empire dropped its guard… and that day had finally come. He'd believed, when he had taken up the office, that it wouldn't come in his lifetime.

But he'd been wrong!

He'd studied the history books endlessly, the ones that talked about the great war waged against the Empire, about how the *Jihadists* had come close to victory before they were betrayed by unbelievers in their own ranks. A force that had almost beaten the mighty Empire had been shattered, the last survivors forced to flee and hide. And hide they had, so well that almost all of Jannah's population hadn't even *known* that they had a Grand Mufti. Or that their planet had covert links to the Empire…

It had been a sign, he knew, that the Founders had selected *this* planet, where God had created a tool they could use against the Empire – if they saw fit to use it. The Empire would pay almost anything for Firewater Mead, funding their own destruction. But that had always been the way with the infidels. When they weren't drugging themselves or drowning their sorrows in alcohol, they were selling the believers the weapons the believers needed to establish themselves as the one true power. The mercenaries training the young men on Jannah in handling starships had no real idea what they were unleashing on the galaxy.

And they wouldn't care either.

The plan was slowly coming to its climax, he told himself. His teams were already poised to head into the Core Worlds, to strike at cloudscoops and other industrial facilities, to set off civil wars and arm insurgents… just to feed the chaos that would consume the remains of the Empire. And, in its wake, his forces would move from world to world, converting the populations and absorbing their industrial bases. Piece by piece, the new Caliphate would be created. The galaxy would finally be set on the proper course.

This time, he promised silently, there would be no mistakes.

The Guardians had weeded the garden of Jannah endlessly. Anyone who showed even a trace of disbelieving thought was removed, along with his family. Disbelief could not be tolerated. No one could question, for questioning led directly to disbelief and sin. It was enough that they had the words of the Founders to point them on their way.

He stood up as he heard the call to prayer echoing through the complex. It would be unseemly for him to be late, or to spend time outside the mosque when he should be paying attention to God. After all, it wouldn't do to court God's anger. Victory could still be snatched away from him.

Behind him, his junior wife scurried in to pick up the coffee cup and replace it with a new one for his return. She'd been defiant at first, when her parents had been convinced to allow him to marry her, but he'd soon taught her how to behave. It hadn't been hard; a few slaps, food restrictions and threats of much worse. She was much more useful and obedient now. And his senior wives were very appreciative of having their own servant.

Yes, he told himself. God's anger should *not* be courted.

Who knew what form His punishment might take?

Chapter
Forty-One

> Supplies from the Core Worlds slowed to a trickle – then stopped altogether. The Imperial Navy was withdrawn from the Rim, leaving defenceless planets wide open to pirate attacks. Entire sectors were simply abandoned…
> - Professor Leo Caesius, *The Science That Isn't: Economics and the Decline and Fall of the Galactic Empire.*

"That man," Jamie said. "Is he really your Uncle?"

"In a manner of speaking," Sameena said. She couldn't help feeling tense. The traders didn't care about where someone came from – and Jamie already knew about Jannah – but the thought of being linked to the raiders was terrifying. "But I separated myself from him."

"I don't blame you," Jamie said. "I spoke to him once and he started raving the moment I told him I was your husband. Apparently I'm failing in my husbandly duties or some such nonsense."

He looked up at her. "Although you really shouldn't have gone to Maxwell," he added. "A little less luck and you might be dead now, or captured."

"I had to go," Sameena said, although she knew that he was right. The prospect of falling into Uncle Muhammad's hands was not an appealing one. "Just as we have to go to Jannah."

Jamie shook his head in awe. "I still can't believe that a low-tech planet managed to put together a viable challenge to the entire sector," he said. "That would be impressive if it wasn't aimed at us."

"The Cartel made vast amounts of money," Sameena said, remembering just how odd it had seemed when she had first researched it. What had it been *doing* with all that money? It could have spent the last few hundred years buying starships and preparing for war. "It all had to go somewhere."

It hadn't taken *her* long to realise that the Empire was in decline, not once she'd had a chance to study some proper history. She could easily see someone else from Jannah coming to the same decision – and then planning to take advantage of it, rather than mitigate the long-term consequences of the Empire's fall. If Uncle Muhammad had been telling the truth, the Founders had planned for this moment. Sameena wasn't sure that she believed him, even though *he* thought that he was being honest. The Guardians had no trouble with the concept of lying.

"If they were buying up starships for hundreds of years, we'd be screwed," Jamie said. "But the Empire might well have noticed if they started too soon."

His eyes narrowed. "Did anyone give you any trouble?"

"No," Sameena said, gratefully. The traders were individualists; they didn't care where someone came from, merely what they made of themselves. And the Imperial Navy had hundreds of thousands of recruits who had joined to leave their homes and families behind. "Well, apart from you."

"Going there *was* stupid," Jamie said, unapologetically. "You're the Head of State, not a simple starship commander. You cannot put your life at risk."

"So you keep saying," Sameena said. "And you're right."

Jamie's wristcom chimed. "Captain Yew has returned," he said, dryly. "It's time for the briefing."

Sameena sighed and reached for her shipsuit. She'd shuttled over to Jamie's destroyer as soon as they arrived at the RV point, then spent the night in his cabin. It had been too long since she'd been with him, she'd told herself, and Jamie seemed to feel the same way. He certainly hadn't raised any objections to her spending the night.

She briefly considered going to the briefing compartment ahead of him, so they entered separately, then laughed at herself. It was an absurd thought. Everyone knew that they were married; there was no point in trying to hide. Besides, it wasn't precisely a forbidden relationship by the Imperial Navy's standards, while the traders simply wouldn't care. It was none of anyone else's business.

Jamie pulled on his trousers and jacket over his shipsuit, then led her out of the cabin and down into the tiny briefing compartment. Thankfully, he'd decided to hold the conference electronically; the destroyer's compartment simply didn't have room for every commanding officer in the small squadron as well as the intelligence officers. Sameena took a seat beside the head of the table – as the starship's CO, Jamie chaired the meeting – and waited for the other officers to appear in front of them.

"Thank you all for coming," Jamie said, once the last hologram had flickered into existence. "As you know, what started as a major pirate raid on Maxwell has become something immeasurably more grave. It is no exaggeration to suggest that the future of humanity itself may ride upon our response to the new threat."

He gave Sameena a brief glance, then looked at Commander Sidney Peterson. "Commander?"

Peterson stood up, activating the holographic display. "Our original assumption – that the raid on Maxwell was merely a looting mission – was badly incorrect," he said. "The raid was actually an invasion, with an overall objective of crushing the planet's independence and incorporating it into a new empire. Furthermore, instead of merely accepting tribute, the planet's new rulers intended to force the population to embrace their religion. In the six weeks they ruled the planet, they destroyed religious buildings, slaughtered religious leaders and imposed religious laws on the planet. Those who failed to abide by them were punished or executed. They are still digging up mass graves on the planet."

Sameena shuddered, feeling a wave of guilt and shame. The occupation force had committed thousands of atrocities, ranging from rape to mass slaughter and child-theft. If the resistance hadn't overrun the camps where the children were being held, they would have been brainwashed into mindless supporters of the regime – or simply killed, if they proved intractable. Even as it was, they were orphans. Their parents had been butchered long ago.

How *could* Jannah have produced such monsters? It had always seemed so peaceful...but she, of all people, ought to know better. If the Guardians had no problems sentencing a young man and his family to death for questioning authority, they wouldn't even *blink* at the prospect of penalising non-believers. Hell, the true believers wouldn't think they had a choice. Any soul that failed to embrace their version of Islam, they believed, would go to Hell upon death. They had to try to save souls.

"We managed to interrogate a number of enemy soldiers before the locals demanded them back," Peterson continued. "They confirmed what we had already discovered" – he nodded to Sameena – "and filled in some of the gaps. The invaders come from Jannah, a low-tech world two weeks from Maxwell. It seems that the planet's rulers have been planning to take advantage of the Empire's collapse for quite some time."

He briefly explained what Sameena had learned from Uncle Muhammad – and then what the interrogators had pulled from him, during the interrogation. Sameena wasn't too surprised to discover that the Guardians hadn't bothered to tell the planet's population much; they'd simply started recruiting young men for the cause, taking them away for training without explanation. Few people would dare to question the Guardians...

But that might change, she told herself, *if few of those young men ever returned.*

The thought made her scowl. Maxwell's resistance – and provisional government - had butchered every member of the occupation force they could get their hands on, despite her objections. They wanted revenge – and she couldn't really blame them. And with so many young men simply *gone*, what would happen on Jannah? She honestly couldn't understand why the Guardians hadn't told their people some version of the truth.

"Those we interrogated claimed that Jannah has millions of starships," Peterson continued. "However, we have good reason to doubt those claims..."

"Sure we do," Captain Yew interrupted. "They'd have won by now if they had millions of ships."

"...And our analysts think that we are looking at upwards of forty starships at most," Peterson said, ignoring the interruption. "However, we have no hard data so we cannot take anything for granted. Given fifty years and the vast monetary resources of the Cartel, they might have built up a formidable force."

He paused. "Their principal weakness lies in poor maintenance and worse training," Peterson continued. "Those we interrogated were almost as ignorant as basic recruits for the Civil Guard" – there were some chuckles, led by Paddy – "and their superiors don't seem to be actually *trying* to educate them. Some of them honestly believed that guns were beyond their comprehension, others had expensive pieces of kit without quite understanding how to use it to best advantage. They had night-vision goggles, for example, but never actually used them on the ground. If they had, the resistance would have had a much tougher time of it.

"The same problems can be seen in their starships. Their training is evidently poor, they make no use of the more advanced functions…and their maintenance is actually lower than that of the average pirate ship. My first thought was that they were suffering from the side effects of an irrational naval expansion program, but after reading the interrogation transcripts I have come to believe that there is a deliberate effort being made to *deny* their trainees useful knowledge. I think that this is likely to bite them hard."

"It already has," Foxglove commented. "If they'd left their computers to handle point defence, the Battle of Maxwell could easily have gone the other way."

Wonderful, Sameena thought, sourly. *We can call this the War of the Poorly-Maintained Starships and Worse-Trained Crews. If we win…*

Peterson scowled. "Despite their general ignorance, many of the prisoners were utterly fanatical when they weren't drugged," he concluded. "They genuinely believed that non-believers were utterly inferior to believers – and that they were forgiven any sin, as long as it was carried out in the name of God. I have no doubt that this military force would happily carry out a whole series of atrocities and never feel the slightest shred of guilt. All those who might have thought for themselves would have been weeded out long ago."

"In short," Sameena said, when Peterson had finished, "we don't dare let them out into the universe. We have to stop them now."

She looked over at Captain Yew. "What did you find when you surveyed their system?"

"They've been preparing for this for a long time," Yew said. "The last known visitor to the system" – he nodded at Captain Hamilton – "saw no space-based presence at all, apart from a pair of communications satellites. When we surveyed the system, we discovered a number of starships and orbital stations in position around the planet. The only thing missing was a cloudscoop."

"There's no gas giant in the system," Sameena said, quietly. "They must have been stockpiling HE3 for a very long time."

"Almost certainly," Peterson confirmed. "Operating a sizable fleet would require secure access to a cloudscoop…"

"They might simply intend to take one," Captain Hamilton pointed out. His presence had been a welcome surprise. "There are five in the sector and we're working on building others."

Sameena nodded, thinking hard. There *had* to be a fuel dump somewhere within the Jannah System – and if it happened to be destroyed, the enemy would become desperate. But fusion was very efficient. It was unlikely that a shortage of fuel would cripple their warships in time to be useful. On the other hand, it might force them to abandon whatever subtle plans they had and go directly for Madagascar. It was still the closest cloudscoop to Jannah.

Captain Yew cleared his throat. "There were fifteen warships, seven of them heavy cruisers, in orbit around the planet," he said. A low groan ran through the room. "However, we do not believe that all of them are operational. We watched them long enough to confirm that their power curves indicate poor maintenance and other telltale signs. I suspect that the crews are simply trying to do too much too quickly. My intelligence officer believes that it will be at least three months before the remainder of those ships are operational.

"There were also a number of freighters in orbit," he continued. "We think that most of them were captured by the enemy – some of the ship losses we attributed to pirates might well be raiding missions from Jannah. Their crews would probably have been pressed into service."

Sameena nodded. Pirate commanders tended to press-gang starship crewmen from captured ships, forcing them to join the pirate crew. Those that agreed were treated relatively well; those that refused were tortured until they broke or were simply killed out of hand. She hadn't been able to understand it until she'd realised just how far most humans would fall just to remain alive. And the pirates were skilled at ensuring their new recruits ended up with blood on their hands. They would soon have nowhere to go.

"I have prepared a complete brief for you," Captain Yew concluded. "However, I believe that our one chance to nip this in the bud is now. We have to squash Jannah before it gets those ships online, or stopping it may become impossible. There is no longer any hope of calling on support from Earth."

"A squadron of battleships would smash them flat inside a day," Foxglove agreed. "But we don't *have* any battleships."

Sameena gritted her teeth. Given a couple of years, Steve's team could *produce* battleships – and plenty of missiles and other advanced weapons systems. If he was actually right about the prospects for future developments, they might certainly create better weapons than Jannah could obtain from the ruins of the Empire. But they didn't have time. It crossed her mind that they could simply withdraw into the trackless wastes of interstellar space and build up their forces, but she knew that was unacceptable. She had pledged to protect every world that had signed up with her government and she wasn't about to abandon them.

She looked over at Yew. "What sort of production plants do they have?"

"We saw none," Yew said. "However, that doesn't mean anything. A survey of this sector wouldn't find our industrial nodes either."

Sameena had to admit that he had a point. It was unlikely that *any* competent planner would turn Jannah into an industrial node; the lack of a gas giant alone would cripple it. If *she'd* been in charge, she would have taken over a system like Madagascar and established the industrial node there. But would Jannah's planners have wanted to separate themselves so much from their homeworld?

A thought struck her and she smiled. What if there was *no* industrial base?

"That doesn't seem too likely," Jamie objected, when she said it out loud. "They have to know that they won't be getting supplies from the Empire."

"I wouldn't trust their people to produce anything more complex than hand-powered tools, if that," Patterson said. "It's possible that they built up a really immense store of weapons and spare parts – hell, they might have helped to drive the price up over the last ten years. Or maybe they intend to construct the production plant later, once they have more engineers trained up."

"Assuming they can," Captain Hamilton said doubtfully. "Engineers and religious fanatics really don't mix."

Sameena tapped the table. "We have to deal with this problem now," she said, firmly. "Do we have enough firepower here to actually win?"

Jamie scowled. "It depends how many of those ships are actually functional," he admitted. "If those ships were crewed by the dregs of the Imperial Navy, they'd still have a colossal firepower advantage. But if the crews are actually untrained idiots…we might have a chance. But I'd hesitate to launch an attack unless there was no other choice."

His scowl deepened. "We could try to lure them into a trap," he said. "If we use our spare missiles as mines…old tactic, but it does work."

"Tricky," Yew said. "A plan that depends on the enemy doing what you want is a very bad plan indeed."

"True," Jamie agreed. "We'd have to give them some reason to try and chase us down."

Sameena smiled. "I can provide that," she said, as an idea blossomed to life in her mind. "We will broadcast to the entire planet. Our captive" – she'd almost called him Uncle – "will record a message for us in Arabic, revealing precisely what the Guardians have been doing."

"Sneaky," Yew said. "But what happens if they jam it?"

"I bet they can't," Foxglove said. "Jamming signals from Imperial Navy ships would require actual understanding of what they're doing. It's not meant to be *easy*."

"And they'd take the bait," Jamie said. "And we'd lure them right into a trap."

Sameena nodded. "It will take us two weeks to get from here to Jannah, then we can lay our trap and advance into the system," she said. "If we're lucky, we can nip this in the bud."

It was going to be difficult, she knew, as she studied the enemy starships hanging in orbit around her homeworld. Even if only half of them were fully-functional – or at least operational – they would have one hell of an advantage in firepower. And they probably wouldn't be fooled by the q-ships a third time. The ship that had fled Maxwell would have alerted them to the trick by now.

But how would they respond? It was almost impossible to predict how religious fanatics would respond to almost anything. They might send another fleet to Maxwell – or they might pull in their horns and try to discover just what happened to the first invasion force. There was no way to be *sure*. Her only hope was to come down on Jannah as hard as possible before its leaders reacted. If it wasn't already too late.

And if we're not lucky, she added, in the privacy of her own mind, *Steve is going to have to remain in hiding and build up his fleet to liberate the sector.*

CHAPTER FORTY-TWO

...Leaving a power vacuum waiting to be filled. Some planets with long-buried dreams of independence sought to carve out their own empires, or secure territory for later expansion. Others were unable to survive without outside help; those unlucky enough to drop out of contact entirely died out. Newer political units expanded into the ruins of the Empire.
- Professor Leo Caesius, *The Science That Isn't: Economics and the Decline and Fall of the Galactic Empire.*

Sameena had been expecting to feel *something* when she returned to Jannah – or at least to the Jannah System – but there was nothing, apart from a grim sense that there was work to be done. The sun that had given Jannah light and heat was nothing more than a glowing spark of light in the distance, perhaps a little bigger and brighter than the rest. There was no trace of activity along the Phase Limit. If she hadn't known that the raiders were there, she would have doubted herself. The destroyer's sensors were picking up almost nothing from the inner system.

"Put the freighters under cloak," Jamie ordered. "And then monitor their positions. I want to be sure the cloaks are working."

"Cloaks operational," Foxglove reported. He'd transferred to *Pinafore* after *Sneaky Bastard* had been towed to the edge of the Maxwell System and decommissioned. "Only a very savvy sensor operator would be able to detect them."

"Very good," Jamie said. He gave Sameena a grin, then looked over at the helmsman. "Cloak us, then take us into the system. I want to be at the first waypoint within three hours."

Sameena sat back in her chair and tried to concentrate. It felt odd to be on someone else's bridge – and she couldn't bark orders to Jamie's crew, something she had to force herself to remember. She'd been a Captain too long, she realised. She watched grimly as the sensor reports came in, noting the presence of a number of energy signatures near Jannah…and very little else. Her thought that the Guardians might have been unable or unwilling to build up an industrial base might have been right after all. They weren't even *trying* to mine the asteroids.

The bridge crews spoke in hushed voices as they drew closer to the first waypoint. Sameena had to smile; there was no way that the enemy could hear their words, yet they were quiet. The dim lighting that signified that the cloaking device was active seemed oppressive, almost spooky. It was a relief when they finally reached their destination without being detected.

"Start unloading the missiles," Jamie ordered the freighter crews. "And then sneak back out of the system and wait for us just past the Phase Limit."

The missiles were too small to carry cloaking devices, even if the designers had been inclined to waste money on such trivial considerations. But they were tiny on the standards of interstellar space and, as long as they were powered down, completely undetectable. Sameena watched as the missiles were unloaded – it had taken Steve two months to produce them – and placed in position, waiting for their time to shine.

And if this goes wrong, she thought, coldly, *this entire plan will be worse than useless.*

"All missiles deployed," Foxglove reported. "Laser command-and-control is online; IFF signal trackers are online."

"Let's hope so," Jamie muttered. He'd told her that IFF mishaps resulted in friendly fire incidents. Paddy had chimed in with a droll observation about friendly fire being nothing of the sort. "If this goes wrong, we are all in deep shit."

Sameena couldn't disagree.

"Launch probes," Jamie ordered. "I want a clear view of the planet before we advance."

Pinafore shuddered slightly as she launched a set of recon probes, hurling them down towards Jannah. Sameena watched as her homeworld appeared in the display, glowing blue-green against the inky darkness of space. It didn't feel any different to Rosa or Maxwell or any of the other worlds she'd visited, she realised. Living in space was her life now.

"Four orbital stations, one of which is definitely still under construction," Foxglove reported. "Seventeen warships in planetary orbit, seven of them heavy cruisers." He sucked in a breath. "One of the others is an Imperial Navy battlecruiser!"

Jamie leaned forward. "Where the hell did that come from?"

"The breakers, judging by its power curves," Foxglove said. "I think they're trying to refit it and not having much luck."

Sameena smiled, even though the presence of the battlecruiser was a nasty shock. Jamie had told her that many system-defence forces tended to go for larger ships, even though they didn't have the trained manpower base to operate them. They would be better off, he'd explained, going for destroyers and light cruisers, then slowly working their way up to battlecruisers and battleships. By the time they obtained them, they should have crews capable of operating them. But Jannah's reserves of trained manpower were almost non-existent.

Jamie gave her a sharp look, then looked back at Foxglove. "Is she armed?"

"Unknown," Foxglove said. "But I am picking up no targeting sensors, not even standby signals. I suspect that she isn't capable of military operations."

"Show us the remaining ships," Jamie ordered. "What are we looking at?"

"Six destroyers and two light cruisers," Foxglove said. "Plus one ship of indeterminate design. It looks like a heavily-modified medium cruiser, but there's no record of anything comparable in the datafiles."

"Probably a custom design," Jamie said. "How many of those ships are operational?"

"Uncertain," Foxglove admitted. "I think about half of them are operational, but it's hard to be sure at this range."

Downright impossible, Sameena thought grimly.

It took another hour before Jamie was sure that they had surveyed the system thoroughly, although they both knew how easy it was to hide something as tiny as a starship in outer space. Sameena watched the endless stream of data flowing into the display, realising – not for the first time – just how strange the whole set-up was. Jannah had nothing in the outer system, not even a handful of observation posts…and yet there were starships in orbit around the planet and four orbital stations.

They must be planning on capturing my industrial nodes, she thought, coldly. *Nothing else makes sense, unless they plan to embrace the destruction of technology.*

"The freighters are clear," Jamie said, finally. He keyed his console. "All ships, prepare to execute Plan Alpha on my mark."

Sameena settled back into her chair and braced herself. This could go horrendously wrong.

"Mark," Jamie ordered.

As one, the squadron decloaked and accelerated towards the planet. They would have been picked up instantly by any competent sensor crew, but no one was entirely sure just what – if anything – was guarding Jannah. There had certainly been no trace of a sensor network watching orbital space when Captain Hamilton had visited the system – and picked up an unexpected stowaway. But the ships in orbit should have been able to detect their presence…

"They've seen us," Foxglove said. "But they haven't focused their sensors on us. I think they're having trouble locking on."

He scowled down at his console. "I'm picking up increased drive emissions from a dozen ships, *not* including the battlecruiser," he added. "They're coming to battlestations."

"Oh, for a battleship or two," Jamie muttered in her ear.

Sameena nodded. A squadron of battleships could simply have sneaked up on the planet, then blown most of the enemy force out of space with the opening salvo. Instead, her little squadron might have inflicted damage with a surprise attack, but not enough to utterly destroy the enemy. It was easy to see how quickly they would have been destroyed once the enemy recovered from their shock.

"Taking their sweet time about it," the helmsman muttered. "I would have been booted out an airlock if it took me *that* long to get underway."

"Be grateful for small mercies," Sameena advised.

Jamie snorted, then keyed his console. "Begin transmission," he ordered. "Make sure the entire planet hears it."

"Message transmitting," the communications officer said. "They'll hear it, sir."

Sameena smiled, very coldly. It had taken some...*persuasion* to convince Uncle Muhammad to read the script she'd prepared, but he'd eventually surrendered to the inevitable. She'd considered reading it herself, as Jamie had suggested, yet she'd known that much of the planet's male population would simply have ignored a feminine voice. They'd be more likely to believe a man.

That will change, she promised her mother's shade. *The entire planet will be reformed.*

The speech had been carefully written to be absolutely truthful – and drive the Guardians insane with rage. And, as it was broadcast on the channels their religious programs used, they had no way to prevent the entire planet from listening to them. Even a complete blackout would not stop battery-operated radios from picking up the speech. Their only hope was to come after her squadron with everything they had.

"They're getting underway," Foxglove reported. "Recalculating engagement range now; seven minutes to outer edge of our missile envelope."

"Open fire as soon as we enter missile range," Jamie ordered. "And prepare to deploy drones the moment they return fire."

We should have the advantage in a long-range missile duel, Sameena told herself, as the enemy starships slowly started to inch out of orbit. Was it her imagination – or did they look like they were nervous at the prospect of leaving the comfort of planetary orbit? She'd had few problems coming to terms with the vastness of space, but she hadn't really had a choice – well, not unless she'd stayed on Madagascar or gone to a low-tech world. The crewmen on the enemy ships might have been offered a choice...

"Entering missile range," Foxglove reported.

"Opening fire," the tactical officer added.

Pinafore shivered as she launched her first salvo of missiles, targeted directly on the enemy craft heading towards them. One of the ships was showing definite signs of drive problems, Sameena noted; the others seemed sturdy enough to keep going, no matter what else happened. Moments later, they belched a swarm of missiles back towards Jamie's squadron, intent on destroying them.

"Hold the range open," Jamie ordered. "Just keep tempting them to shoot their magazines dry."

Pinafore twisted in space, reversing course…and drawing the enemy craft after her. The rest of the squadron followed suit, belching out a second wave of missiles. Sameena couldn't help shivering as she realised how puny their barrages were compared to what the enemy craft could pump out, even though their targeting and point defence was much better. The enemy might manage to swamp them by sheer weight of fire.

"The enemy doesn't have a working point defence datanet," Foxglove observed. "If they did, we wouldn't have scored a single hit."

Sameena scowled. Even with each ship defending itself, rather than fighting as a team and combining their firepower, the enemy had clearly managed to improve their point defence. Only three missiles made it through to slam into enemy hulls, doing minimal damage.

"Their fire control isn't much better," Jamie commented, quietly. "They should have been able to score at least one hit by now. Keeping the range open only goes so far."

"Don't give them any ideas," Sameena muttered back. The enemy ships were firing again, trying to wear the defences down. So far, they hadn't scored a single hit…but everyone knew that it was only a matter of time. "We want them angry, not murderous."

It was a balancing act, she knew. Jamie's squadron had to seem like a reasonable target to keep the enemy in pursuit, but they didn't dare let the range fall enough so that the enemy was assured of scoring hits. It would be easy to simply escape enemy missile range, yet if they did the enemy might simply give up pursuit, even if they were still pumping out the message towards Jannah.

"*Sir Porter* just took two direct hits," Foxglove reported, suddenly. "She's falling out of formation."

Jamie cursed. "Order her commander to evade laterally and escape," he snapped. "And to stop broadcasting the message…"

It was too late. As if they sensed the ship's weakness, enemy missiles homed in on *Sir Porter* and overwhelmed her, slamming into her hull until it disintegrated into a radioactive ball of plasma. Part of Sameena's mind was horrified at watching a crew die so brutally, part of her was disgusted at the waste. There had been no need to expend so many missiles on killing such a small destroyer.

"*Sir Porter* has been destroyed," Foxglove said. "There are no signs of any lifepods."

Sameena forced herself to sit still, even though her instincts called for pouring on the speed and escaping the enemy ships. The cold equations that governed spaceflight ensured that failure – the loss of even a single drive section – would mean certain destruction. She doubted her crews would surrender, even if the enemy was in the mood to accept them. They all knew what had happened to prisoners on Maxwell.

The damage kept mounting up as the enemy force chased them, never showing a hint of giving up. *Pinafore* took a nasty blow that destroyed two of her missile launchers and came alarmingly close to crippling the ship; two other starships fell out of formation and were rapidly targeted by the enemy, one of them blown to rubble as quickly as the first. The second steered a direct course towards an enemy heavy cruiser and ploughed into her hull, destroying both ships in a single explosion. Sameena looked towards the system display, then back at the tactical display, wondering if they'd miscalculated. There might be nothing left of the squadron by the time they reached the emplaced missiles.

"Two direct hits," Foxglove observed. On the display, an enemy destroyer fell out of formation, her drive field spluttering into non-existence. "But their point defence is getting better."

Sameena wasn't too surprised. Experience was a great teacher. The enemy had a major weakness; the closing speed between her missiles and their ships was much faster than the closing speed between her ships and their missiles. Improving their point defence was the only logical solution, although they didn't seem to realise the potential of their own datanet.

Thank God for small mercies, she told herself. If they had, the battle would suddenly have become a great deal harder. They might well lose by the time they reached the missiles.

"Approaching outer edge of emplaced missile range," the helmsman snapped, suddenly.

"Bring up the command links," Jamie ordered. "And make damn sure you triple-check our IFF signals."

"Aye, sir," Foxglove said. *Pinafore* heaved as another enemy missile slammed into the hull, wiping out a handful of point defence nodes. Red lights flared up on the status display, then faded away. "Missiles are ready, sir. They've recognised our IFF codes."

"Let's hope so," Jamie grunted. "Fire the missiles on my command."

Sameena braced herself. Ideally, the missiles should be launched from the closest approach point, just to give the enemy as little chance as possible to prepare to face them. But the closer the enemy came to the missiles, the greater the chance they might detect the missiles and take precautions. It was yet another balancing act, one they'd simulated time and time again without finding a real answer. Too much depended on how the enemy chose to react to their actions.

"Wait for it," Jamie ordered. He studied the display, timing it mentally. They inched through the missile cloud, shortening the range still further. There would be nothing between the missiles and their targets. "*Fire!*"

The missiles came online and lunged towards their targets. Sameena could have sworn that the enemy craft *flinched* as the missiles appeared. They were far too close for any form of evasive manoeuvres; the only thing they could do was try to ward them off with their point defence. But there were too many missiles for that…Sameena watched, feeling cold pleasure, as the missiles slammed into their targets. Laser heads burned through hullmetal, stabbing deep into the starship's vitals, while nukes slammed through hulls and detonated inside ships. One by one, the enemy starships died until there was nothing left, but debris.

Sameena could imagine the last nightmarish moments of the enemy ships. The sudden realisation that they'd been led into a trap, the awareness of the missile swarm bearing down on them, the desperate attempts to fend it off…and the certainty that there was no escape. Hulls would have been torn open, power would have been lost and fusion cores, normally so stable, would have blown. There would have been little time to run to the lifepods before it ran out forever.

"All targets destroyed," Foxglove reported, with heavy satisfaction. On the display, the last traces of the enemy starships faded away. "I say again, all targets destroyed."

"Take us back to the planet, doglegging around the stranded enemy ships," Jamie ordered, sharply. "They can be left to die on the vine."

He sounded pleased, although they would have to move fast to capitalise on their victory. "Order the troop transports to advance into the system," he ordered. Paddy and the ground assault force had remained on the edge of the Phase Limit, ready to retreat if things went badly wrong. "Tell the CO that we're going to need them to secure the orbital stations and the remaining starships. And broadcast a demand for surrender."

Sameena scowled. A planet was largely helpless once its orbital defences – starships or defence platforms – were destroyed, which tended to encourage surrender once the high orbitals had fallen. After all, the attackers could simply blast any resistance on the ground from orbit, with all the attendant civilian casualties. The Imperial Navy ensured that almost all of its ships were capable of orbital bombardment if necessary.

But she was sure of one thing, unfortunately.

The Guardians were unlikely to surrender.

CHAPTER FORTY-THREE

> But all of the savings were just not enough to prevent the Empire's final collapse. Abandoning bases and garrisons saved nothing. As the Empire's grip weakened – and Earth itself collapsed into the chaos of a multi-sided civil war – entire Core World sectors began to break away from the Empire. Ambitious officers did not hold back. They knew that they would never have a better chance at supreme power.
> - Professor Leo Caesius, *The Science That Isn't: Economics and the Decline and Fall of the Galactic Empire.*

"We're picking up no response from the planet," Foxglove reported. "They haven't replied at all."

"Keep broadcasting the demand," Jamie ordered. He looked over at Sameena and lowered her voice. "You think they'll listen to reason?"

"Probably not," Sameena admitted. On the display, the enemy were trying desperately to get the remaining ships into action. It was clear that they weren't going to succeed, certainly not in time to make a difference. Jannah's orbital defences were minimal, assuming that the stations were armed. "But we have to try."

She gritted her teeth as they closed in on the planet. Jannah's government deserved to die – and she would show no hesitation in putting them on trial for their crimes against the universe, then executing them – but most of the population was innocent. Bombarding the entire planet would be a crime fully as great as the invasion and occupation of Maxwell, with a far greater body count. And yet the Guardians had had plenty of time to lay the groundwork for an insurgency. She hadn't realised just how little she had known about her homeworld until after sitting down with the intelligence officers and trying to write down everything she knew.

I was kept deliberately ignorant, she thought, bitterly. *How many others were kept that way too?*

Abdul's education had been more formalised than hers, but it had also been very limited. He'd been taught how to recite religious texts, forced to memorise vast quantities of approved books…and he'd *still* managed to ask questions that had convinced the Guardians that he was a disbeliever, along with his family. She supposed she should be proud of that, even though he had gotten his parents killed. And if Sameena hadn't fled, she would have been killed too.

But how many others would have the potential for greatness, if they had some proper education?

"I wish we had a division of Marines," Jamie admitted. "They could secure those ships easily."

Sameena gave him a sharp look. "How does one secure a ship when the crew are prepared to blow it to take your boarding party with them?"

"You don't," Jamie said. "Standard procedure would be to blow the ship away."

Foxglove coughed. "We're picking up a message," he reported. "They're responding to our demand."

"Put it on," Jamie ordered.

Sameena almost flinched as a thick torrent of Arabic echoed over the bridge. The speaker didn't sound as if he wanted to surrender; instead, he seemed confident that God would grant him and his forces certain victory. Sameena couldn't help thinking of one of Brad's favourite movies, where a Knight had kept trying to fight despite losing all of his limbs, even though she knew that he was being stupid.

Jamie elbowed her. "What's he saying?"

"No, basically," Sameena said. Some of the insults were imaginative, but he was mainly refusing to surrender…again and again and again. "Can you pinpoint the source of the transmission?"

"Abdullah," Foxglove said. "Right in the centre of the capital city."

"Asshole," Jamie said. "If we drop a KEW on the source, it will certainly cause civilian causalities."

"Paddy and his men can handle the orbital stations and starships first," Sameena said. "Once we get complete control of the orbitals we can deal with the folks on the ground."

Somewhat to her surprise, securing the orbital stations was easy. The crews were either press-ganged engineers from captured ships or ignorant trainees from the planet below, all thoroughly demoralised by watching the destruction of the active fleet. Most of the press-ganged engineers were quite happy to tell their stories, including a grim warning that all of the female members of their crews had been taken down to the planet. They hadn't been seen since.

"The battlecruiser will require at least a year to restore to full fighting trim," an engineer reported, after Paddy's team had secured it. "Whoever sold her to them took the money and ran. The interior was more or less completely gutted; they even tore out four of the six fusion cores. She's a right ghastly mess."

"We can put her back into service," Jamie muttered. "Steve might be able to work more of his wonders on her."

"It will take us years to build up the manpower base to crew the captured ships," Sameena reminded him. "But you're right. It might be very useful."

She scowled at Jannah as her ships entered orbit. There were no planetary defences, as far as she could see – but then, only a handful of worlds had fixed defences on the planet's surface, where they might draw fire from high overhead. But there might be other weapons to make an occupation difficult...hell, even if the vast majority of the population welcomed them, the Guardians would definitely have a chance to make everyone's lives miserable.

"We're tracking some military vehicles and bases," Foxglove reported. "It would be simple enough to take them out from orbit, then land troops."

"I can't disagree," Paddy said, through the intercom. "We have the firepower advantage for once. We should take advantage of it."

Sameena scowled, but nodded. "Land your troops," she ordered. "Call for bombardment as you need it."

She looked over at Jamie. "I should be going down there," she muttered. She hated the thought of sending people into danger without sharing it for herself. "All I can do is watch."

"Don't even *think* about it," Jamie muttered back. "I'll bet you're their principle target right now, the person who brought their utopia crashing down in rubble. They'll do whatever it takes to kill you."

He was right, Sameena realised, as the invasion unfolded on the display. The spaceport had fallen quickly, but they needed to land troops up closer to the capital. Once the shuttles were down, the Guardians directed mobs of unarmed men, women and children at the advance parties, using the civilians as human shields to cover their advance. Even after snipers started to pick them off, the civilians kept coming. The obedience the Guardians had instilled in them over the years was terrifying.

"When this is finished," Jamie muttered to her, "there won't be much left of Jannah."

"Good," Sameena muttered back. A display showed a young boy, barely old enough to walk, carrying an explosive charge towards her troops. The charge, apparently timed poorly, exploded in his hands, blowing him to bits. She fought down the urge to vomit as other civilians joined the mad rush, or were caught up in chaos as the Guardians pressed the counterattack. "This is sickening."

She looked down at the display and saw a pattern emerging. "Target the Guardians here," she ordered, pointing to posts just outside the city. "See if we can encourage people to flee, rather than get caught up in the madness."

"I'd suggest taking out the transmitters too," Jamie added. "Their radio keeps pouring fuel on the fire."

"See to it," Sameena ordered. "And then start broadcasting suggestions that people stay in their homes, out of the firing line."

It was nearly four hours before Abdullah fell, Paddy leading his troops to seize the mosques and government buildings at the heart of the city. Sameena looked down from high overhead and watched rivers of blood pouring into gutters and down towards the sea, unable to avoid feeling sick. She'd delighted in the thought of coming home and rubbing her success in the Guardians collective face, of using her firepower to blast them off the planet and avenge her family, but the reality was sickening. How many innocents had been mashed in the gears because the Guardians had turned them into weapons.

They will have been taught to be obedient and never to question, right from birth, she thought, mutely. *How lucky Abdul was to be able to think at all!*

"We found their supreme leader," Paddy reported. "The Grand Mufti won't be standing trial, I'm afraid."

Sameena scowled. She hadn't even known that the Council of Guardians had a Grand Mufti until the interrogations had revealed his existence – and a version of history that was considerably more violent than any she'd learned since leaving the planet. It hadn't taken long to realise that most of it was nothing more than lies; there was no way that Jannah's Founders had posed a serious threat to the Empire, even during the height of the Unification Wars. They'd turned what was, at best, a cowardly flight into a dignified retreat, laying the groundwork for a later return to power. But it had been nipped in the bud.

Whoever controls the past controls the future, she thought. *And the Empire did its level best to forget that it had had a past.*

"Oh," she said. She'd lost any reverence she might have had for religious figures a long time ago. "What happened to him?"

"His wives did," Paddy said. He sounded thoroughly disgusted. "He had *ten* poor bitches in his private quarters, half of them badly bruised. When we attacked the outside, they attacked him. I have them all in protective custody now."

"Excellent," Sameena said, although she knew that it might well be a problem. The Grand Mufti could have been convinced to order the holdouts to surrender. She just didn't have the manpower to even begin to occupy the entire planet. "Keep the capital city under control. I wish to visit later."

She looked over at Jamie. "Stand the fleet down from battlestations, but be ready to provide fire support to the forces on the ground if necessary," she ordered. Between Paddy and Jamie, the Imperial Navy's standing orders on bombardment had been heavily revised. "And detach one of the destroyers and send it to Madagascar. The Meet needs to know what happened here."

They'd be behind the times, she knew. At full speed, it would still take two weeks for the destroyer to reach Madagascar, leaving the Meet wondering just what had happened at Maxwell. Just another reason, she told herself, why the Grand Senate had had so many problems controlling the Empire. *She* would just have to keep delegating her authority, no matter how much she disliked it. But there was no choice.

Jamie objected strongly when she insisted on going down to the planet the following morning, but Paddy – who Sameena had expected to agree with Jamie – understood at once and only insisted that she wear armour and take other armoured guards with her. Feeling uncomfortable in the powered combat suit, Sameena waited until the shuttle had landed outside the town and walked inside, surrounded by her guards. The population had made themselves scarce.

She felt an odd aching pain in her chest as she strode up towards her father's house. It was smaller than she remembered – but then, she'd been smaller and younger too. She half-expected to see her mother as she stepped into the garden, but saw nothing. A red sign, painted on the door, indicated that the house had been sealed by the Guardians. The population had been so terrified that they'd left it alone for *five* years.

"Stay here," she ordered, pushing open the door. "I'll be fine."

The door was locked, but the suit's servomotors had no difficulty smashing it down. She hesitated, then opened the suit and walked into her house. Memories rose up around her as she peered around, remembering how many people had questioned her father's decision not to build a separate section for his womenfolk. His enemies had lost no time in denouncing him once Abdul had run into *real* trouble. A faint smell taunted her as she stepped into the kitchen, the remains of the meat and vegetables her mother had intended to cook. The stench would merely have added to the sense of a house of disbelief, before it wasted away to dust.

Upstairs, she looked into her room and saw the opened window she'd used to make her escape. Her clothes and everything else had simply been left to rot, like the rest of the house. She picked up one of her stuffed toys and hugged it to her chest, then walked down to Abdul's room. They'd taken his books, she noted, and a few other things. Everything else had simply been abandoned.

Tears pricked at the corner of her eyes as she walked back into her bedroom. Her father had been a good man, better than most on Jannah. He'd seen to it that she had an education, even if he'd never envisaged where it would take her, and he'd tried to ensure that she had some choice in who she married. And he'd done it despite his culture, despite the Guardians. The fact he'd failed, in the end, didn't make him any less of a man.

The family photo album had been abandoned in her parent's room, she discovered, even though the Guardians had clearly taken her father's books too. She looked down at the yellowed photos, feeling the urge to cry as she saw her mother and father looking back at her. And her maternal grandfather with his four wives…Abdul hadn't been welcome at his house after he'd questioned the point of the photographs. All four of the women wore the complete face veil.

Sameena took the photo album and walked back downstairs, then climbed back into her armour and left the house behind. There was nothing there she wanted, not any longer. Let the local population take the rest of her father's goods. She said nothing, apart from brief orders, as they returned to the shuttle and headed to Abdullah. Part of her just wanted to hunch up inside the suit and cry.

A mistake, she told herself. Her home no longer felt like home. *I shouldn't have come here.*

Abdullah, she'd been told, had been the most beautiful city in the universe. She'd never actually visited before returning to her homeworld. Perhaps it had been beautiful once, but the destruction and carnage of the brief battle had wreaked havoc on the city. Entire buildings had been destroyed, the streets were stained with blood…even though teams of prisoners had been forced to help clear up the debris. The thought of mass graves revolted Sameena, but there was no choice. Even identifying the dead would be impossible. Jannah, as far as she knew, didn't keep DNA records of its citizens.

The clerk looked scandalised at seeing a woman in armour, carrying weapons and not wearing a headscarf, but he had enough intelligence not to say it out loud. Instead, he pulled up the paper file Sameena had requested – the whole system was frustratingly primitive – and passed it to her, then sneered until one of her guards dragged him away. It was precisely the same attitude Sameena had seen from the Empire's bureaucrats, although she had to admit that it was slightly more justified. Searching vast stacks of paper documents would be much harder than scanning a computer file.

She read the file and shuddered, inwardly. Abdul Hussein had been taken into custody, as had his mother and father. In neat precise script, the bureaucrats had recorded their judgement; the three of them had been sent to a work camp, where his parents had died the following year. Abdul himself had lasted another few months before following his parents into the grave. There was no mention of Sameena at all. No doubt they'd decided that a mere girl wasn't worth worrying about; if she'd escaped, she had probably starved to death or been taken in as an unregistered wife. None of them had ever considered that she might have made it off-planet.

Below her family's name, there was another. Judge Al-Haran hadn't even lasted six months in a work camp – and he had only been slightly involved with Abdul, if at all. His wives, she discovered, had been forced into prostitution. Sameena had been right to run, she knew, yet the thought brought her no pleasure. All that flowed through her mind was a cold determination that such crimes would be avenged.

The Guardians would die, she promised herself, silently. For all of their secret links to the greater universe, they had no real conception of how the Empire could track someone who wanted to remain hidden. Her occupation force wouldn't be brutal, but it would be relentless and difficult to fool. There would be no mercy when they finally caught up with the Guardians. She would authorise the use of truth drugs and whatever else it took to burn them out, root and branch. Whatever Jannah's future might hold, it would not be dictated by the Guardians.

It will be dictated by me, she thought. She would extend the scholarship program to Jannah and ensure that the children received a better introduction to the outside universe. And anyone who wanted to leave would be welcome to try and make a life among the traders, or even settling a very different world. Her lips thinned as she realised just how many other changes she could make. If wife and daughter abuse was harshly punished, just how long would it continue?

Her father would have approved, she felt.

She stood up, still carrying the file, and headed back to the shuttle. Part of her was tempted to stay on Jannah, but she knew that she had neglected her duties at Madagascar long enough. Besides, she had to report to the Meet personally. They'd want to hear what had happened from her own lips.

"It's over," she told Jamie, as the shuttle took her back into space. "We can go home now."

CHAPTER FORTY-FOUR

No one knows just how many people died with the Empire. Eighty billion on Earth, assuming that the official figures were accurate. (Some estimates of Earth's population were far higher.) Billions more on the Core Worlds; millions more on Rim-ward colonies that were abandoned and left at the mercy of outside forces. The full human cost can never be calculated.
- Professor Leo Caesius, *The Science That Isn't: Economics and the Decline and Fall of the Galactic Empire.*

"The stockpile of supplies from Jannah will come in very useful," Steve confirmed, after the Meet. "We should be able to put the remaining ships into active service within a few months."

Sameena nodded. The Meet had been exhausting, particularly when she wanted desperately to talk to her husband in private. She had important news to share. But everyone wanted their say about the Jannah War, even though it had firmly been nipped in the bud. Not that she could really blame them. Maxwell was one of the more populous worlds in the growing Trade Federation – the name had finally stuck – and whatever happened to it could easily happen to someone else. And then there was the blight on Dueller.

At least that was stopped before it got anywhere else, she thought. They'd discovered that the Guardians had intended to spread it into the Core Worlds, but none of their ships had left Jannah before the hammer came down. And now that the biologists had access to the original research notes, creating a counter-agent had been simple. Dueller would recover within a couple of years, she knew. Maxwell would take far longer.

She smiled to herself. Saving them personally had been risky, but it had definitely paid off. Representatives from both planets had been singing her praises, as well as offering to provide more resources and manpower for the Federation. Her position was, for the moment, invulnerable, although she knew better than to expect that to continue indefinitely. The Trade Federation wasn't designed to have a single permanent leader.

And my factories won't matter so much when others start producing their own factories, she reminded herself. She had had to remind herself not to use her position to block the foundation of other factories, even though she *knew* that such attitudes had played a large role in demolishing the Empire's economy. It would have been easy to fall into the trap and sow the seeds of her own destruction. Instead, she'd honoured the laws she'd written and watched as others planned their own factories.

"Always a very good thing," she said, once Steve had finished. Even with Jannah out of commission, there was still no shortage of pirate ships probing the Federation's loose borders. And then there was always the possibility of running into another successor state, another piece of the Empire that had managed to survive separation from the whole. "And our planned warship production?"

"We have an upgraded destroyer design," Steve assured her. "In six months, we should have a testbed prototype and then we can start mass production."

Jamie scowled. "It might be better to start producing designs we already *know* work," he pointed out. "We still have a critical shortage of ships."

"But those designs are outdated," Steve countered. It was an old argument. "Besides, there would still be delays before we managed to build new construction slips. By then, we'd know the flaws in the new design and how to counter them."

"You just want to build something new," Jamie accused.

"You cannot deny that there's room for improvement," Steve said. "In many ways, the standard design is inefficient."

Sameena sighed and tuned out the argument. They'd had it every time the subject had been broached, leaving her caught between an enthusiastic engineer and her husband. Irritatingly, she could see both sides of the argument. A new destroyer class would give them more flexibility – and unexpected capabilities, assuming that no one else was producing their own ships – but if there were problems with the design, they might only become apparent when the prototype was built, forcing them to either redesign the ship or scrap it altogether.

She reached for her datapad and read through the latest report from Paddy. Six months after the occupation and Jannah was *still* in a state of shock. It was hard to tell, Paddy noted, if they were more surprised by the discovery that their leaders were mounting an interstellar war or by the presence of an occupation force. Unsurprisingly, few had mourned the Guardians, but there was some question over what to do next.

Sameena scowled as she read the next section. She hadn't been the only person with grudges against the Guardians – or the people who had supported them. Quite a few people had found the nerve to strike back at their tormentors after Abdullah had fallen, while wives had fled abusive husbands and gone to the occupation force for protection. Sameena had already ordered that they would *have* protection, even though she knew it would annoy the traditionalists. The traditionalists could be as traditional as they liked, as long as no one was hurt – or forced into following their way of life. It would be a long time, she knew, before Jannah recovered from the shock. And they'd probably be an agricultural world permanently.

But if everyone who wants to leave does leave, she thought, *it may teach those who remain a lesson.*

She still didn't understand just how the Guardians had thought they could win. They had no industrial base – and, therefore, no way of replenishing their war stocks. Indeed, they'd had fewer ships than she'd been led to suspect, which meant…what? Was someone else *also* building up their own fleet? Or had Intelligence gotten it wrong, again? There was no way to know.

But the Guardians had inadvertently done the Trade Federation a favour. The captured ships would be extremely useful. It was just a shame that whatever credits the Cartel had saved were effectively useless now. The Imperial Bank had evaporated in the wake of the Empire's departure from the sector. God alone knew what had happened to the Core Worlds if the bank had collapsed completely.

"We will be running additional patrols through the Rim-ward zones," Jamie said, changing the subject. "There have been several nasty pirate attacks and I'd like to discourage them."

"Once we get more armed ships up and running, they will be discouraged," Steve said. "We can also spread more rumours about q-ships too."

Sameena grinned. "Or just share the footage from Maxwell," she said. "If two q-ships can take out a heavy cruiser, they won't have any problems taking out pirate ships."

Jamie nodded. "That would definitely make them think twice," he agreed. "And we can release false data too, claiming that we have q-ships of all classes."

"One final item on the agenda, then," Steve said. "The construction of the Meet ship."

Sameena nodded. Madagascar was effectively serving as the Trade Federation's capital, but no one wanted that to last, not when it would warp the asteroid's development. Earth hadn't benefited in the long run from being the capital of an interstellar empire…and besides, it had eventually developed a colossal army of bureaucrats, who had contributed to the Empire's destruction. The Trade Federation was much less inclined to interfere in the internal affairs of its member states, but Sameena knew that the bureaucracy would grow, given half a chance.

Steve's proposal solution had been simple, although she hadn't been entirely convinced that it was *practical*. A giant starship would house the central government, moving from world to world as necessary, ensuring that the government always remained in touch with the realities on the ground. The Meet had, surprisingly, accepted the proposal at once, even though it would take at least three years to build the new ship. It fitted in, they claimed, with the trader ethos.

"We have finalised the design," Steve continued. "She will actually be bigger than a battleship, but only carrying a third of the weapons."

Jamie sighed. "You do realise that building this giant ship will take up resources we need to devote to smaller ships?"

"I don't intend to start building for another year, at least," Steve admitted. "By then, we should have a larger shipyard and a much greater production facility. If worst comes to worst, we can delay construction for another year."

"The Empire could have built entire squadrons of destroyers for the cost of one battleship," Jamie muttered. "This is a waste of resources."

The remainder of the meeting passed quickly, much to Sameena's relief. There were other issues on the agenda, but most of them needed to be left alone to mature before she – or anyone else – could do anything about them. One planet was unsure if it should join the Federation or not, another had seized a trader ship and his family was demanding immediate action. *That* would require some careful handling – and the personal touch. She intended to leave Madagascar tomorrow.

"It could be worse," she said, as soon as they were alone. "They might want an entire squadron of such ships."

"The whole thing is a nightmare," Jamie said, crossly. "We'll have to ensure that the ship is escorted at all times, not to mention being kept out of danger. What happens if some bright spark decides to ram her? The entire government would be destroyed."

"Not *all* of it," Sameena murmured.

"And if we still use Madagascar as a central base, we will see the bureaucracy develop anyway," Jamie continued. "Can't you talk them out of it?"

Sameena shook her head. "They're willing to do whatever it takes to avoid creating a capital world," she said. "The Meet even rejected the idea of using one of our hallowed locations, or constructing a colossal space station."

"Bunch of fools," Jamie said. There was no real anger in his voice. "I thought that traders would have more sense."

"They can be just as silly as groundhogs," Sameena said, pulling her husband to her. "And I have another piece of news for you."

Jamie looked at her, his face concerned. "What's happened?"

Sameena touched her belly. "I'm pregnant," she said, simply. She smiled at his half-stunned, half-delighted expression. "You're going to be a father."

"I…" Jamie cleared his throat and started again. "You're sure?"

"Yes," Sameena said.

She'd been in two minds about keeping the implant after marrying Jamie. Trader tradition said that such a marriage should produce children, but she knew that she hadn't been the best of mothers to Brad Junior. In the end, she'd had the implant removed and left the rest of it up to chance – or God. It had still been several months before her menstrual cycle had failed to appear, convincing her to go to Jayne for a check-up. Jayne had confirmed that she was pregnant – and strongly advised her to carry the baby to term naturally.

Sameena had hesitated, until she'd remembered her own problems in accepting Brad Junior and her own limited feelings for her son. Her mother would have been shocked and ashamed at such lack of concern; Sameena couldn't help wondering if she'd failed to develop any real feelings for him because he'd been brought to terms in an external womb. This time, she promised herself, she would give birth naturally, even if it did mean that she would have to spend the last five months of pregnancy on Madagascar. *And* she would try to work harder with Brad. It was downright shameful that his adopted father spent more time with him than his mother.

"That's wonderful," Jamie said. "Is it a he or a she?"

"I haven't looked yet," Sameena admitted. "And I don't think I'm going to look."

It was strange to think that Jannah's low-tech society might have been a blessing in disguise, but Jayne had explained that some planets, where one sex was valued over the other, often aborted children with the wrong sex or simply manipulated the fertilization process to ensure that the child would always have the right sex. Societies where women were valued over men seemed to work better than the other way round – she knew that Jannah's population would have always selected for men, if they'd had the choice – but they were still fundamentally distorted.

"Better make sure Jayne knows not to tell you," Jamie said. He hugged her tightly, one hand reaching down to caress her chest. "Are you sure you should go tomorrow?"

Sameena had to laugh. "*Men*," she said. "I should be fine."

"You know what I mean," Jamie said, a little stiffly. "You'd be risking our child as well as yourself."

"I'll stay on Madagascar afterwards," Sameena promised. It would be hard, remaining in one place for so long, but he was right. She needed to ensure that she had the baby somewhere safe. "But for the moment, I need to keep papering over the cracks until the Trade Federation is firmly established."

She shook her head, tiredly. There was just so much to do!

"The traders are likely to go further than you expect," Jamie warned. "I heard that some of them were even planning to head into the Core Worlds, just to see what happened to Earth."

"It'll take us years to rebuild the trade networks to that point," Sameena said. "Unless they make other friends and allies along the way."

Jamie shrugged. Once, they would have *known* what to expect as they travelled Core-wards. Now, no one knew what might greet them when they left the sector. Sameena's newborn intelligence network tried to collect rumours – and there were millions of them - but no one seemed to know anything for sure. It was as if an unholy silence had descended over what was once the most populous sector in human history.

The Empire had been founded on force, naked brutal force. In the end, it had proved unreliable to keep the Empire together. Trade, she hoped, would work better, if only because it would work in everyone's interests. And the Trade Federation would try to maintain the balance between traders and planet-bound populations.

She shook her head as she held her husband tightly, remembering what her mother had used to say on Jannah, before she'd been taken away by the Guardians.

A woman's work was never done.

EPILOGUE

In the end, the Empire's fall was predicable – and preventable. But no one saw clearly enough to try. Let the final word be, then, that the Empire was a victim of its own success – and of those who chose to cling to their power, rather than change with the times. A fitting epigraph, I feel, for a society that had forgotten how to change.
- Professor Leo Caesius, *The Science That Isn't: Economics and the Decline and Fall of the Galactic Empire.*

Anisa Hussein-Cook was a darling little girl.

Or so Sameena told herself. Every mother, according to Lamina, saw their children as *special*, but Anisa definitely was. At two years old, she was already preparing for a life in space by exploring every last inch of the asteroid settlement. And her older brother wasn't much better...Jamie, of course, saw it as a good sign. The kids would be adventurous when they grew up.

Heirs to an empire, Sameena thought. The Trade Federation might not be a proper empire, but she owned two-thirds of it personally. It gave her immense political power, even though she was careful not to use it too blatantly. *Trading will teach them how to handle people and make the best deals.*

She still felt a twinge of guilt when she looked at Brad Junior, but spending so much time on the asteroid had been good for their relationship. It was easier to consider him her son now, even though she would have to sit down with him one day and explain the circumstances of his birth. Captain Hamilton had warned her that she might have to do it sooner rather than later, if only to prevent him hearing rumours about his mother's relationship with his true father. Other lives had been screwed up by parents not being honest with their children.

Her wristcom buzzed, breaking into her thoughts. "Captain" – it was the only title she'd kept, even though everyone called her the Trader Queen – "the envoy from Avalon is waiting in your office."

"Understood," Sameena said. Despite her best efforts., a bureaucracy *had* grown up on Madagascar. At least she did manage to trim it down each year by insisting that the workers had some proper experience – and returned to the field every so often to get more. "I'm on my way."

Her office was as simple as she could make it, with a handful of comfortable chairs, a single holographic display, a handful of pictures and a portrait of her trader family placed against one rocky wall. It had always amused her how many visitors seemed to assume that she had another office, perhaps one hidden from casual view. The luxury the Imperial Navy's officers and the Empire's Governors took for granted wasn't something Sameena wanted to emulate.

The envoy didn't look much older than Sameena herself, she realised, as the girl turned to face her. She was tall, with long red hair and a hardness in her eyes that suggested that she had seen terrible things. Sameena understood; no matter how innocent one tried to remain, the choices one had to make risked staining one's soul. She'd felt a little part of herself die every time she'd used force to get her way.

"Captain," the envoy said. Her accent held traces of Earth, although it seemed to have been dulled slightly by the looser speech of the Rim. "Thank you for seeing me on such short notice."

Sameena nodded, waving the envoy to a seat. It had been a surprise when one of her trading ships had encountered a ship from the Commonwealth of Avalon – their records showed that Avalon had been a small colony, although it did have a cloudscoop for reasons that hadn't been recorded properly – but at least they *seemed* friendly. Their one brush with Admiral Singh's growing empire had convinced her that there would be war. At least *that* problem seemed to have been removed.

"You're welcome," she said, dryly. If the Commonwealth was another multi-system power, good relationships would be vital. The Trade Federation would find it harder to avoid or ignore a spacefaring force. "Please, call me Sameena."

"Mandy," the envoy said, holding out a hand. "Mandy Caesius."

The End

AFTERWORD

[I should mention before I start that all of the figures in this afterword were chosen for ease of calculation. Any resemblance to reality is purely coincidental (and unlikely).]

Politicians rarely understand economics.

That isn't too surprising. Economics is one of those fields that is actually quite hard to define, let alone follow and control. Time after time, people make economic decisions, based on something that sounds like logical thinking, and discover that the real world simply doesn't work like that. On paper, the grand economic plans the Soviet Union produced were perfect – it was reality, the planners concluded, that was wrong. Of course, there's only so far you can go before reality knocks you down.

The problem with intellectuals, as a general rule, is not that they're stupid. There are plenty of very smart intellectuals. The problem is that intellectuals can fall into the very simple trap of mistaking theory for reality. To borrow a line from Sherlock Holmes, when you make theories before you have facts, you start twisting the facts to fit the theories – as opposed to the other way round. Communism, for example, was the brainchild of Karl Marx, one of the world's intellectuals. In practice, communism fails spectacularly every time it is tried. And yet the intellectuals will insist that communism hasn't failed, it just wasn't done right.

It's quite easy to be seduced by a good-sounding theory. Witness, for example, the colossal market for management trends. Or military theories such as 'the bomber will always get through,' 'battleships rule the seas' or even 'shock and awe saves us from mass troop deployments.' The problem, of course, is that such theories can be misleading and often cause major problems for anyone who believes them uncritically.

When it comes to economics, there are millions of theories. How many of them have really been tested? And how many of them are understood by the governments?

Let me start with a simple statement and go on from there. People respond to incentives and disincentives. If someone sees an offer for 50% off dinner, that's an incentive to go to that particular place to eat. On the other hand, if the restaurant is hugely expensive instead, that's a *disincentive* to anyone with one eye on their pocketbook.

This applies almost everywhere – and not just in economics. If one provides support for unwed mothers, expect a rise in the number of unwed mothers. Why not? The incentives they are offered make the best choice for them personally not to wed. People are governed, largely, by rational self-interest. They will do what is in their own best interests, as they see them, and not what might be in *society's* best interests.

Politicians tend not to understand that, simply because politicians (like aristocrats or the very wealthy) are largely insulated from reality. The money they distribute in the form of tax-funded endeavours doesn't come from their pocket, it comes directly from the taxpayer. This has two dangerous effects; it convinces many of them that the government can pay for everything and it blinds them to the dangers of taking too much money.

I shall start with a simple (and partly silly) example to illustrate my point.

Let us assume, for the sake of argument, that Fred wishes to open a business selling homemade cakes. He can just do it, right?

Well, no – he needs to do some planning.

First, he needs the tools of his trade. He needs bowls, spoons, mixers, a cooker and whatever else is needed to actually make cakes. Let us assume, for the sake of argument, that all of this costs £1000. Second, he needs a shop, where he can both sell cakes and produce more. The deposit is another £1000 and the monthly rent is £100. Third, he needs working materials. We will stipulate that a month's supply of everything he needs, from flour to baking powder, is £1000.

His first investment, therefore, looks a little like this:

Tools - £1000
Shop - £1100
Materials - £1000
Total: £3100

What that means, in essence, is that he must be prepared to pay £3100 *before* he actually starts producing cakes. Fred cannot start from nothing. He must spend money *before* actually making money.

However, we're still not done. Next month, he will have to pay:

Shop - £100
Materials - £1000
Total: £1100

On the face of it, it seems that once he has met the first investment, he can get away with paying £1100 every month. This is not, of course, entirely accurate. What happens if he breaks a tool, something that will happen sooner or later. Let us assume that he needs to have at least £200 ready to replace lost or damaged tools. Failure to have this ready may well mean that he can no longer cook, therefore destroying the business when he runs out of cakes.

So his monthly requirement ranges from £1100 to - £1300.

It is a basic law of small business economics that you cannot spend more than you earn. If Fred, each month, earns a gross (before tax, running costs, etc) profit of precisely £1300, he won't be making any profit because all of his earnings are going directly to replace what he spent to start the business in the first place. If Fred earns £1500 each month, he will have a net profit of £200 per month and a yearly profit of £2400 (assuming that there are no unanticipated costs.)

This is important because Fred isn't making cakes out of the goodness of his heart. Oh no, he wants to run a *business*. His incentive to produce cakes is the lust for profit, for money he's earned with his sweat and blood.

From all this, we can draw another economic law. Businesses that can't pay their own way will go bust, eventually.

What, you might reasonably ask, does this have to do with governments?

The fundamental problem is that governments cannot, as a general rule, create economic growth. If that was possible, the communist nations would have worked splendidly. In reality, politicians can do a handful of things to *encourage* economic growth, but the key to making it work is to do as little direct interference as possible.

What a government *can* do is *discourage* economic growth.

You might think that sounds insane – and you would be right. Why should a government wish to discourage economic growth? The bigger the economy, the more money can be skimmed off in tax and plunged back into working for the population. What sort of idiot would interfere with that? Absurd, right?

Politicians *do* interfere – and quite often, the results of their interference is to cause economic depression and, more dangerously, a lack of faith in the government.

One of the primary products of a government is bureaucratic paperwork. This is understandable; pretty much anyone, employed anywhere, will work hard to make it seem that they are indispensible. Given time, the bureaucrats, sometimes encouraged by their elected masters, will start sticking their noses into just about everything. And the cost of meeting their demands increases exponentially.

Go back to Fred's baking shop for a moment. Let's add another cost, the cost of complying with government regulations. Fred, being a baker, will know, better than any civil servant, that the regulations are largely nonsense. But he will not be free to simply ignore them. No, if he is caught ignoring regulations written by the ignorant for the fools, he will be fined, arrested and/or forced out of business. Let us assume that the total monthly cost for complying with regulations is £500:

Shop: £100
Materials: £1000

Regulations: £500
Total: £1600

Anyone seeing a problem here?

Monthly costs: £1600
Gross profit: £1500
Net profit: -£100

Put bluntly, Fred is in the red. He needs another £100 to meet his operating costs.

So…what does he do? What *can* he do?

You cannot run a business at a loss indefinitely. Yes, if you have savings or a convincing reason to think that profits will improve in the future, you can endure for some time before it catches up with you. Fred's business is doomed for two reasons; he cannot meet his costs and he isn't making any profit. Why should he be putting forward the effort when he gets nothing out of it?

Regulations and taxes aren't the only way the government forces business costs upwards and puts those who can't meet them out of business. One example is the minimum wage, which is largely spun as being good for people just entering employment, who might well be paid peanuts if there wasn't a minimum wage. BUT…if the cost of paying your workers gets too high, small businesses will have no choice, but to fire the workers. Or…what if they're expected to provide medical coverage for the workers? This is a tiny cost for a massive corporation, but lethal for a small business like Fred's bakery.

This isn't the worst idea to come out of whatever politicians use for brains. One idea, from Hawaii, insists that anyone who buys a struggling business has to keep the old workforce. That doesn't sound like a bad idea, until you realise that the business might well have been struggling because it had too many workers and the new owners are stuck with them. In practice, business owners will probably end up letting their business collapse rather than trying to sell them to someone who might make them into a success.

The path to economic hell is paved with good intentions. In order to avert unemployment, one idea seriously proposed in France was to order business to take employees they didn't want, let alone need. The costs would have been staggering. Or, to comply with new European Regulations, hundreds of British farms had to either make vast payments or collapse (most collapsed). Or, if that wasn't bad enough, liability became such a problem that the merest whiff of a lawsuit could ruin a small business, while large corporations had armies of lawyers to defend themselves.

Political interference is partly to blame for the problems confronting Europe right now. The blunt truth is that Greece, Spain, Portugal and – to some extent – Italy were ill-prepared to meet their EU requirements. Their financial sectors were effectively black holes; giving them access to lines of credit from the EU was foolish in the extreme. And yet that is exactly what the EU – after having managed to avoid doing due diligence – did. The results should not have been a surprise.

But, some critics will say, how can you trust the corporate lackeys to actually do the right thing without government regulation? Won't an absence of regulation lead to outright chaos and mass exploitation?

To some extent, the critics have a point. There *is* a need for supervision of the economy. However, it needs to be strongly limited, based around ensuring fair play rather than trying to control and direct every last aspect of the economy. Furthermore, it needs to be watched to ensure that it doesn't inadvertently provide *disincentives* that prevent people from engaging in economic activity. Finally, it needs to be supervised to ensure that it doesn't create an army of assholes in suits who, like gangsters of old, walk around brandishing their credentials and demanding the equivalent of protection money from helpless businessmen.

Is there any way, therefore, that we can bring this monster under control?

Yes, there is – but I rather doubt that the politicians will implement them without being pushed.

First, remove the arbitrary power of civil servant bureaucrats. Little details like the precise details of a weapon (which can move it from legal to illegal) should not matter. Instead, the bureaucrats should make recommendations to a jury of citizens, who will decide if the complaint has merit. A small business owner threatened with a fine will have a chance to defend himself in front of his peers, instead of facing a mass of faceless bureaucrats who will hide behind the letter of the law and refuse to discuss specifics. I would go so far as to give that jury the power to order the bureaucrat sacked, if the complaint is silly enough.

As I have lectured before, arbitrary power is a dangerous weapon. It would be better to keep it out of an unaccountable person's hands.

Second, reform the compensation culture, particularly by banning 'no win, no fee' lawsuits (at least against small businesses). Silly complaints (such as suing a company for a problem you yourself caused) not only to be thrown out, but actively punished.

This isn't to suggest that Fred, if he fails to keep his eggs cool overnight, should escape punishment. If he serves tainted food and people get ill, *then* you can prosecute him! Make examples out of people too stupid to follow common sense rules like keeping the refrigerator cool and the smart ones will take sane precautions. It will work far better, I assume, than creating a situation where someone can hide behind the letter of the rules and ignore the spirit.

All of this, of course, requires a major infusion of common sense. I wish I could be hopeful.

Christopher G. Nuttall
Kuala Lumpur, 2013

PS. If you enjoyed reading this essay, Google 'The Voodoo Sciences.' It's well worth a read.
PPS. Please turn the page for a free sample from Book VI - *To The Shores*.

If you liked *The Outcast*, you might like

TO THE SHORES

Four years after their abandonment by the now-fallen Empire, the Commonwealth of Avalon is expanding into interstellar space and making contact with other successor states. With suspicion high on both sides, the Commonwealth and the enigmatic Wolfbane agree to hold a diplomatic meeting on Lakshmibai, a neutral world.

But Lakshmibai's government hates off-worlders and, with the fall of the Empire, sees its chance to be rid of the hated intruders once and for all. While Edward Stalker is besieged in their capital city, Jasmine Yamane must lead an untested army on a race against time to save the diplomats from annihilation.

And if she fails, the Battle of Lakshmibai may be the first shot in a new interstellar war.

CHAPTER ONE

> The simplest definition of diplomacy might be the art of dealing with people in a sensitive and effective way. People use diplomacy every day, from negotiating with their partners to trying to convince their boss that they're worthy of a raise. However, in this article, we are primarily concerned with international diplomacy.
> -Professor Leo Caesius, *Diplomacy: The Lessons of the Past.*

Colonel Edward Stalker, Terran Marine Corps, rose to his feet as Lieutenant Jasmine Yamane entered his office and saluted smartly. Edward returned the salute and then motioned for her to take a seat, which she did, never taking her eyes off him. He studied her back, looking for signs that her ordeal on Corinthian hadn't crippled her permanently. No one became a Marine without an inhuman ability to handle pain and stress, but torture could break even the strongest minds.

She was tall and muscular, her hair grown out slightly in the months she'd been on the beach while the medics and headshrinkers put her back together again. Vanity was not a common Marine failing, but Edward couldn't help noticing that she'd had the scars on her face surgically removed, leaving her looking like a very dangerous predator. She might not be beautiful in the classical sense, certainly not like the holographic stars who had dominated the arena and public viewscreens before the Empire had collapsed, but she was definitely striking. And, he could tell, impatient to return to work.

"I received the final report from the medics yesterday," he said, without preamble. Marines rarely had time for small talk. "You are cleared to return to duty."

Jasmine nodded, slowly. Her face seemed unreadable, but Edward picked up the subtle signs of relief that showed just how concerned she'd been, even after passing a series of increasingly difficult tests intended to weed out the unsuitable or the unfit. Like Edward himself, she'd spent years turning herself into a Marine – and losing it might well have crippled her.

"Thank you, sir," she said, finally.

"However, there are other issues," Edward admitted. He winced inwardly as her shoulders twitched, slightly. "I cannot return you to 1st Platoon."

"I understand," Jasmine said, tonelessly.

Edward felt her pain. Command of a Marine formation was a honour – and Jasmine had commanded 1st Platoon during the covert operation against Admiral Singh. But she'd been taken off duty just after the operation had concluded, forcing him to place command of 1st Platoon into the hands of Blake Coleman, who still held the post. Before the Empire had withdrawn and then collapsed, a Marine officer who returned to duty could be assigned to a different company or spend a few months attached to a headquarters platoon. Neither one was an option on Avalon.

Traditionally, few Marine ranks were permanent – and an unsuitable officer could be reassigned without denting his pride or setting a bad example. But Blake Coleman seemed to have matured since his shaky start and there were no grounds to deprive him of his new post, even though he'd replaced his former commander and teammate. Besides, he did have another post in mind for Jasmine.

"Tell me," he said, falling into the informality that Marines adopted for private discussions, "where do you see your career going?"

Jasmine blinked in surprise – and Edward smiled, amused at her expression. It *did* sound like a silly question, particularly with so few Marines within the Commonwealth. Jasmine couldn't replace Edward himself – the company's CO – or take command of one of the five remaining full-strength platoons. Her career, on the face of it, had nowhere to go.

"I honestly don't know," she said, carefully. "I could return to the ranks…"

"You could," Edward agreed. Even among Marines, it would be impolite for her to suggest that she might take *his* place. If the Empire had still been in existence, she might well have been a Captain by now. But the Empire was gone. "I had something else in mind."

He met her eyes. "Have you been following the diplomatic updates?"

Jasmine nodded. "The Wolfbane Sector?"

"Yes," Edward said, simply. "Governor Brown may pose a significant threat to the Commonwealth."

The thought made him scowl. Four years ago, there had been the Empire…and no significant independent states worthy of the name. Everyone had known that even a nominally independent star system wouldn't stand a chance if the Imperial Navy came knocking one day. Now, there was the Commonwealth and a handful of other successor states taking shape among the stars. One of them had already posed a major threat to the Commonwealth. Another might be far harder to take down before it was too late.

Little was known of Governor Brown. According to the files, he'd been third or fourth in line to the sector governorship of the Wolfbane Sector, a man so unremarkable that the famously-complete files gathered by the Imperial Civil Service said very little about him. Edward could only imagine what might have happened to boost him into a position of power; civil war, a coup, perhaps even the mass desertion of his superiors. It wouldn't be the only time that high-ranking officials had fled the chaos looming along the Rim for the bright lights of Earth, if Earth was still intact. Some of the rumours that had reached them through the Trade Federation – another successor state – had been horrifying.

Edward tapped a control and a holographic star chart shimmered into existence. "We have no way of knowing just how powerful the Wolfbane Sector is," he admitted. "In theory, he should have five squadrons of battleships and several hundred smaller craft under his command, but we don't know how many of them are still there – and in working order. We *do* know that we want to establish diplomatic relationships and eventually determine a practical border."

Jasmine frowned, one finger stroking her chin as she studied the chart. "You don't intend to try to convince him to join us?"

"We don't know enough about him to even *guess* at how successful such a ploy would be," Edward said. It was galling to admit that his long-term objective, the restoration of humanity's unity without the cracks in the Empire that had eventually torn it apart, might be in jeopardy, but he couldn't avoid considering the possibility. "For the moment, we merely want to establish relations and trading links."

He pointed to one of the stars, situated roughly midway between Avalon and Wolfbane. "We've been talking to his representatives through the good offices of the Trade Federation," he continued. "Eventually, the Governor agreed to a conference between our representatives and his here, on Lakshmibai. We will be sending an Ambassador with authority to negotiate on the issues that concern us, as will he."

"That should be interesting," Jasmine said. "Why *there*?"

"Lakshmibai has nothing that anyone wants, us included," Edward said. "The planet is neutral by default. According to the files, there was little contact between it and the Empire, apart from a half-hearted attempt to intervene in the planet's civil war. Brown…seems to feel that it is a suitable place for two interstellar powers to hold talks."

He shrugged. "I would prefer to send a mission to Wolfbane, but that suggestion was rejected," he added. "To be fair, we rejected their suggestion of sending a mission to Avalon too."

"Because they might be trying to spy on us," Jasmine agreed. "And they have the same worries about us."

"They would be right," Edward said, wryly. He switched off the hologram and leaned back in his chair. "After a great deal of argument in the Council, it has been decided that we cannot afford to refuse his offer of talks. Accordingly, a mission will be setting out to Lakshmibai. That mission will be headed by me."

Jasmine scowled. "Sir," she said slowly, "with all due respect, it might be a trap."

"It might be," Edward agreed, unemotionally. It was equally galling to realise that he might be irreplaceable on Avalon, even though he was a mere Colonel. "But the mission needs ambassadors of considerable authority. Professor Caesius will make up the other half of the ambassadorial team."

He smiled at Jasmine's expression. No one would have expected the professor and her to have become friends, but they had. And Jasmine was also a close friend of both of the professor's daughters. Having relationships outside the Corps was good for his Marines, even if civilians did have the strangest ideas of what the Marines did for a living.

"There will be a substantial security element embarked on the transport," he continued, putting that thought aside for the moment. "I believe that this is a good opportunity to carry out a deployment of the 1st Commonwealth Expeditionary Force, now that we have *finally* put most of its order of battle together. You will be given the brevet rank of Brigadier and take command of the force."

Jasmine stared at him, no longer able to *try* to hide her surprise. It was a colossal jump in rank and responsibility – and it would have been unthinkable before the fall of the Empire, where an officer required years of seasoning or extensive political connections to rise so high. Even in the Marine Corps, it could be decades before an officer had a chance at divisional command. But Avalon had a shortage of experienced officers, particularly ones who had served on multiple worlds. Jasmine was among the handful of relatively experienced officers under his command.

There were other considerations, he knew. The Commonwealth's constitution limited the deployable forces available to the central government. In theory, the Marines should be able to provide reinforcements if they were needed at short notice – it had been one of their roles in the Empire – but there simply weren't enough Marines to handle the task. Instead, they had to put together a light force from Avalon, which had its own problems. Few Knights of Avalon had any experience operating at the end of a shoestring logistics chain.

And then there are the political faultlines between the former Civil Guardsmen and the Crackers, he thought. *And the reluctance of Avalon's Knights to serve off-world...*

He pushed the thought aside and smiled at her. "Hopefully, this will be nothing more than a full-scale exercise," he informed her. "An exercise conducted under extremely realistic conditions. However, just in case we do run into trouble…"

"It would be well to have a large force accompanying us," Jasmine finished. "What is the situation on the planet's surface?"

"Good question," Edward said. "Unfortunately, the last update in the files from Lakshmibai is over seven years old. At the time, there was a large Imperial Army garrison and supply dump on the planet's surface. Now…we don't know."

"It's unlikely that the garrison is still there," Jasmine said, thoughtfully. "And the weapons in the supply dump might have been taken by one of the factions on the planet's surface."

Edward nodded, concealing his annoyance. If the files were to be believed – and he knew through experience that the Imperial Army's manifests were sometimes nothing more than elaborate works of fiction – there was enough war material on Lakshmibai's surface to outfit several full-sized divisions of troops. He would have given his right arm for such a supply dump during the war against the Crackers on Avalon; now, however, it wouldn't be so useful for the Commonwealth. One of the major differences between the Marine Corps and the Imperial Army was that the former's weapons and vehicles were lightened to make them more deployable, while the latter could take months or years to build up the logistics base for operations. Hauling supplies from Lakshmibai to Avalon – or anywhere else in the Commonwealth – might be more trouble than it was worth.

"It is unlikely," he agreed. "And it's even more unlikely that there was anything in the supply dumps that would make a difference now. But I'd still like to know what happened to the planet, if only to add to the files."

He shrugged. "Assuming all goes to plan, you will have several months to run exercises on the planet's surface while I and the professor take part in the discussions," he informed her. "If not…we may have to improvise."

Jasmine didn't look daunted, he was pleased to see. But then, she'd never had to command such a large force on exercise, let alone in actual combat. She didn't really know what she was getting into, any more than Edward had truly realised it when he'd been offered command of the company.

Sink or swim, he reminded himself.

"You'll assume command of the assembling force tomorrow," he concluded. "Do you have any specific requests or requirements you wish to raise?"

Jasmine hesitated, then nodded. "I would like to request that Joe Buckley be assigned to my command," she said. "He…is running out of patience on the training grounds."

Edward smiled, rather dryly. The Marine Corps had a proud tradition of rotating training officers through combat units on a regular basis, a tradition that the Knights had copied…but there were still considerable shortages of experienced training officers. It required officers and sergeants who could come across as sadistic brutes, while carefully not *becoming* monsters who abused their trainees or pushed them too far. Joe Buckley had been doing an excellent job, ever since his marriage, but Edward could understand his wish to return to active duty.

"I dare say that he can be spared," he said, after a moment's thought. "I'll have a word with Howell and have him attached to your command. He'll have to deal with his wife on his own, though."

"I think Lila will understand," Jasmine said. "She did know what she was marrying."

Edward wasn't so sure. Military wives *might* be able to deploy with their husbands – or they might be left behind, to make do as best as they could while their partner did his duty in another star system. The military wasn't kind to married soldiers; it wasn't unknown for a soldier to return home, only to discover that his wife had left him for another man. Even the Marine Corps had problems handling married Marines. The stresses of never knowing when one's husband might be called away – or die in the line of duty – placed colossal stress on even the strongest marriages.

"Let us hope so," he said, neutrally. Had Lila and Joe Buckley been separated for more than a week since they'd married? It was unlikely; Buckley was currently based at Castle Rock, where there was more than enough room for married couples. As a training officer, he was entitled to quarters suitable for both himself and his wife. "You should tell him that the whole deployment will take at least four months."

Jasmine nodded. "I'll brief him personally," she said.

"There is one other issue," Edward said, diffidently. He didn't miss Jasmine's eyes narrowing as she registered his tone. "You will be...*shadowed* by a reporter."

"A reporter?" Jasmine repeated. "Why?"

"It is important to showcase how far we've come since the Cracker War," Edward said, truthfully. "And equally important to show Avalon the importance of the Commonwealth to their security. We cannot risk losing public support."

He couldn't blame Jasmine for being irritated by the mere suggestion. The Empire's corps of reporters had been staunchly anti-military – or at least their editors, who took orders from the Grand Senate's vested interests, had been anti-military. Every commanding officer had learned to dread the well-connected reporter sticking his nose into military affairs, asking stupid questions on one hand and breaching operational security on the other. Edward had heard rumours that half of the problems on Han wouldn't have occurred if a handful of reporters hadn't leaked military secrets to the rebels. It didn't strike him as particularly unlikely.

"This reporter does have some experience from the war," he added, as reassuringly as he could. "And besides, he won't be sending live dispatches from the battlefield."

"Good," Jasmine said. She still didn't sound pleased. "I look forward to meeting him."

"You'll have a chance to review some of his work tonight," Edward said, picking a datachip off his desk and passing it to her. "He hasn't broken any of the agreements he made when he started his relationship with the military, at least as far as we have been able to determine. And he's going to be under military discipline while on deployment. If he gets in the way, feel free to put him in cuffs somewhere out of the way."

Jasmine snorted. In the Empire, an officer who put a reporter in irons could kiss any future career advancement goodbye, even if his peers silently cheered him on. But Edward had written the new protocols for interacting with reporters personally. If they did give one of his officers real trouble, they could spend the rest of the trip as a prisoner; Edward would back the officer responsible to the hilt.

"We need to have the CEF ready for deployment as soon as possible," Edward concluded. "I don't know where the next threat will come from, but there *will* be a next threat. We *still* don't know what happened to Admiral Singh, among other things."

"Yes, sir," Jasmine said. She *sounded* confident, he noted, although Marines were taught to sound confident at all times. It helped reassure the civilians – and the Civil Guard, when Marines were deployed to stiffen their spines. "I won't let you down."

She saluted, then turned and marched out of the office. Edward watched her go, then looked down at the papers on his desk. There was just more and more paperwork for him and the other senior officers, no matter how hard he struggled to keep it under control. The rapidly-expanding military seemed to practically *breed* paperwork.

That's why I have to go on the mission, he told himself. *It will be a change from paperwork.*

Pushing that thought aside too, he picked up a datapad and returned to work.

CHAPTER TWO

International Diplomacy can be defined as the profession, activity, or skill of managing international relations, typically by a country's representatives abroad. This is, however, the simplest possible view.
-Professor Leo Caesius, *Diplomacy: The Lessons of the Past.*

"Damn it," Lieutenant Michael Volpe muttered as his wristcom started to bleep urgently, driving away the last vestiges of sleep from his mind. "All right, all right."

He picked up the wristcom from where he'd left it on the bedside table, checked to ensure that he wasn't being summoned back urgently, then clicked off the alarm. The temptation to stay in bed was almost overwhelming, but he knew better than to delay his return to the base any longer than strictly necessary. Instead, he looked over at where the girl was buried under the blankets and then around her apartment. He hadn't had a chance to take in the decor when he'd picked her up last night and allowed her to take him home.

"Hey," he said, poking the girl's shoulder. He realised suddenly that he didn't even know her name! "Where's the shower?"

"Next room," the girl muttered, sleepily. "What time is it?"

"Seven in the morning," Michael said, as he pulled himself out of bed and stood upright. "I'll leave you in bed, if you like."

He fought down a sense of embarrassment as he padded across to the door and opened it, wishing that he'd thought to ask more questions before going to bed with her. There was no way to know if she shared her apartment with other girls, her parents or if she was alone…no, that was unlikely. His memories of the previous night were a blur, but he was fairly sure that she was a student and few students could afford to live on their own. The bathroom held enough supplies, he decided as he stepped inside, for a small army of girls. He stepped under the shower, lowered the temperature as much as possible and closed his eyes as the cold water washed away the last remnants of exhaustion. Just how much sleep had he gotten last night?

Not much, he thought, with a sense of heavy satisfaction. Two weeks spent preparing the 1st Avalon Mechanized Infantry Battalion for deployment had been rewarded by four days leave, which he'd spent in Camelot. Like almost all of the battalion, he'd spent the time looking for sexual partners and trying to relax. The girl – and he still couldn't remember her name – had merely been the last of a string of partners.

He stepped out of the shower, dried himself with a towel that was almost ludicrously small for him and walked back into the hallway. There was a gasp from behind him and he turned to see another girl wearing a nightgown that left almost nothing to the imagination. Michael, who had lost any sense of body modesty he might have had in training – or when he'd been a pirate captive – merely nodded to her and stepped back into *his* girl's room. She was sitting upright in bed, her bare breasts marked from their lovemaking. Michael felt a surge of lust which he ruthlessly pushed aside. There wasn't time for any more fun and games.

"Look me up when you come back to the city," the girl ordered, as he pulled on his uniform and inspected himself in the mirror. All the nice girls on Avalon loved a uniform, he'd discovered; it was almost a guaranteed lay to wear one's uniform on leave. The Empire might have banned its soldiers from wearing uniforms when they weren't on duty, but there was no such rule on Avalon. "And thank you."

Michael shrugged, fought down the temptation to ask for her contact code and walked downstairs, leaving her behind. Outside, the streets were already starting to fill up with people, mainly soldiers and spacers in uniform. He wasn't the only person who was expected to report back to base early in the morning, or the only soldier who had tried to spend his last hours of freedom with a pretty girl. Quite a few of the men on the streets looked considerably worse for wear. He hoped that they would have the presence of mind to use sober-up tabs before reporting for duty. A soldier who turned up unfit would be lucky if he merely spent the next week in the guardhouse.

Churchill Garrison was located to the east of Camelot, close to a small port that provided a sea link to Castle Rock, where the Marines and most of the training facilities were based. It had expanded rapidly ever since it had been founded, during the height of the Cracker War, until it consisted of over a hundred barracks, hangers and supply depots. A chain link fence ran around the complex, guarded by armed soldiers with authority to shoot anyone who tried to enter without authorisation. The Crackers might have been largely defeated and assimilated into the new order, but everyone knew that there were some factions that remained as unrelentingly hostile to the Commonwealth as they had been to the Empire. No one expected them to remain silent forever.

At least the bandits are gone, he thought, as he signed in at the guardhouse and entered the garrison. Thousands of uniformed soldiers were thronging over the base, most of them heading for the barracks where their sergeants would sort them out, match them up with their vehicles and equipment and then take them out to the exercise grounds. In the distance, he could hear the sounds of shooting as the infantrymen practiced on the shooting ranges. The sharpshooting competitions between the different units were intense, deliberately encouraged by senior officers. Michael took some pride in knowing that his unit had taken the cup for sharpshooting several times before losing it to other units.

His wristcom bleeped, ordering him to report to the briefing complex. Shaking his head, he turned and walked down towards the large concrete building. They'd been promised that there would – finally – be answers about their planned off-world deployment. Despite his curiosity, Michael was almost disappointed. The rumours had been fun.

There was a refreshing air of informality, Jasmine was pleased to note, as she entered the briefing room. Unlike the Imperial Army, which had over three thousand years of precedent and protocol to draw on, the Knights of Avalon and the other Commonwealth military organisations were new. Given time, Jasmine was sure that they would evolve traditions of their own, but for the moment they were not burdened by the past. It should give them more flexibility, she told herself, than the Imperial Army had ever shown.

The officers came to attention as she took the stand, looking at her with obvious curiosity. A gathering of Imperial Army officers would have found her beneath their notice, even though she was a Marine; she was just too junior to garner their attention. And the Imperial Army officers would probably have been decades older than her, at the very least. Rejuvenation treatments had ensured that officers held their posts for *years* before finally moving on or retiring from the service. But the Knights were young…even their senior officers were younger than Jasmine herself. Only a handful had served in the military for longer than any of the junior Marines.

The Colonel was right, she realised, as silence fell over the assembly. *They don't have the experience they desperately need.*

"At ease," she ordered, projecting as much confidence and command personality into her voice as she could. "We have a great deal of ground to cover."

She paused, then pushed onwards. "We will be deploying to Lakshmibai," she continued, knowing that few of them would have *heard* of their destination. A handful of officers began to surreptitiously look it up on their datapads. "Once there, we will provide security for a diplomatic mission and exercise as a combined unit on hostile soil, away from our logistics bases on Avalon or any other Commonwealth world."

The officers didn't have the experience to hide their reactions, she noted. Several of them looked confident, others looked worried at the prospect of operating away from their homeworld. A handful definitely seemed to relish the challenge. None of them, even the ex-Civil Guard officers, seemed to show any resentment at her being placed in command. They knew their limits. Besides, Avalon knew how much it owed to the Marines.

She smiled to herself as she caught sight of Michael Volpe – Mandy's former lover – in the audience, then looked away from him. There would be time to catch up with him later.

"We are expected to embark on the transports in three days," Jasmine informed them. "That gives us two days to carry out what joint planning and exercising we can before we leave."

She'd deliberately picked a deadline she didn't expect to meet, knowing that it would encourage her new subordinates to look for ways to speed up the process. Embarking even a relatively small military unit on a transport could take hours, particularly when it included tanks, aircraft or other vehicles. The entire CEF might take *days* to embark on the four purpose-built transport starships. Still, the only way to practice the operation was to actually *do* it. Paper exercises *never* worked out well in real life.

"I have worked out a rough deployment plan for you to consider prior to departure," she said. There were officers who would have refused to consider asking their subordinates to comment on their plans, but Jasmine knew that the men who'd handled their units since they'd come into existence would know more about their operations than she did, even though she'd spent most of the evening skimming through their reports. "However, our first priority remains the security of the diplomatic team."

She scowled at the thought. There was relatively little information on Lakshmibai in the databanks, even though the Imperial Library was supposed to contain exhaustive information on every world within the Empire – and she knew that it was outdated by several years, at the very least. The situation on the ground had been nasty even before the fall of the Empire; there was almost nothing to suggest what it might be like now. It was possible, she supposed, that peace and prosperity might have broken out, but that struck her as unlikely. Civil war seemed a much more definite possibility.

Which leads one to wonder why Governor Brown picked the system in the first place, she thought, sourly. *What was he thinking?*

"I would suggest that you review the information on our destination once we're on our way," she concluded. "I want to run a full-scale exercise tomorrow, if possible, and that must take priority. We need to be as practiced as possible by the time we leave."

She looked around the room, her eyes moving from face to face. "I don't need to tell you just how important this operation is," she said, firmly. "Failure is not an option. Dismissed!"

The officers saluted, then stood up and headed for the doors. Jasmine watched them go, feeling the weight of responsibility settling down on her shoulders. The 1st Commonwealth Expeditionary Force was a new formation, composed largely of individual units that had barely even *practiced* working together. They really needed several months to practice and prepare for their first off-world deployment.

But we need to practice rapid deployment, she told herself, remembering why the Marines had been called the Emperor's Firemen. A Marine unit could expect to be summoned at a moment's notice and then thrown into battle, without time to muster a colossal logistics base to support its operations. The 1st Commonwealth Expeditionary Force had to function along the same lines, which wouldn't stop the whole experience from being painful for everyone involved. They'd learn lessons, all right, but they'd also be dispirited...

Her wristcom buzzed. "Brigadier," Joe Buckley said, "you have a visitor waiting for you in your office."

Jasmine nodded, even though she knew he couldn't see her. "Understood," she said. Joe Buckley had politely but firmly taken a place as her aide as soon as he had arrived on the base. "I'm on my way."

One of Colonel Stalker's decisions when he'd been creating the new army had been to ban comfortable offices. Jasmine had approved, although she hadn't really understood why it had been necessary until she'd assumed command of 1st Platoon. There had been a temptation – a very slight one - to withdraw into seclusion and leave the platoon to the sergeants. It had to be much stronger, she suspected, if the unit she commanded was large enough to prevent her having such strong emotional ties to its personnel. No wonder some of the Imperial Army officers had created luxurious offices for themselves and then hidden inside. The weight of the responsibility had beaten them.

Assuming they were aware of their responsibilities, she told herself, darkly. *Some of them didn't seem to know what planet they were on, let alone which units they commanded.*

Her office was a simple concrete room, furnished with a desk, a computer terminal, a handful of metal chairs, a coffee machine and little else. One wall was covered with operational diagrams, including the CEF's order of battle; the other three were bare, leaving her with the uncomfortable sensation that the walls were closing in on her. Jasmine was hardly claustrophobic – and if she had been, she would have been unlikely to graduate from the Slaughterhouse – but she couldn't escape the urge to leave the office and go out onto the field.

A man was seated on one of the chairs, watched by a scowling Joe Buckley. Jasmine studied him as he rose to his feet, quietly evaluating the reporter as best as she could. He was of medium height and very thin, with strikingly pale skin that contrasted oddly against very brown hair and eyes. The coverall he wore hid most of his body from her eyes, but what little she could see suggested that he was more muscular than she had expected. Not up to Marine standards, or even those upheld by the Knights, yet hardly a weakling.

"You must be Brigadier Yamane," the reporter said. His accent was pure Avalon, although his face suggested a level of genetic modification that was somewhat unusual for a world settled by the Empire. "I am Emmanuel Alves, *Avalon Central*."

"Pleased to meet you," Jasmine lied, as he held out his hand. She took it, taking the opportunity to further gauge his strength. Definitely not a weakling. "Welcome to the 1st CEF."

She hadn't had to deal with reporters personally before, certainly not as a senior officer. There had been thousands of reporters on Han, but most of them had largely ignored the junior Marines as being beneath their notice. Besides, only a couple of the hordes had gone out into the field with the soldiers, even in the safer regions of the planet. Most of them, from what she'd heard, had preferred to file largely fictitious dispatches from the secure zones and reap the plaudits from their fellows who hadn't even dared to go within light years of the planet.

"Thank you," Alves said. He sounded as though he actually meant it. "It is a honour to be here."

Jasmine nodded, impatiently. "I understand that you have reviewed the operational requirements," she said. "Is that correct?"

"I *have* embedded before," Alves assured her. "*And* I do understand the value of security. I was trying to outsmart the Council a long time before you arrived."

"So I heard," Jasmine said.

She *had* taken the time to review his file – and she had to admit that it was impressive. The Council that had ruled Avalon – and fought a losing war with the Crackers – had clamped down on the media, turning the few reporters that lived and worked on Avalon into their propaganda department. Alves had been one of the handful who had tried to set up an independent newspaper, something that had been technically illegal in the Empire without the proper permits. Under the circumstances, he'd been lucky to merely be thrown in jail by the Council. The Crackers had broken him out a few months before the Marines had arrived and he'd helped to run an underground newspaper that had gone mainstream after the Battle of Camelot and the truce that had ended the war.

"I don't think that you will be able to file dispatches until we return home," she said, shortly. One of the other requirements for the diplomatic summit was that both parties would keep their ships outside the Lakshmibai Star System, at least until there was some level of mutual trust. "However, I must caution you that revealing any sensitive data will have the most unpleasant consequences."

"I do understand," Alves reassured her. "And besides, I doubt that anyone on that world has access to a computer datanet."

Jasmine shrugged. The reports on the planet's exact level of technological development were contradictory, as well as outdated. Some of them had suggested that the world was effectively an agricultural planet, with no modern technology; others had implied that outside traders had shipped in everything from fusion power plants to modern weapons and equipment. There was simply no way to know what they were getting into until they arrived.

"We will see," she said, softly. She sat down on one of the uncomfortable chairs and crossed her legs. "I will do my best to make time for you, but when I don't have time to talk I suggest that you stay out of the way. You are welcome to interview soldiers who *volunteer* to be interviewed; you are *not* welcome to push them into an interview or film them without their permission. Do you understand me?"

"Yes," Alves said. "I understand perfectly."

"Good," Jasmine said. She stood upright and grinned at him. If he wanted to follow her around all day, she'd see just how long he could keep it up. "Now that we have that clear in our minds, let's go inspect the troops."

Purchase Now!

Printed in Great Britain
by Amazon